TO CHARM A HAWK

CONTENTS

A NOTE ON LANGUAGE

This is just to let you know that I'm from Australia.

The English I use is Australian English, which is not the same as American English. In Australia, we like S, not Z. The letter U appears in words where it does not in American. Smelt is the past tense for smell. There are certain words that we use on a regular basis which make Americans blush. I'm sorry. Not really. It's all English in the end.

So, I love you readers from America, but please remember that my spelling is not incorrect, it's simply a different version of English to what you use.

Trigger Warning

Please only read this if you have triggers, otherwise you may spoil yourself. This book is about regret, guilt and fighting to fix what the FMC broke. It is about a family finding their way back to each other in the face of grief. It does have a HEA.

To start, I will tell you what isn't in the book. There is no rape, no cheating, no incest, no minors, no pregnancy, and no substance abuse.

However, there are depictions of violence and sex. People are burnt alive. Children are kidnapped. The FMC has terminal cancer. The FMC had her memories altered. There is mild consensual bondage. Various characters discuss past atrocities they committed, but not in detail.

Please always put your mental health first.

ASTORIA

DAWN

CHARNEL

GENERAL VESTA

This is for the ones who regret their mistakes.

Sometimes fixing them is worth it.

Sometimes the best thing you can do is forgive yourself and walk away.

And sometimes it's better to just set it all on fire and call it a day.

Okay Kyle, I'm once again begging you not to read this. Pretty please.
Last I checked, nothing had changed.
You're still my brother-in-law.

PROLOGUE

"Again!"

Her fingers curled into the grass, knuckles protesting the movement. Every joint ached from the continuous shift back and forth between her natural form and her animal one. Sinking her mind into the well of magic simmering beneath her skin, Astoria summoned the will to force her body to obey the command of the god standing over her. It hurt, it always hurt, all daoine knew the pain of the shape change, but to keep pushing it as much as he expected required a willingness to forge the pain into something else.

"You must be faster," he said, mouth twisting as he gazed at the tired hawk on the ground at his feet. "No duine will ever master the shift like you, Astoria Havard, but you must do better. I know it hurts, and if you allow me, I can do something about that."

Lifting her head, Astoria snapped her beak at the hand he extended towards her. Anyone else would have lost a finger, but he simply laughed, tapping the side of her beak when she released it. No blood seeped from his skin, no mark remaining where she bit him. Dark lines wrapped across darker skin, the shimmer of his boundless power flaring along them. Tiny stars sparked from his fingertips, showering her rich brown plumage with lights that faded quickly. Astoria ruffled her feathers, chirping at the god.

"How will you do something about the pain?"

The god tutted, crouching in front of her to run his hand over one of her wings. "I can make the shift easier by changing the aspect of your magic that allows for it. After all, I spun the ability from a thread of chaos, so it's well within my rights."

Cocking her head, Astoria blinked. *"And if the Great Queen finds out?"*

"Oh, I'm not concerned about her. You could fill a library with all the things we do behind Shianeni's back. She might be the god of life, but she's the most self-centred being to walk through existence with unfathomable power. It never occurs to her that some of us might just be more powerful than she is. As far as the Great Queen is concerned, she is everything and the rest of us are simply shadows of her magnificence."

Her wings spread, power warming the feathers as she basked in the god's glow. Beneath the leafy canopy of the forest, they were shaded from the sun, but it hardly mattered to Astoria when the thrum of chaos filled the glen they used for her training. There was no need for space to fly when it was the act of shifting she was supposed to master. His fingers traced the smattering of marks on her feathers that resembled flames, a smile lifting the corners of his lips. If he had been a different god, Astoria would have feared the grin.

"You are so different from your sister, young hawk. It will serve you well in the future."

My job is to protect Eivor. Father always tells me—"

Tapping her beak, the god chuckled. "I know what Craven tells you, and I know what Malena tells you. Just because they are your parents does not mean they're right. Or that they know everything. Your mother is a Raven. I spun her power from the space between this existence and the next, weaving it into the threads Lord Death covered her in. I created the power of the husk makers. As for your father? His years in the arena damaged him."

Screeching in protest, Astoria grabbed for her power and forced herself to change back into her natural form. "My father is not damaged!"

"Oh, my sweet little bird, he is." Ignoring her defiant glare, the god cupped her cheek. "But because of it, you will learn things your sister will not. Those are lessons you must endure. Alyah has seen it. There will be days when you question your purpose."

"And what is my purpose, oh great and powerful, Lord Xhaiden?" she growled, resisting the urge to lash out when her warrior's magic flared.

"Careful, my friend. We don't want to modify her memories more than necessary."

Power sung through the glade; a whisper of battle entwined with the soft coo of peace. It called to Astoria, and she rolled her shoulders, wishing she had a weapon to grasp. She was a warrior like her father, gifted with a connection to the god standing a short distance away. Diwan, the kingdom her parents ruled, had been a reward given to Craven Havard by the god of war for his valour in the arenas. Part of her wanted to make her mark on them like he had, but Astoria knew they would never allow her to compete.

Xhaiden shifted his focus to the newcomer. "Neriwyn. I wasn't expecting you."

"Your wife didn't tell you?" Prowling closer, War brushed a hand over Astoria's hair. "So much like your father, my dear Battle Hawk. But unlike Craven, you'll always be the loyal soldier. My perfect warrior forged to temper storms."

"My Lord War," Astoria murmured.

He leaned down to press a kiss to the top of her head, the wrap of his power calming her battle lust. "I wanted to check on your progress with her, Xhaiden."

"She's already better than most Ravens at consecutive shifts, but I have yet to make the necessary changes to her magic. I was about to do so when you arrived," Xhaiden replied, dark eyes narrowing in annoyance when the other god crouched next to Astoria.

"Show me, Battle Hawk. Shift."

The command whispered through her, filling her mind with the desire to demonstrate her abilities to the god. Astoria sunk into the magic, letting it spread her wings wide as the pain ripped down her spine. A small part of her wondered if each shift between forms would chip away at her sanity, carving the cost from what made her who she was. Neriwyn's hand ran through her feathers, scratching a spot behind Astoria's ears to coax a trill of pleasure from her. His knowing chuckle had her ruffling her feathers in embarrassment.

"Now shift back and repeat it twice without hesitation."

Giving a screech of protest, Astoria spread her wings and snapped her beak at the god. "*That is too much without stopping.*"

Neriwyn's eyes narrowed, mouth twisting in displeasure. "You will do it, or I will increase the amount. The pain is your enemy, and you will defeat it."

Directing a pleading look in Xhaiden's direction, Astoria waited to see if the other god would intervene on her behalf. Stars swirled in the depths of his gaze, a flare of power trailing gentle fingers down her spine. Realising he had no intention of doing what she hoped, the duine reached for the magic that allowed her to shift forms. Feathers reverted to skin, wings melting back into her body as Astoria returned to her natural form. Only to gulp down a single breath before repeating the process to become a hawk again.

"This is not helpful." Xhaiden crossed his arms, glaring at the other god.

"Then do what you need to do, my friend. Make it easier for her."

Lifting his chin, he returned his gaze to the woman shifting forms at his feet. Power crackled in the air, sinking needles into Astoria's body to banish the agony. It slid through her skin, melting into the magic that allowed for the shape changing. As her bones cracked and changed, Xhaiden's power wove through them, easing the pain that made her baulk at following the command of the god of war. When it all vanished, leaving the shift as easy and painless as breathing, she became eager to do it again to prove she could.

Astoria tossed her head back, rich brown hair pooling over her shoulders as she gazed at the god of chaos. "What did you do to my magic?"

"I am not simply the god of chaos, Princess. It is well within my power to change the manner in which things exist. All those with the ability to shapeshift gained that gift from me, so making some adjustments to it is easy."

Rising, Neriwyn chuckled in delight. "Perfect. The variations have improved."

The desire to shift to confirm that she had not imagined the lack of pain overcame Astoria. Once in her hawk form, she flapped her wings, eyeing the space in the glade in annoyance. If there had been more room, she would have taken flight. Snapping her wings back, the duine returned to her natural state, stretching in delight when no pain lingered in her joints. There was still a trace of exhaustion from so many shifts, but that was the worst of it. A welcome change when she would have otherwise been in agony.

"It feels good, doesn't it?" Xhaiden smirked, stars shooting along the lines on his skin. "This is how you will make your mark on the world. Diwan's second princess, the loyal Battle Hawk, who slips between forms in a fight as easily as breathing and claws out the eyes of her enemies. And those who bear the scars will never forget you."

"Don't you think that's enough? Remember, the more you tell her, the more she must forget." Tutting at his fellow god, Neriwyn offered a hand to Astoria so she could stand.

"Must you take my memories?" she whispered, meeting his gaze.

"Yes. Your father has a deal with Annawyn, and it's important you don't attract her attention. The survival of so many depends on you never drawing my wife's attention. Eivor has her role to play, as do you. But for our plans to work, you cannot remember."

Xhaiden stretched out his hand, stroking her cheek to draw her attention. "You are more than you realise, Astoria. When the time comes, you will understand."

Staring into the starry depths of his eyes, she felt like she was falling into the darkness. There was a soothing chill that wrapped comforting arms around her, and Astoria wanted to bury her face in the neck of the man guiding her to the ground. He smelt of sandy beaches and the ocean, and it called her home. Lips pressed to her forehead, accompanying a soft murmur of words her clouded mind could not grasp.

"Sleep, my sweet Fire Hawk."

ONE

The wind was a gentle caress over her feathers, helping her maintain a position hovering above *The Storm Bird*. Far below, her fellow crew members were busy preparing the ship to drop anchor in the bay. She knew she should have been on deck with them, but waking to find an empty bed again had left Astoria with a desperate urge to fly. No one had criticised her for walking naked from the captain's cabin, or for transforming into the massive brown hawk they were used to watching her become. It was not the first time, and while she remained one of the crew, it would not be the last.

Astoria banked, letting the currents carry her closer to the ship. The sea was a glittering blanket of reflected sunlight. Small waves crested before smoothing out to blend back into the water, but every sailor knew how quickly things could change. Especially since the captain of their ship was the god of the sky. As her lover, Astoria knew better than most how swiftly Dawn's mood changed, and how closely tied it was to the weather. After 175 years, she was questioning how much longer she could deal with the ever-changing moods of the Storm Queen. She loved her life as a pirate, and the freedom of the skies that came with sailing on open seas, but there were only so many times she could bear the brunt of the younger woman's temper when something did not go as planned.

She dipped a wing, circling *The Storm Bird* to let her crew mates know she was there. Whistles and cheers assured the hawk they did not mind her lack of help. With steady flaps of her wings, Astoria lifted higher, her keen eyes taking in the busy shore surrounding the bay. It was a reminder that her primary job was to scout ahead of the ship. They relied on her sharp sight to see farther than the person stuck in the crow's nest. Few things saw as clearly as a predator with wings. Tugs of wind encouraged her to drift closer to the town nestled in the valley. Circling it, Astoria searched for the usual signs warning of an attempt to capture the pirates.

Despite their reputation, the crew of *The Storm Bird* were not cutthroat killers determined to rob every ship that crossed their path. Their enemies spread those stories to discourage people from giving help to any who sailed in the Storm Queen's fleet. Dawn was the leader of the pirates, and among those who knew the truth, she was worshipped for what she did. They fought to free slaves in transport across the seas. It was their primary task, and one which gained them goodwill in many places across Tir. It even left them in a tentative alliance with those who owed their allegiance to the Unseelie Council—something Astoria found disconcerting when she considered where they were based, and who ruled over them.

Satisfied they would not be in danger when they went ashore, the hawk drifted back to the ship. They had established a signal soon after she joined the crew, and she let out a shrill whistle. It always felt strange to use the voice of her animal form, but few of the pirates were capable of mind speaking with her kind. The selkies, kelpies, and merfolk could, but it was always uncomfortable over distances. Astoria knew it was because their magic was for use in water, while she belonged to a land-bound race. Daoine rarely possessed an aquatic animal form, and there were none of them on *The Storm Bird*'s crew. She was the only duine, and sometimes the hawk wished she was not.

Tempted to land on the ship to lend a hand, Astoria felt a shift in the wind. Her gaze drifted over the people scurrying around on deck, settling on the figure of the woman standing with her hands on her hips by the wheel. Annoyance flickered through her when Dawn tilted her head back to wave, her other hand holding tight to her tricorn hat. It was both a greeting and a summons. One Astoria did not feel like answering. Adjusting her path, she flew back towards the shore, making it clear to the waiting god that she had no intention of joining her on deck. She knew it was petty, but being left alone in bed with no idea of where the other woman had gone stirred that emotion in her. All she ever wanted was for Dawn to tell her she was going.

"Don't be like that, Tory." Dawn's voice caressed her mind. *"I have something for you."*

If she had been in her natural form, Astoria suspected she would have been grinding her teeth. Following the shoreline, she studied the tiny huts sitting farther back from the water, keeping out of reach of the greedy fingers of the sea. She was tempted to search for the god of water, knowing he was rarely far away, even if he refused to have anything to do with Dawn. He was one of the few people she could talk to. Charnel always understood. Folding her wings back, she plunged through the air towards the waiting land, eager to feel sand beneath her feet. If the pirate queen wanted to talk, then she could come to her.

There was a thrill in the unchecked plummet that filled Astoria with joy. All it would take was a slight miscalculation on her part, and instead of landing intact, she would crash into the ground with enough force to end her life. Her mother had dubbed her the reckless one, and Dawn had done nothing but encourage the side of her that thrived on danger. Part of her was glad the late queen of Diwan could not see her now. It made it easier to deal with the guilt of running from her home when war came to claim it. Every time she threw herself into a fight, naked and shifting between forms as she dragged her talons through the flesh of the enemy, Astoria could forget she had abandoned her sisters. They were flourishing now, free to build their lives as they saw fit, but it did not change what she had done.

Extending her feet, she spread her wings, catching the draft she needed to slow her descent before she hit the ground. Thousands of years of experience kicked in, overruling the instinct to wait a moment longer before she landed. Scaled claws dug into the sand, transforming into bare feet and toes that wriggled to feel the scratch of the grains. Feathers merged into smooth skin, the breeze becoming a tickle. Arching her back, Astoria bathed in the sunlight's warmth. She welcomed the change to her sight as colours lost some of their sharpness, and she stopped being able to see as far as she did in her hawk form. Laughing, she tumbled to the ground, lying back on the sand simply to enjoy the feel of solid ground while she took stock of the persistent ache in her limbs.

"Are you avoiding me or your duties?"

Her joy faded, replaced with frustration. "You. Always you."

Looming over her, the god looked upset by her words. "What's wrong, Tory? When I left, things were fine. What did I do this time?"

"The same as you always do, Dawn. Is it really too much to ask for you to wake me before you vanish from bed? I hate waking up to find you're gone, and I have no idea where or when to expect you back."

"You know I don't do it on purpose."

Slinging an arm over her face, Astoria blocked out the view of the woman standing at her head. It was easier if she avoided looking at Dawn when they argued. Too often she had forgotten what she was saying because the god would cock her head with a mischievous grin that had desire pooling between her legs. She hated her inability to resist the other woman, even when she was furious with her. Even when touching her was agony.

"That's what you tell me every time, and yet, you make no effort to change."

Dawn grunted and dropped a bundle beside Astoria. "I brought your clothes in case you wanted to walk to the town with me. Though I left your present back on board. Of course, we can always just go to bed…"

"Is that your solution to everything, Dawn?"

There was no need to uncover her eyes to know the god was giving her an incredulous look. She did not need to see the warm brown eyes filled with confusion or watch how the breeze caressed the deep brown hair Astoria loved to run her hands through. So many of the tiny braids had been woven by her fingers and decorated with beads of her choice. Jaw clenched, the duine forced her thoughts away from the image of Dawn's body. It was not what she needed when she was trying to get her point across to the god. All it would do was land her back in the same bed she had woken alone in.

"You say it like it's a bad thing, Tory."

"Because it is!" Wrenching her arm away from her eyes, Astoria sat up, nose crinkling at the sand stuck to her skin. "I've spent the last 175 years warming your bed and stopping you from crossing the line, and all I ask is for you to tell me before you leave. I hate waking up alone!"

Recoiling from the angry magic swirling around Astoria, Dawn wished her father was there to help her make sense of it. It was not the blood lust of a warrior; it was something else. Something hot that wanted to consume everything within reach. Tentatively reaching out, she touched the duine's shoulder, hoping it would not cause further arguments. Her skin was warm, too warm, reminding the god of when she had first joined the crew. The sun had left its mark on the pale glow of Astoria's body, and Dawn sometimes wished she was still the unblemished woman she had found crouched on the floor of her cabin.

"I'm sorry, Tory. I can't help it. You're always so soundly asleep when I get bored, and I don't like to disturb you. Most of the time I'm not even going anywhere, really."

"Then why leave at all? When I wake up and find you on deck, that's one thing. But you're almost never onboard. Why can't you deal with your restlessness by commanding your ship?"

Resting her arms on her knees, Astoria watched the waves breaking over the sand, fingers of water gorging on the earth. She had come to appreciate the delicate balance of things over the years. Before meeting Dawn, her knowledge had been limited to what she had bothered to learn. Her sisters were the ones who took the time to read while she spent long days in the training yards. They had called her the Battle Hawk, and Astoria had welcomed the name. Yet, when battle had come to Diwan, she had taken to the sky without looking back.

"What's really wrong, Astoria?" Dawn sat beside her, keeping her hands to herself. "I feel like you're angry about something else, and you're using me as an easy target."

"It was Eivor's birthday recently," she whispered, watching a larger wave crash upon the beach.

Stiffening, the god gave her a look at the mention of the Unseelie leader. "Do you miss your sister?"

"Yes... no... I don't... it's hard to miss someone you barely knew. Our parents were careful to space us out, so we never really knew what the others were capable of. Except Silaine."

"I can arrange for you to visit her in the Vale. Every time I see Uncle Tigs, he tells me she asks after you. But if it's your other sister you want to see, I can't help."

"You don't need to remind me that the gods are forbidden from entering Diwan. It should hurt more than it does to know how much Eivor hates you just for being born. But it doesn't. I understand."

Giving a laugh of confusion, Dawn poked her arm. "Are you saying you hate me?"

"No, never. I love you, you stupid woman. Even if you can't say it back. You're mine until the day the gods bound to you come to claim you. Which is a long way away, considering two of them don't exist, and Charnel can't stand the sight of you."

"He despises me. I've never been able to work out why."

Lips thinning, Astoria gave Dawn a knowing look. She had spoken with the god of water in depth about his unwillingness to go near the woman he was bound to. It was easy for her to understand, but the younger woman had been born into a time of peace among the gods. Dawn carried no scars of the war that had torn the old gods apart and nearly destroyed the world they created. While she was only around 2500 years old, Astoria remembered the first war. Her parents had been spun from stardust by the gods and bound in servitude to them. The world they lived in now was a very different place.

"Charnel doesn't despise you. He believes you're immature and need time to grow." Winking, Astoria stood unsteadily, and Dawn shot to her feet to support her. "And I'm getting too old for this. I don't know what you see in this old woman. Soon enough, my age is going to catch up with me, and you'll leave me for someone younger."

Snarling at the suggestion, Dawn buried a hand in Astoria's dark hair, pulling her face around so she could kiss her. She tasted like pure mountain air, lightning, and the moment before rain fell. Slinging an arm around the god's waist, the hawk did not pull away, even though she knew it would lead her back to the place she was avoiding. The Storm Queen was an addiction she could not shake, and Astoria had a deep-seated fear it was going to destroy her.

"I want to love you, Tory," Dawn whispered against her lips. "I really do."

TWO

No one noticed how forced her smile was, not even the god clinging to her side. The town had opened their doors to the crew of *The Storm Bird*, welcoming the visiting god. Astoria was the silent sailor waiting to be commanded, her blue gaze constantly searching the surrounding crowd for any signs of a threat. Not that anyone could harm Dawn, but that did not mean people had not tried. She had several scars from taking blows intended for the younger woman. They were reminders she needed to stop acting first and to think about what she was doing. Because if she had thought twice about getting between a god and a knife, she would not have those scars.

The tavern was larger than she expected for the size of the town. Filled with people eager to spend time with the Storm Queen and her infamous crew, the buzz of energy was contagious. It was a battle to keep her magic from latching on, stirring the more positive side of her gifts from the god of war. Astoria wanted to stoke the fires of camaraderie among the crowd, but her thoughts were too busy circling the frustration refusing to dislodge from its perch in her gut. If Dawn would leave her alone, she could settle into a corner and wallow while staring into a tankard of whatever piss weak drink they called alcohol. But the god would not go, nor would she stop touching Astoria whenever she got the chance.

Catching the gaze of the first mate, Astoria saw the concerned frown of the other woman. Cass knew her too well. Whenever Dawn lost her temper, Cass was the one she went to. The other pirate had been the first to join the sky god, but she was not blinded by loyalty. If she could see how unhappy the former princess was, it would not be long before other crew members noticed. Most would side with Astoria, supporting her in whatever argument was unfolding. She found it incredibly hilarious the pirates sailing under the flag of the Storm Queen were more than happy to tell said god when she had fucked up. Especially when it came to the woman who showed her more loyalty than anyone else. Including the one she refused to stop chasing even though she could never be what Dawn wished her to be.

Astoria bit her lip, refusing to think badly of Jen. The daughter of Chaos had only ever denied Dawn's advances. It was not her fault the foolish pirate queen would not accept that she was not interested, and it certainly was not her fault that when she was reborn as the god of learning, Dawn had wreaked havoc on Tir's weather for months in a temper. Not even her parents had been able to calm the tempest. Then one day, Dawn had come back from one of her vanishing acts, and the skies were perfect. The balance was restored across the world. Charnel had told her only one person could calm the Storm Queen, and that the god of time had shown Dawn something important to their future. Whatever it was, the duine suspected she would not be around to see it.

But part of her wanted to know if Dawn would rain destruction on Tir if she left. For all her claims of not being able to love her, Astoria believed there was something between them. She felt it every time her captain stopped to watch her, and every time they touched. It was happening with an alarming frequency. Things would be fine, then she would turn around and Dawn would be frozen in place, following her every move as though she were a lifeline in the raging sea. Those moments always ended with them in bed. Afterwards, the god would dismiss her questions, and Astoria would turn to a bottle of whatever was at hand to banish the memory of stormy eyes locked on her.

"Sing for me, pretty Battle Hawk," Dawn murmured, lips trailing over her jaw with the promise of kisses. "I love hearing you perform in taverns. Well, anywhere really. You are so beautiful."

Mouth twisting, she attempted to wriggle out of the god's grasp. "I'm not in the mood to sing. Why don't you?"

"Because the people here aren't nearly drunk enough to listen to me."

"Then maybe don't sing your favourite bawdy songs? Just because you like them doesn't mean they need to be the only ones you remember. Perhaps it's time to pick up a few new ones. You visit the Vale often enough. Ask my sister."

Tightening the arm around Astoria's waist, Dawn chuckled. "Where's the fun in that?"

"Not everything has to be fun all the time."

Her mirth faded, and the god sighed, releasing Astoria. Free to step away, she glanced around for Cass but could not locate the first mate in the crowd. Humans and elves happily mingled with kelpies and selkies, while merfolk perched on whatever they could find to watch over their friends. She remembered the time before the old gods were reborn, when the First People were immortal and many of them would have happily killed the town's folk.

It felt like another life and Astoria wanted to bury those memories somewhere far away where she never had to remember the sight of a mutilated person, half eaten by a goblin. Every time they sailed past a certain peninsular where magic clung heavily to the land, calling to her like a crackling fire, she was drawn back into the war she had taken part in at the side of her mother. A war that had left her intrinsically changed.

"Do you want to return to the ship?" Dawn made to grab her wrist, but the look Astoria gave her had her recoiling. "I'm sorry, Tory. How many times do I have to say it?"

"I don't need your apologies, Captain. Just let me have some time to myself."

People were watching, their eyes wide with mixed emotions over the exchange. Only the crew ignored the two women, knowing it was nothing unusual. Letting Astoria slip through the crowd, Dawn slumped and signalled for the man behind the counter to pour her a drink. Pushing her way over, she leaned on the cool timber, wishing she could get drunk. There were few things she disliked about being a god, and one of them was never knowing the delights of intoxication.

"Are you ever going to grow out of this stupid girl stage?" Cass joined her at the counter, shoving her elbow into Dawn's side with enough force to make the god grunt. "You're going to lose her."

"Of course I am. She's mortal. You're all mortal. I will lose all of you."

"That's not what I mean, and you know it. Fuck Dawn, seriously. Astoria is the best thing that has ever walked into your life, and you are one mistake away from ruining it."

Glaring at the dark liquid in the tankard in front of her, the Storm Queen said, "I can't give her what she needs. Tory is mortal, and I'm a god. It doesn't matter how much I crave her; she'll never be part of me."

"Doesn't mean you can't love her back. Sure, you'll end up with a broken heart, but how else will you learn to value what's right in front of you? I bet that's why Charnel won't pass over yet. Because you don't deserve to have one of the other parts of you until you learn to appreciate the people who love you."

"Oh, fuck off, Cass. What would you know about it?"

Sneering, the kelpie grabbed one of Dawn's braids and yanked on it. "I've lived longer than you can imagine, you impertinent little brat. As has most of your crew. We're thousands of years old, and we're here because we believe in what we're doing. Doesn't mean we have to stay."

"Maybe she should leave," Dawn muttered before sculling her drink. "She deserves to find someone who can love her back and who won't ruin what is left of her life."

"Yes, she bloody well should. And we'll help her do it because she's one of us. If Tory goes, we'll take her wherever she wants, and if you try to stop her, you'll find yourself without a fleet."

Leaving the god at the counter, Cass turned to locate Astoria. She had found a spot in a corner where people did not want to linger. It was tucked beneath the stairs to the upper levels of the tavern, where those wanting to get a little better acquainted with a pirate were free to pay for a room for the night. The only ones who never took up the offer of a room were Dawn and Astoria. They always returned to the ship, taking the time to stretch their wings together.

Glancing back at her god, Cass wanted to beat the fool over her head with something heavy. Or drown her repeatedly until she got it through her thick skull that she would regret letting Astoria go. No one else was stupid enough to fall in love with the one god who was a walking tempest in a teacup except the daughter of the woman who had gotten between the mad god and the victims of the Sundering. She had seen the late Queen Malena in action as one of Death's Ravens, and she knew Astoria did her mother proud, even if the younger woman could not see it for herself.

"Need to talk?" Sliding onto the bench opposite Astoria, Cass gave her a grim smile. "She's an idiot."

"Yes, she is, but I think I'm insane."

"Don't know about that."

Astoria arched a brow and kicked her under the table. "Considering I keep expecting her to change, I think I'm living the definition of insanity. I do the same thing over and over, and the results never fucking change. Why? What stupidity drives me to stay with her?"

"Love is stupid."

"She'll never love me back, Cass! I need to let go of her."

Cass leaned against the wall, listening to the hum of the crowd. "Look, I won't argue because you're right. You need to let go of her. Dawn is a child compared to us, and sometimes children learn best when they lose their favourite toys. She takes you for granted. It's time that stopped, but you're the only one who can make that choice."

"I keep thinking it's time I went home," Astoria replied, rubbing her chin nervously. "I have a lot to make up for, and sometimes it feels like there is this huge gnawing pit in my heart that's slowly consuming me with guilt. It's burning me up. Silaine might have forgiven me for abandoning her after I got her out of the castle that day, but what about Eivor? I turned my back on my sister, my queen, and it's time I answered for that."

"That's heavy thinking for anyone, Tory. Your sister has done well for herself. You've met one of her consorts, and did Thorne give you any reason to think she wanted you to return?"

"No, quite the contrary. Doesn't mean I shouldn't. A weariness has burrowed into my bones and I'm tired, Cass. Aren't you?"

"We'll sail for whatever port you want us to, but if you choose to go to Diwan, we cannot walk that path with you. It's one journey you'll take alone. And Dawn won't follow. She cannot."

Humming thoughtfully, Astoria located the god on the other side of the tavern. People surrounded her, eager to be as close to a divine being as possible. It was laughable to imagine Dawn as an answer to anyone's prayers, but she knew better. The god of air did her best to help people who needed it without disrupting the delicate balance of the world. Of course, that did not extend to her temper tantrums and the effect they had on Tir. Wishing she had a drink, Astoria contemplated slipping from the tavern to return to the ship. She knew where Dawn kept a stash of wine from the eternal valley of spring, and it was a far better option for getting drunk than anything the town offered.

"I heard something interesting before the two of you got cranky with each other again," Cass said, propping her legs up on the bench. "Something about your sister."

Studying the strand of kelp growing amongst Cass's hair, Astoria grunted. "Did you?"

"Seems her eldest child just turned 70, and they threw a big party in spite of the threats after they broke the treaty between Diwan and the Spire."

"That sounds like my sister. Eivor was always the most family oriented of us. Our parents doted on her."

"And yet, you're the daughter Malena snuck away to fight in a war with. I wonder if the dullaghan has told your sister about it. Princess Astoria, the Battle Hawk who fought beside dragons, and saved the lives of the women who locked the mad god in her prison. You'd think the gods owed you one."

Looking away guiltily, she knew it was an ill-kept secret. Dawn never asked about it, but Astoria suspected she was aware of details of her past she had not shared, considering Death had thanked her for her part all those years ago. Not the god of death she had met on the battlefield, but the one who had destroyed the mad god before she burned Tir to a husk. The battle often haunted her dreams, and she hated waking alone, upset over the memories.

"Do you have nightmares of the things you've done?"

"Sometimes. I've eaten my share of innocents. The difference between us is the gods made me this way. I had no say over the hunger for flesh that eats at me. You chose to claw the eyes out of a few goblins before they were roasted by a dragon or killed by the Executioner. You coated your feathers in the dust of those turned to husks by your mother and the other Ravens. Free will and all that fun stuff."

Snorting, Astoria wished she had Cass's ability to make things seem lighter than they were. She knew the secrets her mother had sworn her to keep were part of the reason guilt ate at her. As the middle child, people had often forgotten she was there. Her parents included. King Craven Havard had made his deals with the mad god and with Death, and Eivor, with her terrifying powers, was the product of those. And she knew all about her mother's deal with Oblivion that had seen her offer Silaine to War and his winged warriors to bring back the Ravens. No one ever realised how much she knew.

"I'm just the dismissed warrior. The one daughter who wasn't special."

"Are you sure about that?"

Remembering the feel of fire caressing her feathers as she flew alongside her dragon allies, Astoria shrugged. She had always questioned how she survived the battle to protect the humans and elves of the twin cities of Endara and Ensaycal. The first time she saw a map of the land where Dawn's parents had been born, she had felt like she had been gutted. Finding the names of those ancient cities scrawled across kingdoms was a step back into the smoke, and the blood, and the fires. It had fed a hungry ember she had kept buried since then, and the Storm Queen had weathered the brunt of her fury over what she viewed as blatant disrespect for the dead. But she had visited those lands, drifting over them on unburnt wings, and saw how different they were to the land she had shed blood for.

"You know, I'd love to see Dawn go toe to toe with Oblivion."

Snorting, Cass covered her mouth and shook her head, so she did not draw unwanted attention. "Me too. It would be hilarious... and then the Executioner would run her through with that nasty sword of hers."

"If anyone deserved it."

"You should fly back to the ship and get some rest. Those shadows under your eyes concern me."

Eyeing the crowd, Astoria contemplated picking a random person from the town and heading upstairs to a room for the night. "I'll think about it."

"And while you're thinking about it, don't do anything that will make our brat of a captain decide to gift this lovely little town with a cyclone. You know Charnel gets fed up with fixing her messes."

"True, and I like him. He doesn't deserve to put up with her shit."

Cass leaned across the table to poke her chest. "Neither do you, and it's time you remembered that."

"Why do you put up with her?"

"Mine is an entirely different type of putting up with her. I'm not the one keeping her bed warm and waiting desperately for the day she wakes up and realises how good she's got it. That's all you, Tory."

Her gaze found Dawn across the tavern. The god was staring, and Astoria felt a need to go to her. It was an agonising pull, a craving she had to deny. Clenching her jaw, she turned away. Everything Cass said was true. She was the one desperately waiting for something to change, and it was about time it did. But nothing would until she made it happen. Wrapping her magic around herself, she tapped her nails against the timber of the table.

"I'm going home, Cass. It's time. Especially since the Blood Queen is becoming a bigger threat. I fear what will happen when she turns her sights on Diwan."

"Good girl. We'll get you there, no matter what the captain might threaten. You have my word."

THREE

"Trust the fire."

Jolting awake, Astoria pressed a hand to her chest, feeling the hammering of her heart against its cage of bones. The linen blanket clung to her sweaty body, refusing to fall easily as she sat up. Sprawled across the other half of the bed, Dawn had her head buried under a pillow. More concerned with the burning of her limbs, the duine did not spare a surprised thought over finding the god still present. Closing her eyes, she breathed deeply, tasting the ever-present promise of rain accompanying the woman beside her. With each slow breath, Astoria focused on calming her racing heart and examining the magic raging through her veins. There was no blood lust, no desperate fury of a warrior demanding to be let loose. It was simply there, burning as though she was a piece of timber thrown into a fire.

Dragging a hand over her face, she shoved the tousled brown locks out of the way of her eyes and slid her legs over the edge of the bed. There was no point staying where she was. Glancing at Dawn, she considered waking the god and extended a hand to shake her. Yanking it back, Astoria decided not to bother. Whatever was going on with her magic and her nightmares had nothing to do with her lover. Besides, she could not see the point of sharing it since she planned to leave *The Storm Bird* when they sailed into the port nearest Diwan. When her mind turned to her former home, the princess suspected it was the source of her problems, and nothing Dawn could say or do would solve it for her.

Astoria staggered to the washbasin, dipping her hands into the water. It was ice cold, and she hissed through bared teeth. Scooping some to splash over her face, she enjoyed the trickle down her skin and the drips from her chin left an odd sensation behind them. Beneath her feet, she felt the gentle motion of the sea as it carried the ship across its surface. No vessel in Dawn's fleet ever sank or sailed into unpleasant weather. Even though the sleeping woman was the god of air, Astoria knew it was the god of water who kept them truly safe. Charnel drifted through the waters of Tir, guarding the ships sailing under the Storm Queen's flag. There was always fresh water, and they were never becalmed. Sometimes she wondered if he did it for her rather than Dawn.

"I thought I heard you wake up," Dawn said, sticking her head out from under the pillow. "Are you coming back to bed? It's still dark outside, and I can think of a few things to do."

She felt too hot to go back to sleep. "Can you make it cooler in here? I'm worried I might be sick. If I don't feel any better, I'll go see Marija for something to help."

Almost instantly, the temperature in the cabin dropped, and Astoria shivered. It was too soon to tell if it helped, but Dawn rolled out of the bed to approach her in concern. She wanted to laugh at the fearful way the god eyed her, but it faded into tenderness when she began examining her. The god had never experienced illness for herself, but she had seen enough of her people go through various afflictions. Cass liked to laugh about the first time the crew brought a vomiting sickness onboard, boasting it had sent Dawn running for her mother to heal everyone because they were clearly dying. They were not, but the young god did not know how to deal with such a thing when her mother was the god of life, and the mortals who circled around her were immune to illness because of her power.

"Come on, let's get you back into bed. Is it your stomach, Tory? Or your head? Tell me because I can't figure it out alone."

Dawn's hands were soothing, and Astoria leaned into her, inhaling the scent of a building storm. "I don't know what it is. I'm just so hot, and my magic is being difficult."

"You're burning up. I'll get Marija."

"No! Just lie down with me for a little while. I was having a nightmare, so maybe this is a reaction to that. Besides, you feel nice, and I think it'll help if we just cuddle."

Stumbling over to the bed, Astoria sat on the end while the god stared at her in concern. Away from Dawn's touch, her skin felt like it was going to catch on fire again. For a moment, she considered going outside and jumping overboard to use the sea to quench the heat burning through her. She knew Charnel would be there to keep her afloat for as long as she needed. Eyes darting to the covered window, Astoria could not help wondering if he might know what was going on with her.

"Are you sure that's what you want?" Dawn sounded small, the uncertainty on her face surprising Astoria. "I don't want you to be sick, Tory. Marija can help before you get worse."

Holding out a hand, she nodded. "While you were touching me, I felt a little better. You're nice and cool, Dawn, and it felt so good."

"The cooler air in the cabin isn't helping?"

"A little. Now, come hold me before I decide to jump overboard."

Scowling, Dawn crossed to the bed and sat. Her arm settled around Astoria's back, a cool line of comfort seeping through the blanket of fire her skin had become. Their gazes met, and the god bit her lip, worry banishing any thoughts of taking advantage of the naked woman pressed to her. It did not have the same effect on the duine, and she leaned in close enough to kiss without going through with it. The cool touch of Dawn's breath, and the magic coating her, was intoxicating. Astoria wanted nothing more than to push her back and lay on top, melding as much of their bodies together as possible.

"Fuck," she murmured. "I think maybe you should get Marija before I take advantage of you."

Dawn's hands slid over her gently. "You might need to move out of the way first."

"I don't want to." Grazing her cheek against Dawn's, Astoria groaned when it felt like ice sliding over her skin. "Why do you feel so agonisingly wonderful? Have you done something to me, oh mighty god of the sky?"

"No, I'm just cooler than you are. You feel hotter than my mother."

Being compared to the god of life turned her desire into discomfort, and the duine jerked back. Taking the chance to jump away, Dawn stood a short distance from the bed, staring at her in bafflement. Clenching her hands in the sheets, Astoria swallowed, closing her eyes while she attempted to rein in her magic again.

"Maybe I should get my mother instead of Marija." Cocking her head, Dawn chewed on her bottom lip. "This doesn't seem right. Your magic isn't like it normally is."

"Just get the fucking healer, please, Dawn."

"Fine. But don't go anywhere."

Watching her stomp over to the door, Astoria said, "Marija, not your mother. I don't feel like having the god of life poking me. You know she makes me uncomfortable."

"She's just my mother!"

"She looks at me strangely. Your uncle is worse. If I never have to see Lord Time again, it would be too soon. I'd rather ask Charnel to drown me than to deal with your family."

Hurt crossed Dawn's face before she turned to yank open the door. With so many shape shifters onboard, the crew did not care about nakedness, so no one batted an eye at the sight of their naked captain stalking through the ship. She found the healer in the small room set aside as an infirmary. *The Storm Bird* was a large vessel, but space was a limited thing. When Dawn entered, Marija arched a brow.

"What have you done this time?"

"Nothing! Why would you assume I've done something wrong?"

Marija snorted, putting her hands on her hips. "Because it's normally the safest assumption."

"Tory woke up burning hot. We think she's sick. Can you come?" Dawn glanced over the room, chewing the inside of her cheek. "Sorry, I don't know if you were doing something important."

Waving at the shelves of supplies, the woman shrugged. "Taking inventory. I restocked a few things in the last town, but you know what this bunch of idiots is like. None of you can avoid hurting yourselves for long. It's like they're encouraged by your insanity."

She huffed, debating if arguing with the healer was worth the time when Astoria was back in their cabin with a fever. "Yes, yes, my insanity is infectious. Let's hope Tory isn't."

Fussing around the room, Marija gathered a few things, tucking them into the pockets of her apron. Like most of the crew capable of changing forms, she wore simple clothes for ease of stripping when needed. Patches of brightly coloured scales decorated her skin, matched by the colours of her hair. When she was in her merform, the healer was one of the most beautiful women Dawn had ever seen. Her beckoning call had lured many an enemy sailor from the decks of their ships, where they fell prey to her claws and fangs.

"Tell me what other symptoms Tory has?"

"Nothing. Just a fever and her magic feels weird."

Humming, Marija stared into the distance, her gaze losing focus as she ran through her options. "Not much point taking anything else until I know what's wrong with her. She probably picked up something from the town while we were there. I'll monitor the rest of the crew."

Prompted by her shooing gestures, Dawn led the way through the ship towards her cabin. When they got there, the door was open, and rushing in, she snarled upon finding the room empty. Standing in the doorway, Marija eyed the angry woman in understanding. The crackle of lightning tainted the air, fuelled by the temper of the sky god. Grinding her teeth, Dawn shoved past the healer, stomping her way out on deck.

"Where is Astoria?"

Her shout drew attention, and Cass hollered from her place at the wheel. "She's gone flying."

"Fuck!" Throwing her hands in the air, Dawn spun around to share an exasperated look with Marija. "I better go after her. If she's sick, and flying out there, she could kill herself."

"You're right. This isn't your fault, Captain."

"I should have made her come with me to see you, but she wasn't right, and I wasn't thinking."

Another member of the crew had taken over the wheel, and Cass marched down the steps to join them. "What's going on? Has something happened to

Tory? She said nothing when she came out here. Just shifted forms and took off. I figured you'd been arguing again."

Gazing at the glittering night sky, Dawn opened her mind to her power. "She's sick. Woke up with a terrible fever, and I left her alone to get Marija. I need to go after her. Flying at night is dangerous enough for her but doing so while battling a fever is more than risky."

"Can birds have a fever?" Marija looked at Cass.

"Why are you asking me?" The kelpie held her hands up. "I turn into a horse and a seahorse. Why would I know if a bird can have a fever? Not to mention the part where she's a duine and not a true bird."

Thankful she was naked and did not need to worry about ruining any clothes, Dawn drew her power through her body. Wings burst from her back, their weight taking a moment to adjust to. She could sense every change in the air, the way the currents interacted with each other. So far out at sea, there were few birds to be found, so she was confident it would be a straightforward task to locate Astoria before something terrible happened to her. Giving her space to flap the massive limbs, Marija and Cass exchanged worried looks.

"Do you want us to take to the water?" Cass inclined her head at the rail.

"No. If she hits the sea, Charnel will save her. Stars know, he's always around."

Launching into the air, Dawn relished the rush through her feathers. Flying gave her a pleasure that was unmatched. When she first decided she wanted wings, her parents had laughed and told her she would have to change her entire existence to manage it. So she had. They had stopped laughing after the wings appeared, her feathers the colour of a stormy dawn sky. Tigernach, king of the danann, had taught her to use them, and she knew he never let her father live it down.

"I'll bring her back."

The ship grew smaller the higher she went. Hovering far above the sea, Dawn cast her power out like a net, seeking the familiar ripple of her hawk. When she wanted to, she could connect with the entire sky, feeling every particle. She rarely did, fearful of the results if she lost her mind in the sensation. Having watched her mother become lost in her power for days, the young god knew better than to risk finding out what happened when she fucked around with the power fuelling her existence. Continuing to reach across the sky, Dawn grew increasingly concerned when she could not find Astoria.

"Where are you, my Battle Hawk?" she muttered, drifting along the strongest air current. "You should be here somewhere. I wasn't gone that long, and it's dark."

Remembering Astoria's comment about throwing herself overboard, Dawn stared at the dark entity far below. Despite the clear night sky, she was too far away for the sea to be anything more than a shadowy beast waiting to swallow any unfortunate fool who tried to tame it. Panic raced through her, fuelling thoughts of what might happen if their comments about Charnel being around to save Astoria were wrong. In her fevered state, the duine might have shifted back while flying, expecting the god of water to be there to catch her, only to succumb to the depths when the god of water proved her faith wrong.

"Fuck, fuck, fuck."

Delving into her mind, Dawn reached for the chain connecting her to the other god. It was always there, tucked away in a corner, reminding her he was one part of her essence. They avoided each other as much as possible, refusing to acknowledge their bond. Air and water, two lonely gods waiting for the other parts of their power to come into existence. She had hoped for so many years that Jen would become her god of the earth, but the other woman had decided on a different path. All these years later, and it still hurt like someone had taken a knife to her heart. Everyone had told her not to set her sights on the daughter of Chaos, that Jen could not be Earth, but Dawn had stubbornly clung to her dream.

Leaving her power to soak in the sky, the pirate captain drifted towards the sea in a downward current. Her fear for Astoria had spread through the air, becoming clouds that would have appeared ominous if their part of Tir had been facing the sun. The thread linking her to Charnel drew her, but despite his proximity to *The Storm Bird*, Dawn did not feel relief. She needed to get the sick woman back to their ship, where Marija could tend to her.

Remaining in the air above where she sensed the other god, she clenched her fists and contemplated how to approach the situation. Charnel was beneath the surface, bundled up in a massive air bubble that she could extend her power to. If it had been just him, Dawn would have popped it, but the fact it even existed confirmed he had Astoria.

She stared at the murky waters, watching the battling waves that seemed angered by her presence. Whenever Dawn dared put a toe in the sea, it lashed out at her. The crew thought it was hilarious to push her overboard, only to have her slammed back on deck by a furious wave controlled by the water god. Sometimes it felt like a game Charnel had going with her crew to make her suffer. If anyone else went overboard, he returned them gently, held aloft by a cradling hand of water. Astoria received the best treatment, which confirmed to Dawn that it was just her he hated.

"Charnel! I need her back. She's sick," Dawn shouted at the sea, reluctant to reach across the bond to speak into his mind. "Please, Charnel. Tory needs to see Marija before she gets worse."

The sea lashed out at her; a furious spray that left the feathers of her wings soaked. Huffing, Dawn swiped a hand across her face to dislodge the sodden strands of hair sticking to it. If she tried to transport herself into the bubble, it could harm Astoria. All she could do was plead with the other god to return the duine to her before it was too late.

"I know you can hear me, Charnel. Just tell me she's alive."

"Go away, Tempest. Tory is safe with me. I'll return her to the ship when she's ready." His voice sent unwelcome shivers down her spine as it caressed her mind. *"She needs my help."*

Snarling at the water, Dawn knew she had no other choice. *"Fine. But if she gets worse because of this, I'm telling Mother. I know how much you like it when she makes islands."*

"There's no need to be a brat. I would never let harm come to Tory."

FOUR

It was easier to breathe inside Charnel's bubble beneath the surface of the sea than it had been onboard the ship. Curled up in his lap, she gazed at the murky waters that seemed to possess a glow. His hand stroked her hair gently, the silky thrum of his power a cool blanket that soothed Astoria far better than Dawn's attempt. A small part of her felt guilty for leaving the ship, and for running from her lover without telling anyone what was going on. The fever had addled her thoughts to where the only instinct left in Astoria's mind had been to seek the god of water for help.

"Dawn is worried about you," he murmured, tracing the line of her jaw with a chilled fingertip. "You can't stay here indefinitely, my Fire Hawk. If I don't take you back, she will get her mother."

Rubbing her cheek against his leg, Astoria did not want to talk about Dawn. "I'm planning to go home to face my sister. Do you think she'll welcome me with open arms?"

"You want to return to Diwan after all this time?"

"I need to."

Charnel sighed, and the lights in the water flickered. "Perhaps you're right, though I don't imagine you'll receive a warm welcome from Queen Eivor. It's no secret you've been the lover of a god since you fled Diwan. Are you sure you want to risk what she might do to you?"

"Yes. Don't tell Dawn, but I'm tired. So tired. Let me go home, and at least apologise to my sister for doing her wrong. She didn't deserve to be abandoned by me."

Without the feeling of being burnt from the inside out, Astoria could relax. Her eyes drifted closed, lulled by the safety she felt while wrapped in his watery power. It was one reason she enjoyed Charnel's company, despite knowing it drove Dawn crazy. He never questioned it, or attempted to make her feel guilty for her choices when the duine needed someone willing to hold her without speaking.

"She's going to find out the truth as soon as I return you to the ship," he replied, running his fingers through her hair. "As soon as she gets her hands on you, she'll have Marija work her healing magic, and they'll find out what's wrong with you. There's nothing I can do to prevent it."

"Wait, what do you mean? It's just some sickness I picked up at the last port."

"Tory, no, my precious Fire Hawk. It's not. I can feel it in your blood, and it's killing you."

Astoria opened her eyes, turning her head to gaze up at him. "Then I should hurry home. At least Eivor won't need to worry about looking bad by executing her sister."

A surprising gleam of mischief appeared in his eyes, and Charnel tapped her nose. "Perhaps this is what Dawn needs. I can get you to the Diwanian border, but the rest would be up to you."

"Must you make it about her? You tell me I'm dying, and somehow, it's still about her."

If it had been anyone else, Astoria would have pulled away in annoyance. But it was Charnel, and whatever influence his power had over the sickness he claimed to be killing her was not something she wanted to give up. Settling her head back into a comfortable position, she wondered what Eivor would say when she arrived in Diwan. The more she pondered it, the more Astoria questioned if the dreams had been trying to tell her she was running out of time.

"Do you want me to help you?"

Grunting, she wriggled an arm free and stretched it out to brush against the wall of the bubble. "Why won't you ask me properly? Are you afraid of what Dawn will say if she finds out?"

"It's got nothing to do with her, and everything to do with me, Astoria. I have choices in this, but most of them mean going against what you want. I could return you to Dawn where they will discover your illness, and she'll get her mother to heal you. Or I could fetch Eirian myself to do the same thing. Then there is the option wherein I help you get to Diwan, so you can seek the absolution you feel you need. Once there, I can either let you die, or once again, speak to the god of life about saving you."

"We're all dying, Charnel. I don't want to be saved because I'm the plaything of a god. Especially one who is incapable of loving me back. Let me go home where I can quietly fade away, surrounded by memories of happier times. If you want to make me feel better, then you can tell Silaine what is happening once I'm in Diwan. Maybe my death will fix things between her and Eivor."

A dark shape approached the bubble, and the god slumped in defeat. Watching the whale investigate their presence, Astoria wondered what it would be like to have such a form. She loved being a bird, and feeling the wind beneath her wings, but there were so many animals in the world she wished she could experience. Stretching a leg out, the duine touched the wall where air and water met, trailing a toe across it and giggling at the trickle that curled around her foot.

"Careful, Fire Hawk," Charnel grumbled. "Are you sure this is what you want?"

"Going back to Diwan? I'd already made that decision before this revelation."

Staring towards the surface of the sea, the god contemplated his options. His silence had Astoria shifting in his lap to study the line of his face. Compared to some of the other gods, Charnel was someone most people would pass by on a crowded street without sparing him a second glance. She knew he liked that about himself, preferring to avoid company as much as possible. The colour of his hair reminded her of slightly wet sand, where the sea had tried to soak it but the sun had done its best to dry it out. Remembering the first time she had buried her hands in it and stolen a kiss, Astoria reached up to wrap a curl around her finger. His gaze dropped, and she smiled at the bright blue of his eyes.

"Dawn will tear Tir apart over this."

"No, I don't think she will." She brushed her thumb over his lips. "She knows I'm planning to leave. If I go now without saying goodbye, it'll make her angry, but it will pass."

Guilt flickered across his face when he could not resist pressing a small kiss to her thumb. "When she finds out why you slipped away with me, she will be furious. Dawn is a child with a temper, and if you deny her the chance to save you? Everyone will suffer."

"It's been 175 years, Charnel. I have tried my best to help her learn to control her temper, and all it has done is break my heart, and yours. But maybe my death is what she needs, and you'll be able to pass over to your heir. A pity we won't be able to find each other on the other side to watch her grow."

Movement beyond the bubble drew her attention away from the god. Realising they were drifting away from the ship, Astoria let her thoughts go still. It was soothing to watch the swirl of the sea as Charnel used his power to create currents to carry them along as quick as any ship under Dawn's influence. She knew if the sky god wanted to, she could find them wherever he took her. An unbreakable bond entwined the two gods, and she was the foolish mortal who had thought she could repair the rift between them. More whales surrounded the orb, dark figures looming through murky shadows to take advantage of the swift current their god had summoned.

Listening to them, Astoria sighed in delight. "They're singing. It's beautiful. I wish I could capture it in a bottle to give to Silaine. She would appreciate it more than anything else I could give her."

"How do you shoulder the weight of all you know?"

"Terribly. Perhaps that's what is killing me."

Charnel stroked her cheek. "No. Cancer is killing you. Something only Eirian can heal."

"Or Death."

"What he does is not healing."

"Isn't it?" She gave him a faint smile and wondered at the way light reflected through the water and the walls of the bubble onto his stubble. "It will free me from the weight and break the chains that prevent me from revealing everything I know. You're the only one I have ever been able to speak with."

"Because I was there."

"Exactly. You, Alyah, Xhaiden, Gebael, Oblivion, my mother, the dragons. Neriwyn. The things we did to bring about the new age that others will never know. I often wonder if anyone ever stopped to think that maybe I was too young for it? Let alone poor Briallen Altira. Sometimes I question my memories of it."

He stiffened, giving her a look that suggested to Astoria she was right to question. Closing her eyes, she cast her mind back to the battle, to fighting side by side with her mother, and the way the lines between skin and feather had blurred as they shifted when they needed to. She remembered the fires, and the screams, the way the dragons had consumed the withered forms of the Unseelie brought down by the husk makers walking among them. That day had been the day her magic raged unchecked, and it had never been the same since. It had burned along with the dragons, leaving her feathers untouched as she plunged from the sky to tear her claws into the faces of unprepared Unseelie soldiers. And Astoria remembered laughing while she did it.

"Some things are better forgotten, Tory," he whispered, leaning down to kiss her gently. "Calm your thoughts and your magic. You need to conserve your strength so you can fix things with your sisters."

"That's not a denial, Charnel. They altered my memories. Is it too much to ask for it to be undone before I die? Let me remember."

Around them, the sea was a lumbering beast that moved with a surprising speed when commanded to. Charnel kept his power woven through the currents, and wrapped around Astoria, cooling the fire burning in her veins. He could do nothing more than ease the symptoms while she was with him. It hurt to witness her pain, especially when he knew it would steadily worsen, and there was little anyone could do to stop it. Healers would offer her pain numbing concoctions that left her mind as addled as the pain itself did, and they would try their best to stem the tide of what was eating away at her body. Despite her comments about not wanting to be healed, Charnel desperately wanted to rush to the side of the person who could save Astoria's life because he was not ready for what was to come.

"I can ask the others to unravel any manipulations their predecessors worked, but you would need to leave Diwan. The gods agreed to remain out of your sister's kingdom, and they're unlikely to go back on their word for you. Not without Eivor's agreement. Maybe it's better to leave things as they are?"

Laughing, Astoria lightly tapped his cheek. "When have I ever done that?"

"It's never too late to change your ways, Fire Hawk."

"In that case, will you tell me the real reason you call me that?"

He screwed up his face, turning it to gaze into the sea above. "It's been long enough that Dawn will be cranky with us. She'll soon realise we're not where she left us, and are, in fact, much farther away. If we're lucky, she won't unleash a storm on us in an attempt to convince me to release you."

"Are you avoiding my question again, Lord Charnel? I'm just going to keep asking it until you answer. This could become an endless journey if you want to play that game."

"Or I could give you back to Dawn. Drown you. Gag you. Take your pick."

It was easy to walk her fingers across his chest, pointedly twisting the sea green linen of his tunic as she went. They followed an unseen pattern of dark lines etched into his skin. Astoria had memorised his, and Dawn's, and no one else knew the differences between them. If either realised the subtle tributes to them decorating her body, they refused to mention it. She loved knowing that written among her tattoos was her devotion to the two people who made her feel most like herself. Not in words so anyone else could read it, but in symbols she knew in her heart held significance to them.

"I do like it when you gag me, Charnel," she replied, grinning at his startled look. "Dawn doesn't know what she's missing. Tell me why you call me Fire Hawk, and I'll be good."

"Perhaps it's just because you shift into a hawk form, and you've got a fiery temper. You need to have one to last for as long as you have at Dawn's side. Does there need to be some deeper meaning to what I call you when I'm not using your name? Would you rather I call you Astoria all the time?"

She wanted to bury her hands in his dishevelled hair while silencing whatever argument he came up with to dissuade all the questions she liked to ask. Laying her hand on his neck, Astoria wondered what he would say if she admitted she had imagined being pressed between him and Dawn. Part of her had always hoped to be around when Charnel either put aside his reservations about the god of air or passed over to his heir. Knowing they would set her aside when it happened had done nothing to dampen the desire she felt over the fantasy woven in her mind. Licking her lips, Astoria caught the flicker in his eyes, the slight shift in the blue that gave it a green tinge, like the clear waters of a bay on a tropical island.

"You know I love you as well, my Lord of the Tides."

Charnel studied her, tracing the line of her face with his gaze. "Don't, Tory. Not now."

"Why? Am I making you feel guilty? You're not the one who started all this. I am. I ran from a war and flew in through the open door of a ship's cabin, where I saw a chance to escape. Dawn didn't try very hard to resist the naked woman on her floor offering her service in return for safety, but you? You resisted for so long before I finally wriggled my way in through the cracks in your defences."

Falling silent, Astoria dropped her hand away from his neck, and curled in on herself. The tiredness was bone deep, and she wondered how she had missed the signs. It had crept up on her like a slow-moving fog, insidious in the way it tricked her into thinking she was pushing too hard at her duties onboard *The Storm Bird*. Not once had it occurred to the duine that the frequent bouts of exhaustion were a sickness staking its claim on her body. But knowing what was going on made her suspect the urge she felt to return to Diwan had struck because her body knew its time was ending and she needed to seek forgiveness.

"When I saw you on the battlefield, my Fire Hawk, you were standing with your mother, waiting for the order to come. I watched you fly through dragon fire, and I understood why Xhaiden said you were special. You are the flame that burns so brightly."

Astoria hummed in appreciation of how he stroked her head, and the gentle lull of his power. "Don't bother giving me some lecture about having the courage to live rather than letting this take me."

"Would you listen?"

"Not today." She wanted to fall asleep, but feared the return of her dreams. "Sing for me, Charnel."

His hand settled on her neck; a comforting weight that encouraged her eyes to flutter shut. "As you wish. But I remind you like I do every time you ask. My voice is not as beautiful as yours."

"And as always, I'll point out that I don't care. It makes me happy to listen to you."

The song he picked was one Charnel knew she liked. It was easy to sink into the words while his mind wandered with the currents of the sea. Better to drift through the water than linger too long on the dying woman in his lap. As long as his voice kept her quiet, he could prepare for when Dawn came in all her storming glory to demand the return of her lover. He wanted to gather Astoria up in his arms, and whisper sweet promises to keep her safe, no matter what. It was an impossibility he knew Dawn would need to face, and the dozing hawk who loved them both would expect him to be there to help the other god.

Stroking her cheek, Charnel sighed in defeat. "You never could leave well enough alone, my precious Fire Hawk. Not back then, and not now. But I'll deal with the consequences when it's time. There may yet be some good to come from this. I just hope your decision to run back to Diwan won't start a war no one wants to fight. Because your sister's heart is full of anger over what happened to her, and I don't think she's going to forgive you. This sickness will make you suffer, but she will make you hurt."

FIVE

Storm clouds smothered the sky, waiting to be unleashed the moment her temper snapped. It felt like the only thing keeping her from losing control was the perfectly calm sea beneath her ship. The crew knew better than to approach, even as she strode back and forth across the deck, peering over the side impatiently. When she returned from locating Astoria, she had gone straight to her cabin and pulled on clothes to distract herself for a moment. Her coat fluttered in the wind, and the sails of *The Storm Bird* were taut. Driven across the sea under the command of her power, the ship continued its path, following the direction the bond pointed her in, chasing the one person she preferred to avoid.

Every moment that slipped past filled Dawn with agitation. All she cared about was retrieving the other woman so the healer could help her. She wanted to see her back on board, tucked up safely in their bed. It was a desperate need clawing at her gut, wriggling thorny vines around her heart that clenched tight every time the god thought about a life without Astoria. No one needed to remind Dawn her lover planned to leave. It was something she needed to come to terms with on her own. What she could not bear was the possibility of having her hawk ripped away from her by death.

Peering over the rail at the calm waters disturbed only by the passing ship, Dawn opened her mind to the bond with Charnel. He was moving away from her instead of bringing Astoria back. The relationship between them had confused her, but it had given her hawk something she could not. Whatever her watery counterpart did for Astoria, Dawn never asked. It was better if she did not, because she wanted no reason to resent them. What she knew was that Charnel cared for Astoria, just as much as she did, and he would not intentionally harm her. Which left her wondering why he was taking her away when she needed to see the healer.

It fed her dread. Dawn could not help but wonder if he knew something was terribly wrong with Astoria and believed he could get her to help faster. Pressing her lips together, she wondered if she needed to go to her mother. They could meet Charnel wherever he surfaced with her hawk, and the god of life could deal with whatever illness had taken hold of her. Then she would make sure Charnel knew exactly what she thought of his actions. If he had taken the time to inform her of the situation, Dawn would have helped him.

"Captain?" Cass approached her cautiously, the wind whipping her hair across her face. "Where are we going? Any sign of them?"

"No, none. He's taking her somewhere, but I don't know where. Or why."

Leaning on the rail, the kelpie watched the swirl of water moving out of the way of the ship. "Maybe you should try talking to him?"

"She's not well, Cass. Why would he take her away? If Charnel knows something is wrong with her that needs help, why not bring her back to me? I could have gotten my mother by now, and Tory would be better." Pinching the bridge of her nose, Dawn considered her options. "I should just get her. Charnel is frightened of her, so he's less likely to resist giving me back my hawk."

"Or you could leave it be."

She spun to face her first mate, staring at Cass in horror. "Excuse me?"

"Maybe it's not an illness. Maybe this is her leaving. Charnel would help Tory if she asked him to. He worships her."

"No, she wouldn't just leave like this."

Cass shook her head, gesturing at her. "Why not? You do it to her. Every time she sets foot out on deck, I see the pain in her eyes when she doesn't find you here. Maybe this is her attempt to make you feel a little of what she feels. Don't go running to your mother, Dawn. Just follow him and see what happens. My guess is the Lord of Tides is taking our hawk home."

Grinding her teeth, Dawn considered what Cass had said. She wanted to dismiss it out of concern for Astoria's health, but she suspected it was true. What stopped her was the memory of how hot the other woman had felt. There had been a glassiness to her eyes that could not be faked. If there was one thing that Dawn knew with certainty, it was that Astoria was unwell. Even if she had asked Charnel to take her away, it did not change the fact she needed a healer.

Dawn stared at the clouds, running her tongue across her teeth as she considered what to do. "He can take her farther inland than we can. If we assume Diwan is the destination, Charnel will need to stop before the border, or he risks the agreement between my parents and the Unseelie."

"Don't, Dawn. Don't stop them." Cass grabbed her arm, ignoring the sudden crack of lightning breaking through the clouds. "If she wants to go, let her. Sometimes that's the best thing you can do for someone. Let them go. If Tory wants to return, she will, but you can't force it to happen."

"She's right. You need to let her go."

The voice of her uncle was one Dawn dreaded hearing. Shoulders slumping, she turned to face him, carefully avoiding his gaze. Cass nodded to the Lord of Time, knowing better than to stick around when it came to issues involving the gods. Other members of the crew made themselves scarce, leaving their tasks if they could without risking the ship.

"Uncle Emlyn."

He studied her before lifting his gaze to the sky. "Astoria needs to return to Diwan, and Charnel will take her without a fight. If she had remained here, you would have tried to stop her from leaving once the ship docked. This isn't about you, Dawn. So please don't make it."

"Will you tell me what's going on? I have a right to know." Crossing her arms, Dawn lifted her chin, tempted to defy his request even though she knew he had already seen all outcomes.

"Come with me."

Extending his hand to her, Emlyn arched his brows. The look he gave her reminded Dawn of her mother, and she huffed, letting her arms drop. As soon as her hand touched his, she felt the shift in the fabric of the world that confirmed his intention. It took a moment to adjust to the feeling of solid ground beneath her feet, and she breathed in deeply, tasting the dirt in the air. She knew where they were, but it was a place she had avoided. Sweeping her gaze over the brittle land, Dawn wondered why he had brought her to the site of a battle long before their time.

"Few people know what happened here, Dawn." Sweeping his arm outward, Emlyn did not look at the land, instead keeping his gaze locked on her. "Astoria is one of them. As is Charnel."

"I know. It's a reason they're friends. They met back then."

"My mother, your grandmother, she never knew the other gods were conspiring against her. That they had been doing so long before the Sundering."

Dawn snorted, giving him a pointed look. "And yet it was her son who brought about her rebirth."

"Indeed. And if my plan had not worked, Gebael would have killed your mother as a newborn. Yet here we are. If you're hoping I'll feel guilty over what happened, you'll be waiting a while."

Nudging a rock with her foot, she wondered why her mother had not brought life back to the region. It remained barren after the battle between the old Unseelie and those who had come to the aid of the ancient cities of Endara and Ensaycal. Her ancestors. If it had not been for them, the mad god would have wiped out her parents' bloodlines. Tir would have changed for the worse. The dragons had fallen in the battle, assisting the last of the original Ravens. Astoria had been there with her mother. She had taken part in the fight, defending the Ravens as they drained the life from the ground and the Unseelie standing upon it. They had blighted the land.

"What does this place have to do with what's going on with Tory?"

Coming to stand beside her, Emlyn shoved his hands into his pockets. "There were choices made that have waited a long time to come to light. Astoria was a witness to many of them, though she doesn't remember most of it. She knows what Gebael and Annawyn did to Eivor, and she knew the truth about those born as husk makers... and she knows about the dragons, Dawn."

Frowning, she glanced at him. "What do you mean? The dragons are gone."

"No, they're not. Not all of them. They're in hiding. Why do you think you avoid the Kutini Peninsula? No ship dares go near that place, not even the one captained by the god of air. Have you never noticed how Astoria stares at it when you sail past? She has been there. Her magic is in the very ground of that place, and it calls for her to return."

"Are you telling me my hawk knows the dragons still live?"

Emlyn did not answer, walking forward to survey the dead land. His power picked up the traces of the choices made that day, offering flickers of alternative paths they could have taken. It had happened before his birth, but if the gods scheming against his mother had not made the decisions they had, he would never have been born. Tir would have burned. A whisper of his power sometimes taunted him with the fact that what the previous gods of choice and chaos had done had led to him being the god of time. Their third. They had quietly pulled the strings of existence, working in the shadows while the other gods fought with each other.

"Uncle Emlyn, there's more to it, isn't there? What did they do to Astoria?"

Closing his eyes, he wished he could tell her everything. "I've had visions of this battle. Your hawk fought with such determination that it changed Charnel. He was there to help keep the dragon fire from destroying the humans and elves fleeing from the Unseelie."

"That's why they're friends? I mean, I can appreciate connecting over a shared experience, but you're almost making it sound like Charnel saw Tory across the battlefield and fell in love."

"I cannot attest to that. You know he calls her Fire Hawk."

Scowling at his back, Dawn waved at the barren land. "Having seen her fight, I can imagine she would have flown through dragon fire during the battle. That would leave an impression on anyone."

A wind stirred, picking up dirt as it whirled a path in front of Emlyn. He glanced back at his niece, arching a brow in annoyance before the willy willy struck. Power rippled outward, freezing it in place. Swiping the particles away from his face, the god of time turned and strode back to stand in front of Dawn.

"You are too much like your mother, Dawn. Always avoiding the truth, even when it's right in front of you. If you interfere with Astoria returning to Diwan, she will never forgive you."

"But why is it so important for her to go back? I know she wanted to make things right with Eivor over the whole abandoning Diwan issue, but that doesn't seem like something you need to become involved in."

Her willy willy dissipated, replaced by a wall of wind capable of ripping rocks from the ground, sending them flying across the land. Emlyn gave her a pointed look; his mouth twisted in an expression she normally only saw on her mother's face. Squinting, Dawn glanced at the sky and wondered if her uncle had warned Life of her daughter's potential upset. Part of her hoped Eirian would show up, because then she could ask her why she had not restored the land they stood on. Then she would demand for her hawk to be healed of whatever ailment had left her fevered, and willing to run away.

"No, your mother is not coming," Emlyn said.

"I hate it when you do that."

"You hate it when I see the likely variations unfolding from an interaction I'm having? Well, I'm sorry if my power is an inconvenience to you, Dawn. Personally, I find it helps me ensure things go the right way."

"Why isn't my mother coming?" She felt an urge to cross her arms and stomp her foot, but Dawn suspected he was expecting her to behave like a bratty child, and she was determined to disappoint him.

Slipping his hand into a pocket of his coat, Emlyn withdrew a long ribbon of burnt orange silk. "You should braid this into your hair."

Eyes narrowing, she did not reach out to take the ribbon. "There's always a reason you want people to wear your gifts. Now tell me why Astoria needs to return to Diwan."

"Because she's going to repair the rift between her sisters caused by her choices. She ran from Diwan, abandoning Silaine to find her own way, and leaving Eivor to suffer for a hundred years at the hands of Oisin. When Astoria landed on your ship, she decided not to ask you to help her home."

"If she had, I would have." Her mouth twisted and Dawn glanced away in shame. "When I found out who she really was, I offered to take her back to Diwan to free it from Oisin, but Pa told me I wasn't allowed to interfere. Uncle Tigs said he was also told to do nothing."

"Because the variations demanded it. Eivor Havard needed to go through what she did, so the Unseelie would have their queen. She has battled every day since her salvation to help others. If we had rescued her, the Unseelie would have remained under the control of the wrong person, and they would have done more harm than good to the people of Tir. Astoria knew this. That is why she didn't ask you for help. That is why she left her sisters and ran."

Shock had Dawn sinking to the ground, covering her mouth as the air went still. Crouching in front of her, Emlyn plucked one of her braids from the mess of her hair, tying the orange ribbon in a bow at the end. When he was done, he cupped her cheek, gazing at her sadly.

"Astoria has done as instructed, even if she's not fully aware of it. She knows her memories have been altered, and gods have manipulated her existence. As does Charnel. It is something they can talk about when they're together. You're so young, Dawn, and war has not touched you like it has them. He offered her something you couldn't, but you knew that, which is why you never stopped her from going to him, even though it hurt."

"So, I'm just to let her go? After all these years, I don't even get a goodbye?"

"What you get is to learn patience. Good things come to those who wait."

Staring across the land, Dawn tried to imagine Astoria flying through dragon fire to attack immortals she had no hope of killing. "Maybe it's better this way. I can't give her what she deserves. Let her go to Diwan to do what she needs to do, and I'll continue as I am."

Resting his hand on her head, Emlyn smiled. "Yes, you should let her go."

"Because it's what you want me to do."

"You're family, Dawn. I want you to be happy, just like I want all of us to be happy. Bide your time, and everything will be as it is supposed to be. This path is the right one for Tir. It avoids a war the Unseelie aren't ready for."

Closing her eyes, the god of air did not bother trying to come up with an argument. There was no point in seeking help from her parents. If Emlyn declared a path had to be taken, none of the other gods would step out of line. He was Time; he saw things they could never fully understand. Anything she might do, he had already seen unfold, and it left her with no choice but to walk the road he chose. Remembering the ribbon, she opened her eyes, peering at it where it dangled on the end of her braid. The colour was an odd shade of orange, reminding Dawn of the glow of embers in a fire.

"I'll play your game, Lord of Time, but if anything happens to Astoria?"

"Fire will consume your rage, Dawn. Trust me, all will be well."

SIX

It felt strange to be carried ashore in Charnel's arms, but considering she felt terrible, Astoria had no desire to complain. She did not want to find out if she could have managed on her own. Collapsing after insisting on walking would have been more embarrassing than accepting his help. Besides, knowing they would soon part ways left the duine with a need to remain curled against him for as long as possible.

With the promise of a slow, painful death hanging over her head, she did not know if she would ever see Charnel again. Or Dawn. She needed to make the best of what little time she had left to memorise the line of his stubbled jaw, and the flutter of his dark eyelashes whenever he stole a glance down at her. Astoria wanted to remember the stray curls stuck to his forehead, and how he shivered whenever she ran her fingers down one of the dark lines decorating his body.

What she did not want to remember was the deep ache of guilt threatening to steal her breath unless she returned to Dawn. Leaving without saying goodbye to the woman she loved was one of the worst things she had done, and Astoria hoped the god would forgive her. On their journey towards Diwan, she had pleaded repeatedly with Charnel to convey her message to the Storm Queen. Even if it meant hurting Tir, she needed Dawn to understand why she had gone. She did not want to be healed of her affliction, and if she had remained, they would have taken the choice from her. There was no way the Air would have let her die when all she had to do was fetch her mother.

"I have no clothes for you," Charnel said, gaze sweeping over the empty bank of the river that fed into Diwan. "And I don't know if shifting forms to fly the rest of the way is a good idea."

Cupping his cheek, she banished her thoughts of Dawn. "I'll be fine. I'm sure the sickness has not progressed so much in this short amount of time as to render me incapable of flying from here to the castle."

"Without my power soothing your fever, you're going to feel worse quickly."

"And then I'll be back where I started, and either my sister will kill me on the spot, or she'll send for a healer when I collapse at her feet in a delirious state, muttering about dying."

He scowled at her, grasp tightening. "I wish I could take you all the way."

"I know, but the agreement is more important than I am. You'll not start a war because of me, Charnel."

Moving towards a patch of grass that looked soft enough to set her down, Water ignored the shrill cries of the birds they disturbed. Tiny finches darted away, landing in a nearby shrub to twitter in annoyance. Far above, shadows circled, and Astoria wondered if they were true birds. She figured she would find out once Charnel let her shift and take off. If they were daoine who answered to her sister, Eivor would soon find out about her return. The grass was strange against her bare skin, but the hawk smiled at her companion thankfully.

"This is a mistake." He refused to let go, pulling her into his lap. "I should get Eirian and fix this."

"No, Charnel. That's not what I want. If I wanted to be healed, I'd have asked you to return me to Dawn. I know this is hard, and we're unlikely to see each other again, but I need you to let me go."

Shaking his head, the god avoided looking her in the eye. Resting her head against his shoulder, Astoria let him struggle with what he needed to do. She did not want to fight after everything that had passed between them. His power twisted outwards, leaving drops of water dangling from the tips of grass and leaves, while the finches chirped in delight. They had not found the courage to venture back to their foraging, and Astoria watched them bopping around in the bush. When she shifted into her hawk form, they would flee in fear. Eyes darting up to study Charnel, she wondered if he knew how much she appreciated his company, regardless of the situation.

"I promise I'll go to the Rainbow Vale and tell your sister about your condition." Dropping his head, he pressed a kiss to her forehead. "I wish we could have gone there together. It's a beautiful place."

"You've taken me to beautiful places, Charnel. They're memories I'll cherish until I cannot remember anything. Do you also promise to ask the other gods to undo what was done to me?"

"Are you sure you want me to?"

Closing her eyes, Astoria let memories of fire and screaming wash across her thoughts before banishing them. "Yes. I'd like to know everything I should feel guilty about. Especially if it's something I need to apologise to my sisters for. If you ever see Briallen Altira again, tell her I said goodbye."

Giving her a baffled look, the god of water asked, "Briallen Altira?"

"Yes, the dragon rider I helped. She saved my life. The one with Eclipse."

"Oh, right, Gebael's precious half-duine. Sorry, Tory, I didn't bother to learn names. I was too busy keeping the dragon fire from spreading to the refugees from Endara and Ensaycal."

"And looking at my arse."

The indignant look on his face made her laugh. It felt good to giggle over something as silly as remembering the name of one person from a battle over a millennium ago. She thought about the sanctuary where they had hidden the survivors, and wondered if those dragon riders who had belonged to the First People had found themselves back there when the Fog was lifted, or if they were wandering Tir searching for their bonded. Chewing her lip, Astoria hoped they had slipped back into their lives without too much pain. The disconnect most of her kind had felt during the Fog would have been that much worse for the dragons who had their bonded ripped away from them for over 1000 years.

"Since the Fog lifted, I've rarely gone a day without wondering what I could have done to change things," Astoria said quietly, struggling to sit up.

For a moment, it seemed like Charnel would not let her go, but his arms loosened. He helped her sit in his lap, her back resting against his chest while his arms curled around her stomach. It was easy to forget what she needed to do and lose herself in the feel of his fingertips tracing patterns on her skin. Sliding her hand up to cup his face, Astoria twisted around to draw him into a kiss.

There was no hungry clash of mouths, simply the slow caress of longing. For all her attempts to push him into a final tryst on their journey, Charnel had remained firm in his refusal. She wanted to sink into his embrace and forget the anguish of saying goodbye.

"Tory, my Fire Hawk," he murmured against her lips. "I don't want this to be how we say goodbye."

"Why not?"

"Because I don't want to say goodbye at all."

The grief in his voice made her close her eyes. Astoria knew she should cry over the unfairness of her situation, but she was aware she was the one being unfair. All she needed to do was say please, and Charnel would fetch the god who could solve her problem. There would be no need to say goodbye, or to shed tears over the tattered dreams of a future that was not hers to claim. Her illness was not a punishment for her crimes, no matter how much she tried to convince herself it was. Life did not work that way.

"I'm sorry, but please don't forgive me. I don't deserve it." Kissing him again, Astoria did her best to pour all the unspoken emotions she possessed into it.

Peeling away, she rolled out of his lap and knelt on the grass. A voice at the back of her mind screamed to return to Charnel's embrace. Reaching for her magic, Astoria wove the strands of it through her body, letting the transformation slide over her as easily as it had thousands of times before. It was better to do it while his power held the fever at bay. Ruffling her feathers, the hawk suspected it would be the last time she could enjoy flying. If her death progressed as quickly as she feared, there would be no more shifting. All she wanted was one more flight beside Eivor in her magpie form. One hunt together as sisters through the forests of their youth.

"*Thank you, my love.*"

Charnel pulled his knees to his chest, staring at her with wide eyes filled with unshed tears. "Don't go, Tory."

Her talons dug into the grass, and the finches screamed in the bush. "*I want to. Tell Dawn I love her, and I said goodbye. Don't let her start a war no one deserves to suffer through. There's been enough of them, and our families have been involved with too many already.*"

"I'll do my best."

"And maybe don't pass over. I know you find her intolerable at the best of times, but Dawn is so very young. She needs someone who understands how hard life can be to guide her. I tried, now it's your turn."

It received the reaction she hoped for, and Astoria chirped when the god raised a brow in disapproval. His expression faded back into sorrow, blue eyes becoming a shade reminiscent of the dirty waters of a flooded river after rain had washed the land clean. Spreading her wings, she walked closer, nipping at his leg with her beak. The click was a threat to the god, but the fussing finches finally gave up on waiting for the giant predator to leave and swarmed away from their bush.

"Look what you've done, my precious Fire Hawk." He stroked her head, fingers seeking the spot behind her ears that always felt delightful when scratched. "You can bite me if you like, but you know it gets you nowhere. Doesn't even give you the satisfaction of drawing blood."

She was tempted to indulge in his suggestion. *"But it's fun."*

"You should go before it gets any later. Enjoy these daylight hours."

Peering at the sky with her keen eyes, Astoria was thankful they had surfaced shortly after sunrise. There was no sign of rain, and the soft white clouds promised a fine day for flying. If she was fortunate, the wind would be in her favour. A small part of her was worried Dawn would have shrouded Diwan in bad weather to spite her. Though Charnel would have known before their arrival and come up with a different plan.

"Unless you've changed your mind..."

"No, I haven't. I won't. Be strong, Charnel. You are more than that old bitch of a god made you believe you were. There is a world of beauty you can share with Dawn. You would be so very good for her if you tried."

"I'll never stop being amazed you think you can tell me what to do."

If she could have grinned at him, Astoria would have. *"I never heard you complaining when I told you to lie back and let me suck your cock."*

He flicked his hand at her, and a light spray of water left her feathers damp. Shaking them out, Astoria snapped her beak, but the god chuckled. Bopping the curved tip he had seen tear through flesh in battle, Charnel traced the line of her hawk shape with his gaze. She was magnificent in both her forms, and he wished he could put his emotions into words in a way that conveyed everything.

"Goodbye, Astoria Havard. I hope we see each other again."

Dipping her head, she accepted a final scratch, and felt the rush of his power through her. They did not know how long it would hold the fever at bay, so she knew she needed to keep her focus on flying to the castle that had been her home. Spreading her wings, Astoria felt any traces of moisture evaporating, and chirped her appreciation. It felt wonderful to take off, even if half of her heart remained on the ground with Charnel. The other half was with Dawn.

"Thank you, Charnel. I love you, and I love her. Remember me."

When she glanced down, Astoria caught him fading from sight. It felt like her heart was going to shatter and she did not know why. Thankful she could not cry in her hawk form, the duine set her mind to locating familiar landmarks to guide her way. She had memorised maps long ago, but they never gave a bird's perspective. As soon as she spotted a tumble-down tower near the river, she knew Charnel had brought them to the edge of the border. There were no signs of patrols, only wandering livestock kept in their fields by stone and timber fences. In the distance, other birds watched her, confirming Astoria's suspicions. Who they were and what they intended to do did not matter as long as she reached the castle before nightfall, and preferably before Charnel's power wore off, leaving her at the mercy of the cancer.

It made her want to laugh as she flew. Her eyes followed the glittering river as her wings carried her towards the place she had happily turned her back on. There was irony to be found in the fact that after everything she had done, it was an illness that would bring her down. Astoria almost hoped Eivor would decide to execute her and put an end to her suffering before it became too apparent. While it was rare for a duine to be stricken with such an affliction, she had witnessed others die from it. Magic could heal a lot of things, but it did not cure. She knew she would steadily waste away until there was nothing left for her body to fight with. A quick beheading was preferable.

Astoria kept low enough over the land to see the changes. There were more towns outside the city, more farms. They had cleared sections of the forests to make way for the increase in population. Roads scarred the ground where there had been none when she left. It filled her with mixed emotions. On one hand, she was thrilled to see Diwan thrive under Eivor's leadership, but she grieved having not played a part in those changes. Guilt beat an angry fist on the shards of her heart, grinding harder the closer her wings brought her to the city.

When she finally set her sights on the towers that haunted her dreams, it did not surprise Astoria to see winged figures circling it. Not just her fellow daoine, but pixies who had joined the Unseelie faction led by Eivor and her consorts. No one attempted to stop her, and the former princess circled the grounds to decide where she would land. In all her thoughts about how things would go when she reached the castle, Astoria had not spared the time to plan her landing. If anything, she had expected to be attacked before it was possible to set down anywhere on her own.

Spotting people gathered in a garden, she decided it was better than nothing and folded her wings back to dive. Wind rushed through her feathers, filling her with a muted version of the delight she usually felt. She could not bring herself to relish it, like she had before she learnt she was dying. All she wanted was to land without being harmed, and to shift back to plead for mercy. Landing on the perfectly maintained lawn surrounded by towering gum trees, Astoria kept her head lowered and wings spread, eyes searching the crowd.

They watched her, no one attempting to approach or to speak to her. The silence in her mind was odd. She had missed the chatter of daoine mind speaking to each other, and to arrive to find no voices whispering across the shared link left her uneasy. Reaching for her magic, she felt a flicker of fear when it was slow to respond to her demand to shift back to her natural form. Pain coursed through her, a deep ache settling into her bones that left Astoria gasping in shock. Burying her hands in the grass, she realised Charnel's power had faded, and she had not known it while transformed.

"Well, look who thought she would come crawling back."

It was an effort to lift her head, but Astoria wanted to see her sister. "Hello Eivor. Have you missed me?"

"Do you mind giving her your coat, Precious?" The black and white-haired duine nodded at the tall man beside her. "You don't look good, Astoria. Has your wonderful god finally grown tired of you?"

Watching the man walking towards her while he peeled off a deep green coat, Astoria frowned. He looked familiar, and when their eyes met, her memory offered her an image of a goblin man in dragon rider's leathers helping her stand after she had transformed in battle to fight a particularly vicious Unseelie aligned goblin.

"Tristan?" She blinked and shook her head in confusion. "What are you doing here?"

The green eyes she remembered clearly widened, and the red-haired goblin dropped to his knees. "How do you know that name? Have you seen him?"

Her memories faded, and Astoria felt like her skin was crawling. Staring at the man in front of her, she realised he was not the goblin she had fought alongside in battle. But he looked like he could have been his brother. Lifting her gaze to find Eivor had joined them, she let her exhaustion show.

"I'm sorry, sister. So very sorry."

There was a soft caress across her mind, and the Diwanian queen sighed. "Someone fetch Jola. Rhyd, help her put the coat on, and then pick her up carefully. It seems the Battle Hawk is dying."

"If it helps, I was already coming back when I found out."

"I'm Rhydwen. I'd say it's nice to meet you, Astoria, but I think it's too soon to say either way." The goblin was gentle as he helped her slide her arms into his coat.

A child ran over to them, giggling as a black-haired woman chased her. "Ma! Ma! Look what I made."

Eivor picked the little girl up, and Astoria wanted to cry at how much like their mother she looked. "This is your Aunty Tory, my little Rose. Say hello."

Bright blue eyes beamed down at her, and the girl wriggled to be let loose. "Hello Aunty Tory."

Covering her face as Rhydwen picked her up, Astoria let her heart be gobbled up by guilt. Tears finally broke free of her walls, flooding her cheeks as he carried her inside.

SEVEN

Her eyes followed the bustling woman, picking up on the smallest things she suspected the healer did not believe she would notice. The chambers they had brought her to were not the ones she had called her own before Talaroo invaded, but the quality of them surprised Astoria. She had expected to be taken to either a cell or some small room in a forgotten corner, where it would be easy to hide her presence from the rest of the court. Instead, Rhydwen had carried her to a set of chambers in the family section of the palace and chatted the entire way there as though she was not the woman who had abandoned his wife to be tortured for a hundred years.

"I feel you watching me, girl." Jola glanced at her, eyes narrowed. "How did you find out about this? You're a warrior, not a healer."

Whatever Eivor had read from her thoughts when she arrived in the garden had been relayed to the healer before any of them arrived in the chamber. Astoria let her head fall back against the pillow, realising it felt strange without the rock of a ship beneath her. The bed was soft, pillows and blankets cushioning her body in a way that did not add to the ache. She missed the soothing chill of Charnel's power, but Jola had already forced a concoction down her throat to take the edge off the fever that had returned in full force, leaving a sheen of sweat coating her skin.

"Charnel told me. I awoke on *The Storm Bird* and the fever had set in, but before Dawn fetched the healer, I fled the ship and ended up with him. His power helped, and he told me he could feel the cancer in my blood. He brought me to the border because I wanted to come back to make my peace."

There was a cup in her hands when Jola returned to the bed. "He's right, you're extremely sick. There's not a lot I can do other than make you comfortable in your final months."

Smiling bitterly, Astoria accepted the drink without commenting on the unpleasant tang of it. "I know, and I'm not asking for anything more than that. If I'd wanted to be healed, I would have gone back to *The Storm Bird*, or let Charnel do what he wanted to do when he realised I'm dying."

"Why didn't you?" Brushing her fingertips over the duine's forehead, Jola frowned. "We know you're the sky god's lover. She would have arranged for you to be healed by her mother."

"I don't want to be healed. It's as simple as that."

"Do you realise how much you're going to suffer? This will ravage your body. From what I've assessed, your power is the source of the fever."

"What do you mean?" She swirled the drink around in the cup before draining the contents.

Jola perched on the edge of the bed beside her, plucking the empty cup from her grasp to place it on the small table. "Your magic is attacking the cancer. It's as though it's trying to burn it out of you. I've not seen anything quite like it before, but I'm also a goblin and until a couple of hundred years ago, mortal ailments were hardly something I had a lot of experience dealing with."

She did not get to respond when the small girl from the garden bolted into the room, throwing herself onto the bed with a wild giggle. Following her, Eivor appeared amused, and less inclined to do anything about her daughter bouncing around her estranged sister than Astoria expected. There was no sign of either of her consorts, which gave the hawk some small sense of relief. Plonking down on the pillows, a grinning Rose rolled over onto her stomach and kicked her legs in the air.

"Aunty Tory, are you ready to play with me?"

"Rosie, sweetheart, your Aunty Tory can't play right now," Eivor said, standing at the end of the bed. "I told you she's not feeling very well. But you can cuddle up and read to her after she's had a bath."

Pouting, the girl refused to move. "But Jola makes everyone feel better."

Meeting her sister's gaze, Astoria saw the tiredness there. "Why don't we make a deal, Rose? I need to have a bath, and something to eat, but you can read to me afterwards. Then tomorrow, when I have a little more energy, we can play a game of your choosing."

"Oh, no, don't suggest that!" Jola cringed, eyeing the girl warily. "She's a handful."

"Just like her aunt was at the same age," Eivor said, smoothing her hands over the fabric of her skirts before gingerly sitting on the end of the bed. "So, is it true? Don't make me violate your thoughts again, Tory. You know I don't like to do it without a good reason."

The child wriggled closer, resting her chin on Astoria's leg. Her blue eyes threatened to send the hawk plunging into the memories that had haunted her for so long. It was strange to see fragments of her sisters, and her parents stitched together with a smattering of someone else. Even the shape of Rose's eyes reminded her of Silaine. She was not the only child Eivor had, which left her wondering who the others looked like the most.

"Yes, it's true." Giving her a wry smile, Astoria ruffled her niece's hair.

"Well then, I suppose there's no point in throwing you in the cells."

Huffing, Jola pointed at the queen. "Don't even think about it. It doesn't matter what she's done, she's still your sister, and she's dying. Not a pleasant death, a horrible one."

It felt uncomfortable to be discussing her illness so openly with a five-year-old girl grinning at her. Covering Rose's ears, Astoria gave the other two women an annoyed look.

"This isn't appropriate for young ears."

Eivor inclined her head, and there was a glimmer of affection in her gaze that took Astoria by surprise. "You're right. Talaith, come get your sister!"

A tall young woman with red hair hurried into the room, her blue eyes a mirror of Eivor's. "Of course, Ma. Rosie, come with me and we can go find Keeran down at the stables."

Squealing, the girl jumped from the bed, forcing her sister to catch her. "Can we go riding?"

"Maybe later if Mama agrees to come with us. You know she doesn't like us riding anywhere without her. Now say bye to Ma, Aunty Jola, and Aunty Tory."

"Bye bye!" Pressing her hand to her mouth, Rose blew kisses to them.

Watching her nieces leave the room, Astoria rubbed her face, and tried to remind the guilt chipping away at her heart that they would never have been born if she had not abandoned Diwan. She had quietly gathered information on how well Eivor was doing in Diwan with her family, and she had met Thorne when Dawn agreed to help deal with a situation involving the Shadforthian Empire. They had come together to fight alongside the dullaghan who remained loyal to Death to liberate the people enslaved by the ambitious emperor of Shadforth. It was one thing Dawn and the Unseelie agreed on.

"She's beautiful, Eivor. They both are," Astoria said. "I haven't met Silaine's son, but I was told he's growing up nicely. You've both done so well for yourselves."

"While you sailed the seas warming a god's bed." Leaning back against the corner post, Eivor lifted her legs onto the bed and studied her sister.

Fussing with the pillows behind Astoria, Jola made no attempt to provide them with the illusion of privacy. "You can't be too angry with her, Eivor. She's been fighting the same battle as you. The Storm Queen and her fleet of pirates have liberated countless people from the flesh traders. They help coastal communities."

"Which is why I didn't have her shot out of the sky."

"I wouldn't have blamed you if you had. It's the least I deserve. This illness is my punishment, Eivor, and the suffering it causes me won't come close to making up for what I left you to endure." Shifting to let Jola move a pillow, Astoria bit back the desire to tell her to stop fussing.

Grief replaced the anger in her sister's gaze. "I don't want you to suffer, Tory. Yes, I'm angry, and I doubt I could ever completely forgive you for abandoning me. But you're still my sister, just like Laine is. I don't hate either of you for your choices, and I'm happy she's thriving with the danann."

"Maybe you don't hate me, but I certainly do."

Lowering the walls in her mind, Astoria left her thoughts and memories open to the older duine. There was no point shielding them anymore, and with her body battling the illness destined to claim her life, she doubted she would spend much time outside the chamber they had brought her to. It would save time and energy if Eivor took the information from her mind instead. A white braid slipped free of the queen's elegant arrangement, dangling across her face as she stared at her sister in horror.

"You can't mean for me to do that!"

"Please, Eivor. I don't know how long I have, so indulge me. You can ask your questions, but it's easier for both of us if you rummage around up here." Tapping the side of her head, Astoria ignored Jola's scowl. "Though I suggest you avoid certain topics… like Dawn. You might not enjoy those memories."

They stared at each other, neither willing to back down. It had always been that way between them, and Astoria was pleased it had not changed. Eivor's magic was a gentle caress across her mind, slipping through her thoughts and memories, dancing across those that filled her with happiness. Closing her eyes, the hawk did not fight the intrusion, knowing it was safer to let her sister pick her path.

"You knew…" Lips parted in shock, Eivor tumbled from the bed in her hurry to put distance between them. "How could you not tell me what you knew?"

"If Annawyn had found out what I knew, what do you think she would have done to me?"

Jola realised what they were talking about and staggered backwards, resting against the wall. "How could you know about the mad god and what she did to your older sister?"

"Because no one really noticed me. I was Craven's little warrior, the Battle Hawk, and Malena's disappointment. You are the result of bargains, and Silaine came about because Gebael and Aunty Liv wanted our mother to try again for a husk maker. No one bothered to see me standing in the shadows, watching. Listening. Gathering information."

"Why don't I remember you and Mother leaving to fight Annawyn's army? You were there when the dragons fell. I saw it in your mind. They still exist. Tory, you know where they are!" Striding over to the bed, Eivor gave Jola a knowing look. "But there are large parts of your memories that have been... manipulated."

"I know. There are things I have conveniently forgotten, and things I cannot speak of. I asked Charnel to speak to the other gods about restoring my mind before I die, but I don't know if he will do it."

Huffing, the goblin pointed at her. "I've seen that look on your sister's face. What else did you ask him?"

"To tell Silaine what was going on. I'm dying. Is it so wrong to want to say goodbye?"

"Leave us, Jola. Please." Climbing in next to Astoria, the queen gave her a little shove to move. "We need to talk about things that should remain between sisters."

"Are you sure, Eivor?" She crossed her arms, scowling at them.

"She's no threat to me."

"Fine, but I'm in the other room. The moment it feels like her fever is increasing, call me."

Eivor frowned at the healer before pressing her lips to Astoria's forehead as though she were a child again. "Noted. Won't your medicine keep it under control for hours yet?"

"If it was a normal fever, I'd say yes. But as I told her, my examination suggests the fever is because of her magic trying to fight the cancer. I've never dealt with anything like it."

Leaning against her sister, Astoria smiled grimly. "I'm sorry. But if it helps, maybe check with the healers in the infirmary who have been here for a long time. I know there have been others who've died of similar illnesses, so maybe they have records that can give us more information."

There was a gleam of begrudging respect in Jola's gaze as she inclined her head. "Good thinking. I'll find out what I can from them. Perhaps this is a normal response."

"Tell Rhydwen and Thorne they don't need to hover like overprotective fools," Eivor said, sliding an arm under her sister so she could pull the younger woman closer. "They may as well go find something to do instead of bothering me with their fretting. It's getting annoying."

Laughing as she turned and walked from the room, the goblin waved dismissively. Resting her head on Eivor's shoulder, Astoria remembered the threats Thorne had levelled at her when they first met. They had wisely waited until Dawn was gone from her side before declaring what they intended to do to her if she ever hurt the Diwanian queen again. She had respected the dullaghan even more for it.

"Why do you love them?" her sister asked quietly.

Closing her eyes, Astoria hummed in amusement. "Why do you love your consorts?"

"Because I want to. Calista demanded I take Rhydwen as my concubine in return for my freedom, so I did, but only after he and I discussed it. We decided to become a team, to build a future together as friends and lovers. I wanted a family filled with the happiness I thought our family had. Never did I realise how much of it was a show. Each of us had a vastly different upbringing."

"Of course we did. We may have had the same parents, but we did not have the same parents. I'm sorry, Eivor. Part of me thinks this illness is my punishment for my part in everything."

"I can't believe you flew through dragon fire and survived!" Giving her an amazed look, Eivor poked her ribs. "I wish I could have seen it! But now I know why Rhydwen is going out of his mind. Who is Tristan? Why was there a goblin who looks like he could be my husband's dark-haired brother fighting with the dragons? He's never mentioned him before, and neither has Thorne. Or the others."

Casting her memories back to the battlefield, Astoria shrugged. "I don't know who he is to Rhydwen, but Tristan was a dragon rider, and he saved my life during the battle. We fought together. The rest? I really don't know."

"Tory, if Laine wishes to come here to visit you before the end, I'll let her. You want to mend things between us, and I understand your desire. But you must see why I cannot bend the knee to the gods."

"Who told you that's what the gods want? And I'll spare you my crude jokes about bending the knee to Dawn because that's an entirely different thing to what you're talking about."

The strangled noise that came from her sister's throat when she let a memory surface to the front of her thoughts brought a smile to her lips. It was only half intentional. Astoria wanted to close her eyes and sink into the ghost of Dawn's touches, and the feel of warm sand beneath her knees as she pleasured the god. Fingers pinched her arm, and suddenly a memory of being pinned between the ice of a dullaghan and the grinning red-haired man who had carried her to the room flooded her mind.

"It's not nice, is it?" Eivor grumbled.

Morbid curiosity had her clinging to her sister's memory even while the queen took it away. "Hey! I was enjoying that. Are dullaghan really that cold? How do you cope with it considering your problem?"

Gasping, Eivor smacked her arm. "You haven't changed a bit!"

"Of course not. But my point was, the gods don't want to be worshipped. Not even Dawn. They're not the gods of our youth who demand our servitude. Many of them were mortals once, who have led lives much like ours. I don't know what Thorne has told you, but I've met them, and I promise they're not terrible. Powerful, yes, they are gods, but they just want to have their peace, and their families, and to watch Tir grow around them, safe in the knowledge people are free to do what they want."

"They left me to suffer."

"Where would you be if they hadn't? Lord Emlyn, the god of time, sees all the possibilities and does his best to guide the other gods down a path that's best for our world. I don't know what he saw happening if you were rescued before you were, but I imagine it was a terrible option. Just like I know the old gods of Death, Chaos, and Paths played a part in the battle to save the people of Endara and Ensaycal. If they hadn't, those people would never have made it to the lands where Vartan Malfaer lived, forcing Lady Shianeni to work with them to imprison Annawyn."

Sitting in silence, the two sisters contemplated the point of continuing the discussion. Eivor's power continued to slither through her mind, reminding Astoria that whatever she thought, her sister already knew. It was easier to let her pick her memories apart. For a moment, she saw a wisp of an image pass behind her eyes. Charnel stood among the flames and the fallen dragons, holding his hand out for her to take.

"Tory, when did you fall in love with him?"

"I don't know. At least with Dawn it was a matter of years. She didn't know who I was at first, and I did my best to hide my identity from the crew for the sake of survival. Oisin had people hunting for me."

Sighing, Eivor cuddled her. "No promises, Tory. But if you hadn't abandoned me, I wouldn't have my wonderful family. I love them, and I wouldn't change what happened if it meant not having them. Ask me, and I will take away the guilt you feel so you might die free of its weight."

"No, thank you. This is about me, Eivor. Don't make my death about you." Snorting, Astoria arched a brow in amusement. "My guilt is my own to resolve."

EIGHT

Wandering the halls of her former home after all it had been through was a strange experience. The hours of rest under the influence of Jola's medicines had done little to fix the exhaustion. She supposed the emotional exchange with Eivor had not helped. Trailing her hands over walls as she drifted with no destination in mind, Astoria marvelled at how different the palace felt. When her parents had been king and queen, there had always been a stifling air of sameness, but under her sister, it felt alive. Power thrummed through the stone, and the shadows seemed to dance. People moved with purpose, barely sparing her more than a cursory glance when they saw the barefoot pirate.

It was equally strange to feel the smooth stone beneath her feet when she had grown used to the timber of ships. Her balance did not seem quite right, so Astoria kept close to the walls just in case she got dizzy. There was no need to pester the healers for an explanation. Many years had passed since she had spent much time on land, and her body would need to adjust. She was thankful it had nothing to do with the sickness. At least, not for the moment. The hawk expected to regain her land legs just in time for the cancer to impact on her sense of balance. She planned to enjoy what she could while she could. Even if it meant holding onto the walls to keep her upright, and facing the pitying looks of people who remembered her as the warrior daughter of the king who had won his kingdom in War's arenas.

"You almost look lost."

Turning to face the woman, Astoria leaned against the wall with a light smile to hide the dizziness her action caused. "Perhaps I am. This is not the home I left behind."

"Indeed," she replied, arching a brow as her gaze assessed the former princess. "I'm General Vesta."

"Ah."

"Is that all you've got to say?"

"What were you expecting from me? To tell you I know your name?" Lifting one shoulder, Astoria dug her nails into the wall behind her and refused to let her smile fade.

Vesta approached, eyes narrowing as she took in the shadows beneath the younger woman's eyes. "I've never forgotten fighting you. It's a pity we cannot repeat it on equal grounds, Battle Hawk."

Confusion ripped through her mind, and Astoria tried to remember if she had faced the goblin before. "I'm sorry. I don't recall our fight, but I'm going to assume it was the day the dragons fell."

"You were magnificent. I'm sorry to hear about your fate."

"A well-deserved one, if you ask me. I'm sure you're not, though. Asking, that is."

Lifting a hand to her face, Vesta touched the scars etched into her face, crossing over her eye. "Anyone capable of leaving a mark on me deserves a better death than the slow agony of cancer."

"Did I do that?" Fascinated, Astoria stretched her fingers out to trace the scars. "I'd apologise, but we were on opposite sides of the war and just doing what they ordered us to do. Though if you want my opinion, they make you look... intimidating. You're welcome."

"If I could have captured you that day, Battle Hawk, I would have kept you."

Smirking, Astoria lifted her chin tauntingly. There was something hungry in the general's eyes that made her feel good despite the effects of the medicines and the cancer. She needed the reminder she was still the warrior who had flown through fire, and the dashing pirate who leapt from ship to ship, cutting throats with blade and talon. Letting her fingers linger on Vesta's face, she tried not to think of Dawn and Charnel, or the family she had made and left behind on *The Storm Bird*.

"You would've regretted it. If you think my sister is a pain in your arse, I would have been so much worse. Still could be. I suspect you just want to know if a certain god is going to vent her anger over my departure by locking Diwan in an unending storm."

"There's that. There's also the part of me who wants to keep you tied up in her chambers for her pleasure. Which would be wrong of me, considering everything has changed. But I still dream of the screaming hawk passing through dragon fire to attack me. The way you shifted between forms, grabbing any weapon you could get your hand on. It is still one of the most magnificent things I've seen in a fight."

Eyes widening, Astoria could not reply before the goblin's mouth crashed into hers. It conveyed the hunger she had seen in her gaze, the graze of sharp teeth promising to draw blood if she resisted. Vesta pressed her against the wall, a hand buried in her hair while the other grabbed the loose fabric of the dress she had pulled on rather than wander naked. A small voice at the back of her mind screamed at Astoria to break away rather than betray her gods, but she buried it, happy to meet the other woman's hunger with her own. Another voice cooed in delight at the taste of Vesta on her lips. Someone cleared their throat, prompting Vesta to break off the kiss with a snarl.

"What do you think you're doing to my sister, General?" Arms crossed, Eivor regarded the two of them with a blank expression Astoria recognised as an attempt to be neutral.

"Getting payback for my scars."

Shrugging, the hawk smiled sheepishly. "Apparently we've met in battle."

"I'm offended you don't remember our fight. Did you really go up against so many goblins that day that you can't remember almost tearing my eye out?"

Eivor's blank look morphed into one of understanding. "Vesta, they manipulated her memories. She doesn't remember everything from that battle, and other times. The gods were involved. Though that doesn't excuse you for not telling me."

The hand in her hair refused to let go, and Astoria felt the prick of claws on her scalp. It sent a shiver down her spine that was not entirely unwelcome. Studying the woman pressed against her, she wondered if letting Vesta have her fantasy was what she needed. As long as Diwan remained forbidden to the gods, Dawn and Charnel were out of her reach, and the general struck her as the sort of person who would not let a little thing like cancer stop her from making the most of what time she had left. Nights spent in her embrace might banish the longing to be back onboard *The Storm Bird* with her captain.

"It's true," she murmured, licking her lips. "There are a lot of things I don't remember."

Groaning, Vesta dragged her nose over Astoria's cheek. "An even greater pity. Perhaps our queen can share my memories of it with you. Would you like to see what I saw? Because I mean it, you were magnificent."

"Obviously I was, or you wouldn't still be thinking about what you want to do to me."

Spluttering, Eivor gestured in frustration. "My sister is dying, General. Accosting her in a hallway when I asked you to fetch her for dinner is not what I expected from you."

"Accosting her? Not yet. Maybe later." Kissing the side of the duine's face, Vesta smirked. "Besides, I didn't hear her complaining. She's a feral little thing, Your Majesty. You should give her to me. I know how to care for feral things."

"Let go of Princess Astoria, or I'll make you."

Happy to remain where she was, Astoria chuckled. "I'm good here, Eivor. There's no need for you to rescue me from your general's claws. She knows what she's doing with them, and I don't have much time left."

"Yes, I'm sure she does. But I wanted you to join us for dinner. Family time. You know that thing you've missed a lot of, and since you're dying..." Eivor spread her hands, her impatience becoming a scratch on the edge of Astoria's mind, urging her to wriggle free.

"Wait, you want me to join your family for dinner?"

"You're my sister, Tory. They're your family."

Laughing nervously, she ran a hand through her hair and glanced at the smirking goblin. "And you sent the general to fetch me to join you? Why?"

"Because I normally attend family dinners. Jola and a few others do as well. We're the ones who helped pick up your sister after what Oisin and Cathair did to her. Does it surprise you she'd welcome us as kin after that?" Pushing away from the wall, Vesta gave her an unreadable look and started down the hallway.

"Well, come on then. Let's not give Thorne a reason to come looking for her wife."

Pointing at Astoria, Eivor scowled. "No. Do not get involved with my general. I'd like to keep her alive, and you're the lover of two gods. One of whom is known for her temper."

"Dawn won't risk breaking the treaty with the Unseelie. She'll leave me be."

"Right. And say she finds out you and Vesta had a thing while you were here, dying, and hiding from her? What will happen the next time my general leaves Diwan? We're a risk of war with the Blood Queen, Tory. I need her to command my army."

It amazed Astoria that she did not fall over as she crossed to her sister so she could sling an arm around her shoulders. "You're implying Dawn loves me when I know for a fact she doesn't. Besides, I don't think she's that possessive."

Huffing, Eivor did not shake her off, and instead slipped an arm around her waist. "Why did you have to go wandering around in this state? You're a mess, Tory."

"I've always been a mess. It's what makes me so much fun."

They followed Vesta slowly, the general making a point to keep just far enough ahead of them to pretend she was out of earshot. Thankful she had not wandered too far from her room, it amazed Astoria when they arrived at a set of doors opening into a room with a massive balcony overlooking the gardens. Someone had pinned the glass doors open, lanterns dangling everywhere while the sunset turned the sky into liquid gold. A long table was set for dinner, bottles of wine already flowing as people laughed at each other. Rose was being chased by her father, and the moment she saw her mother and aunt, she headed straight for them. Launching herself at Astoria, the girl screamed when Vesta caught her before she could send the ailing woman crashing to the ground.

"Little Rosie, you can't just throw yourself at people," Vesta grumbled. "Especially not your aunt. You might hurt her. She's fragile."

Pouting, the girl stared at Astoria with wide, disappointed eyes. "But she's my Aunty Tory!"

Bopping her nose, the hawk smiled. "I've been on a ship for a long time, and I'm not steady on my feet. We could have been hurt if General Vesta hadn't caught you."

"What's a ship?"

Propping Rose on her hip, the goblin chuckled at the question. "It's a boat like the ones you make to race in the creek. But a lot bigger. Your Aunty Tory is an infamous pirate. She stabs bad people and steals things from their ships when she isn't setting slaves free."

Her tiny mouth formed a perfect circle, and Astoria felt a stirring of regret. "That's one way to put it."

"Slavery is bad," Rose said with all the confidence a five-year-old could muster. "Ma, Pa, and Mama said so. They say everyone deserves to be free, and people who make slaves are bad."

"And they're right. Your parents do their best to fight those bad people on the land, but I was fighting them on the sea. Have you ever seen a map of Tir? Our world is enormous, and there are lots of seas."

Catching sight of her sister standing with her consorts, Astoria gave her a small smile. There was something completely unsettling about standing on a balcony surrounded by people she did not know while talking to a small girl about how slavery was wrong. Especially when she met the gaze of the general, who watched her with undisguised desire. Sweeping her focus across the gathered people, she tried to imagine Dawn among them, or Charnel. It was easy to picture the Storm Queen at a family gathering. The younger woman enjoyed being around others and could lay claim to a happy childhood. The god of water was a different matter, and Astoria wished she had coaxed him out of his shell more before her time ran out.

"You should sit down, Astoria," Vesta said when she swayed slightly, and Rose squirmed in her grasp, eager to run around again. "It's fine to acknowledge you're not well. No one begrudges you that."

Lips quirking, she did her best to saunter over to the table. The general could tell her it was fine, but that did not mean she believed it. Selecting a chair midway along the table that she thought would give her the best options for conversation, Astoria was surprised when the young woman who had taken

Rose from her chamber quickly slid into the seat next to her. Free of the boisterous child, Vesta pointedly took the one on the other side, placing a hand on her shoulder as she slid onto the seat.

"I have so much I want to ask you," the young woman said, staring at her in awe. "But Ma said I'm not allowed to pester you too much. Do you mind if I sit here?"

"Talaith?" Astoria ignored the sudden dig of claws in her thigh.

"Yes! Oh, I'm sorry, we haven't actually been introduced. I'm Talaith, your niece. And you're Princess Astoria Havard, second daughter of King Craven and Queen Malena. My mother's sister. I recently turned 70 and one of my wishes was to meet you."

Her niece reminded her of Silaine when she was of a similar age, and Astoria looked around the balcony. It was a fresh cut to her heart to see what she had caused. Their youngest sister should have been there, entertaining them with music and her light chatter. Biting her lip, the hawk glanced down, hiding her gaze from anyone tempted to see the glimmer of tears in her eyes.

"I'm sorry!" Talaith whispered, withdrawing slightly.

"No, don't be. You're fine, girl. I don't mind your questions."

Vesta looked around for Jola, signalling to the healer. "Is she allowed wine?"

The question drew the attention of everyone else, and Astoria wanted to sink beneath the table to avoid their stares. Pressing her lips together, Talaith grabbed her aunt's hand and squeezed it reassuringly. Laughing loudly, Rhydwen waved his glass of dark wine at them before giving Jola a scolding look.

"Don't you dare deny the poor woman the right to drink! Especially not tonight. She's allowed to enjoy what she can while she still can, and it would be awfully rude of you to say no."

"Am I expected to obey Jola?" Leaning closer to Vesta, Astoria whispered, "Because I've met scarier healers and had no issues with telling them where to stick it."

Gawking at her, the general covered her heart. "Everyone does what Jola tells them. Stars bless your courage, Battle Hawk, if you think you can defy her and get away with it."

"My last healer was one of the merfolk."

Sensing a presence behind her, Astoria snorted when Jola leaned over the back of the chair to say, "You're not prepared to fight me, little hawk. But you can drink within reason. I haven't given you anything too strong for the pain. Not when you didn't need it yet. Better to hold off until I don't have a choice."

"Wonderful, thank you," she replied, letting her amusement carry in her voice. "Shall I also call you Mother, since you seem to be the one in charge here?"

"You've certainly got more attitude than your sister. Behave, and you won't find out how truly unpleasant I can make your medicines. Speaking of which, this is for the shaking."

Jola dropped a pouch on the table in front of her. Poking it, Astoria arched a brow in confusion while everyone else pretended to be busy elsewhere. Giggling, Talaith picked it up to take a sniff, and screwed up her face in disgust. A second pouch took its place, and the healer patted her head as though she were an obstinate child.

"As well as some more pain relief. Don't bother trying to say you're not hurting. I can see through your lies, child. If you want to be stubborn, I'm sure Vesta will happily force it down your throat."

"That's not the only thing she'll force down my throat," Astoria muttered. "Do they come with instructions, or am I supposed to guess how to take them?"

"Mix with water. Not wine or anything else. And before you ask, no, we don't have rum."

She gasped dramatically, pressing the back of her hand to her forehead as she pretended to swoon. "I am wounded! Where is the rum? What sort of place is this that you're out of rum?"

"Tory, stop it," Eivor said, sharing a look with Thorne. "I don't need you encouraging my husband to be a fool. He'll take your performance as permission."

Rhydwen poked her arm. "As if I would."

Scoffing, Talaith muttered, "My Pa absolutely would. Ma says he gets too silly sometimes, but I know she enjoys it."

Leaning back on the chair, Astoria listened to the burst of arguments around the balcony. It made her smile, and she only half heard what Jola was saying about the medicines she needed to take. Vesta's hand returned to her leg, the scratch of claws through her skirts oddly comforting. Twilight had settled on the land, the barest smattering of clouds still holding a hint of colour even though the sun had set.

"My parents would be proud of this," she murmured to the general.

"They would. And they would be heartbroken over what you're going through."

Remembering her choices, Astoria grimaced. "Promise to put me out of my misery before the end?"

Vesta sighed, giving her an unreadable look. "Why wouldn't you let your god have you healed?"

"Because she doesn't know about this. Not yet. And because I deserve this suffering. I don't want them to see how terrible things will get before the end, and I'd like to save them from that, if I can."

"Fine. I promise to help you when the time comes, but until then, you owe me, Battle Hawk."

"I'm sure I can think of a few things that will suffice."

NINE

Laughter filled the air, drawing Dawn's attention to a group walking along a terrace without a care in the world for the dark clouds robbing the Rainbow Vale of light. No one could see her, but the chains binding her to Charnel had led her to the mountain city the danann called home. Air wanted to know why Water was there instead of haunting the sea around her ship, and a part of her hoped he had brought Astoria to the Vale instead of Diwan. It made sense when her younger sister lived among all the happy pairings of danann and Ravens. Dawn longed to go to him to find out where her hawk was, but there was a reason they avoided each other as much as possible.

Familiar colourful wings filled her view, and the danann king stared at the spot where she sat in silence. He could not see her, but Dawn had never been able to hide from him. With his hands on his hips, and rainbow feathered wings spread wide, Tigernach tapped his foot impatiently before pointedly looking up at the dark clouds smothering the view of the mountain range. Pressing her lips together, Dawn reined in her emotions, letting the sun break through her shadows. Releasing her power, she shimmered into view, leaning forward with her elbows digging into her knees as she stared at the spray of waterfalls.

"What's wrong, my darling girl?" Tigernach sat beside her, draping a wing over her back to comfort the young god as he had when she was a child. "I'm guessing it has something to do with why the god of water is with my brother and his wives."

"Did he bring Tory with him?" she asked, unable to hide her hopefulness.

"No? Have you misplaced your hawk?"

"She got sick and went to him. Then he took her away, but Uncle Emlyn said I wasn't allowed to go after her. He's supposed to be taking her to Diwan, but when I realised he was here, I thought maybe he'd brought her to her other sister. You know, the one that doesn't hate gods."

Studying her, Tigernach sighed and slid an arm over her shoulders to pull her into a hug. "I'm sorry, Dawn, but she's not here. I was with Red, Moth, and Laine when Charnel arrived. He came alone."

"Then she's in Diwan with the Unseelie. Uncle Tigs, if anything happens to her..." Dawn stared at him, and it felt like her heart was sinking beneath the deepest sea. "I can't bear the thought of Tory being hurt."

"Love is a tricky thing."

Recoiling from him, the god shook her head and rubbed the back of her hand over her eyes. If she had been anyone else, Dawn would have agreed with his comment. But she was not just anyone, she was a god. Anything she felt for those who were not part of her bonded group was not love. Her heart could only belong to those who completed the circle of power fuelling her existence. Like Charnel. She could adore Astoria, and she did, deeply, agonisingly, but she could never love her the way she deserved.

"I don't love Tory. You know I cannot."

The slow arch of his brow suggested the ancient king disagreed. "Can't you? You have no control over who you love or do not love. I know you have this belief that because you're a god, you can only love your mates, but it doesn't work that way. The heart does what it wants without consideration for what the mind thinks is the right thing to do."

"Is that why you fight with Uncle Merle all the time?"

"This isn't about me, Dawn. We're talking about you."

It felt wrong to smirk, but she enjoyed knowing she had turned his comments back on him. "And yet, the two of you are bound in a way Tory and I aren't. Your heart knows what it wants, Uncle Tigs. And it wants to bend a certain captain over the end of your bed to show him who he belongs to."

"Where did I go wrong with you?" Tigernach huffed. "I know your parents made it hard, but I really tried to raise you better than this, Dawn. Just because you're swaggering around leading pirates doesn't mean you need to voice all the crude thoughts that cross your mind in public where respectable people can hear it."

"What respectable people?"

"Me. I am the king of the danann."

Tossing her head back to laugh, Dawn slapped his knee. He stared at her blankly, lips set in a thin line while his wings folded back out of the way. It felt good to laugh as hard as she was, but it was short-lived. A worm of disapproval burrowed into her mirth, reminding her she needed to find out if Astoria was well. Facing Charnel would be a challenge, and the god of air needed Tigernach to support her.

"Sorry, Uncle Tigs, but I've heard you. Don't claim you're some polite king who would never dare speak about such things when you once told me what I should do, in detail, to one of the swan folk."

"Perhaps you should try being polite before you attempt to talk to your mate."

Screwing up her face, Dawn groaned. "Why does he have to be so... stiff?"

"Dawn."

"It's like he's got a pole shoved up his arse."

"Oh, dear stars above, please stop."

"I bet he doesn't even know how to make Tory scream."

Covering his face, Tigernach sighed in defeat before jerking away to blink at her when his brain caught up with what she had said. "Wait, what?"

"Which part?"

"Did you just suggest your little hawk and Charnel, the god of water, are involved?"

Admitting it out loud to someone felt like a knife had been shoved in her gut and twisted. "Yes. Tory and Charnel have been fucking each other. Without me, of course. It's been going on for a long time, Uncle Tigs. They met during the war before the Fog and all that. The one where the dragons fell. If you want more information about it, ask the god of time."

"That's not possible. She can't have been there."

"She told me about it, but we never went into details because she couldn't. It still gives her nightmares. That's why I've never tried to stop her and Charnel. They shared the experience of that war."

Refusing to accept her statement, Tigernach rose to his feet and held out a hand for the god to take. "I need to hear it from him. Our participation in that fight was forbidden. Neriwyn wouldn't let us help. He made us sit back while the Unseelie destroyed the dragons."

Hesitating to take his hand, she considered her options. She needed to speak to Charnel, and it made sense to do so while there were people around. Particularly ones she trusted, like Tigernach. Though the prospect of facing Astoria's younger sister when she did not know the hawk's location did not sit easy. His hand was warm and felt the same as it always had. There were calluses from training that never vanished, and a strength that seemed strange to those who did not know him. The Lord of Rainbows moved like a dancer and looked too beautiful for his reputation.

"At least you'll be able to find out where your hawk is," he muttered, tucking her arm through his elbow. "Why would he take her to Diwan? I didn't think Queen Eivor wanted anything to do with her sisters. Not to mention their increased conflict with the Blood Queen. War is brewing. I feel it in my bones."

"Tory has been struggling with her nightmares recently. She's feeling guilty and wants to fix things with her sister. We were on the way to the nearest port so she could go to Diwan when she got sick."

"Unusual for a duine to get sick."

"I know. We had recently been to a little seaside town. No one else onboard has gotten sick though... so I don't know. I'm just the god of air, not my mother."

There was something odd in his glance that made Dawn want to itch her shoulder. Watching danann flying above the city, she decided she would join them when she was done with Charnel. It was freeing to dance on the breeze with people who understood the joy of it. They appreciated her power and never hesitated to sweep her into a wild swirl. As much as she loved to fly with Astoria, it was never the same. When one of them was a bird, and the other a woman with wings, it was impossible to experience the same rush of pleasure. The wind did not slide through their feathers in the same manner.

Imagining Astoria with wings like her own made Dawn wish she had the power to change people. The god of chaos had managed it with her champion, giving the stalwart elven shield mage a set of wings to match her danann mate. She had marvelled at the gift before spotting the elf's other mate, the dullaghan who had convinced Jen to become the god of learning. If she had the power to give Astoria wings, she doubted they would ever leave the sky. Exploring Tir with her hawk would take on a different appearance. They would fly all day, drifting in the currents until Astoria needed to rest, and then they would find a place to stop with an unmatched view of the world beneath their feet.

"We're your people as much as we're your father's," Tigernach said, joining her in admiring the view of the flying danann. "How could we not be? There's no surprise you're able to give yourself wings. You're the god of the sky, the wind beneath our feet, and the currents that take us far."

"I wish I could give wings to people."

"Your hawk was born with her own."

Giving him an unreadable look, Dawn pulled the dagger from her heart and stabbed it in his. "Did you never wish you could dance beneath the stars with Oblivion? Because that's what I wish I could do with Tory. She has wings, but I cannot kiss her when she wears them. I cannot run my hands through her feathers while she does the same to me in return. It'll never be the same."

"They're not danann."

"Neither am I."

He arched a brow, snorting in amusement. "You and Chaos are the only ones who have wings like ours. Though I suppose if I'm going to suggest the two of you are danann, I may as well lay claim to that pretty little elf who has wings as well. It would not go down well with the dullaghan. They're rather protective of the Master of the Hunt's vicious mate. She is something else."

"You just haven't forgotten she nearly got the better of you in the arena. Have your balls recovered?"

Huffing, Tigernach tugged her towards Redmond's quarters. It was easy to fall into silence as they walked along the winding pathways of the Vale. She loved the city, but not enough to give up her life on the sea. There was freedom in sailing that Dawn had found nowhere else. Some would argue she loved it because the only one of her mates who existed was the god of water. Out on the ocean, it was just the two of them, their powers becoming an ebb and tide of their own. Her parents continuously pointed out that if she wanted to find her Earth and Fire, she needed to spend more time with people who did not belong to the crews of her ships. Chaos could create more gods by connecting a person with the threads of existence, but Dawn could not bring herself to search for her mates. Even thinking about it felt like she was betraying Astoria in some unforgivable manner.

"Do you think I'm making a mistake by not looking for people who could become Earth and Fire?"

Tigernach stiffened, his brows furrowing as he pondered his response. "Maybe. I don't know how these things happen. It seems possible that somehow, the universe will provide the right people to you at the right time. Because how do you know if they're the right ones? For all you know, Astoria might be the right one."

"Like Jen and Nexara?"

"Yes. They've loved each other for a long time, and their existence has always been matched. It made sense they would become the gods of knowledge and learning. I know it hurts you to think of them, but Jen was never meant for you, Dawn, no matter how much you wished it otherwise. All of us told you that from the beginning."

"Maybe it was a lesson I needed to learn on my own, Uncle Tigs."

He nodded sadly, giving her a grim smile before they stopped in front of the door to his brother's quarters. Sensing the other god inside, Dawn hoped he would not run away to avoid her. Before Tigernach could knock, the door was yanked open, and a frustrated Redmond greeted them. Waving for them to enter, he waited until they were through before placing a hand on Dawn's shoulder and squeezing. His crimson wings curled around her in a hint of a hug, but he did nothing more than that. Hearing sobs, she brushed the feathered limb out of the way and spotted Astoria's younger sister huddled in the arms of the grey-winged danann woman while Charnel leaned against a wall, staring at her.

"What's going on?" she asked softly, not daring to take a step towards him.

While she froze, Tigernach had no problems ignoring the scene and striding over to the god of water. "Were you at the battle when the dragons fell? You and the hawk."

"We were. Not that it matters," Charnel replied, dodging around the danann to look at Dawn.

"It does fucking matter!" The king grabbed his shirt, shoving the god back against the wall. "It was the last place anyone saw Oblivion! You're going to tell me what you know."

"I'm not allowed to. Neither is Tory. This has nothing to do with you, Lord of Rainbows. If you want to argue about it, take it up with Aiden, Celiaen, Tessa, Emlyn, and Viv. My role in that battle was to keep the fires from destroying the people of Endara and Ensaycal. Yes, I saw the Executioner. And I watched Tory fly through the fire like she was part of it. I saw the last stand of the old Ravens and the dragons against an army of goblins. And I never forgot. When Tory came into Dawn's life, it was fate."

Dawn staggered, and Redmond caught her before she tripped. "You're in love with Tory?"

"Aren't you?"

Their words brought a fresh sob from Silaine, and Dawn forced herself to return to the reality that there was something else going on. "Why do I have a bad feeling about why you're here, Charnel? Where is my Battle Hawk? I trusted you to look after her, and you didn't bring her back to me."

Free of Tigernach's grasp, Water strode across the room to her, halting a short distance away. "You cannot go to her in Diwan. I did what she asked of me, and I'm past caring if you hate me for it. Tory wanted to return to her home so she could see her sister again. She wants to repair things between the three of them before it's too late."

"What do you mean?"

Her blood had frozen. It was the only reasonable explanation for why she could not move while Charnel reached out to cradle her cheek. His eyes were the clearest ocean blue, and she wanted to hate him for the grief she could see in them. Agony curled through Dawn, exquisite in its reminder the man was part of her in a way no one else ever could be. They were two parts of a shattered whole.

"Tory is sick, Dawn. The sort of sick only your mother can heal. I know what you're feeling right now because I feel it too. She doesn't want to be healed, and despite my desire to deny her request, I took her to Diwan so she could find peace. You don't know how badly I want to go to your mother and beg her to fix this because the thought of losing Tory... it's not fair, Dawn. It really isn't."

"No, I refuse to believe this. I'm going to get my mother, and she will sort this out."

"You can't."

"This is why Uncle Emlyn came to me. He knew."

Charnel clenched his jaw, anger turning his eyes to the grey of a stormy sea. "He visited me as well. Before I came here to see Silaine. Tory wanted me to tell her because if there's a chance she can mend things between her sisters, then she wants to try. We must let her try. If we interfere, if we break the treaty, innocent people will die. Not because that's what we want or what Queen Eivor and the Unseelie Council want, but because there are people out there with fanatical inclinations who would go to war in the name of the gods. Or in defiance of the gods. And no one wants that."

"What do we do?" She wanted to collapse, but his hand was a soothing presence on her cheek.

"We wait. You go back to doing what you do, and I'll keep watch. Tory knows how to call me to her. If she wants to see us, she'll find a way that doesn't violate the treaty."

Shifting her focus to Silaine, Dawn felt a need to apologise, but she did not know why. The wolf regarded her with a tearful curiosity that broke when a young boy wandered in. He had pale blond hair and the blue eyes of his mother and aunt. No wings graced his back, but no one expected them to. It was a coin toss if a child would be born with wings when one of their parents was a duine, and the other a danann. Climbing onto his mother's lap, he cuddled her tightly.

"I'm sorry," Charnel murmured, and his thumb brushed the corner of her mouth. "I wanted to bring her back to you the moment I realised what was wrong. All I did was respect her wishes. Please do the same. You owe it to her."

Shoulders slumping, Dawn nodded slowly. "I'll do my best. But I want to say goodbye to her. Surely Queen Eivor wouldn't deny me the chance? She wouldn't, would she?"

"I don't know."

Anger was a distant whisper beneath the pain of knowing Astoria was dying. She wanted to scream and swear to lock Diwan in an unending storm if the Unseelie Queen denied her the chance to say goodbye. Except the words would not come. Nor would the wrath. Dawn felt hollowed out, and the only thing keeping her standing was the delicious agony of Charnel's touch. The chains linking them urged her to collapse into his arms so he could wash away her grief. It was tempting to let the tide of his power lull the storm of emotions raging through her. Holding his gaze, the sky god acknowledged the grief mirrored back to her.

"I'm sorry as well, Charnel. I promise I'll be patient and wait to hear from her." Smiling sadly, Dawn leaned into his hand. *"Give me a chance, and I'll behave better, I swear."*

He arched a brow, but there was no amusement in his expression. *"We shall see."*

TEN

The gardens had barely changed in all the years of occupation or after the liberation of Diwan. As Astoria wandered the shaded pathways of the maze, she let the memories play out in her mind. She enjoyed listening to the ghost of her father's laughter as he chased her and her sisters around the corners. It should have filled her with grief, but the hawk found little point in mourning his death when she could cherish the life they had together. Stopping to stare at a leaning gumtree in a corner where three pathways met, she remembered her mother sprawled out beneath it, a book in one hand, and a wineglass in the other. No matter what lively activities Craven had planned for their daughters, Malena always had a more subdued option available for when they needed to collapse and catch their breath.

Her legs ached from the effort of walking, but no one had come searching for her yet. Approaching the tree, Astoria was happy to settle on the grass beneath it. Birds flitted about in the branches above her head, their chorus of chirps reminding her of Silaine's fascination with watching everything. She could almost hear her younger sister describing the chords of music no one else could hear. Lying back with her arms folded under her head, Astoria observed the birds, smiling at the flash of colours. Light filtered through the leaves, dappling everything it touched with shadows that shifted with the slightest of breezes.

Closing her eyes, she imagined the touch of the wind was Dawn's fingers over her skin. It had been days since she returned to Diwan, and it had officially become the longest amount of time she had been separated from the god of air. When she lingered too long on the ache in her heart, Astoria felt the urge to run to the border to summon Charnel. She knew he would return her to *The Storm Bird* if she asked. The weather had been too perfect, and she caught the calculating looks sent her way by Eivor and the others. General Vesta was the only one who openly asked if she thought it was Dawn's doing. In all honesty, she admitted she did. What she did not know was if it was because Charnel had told her what was going on and it was her attempt at being nice. It was spring, and there should have been more rain than there had been, so Astoria understood the concern.

"I know you can't hear me, Dawn, but you need to let the weather be," she whispered to the wind, wishing her voice would carry to the ears of her god. "I miss you."

No one tried to berate her for being a god's lover. She watched people in the halls of the palace and in the gardens, admiring the open mix of relationships. They filled her with hope that the future of Tir would be mostly peaceful. Astoria knew better than to believe complete peace everywhere and all the time was possible. There would always be someone with ambition, or the need for revenge. Since the treaty between the Unseelie and the gods had been established, she had suspected there was an underlying reason for it. In her mind, it made sense that their creators would want a faction to stand against them. The Unseelie kept extremists under control. They fought against places like the Shadforthian Empire, which conquered other lands in the name of the gods. As much as Eivor and her council might deny it, they did what the gods needed them to do, and in return, they had their peace.

Feeling a prickle on her arm, she wondered if it was an insect or a message. It crept across her skin, causing an itchy sensation. Her shoulders were burning from being stuck in the same position for so long, and a slight flush to her face suggested her last dose of Jola's medicine was wearing off. The fever attacking her body was returning, and Astoria dreaded the long trudge back to her chambers to prepare another dose. No one had been able to work out why her magic was reacting the way it was to the cancer. She saw the worry in the goblin healer's gaze every time she delivered more pouches of medicine. They had attempted to see if she could ride it out, but Jola had quickly put a stop to it when she realised it would kill her.

Removing her arms from under her head, Astoria stretched, cringing at the pain lancing down her spine. She did not push herself to get up, preferring to let the discomfort in her shoulders settle before she risked a dizzy spell. It was impossible not to be angry with how quickly her body was failing. Especially when she overheard the mutters of the healers tending to her. No one said it where she could hear it, but Astoria did not need them to. Her health was declining faster than it should have been, and they could only blame her magic. But even though she was angry, the hawk refused to let anyone see it. For Eivor's children, she wanted to be the strong aunt they were excited to get to know. She needed it for herself as well. Death might have decided to make her suffer, but she would do so with her head held high.

She sat up slowly, using the trunk of the gum to support herself. The slower she went, the less likely she would end up swimming in dizziness. Resting against it, Astoria swept her gaze over the maze. Nothing seemed out of place, and there was no one openly watching her. Assuming there had been an insect on her arm, she prepared to stand and braced herself against the tree. It was an effort to rise without doing something that would send her back down again. Hands slid under her arms, supporting her weight so she could steady herself. Turning her head carefully, Astoria was unsurprised to find Vesta behind her. A worried gleam in her eyes suggested she had been sent to find her.

"Thank you."

"You shouldn't be out here alone, Battle Hawk." Not letting go until she was certain the younger woman was stable, Vesta examined the creeping bruises on her skin. "You look terrible."

Chuckling, Astoria released the tree. "Sorry, it's out of my control."

"Maybe you should consider talking to your... friends."

"Oh, come now, General, you can say it. My lovers who are gods."

"Yes, them."

Stepping away from the goblin, she dragged up a memory of the maze's layout to recall which way to go. Before the sickness, Astoria would have simply stripped and shifted forms, flying free of the winding puzzle of thick green shrubs. There was no more shape changing unless she wanted to risk killing herself before the sickness could finish the task. Part of her wanted to do it, but the thought of going down in that sort of agony did not appeal to her. Not when there were quicker options available. Glancing at the sky, she squashed down the longing to be in it.

"I'm sorry," Vesta said, joining her.

"What for?"

"You want to fly. I see it in your eyes."

Astoria shrugged, resentment threatening to rise. "As for your suggestion, I've thought about it. I don't really want to die, even if I think I deserve my suffering. The more time I spend here, the more I consider it. I'd like to see Rose grow up, and to be there when she discovers what her other form is."

"Do you think she'll be able to shift?"

"Have you met her? That girl is going to make ripples in the world. She's amazing."

Offering her arm for support, Vesta chuckled knowingly. "I think even her grandmother would cower before her. Talaith keeps asking when she might find out if she'll be able to shift."

"Haven't there been other half-goblin, half-duine's before? I know the old Unseelie kept prisoners, and the Blood Queen enjoyed her share of mortal playthings. Mixes with human or elf normally shift for the first time when they're around 300 years old, just like a pure duine does. But I suppose that had changed with our mortality."

She felt no shame in relying on the general to help her walk. The news of her ailment had spread through the castle quickly, but she had expected nothing less. It was hard to keep it secret after the former princess landed in the middle of a garden and required someone to carry her to a healer. For too long, the daoine had kept things like illness swept into a corner, preferring to pretend to be the untouchable ones who could only be brought down by injury. Astoria was happy to force her kind to acknowledge they were not immune to everything.

"When you were that age, did you have a suspicion about what you would become?"

Humming as she pondered the question, Astoria replied, "I knew I was going to have wings. Mother and Eivor could fly, therefore I would as well. Father used to joke I would end up being something outrageous, like a woman he knew who shifted into a cerapter, but I refused to accept it."

"Do you think you had any influence on your form?"

"Besides the usual?"

Vesta grunted in confirmation, and she frowned. It was strange to reflect on her youth. Who she had been at 300 years old was nothing like the person she had become. She remembered being certain she would throw herself into War's arenas to earn her fame like her father had. From the moment King Craven had pressed the hilt of a blade into her hand, she had dedicated herself to training until the only people willing to spar with her had been her father and his best friend. That had suited her just fine.

"Maybe. You like to jokingly call me savage and feral, and you're right. I've always been the savage one of the three of us. In a fight, I am feral. Eivor is ruthless, calculated, and has no problem ripping a person to shreds, but she doesn't... or didn't enjoy it like I do. Sometimes I think that's why I adapted my style of fighting the way I did. The satisfaction I get from tearing through someone with my talons before shifting to slit their throat with their own weapon. Do you understand what I'm saying?"

"I'm a goblin, Battle Hawk. My primary weapon is my claws."

"If I had been a Raven like my mother, I would have become a different sort of warrior."

They fell silent, passing through an arch that appeared to be struggling beneath the weight of the vine covering it. Pointing in the direction they needed to go, Astoria rolled her shoulders uncomfortably. The fever was steadily rising, and her skin felt wrong. Her body felt like it was crawling with something she could not see. Eyeing her in concern, Vesta drew them to a stop.

"Are you fine to keep walking?"

Lips twitching, Astoria arched a brow. "Trying to be my dashing hero again, are you? I'm beginning to think you're following me around, looking for a reason to sweep me off my feet."

"Would it be so bad if I was?"

"Eivor made her thoughts clear. I'm not allowed to play with you, General. No matter how much I might want to."

A spark of defiance had shadows curling around them, the silky touch reminding Astoria of when Dawn would take her time to use her power to tease her. She understood why her sister was concerned about Vesta's interest in her, and she had every intention of respecting it. Though she was certain the god of air did not love her, Astoria could not be sure she might not take it badly if she became involved with someone else during her last months of life. After everything they had been through together, the duine did not want to disrespect Dawn or Charnel by embracing someone else. Or endanger Diwan.

"If I didn't respect her so much, I'd be tempted to ignore her request." Sighing, the general recalled her shadows. "When Queen Calista commanded me to lead the army to liberate Diwan, I really hoped I'd get to meet you again. By then, it was no secret you were not Oisin's captive like he claimed, but we weren't about to attack the Storm Queen's fleet. I thought you might come back when you learnt your home had been freed from Talaroo."

"This obsession you've had with me all these years is both flattering and concerning."

"I wouldn't call it an obsession."

Chuckling, Astoria decided not to press. They drew close to the edge of the maze, and she heard laughter beyond the wall of green. Music drifted on the breeze, making her miss Silaine's presence. Leaning into Vesta, she did not hide how she felt, and the general's lips thinned.

"I should start carrying a flask of Jola's bitter torture around so I can pour it down your throat whenever I find you somewhere you shouldn't be."

"Don't you have more important things to do, General?"

"Yes, but here I am."

Crinkling her nose, the hawk smiled. "Can't get me out of your mind?"

"No. I've never been able to banish you from my thoughts."

A fast-moving shadow passed over them, and they lifted their eyes to the sky. Startled to see a trio of danann flying toward the castle, Astoria clutched Vesta's arm tightly. Her heart knocked a quick beat against her ribs, leaving her flustered. There was only one reason she could think of that would bring the winged warriors to Diwan, and the twitch in the general's cheek suggested she knew it as well.

"Would I be wrong in guessing that your other sister is aware of your condition?"

"No. I asked Charnel to tell her. Am I wrong for wanting to fix things between Silaine and Eivor?"

Vesta did not respond. They kept walking as quickly as she could manage, but the duine knew it was frustrating the older woman. She wanted to be present when Eivor dealt with the danann, and Astoria's weakness prevented that. Eyeing a chair as they passed it by, the pirate was tempted to ask to be left there for a while, freeing the general to hurry along to the meeting. Before she could say anything, Vesta let out a huff and yanked her close so she could scoop her up in her arms.

"You need to stop doing this," she muttered, feeling the warning prick of claws through her clothes.

"No."

"I'm not exactly light."

The answering smirk revealed the points of several teeth, and Vesta kept her gaze locked on the palace as she strode along quicker than they had been walking. "If you think you're too heavy for me, Battle Hawk, then I've got news for you. Goblins are naturally stronger than daoine."

"I know."

"You're all muscle, but I know that's going to waste away. Let me enjoy the feeling of having a very capable warrior in my arms, even if I can't take advantage of you."

Snorting, Astoria realised the other woman was feeding her own ego. "You really do like to think you're rescuing me."

"Maybe."

They did not make it all the way to the castle before they encountered Eivor and the danann. Eyes widening when she recognised the vibrant purple wings of the lead warrior, Astoria attempted to wriggle free of Vesta's grasp. Snarling, the general refused to let go, drawing her tighter to her chest.

"General Irisa! What are you doing here?" Astoria felt her cheeks burn with more than the fever when the purple winged danann blinked at them in confusion. "How's the Vale?"

Dismissing the greetings, Eivor hurried over to them, pressing her hand to Astoria's forehead. "When did you take your last dose of medicine? You're burning up, Tory."

"I was taking her back to her quarters to deal with it," Vesta replied, eyes never leaving the trio of danann. "She was in the maze, alone, when I found her. Might I suggest she have a permanent escort?"

"What your general neglects to mention is that I was about to make my way back before she swept in to be my dashing saviour. Sorry, Irisa, but they like to fuss over me these days."

Spreading her wings, the danann's composure broke, and she gave them a faint smile. "I'm not surprised. We heard what's wrong, and I've been sent to negotiate. Your other sister wants you brought to the Vale."

"Out of the question!" Eivor snarled, turning back to the danann.

Frowning, Astoria considered her choices. She suspected it was a trap, and if she agreed to go to the Vale to see Silaine, Dawn would sweep in and whisk her away to the valley of spring where the god of life would heal her. Chewing her bottom lip, the hawk stared at her older sister, wondering if Eivor had considered what the request really meant.

"Did Silaine ask for it, or did the Storm Queen?" She kept her voice low, not wanting the words to be heard by the gathering crowd of onlookers. "Because I know what will happen if I leave Diwan."

Recoiling, Eivor stared at her. "Wait, what do you mean?"

"What do you think I mean?"

Her power slipped through the cracks in Astoria's mind, gathering the information it needed. Shoulders slumping, Eivor pressed her hand to her forehead and sighed heavily. Fear coiled in her gut, reminding the hawk her sister might decide that treating with the gods was worth it if it meant she survived. Glancing at Vesta, she saw a mixture of determination and resignation in the goblin's eyes.

"Please don't send me to the Vale, Eivor," Astoria said. "If I wanted to be healed, I would have let Charnel fetch Lady Eirian himself instead of bringing me here. Let me die."

Giving her a nod, the Unseelie Queen settled her gaze on the danann general. "Tell my sister she and her family are welcome here for as long as Astoria breathes. The rest is something the three of us can argue about once we're together. It's a long flight back to the Rainbow Vale, so please take some time to rest before you depart. No one will harm you."

Lowering her head to Astoria's ear, Vesta murmured, "We need to talk about you seeing reason."

"It's my decision to make."

"When does it stop being your punishment and start being theirs? Don't you see what you're doing to your family, Battle Hawk? After everything that happened, your sisters still love you. They don't have to suffer when you have a perfectly legitimate opportunity to be healed. One none of us would fault you for accepting."

Clenching her jaw, Astoria refused to give in to the guilt stirred by Vesta's words. "Take me back to my room, General. I would hate for Jola to yell at me for not taking my medicine on time."

ELEVEN

Rain cascaded over everything, grey clouds stretching as far as her hawkish vision could see. People remained ensconced in the castle, hallways filled with their drifting forms as they fluttered from one communal location to the next. Every time she encountered an amorous couple too eager to make it to a private chamber, it reminded Astoria of a time when it had seemed normal to her. The gods had created the daoine as entertainment. It was their nature to seek pleasure, and rare for them to deny those urges. Before the invasion, she had never thought twice about doing the same, and the hawk felt a pang of regret when she remembered all the times she had shoved someone against a wall without regard for anyone else. Onboard *The Storm Bird*, she had quickly learnt to show respect for the rest of the crew.

With the sickness dragging her down as the days passed by, Astoria found herself happy to avoid being touched by anyone. She missed the press of Dawn's body, and the slide of cool water over her skin when Charnel wanted to drag out her pleasure just to hear her scream, but whenever another person touched her, she felt nothing but regret. It helped that with the fever and the ache of her body battling the cancer, any touch to her skin hurt. The only exception was Vesta. Her touch was soothing when even her clothing was barely tolerable. Eivor had raided her wardrobe for the lightest fabrics she possessed to mitigate her sister's discomfort. Wearing spider silk chemises, trousers, and little else around the castle seemed foolish, but Astoria preferred it to being stuck in her chambers.

Anticipation held them trapped in its claws. Silaine and her family would soon arrive from the Rainbow Vale. Preparations were underway to welcome the very people most considered an enemy on paper, even if they were not fighting each other. She was excited to see her younger sister, and though

Eivor would not admit it, Astoria knew she was as well. The day before Oisin invaded was the last time the three of them had been together. Things would be awkward at first, and they would all be very aware of the fact their parents were gone. But every time Eivor's older children questioned her about Silaine, she remembered that even though Craven and Malena were dead, their grandchildren were not. They would be the ones who turned the reunion from bitter heartbreak to a testament of survival.

Lingering beneath the sloped roof of the walkway, Astoria longed to stick her hand out into the rain. She wanted to run through it, laughing as the water slid across her body, and her hair stuck to her skin. The last time she had enjoyed the rain, it had been with Dawn sprawled out beneath her, completely at her mercy. Closing her eyes, the hawk inhaled deeply, letting the comforting smell fill her lungs. Her thoughts swam under the influence of the pain relief she had drunk while Jola stood glaring on the other side of the table. From the taste alone, Astoria had known it was not the same concoction she had taken previously, but she was not a healer, and if the goblin insisted she drink it, she was not in a position to argue.

But it did not stop her from plucking clearer thoughts out of the whirlpool of demands that she curl up and sleep. Her chambers were not so far away, only up several flights of stairs, and Eivor's family had set up camp in one of the larger private libraries where the children could run around under cover while their older siblings attempted to read or do other activities. She expected her sister to settle down with a sketch book once she finished with her official duties for the day. The Unseelie Council had closed the doors to the meeting chamber shortly after the breakfast bell sounded, and Astoria was glad to be free of Vesta's stalking. It was flattering to be the focus of such an intense person, but she felt like she could not relax without fear of the general waiting in the shadows to swoop in.

Slipping the soft slippers from her feet, she left them undercover and took the few steps needed to emerge from the shelter of the palace. The patter of rain against her skin felt like darts, but Astoria turned her face to the grey sky. Arms spread, she caught water in her hands, and let it soak the silk clothing without a care for what anyone would say. As far as she could tell, no one was around to see her, and the medicines were fresh enough in her system to fuel her confidence she could return to her chambers before anyone found out. Drops clung to her lashes as she searched the sky with a fool's hope of seeing the familiar winged form of Dawn watching for her.

"I hope you're keeping out of trouble, my captain," she said, not bothering to whisper. "And I hope you're not torturing Charnel because he helped me."

There was no answer in the rain or the biting wind ripping across the courtyard. She wanted to pretend they had heard her, but few people knew how gods worked like she did. Prayers meant nothing unless the person uttering them had a connection to a god. Silaine had admitted Death could hear her prayers when she bothered with them, but it was not something she had done since the day Oisin's officers had captured her when she left the safety of the house where she had been living. Astoria had not bothered to mention to the younger princess that when she wanted to pray to Charnel, he always came. Sometimes it had worked with Dawn as well when the conditions were right. She had always assumed it was because of their relationship that they could hear her.

Bringing her hands together to let the water pool in her palms and trickle between her fingers, Astoria held an image of Charnel in her mind. "Thank you for telling Silaine, my Lord of Tides. I miss you."

It was unlikely he would hear her, but it made Astoria feel better to utter the words. A part of her heart wanted the two gods to sense how much she missed them, and rush to her side. That was the dream that cut through the nightmares plaguing her sleep. When she was fortunate, Astoria was granted images of Charnel and Dawn holding her, their hands banishing the terrible memories tormenting her.

"You shouldn't be in the rain."

At her feet, a puddle remained while the sheen of water covering the stone pavers became brittle with frost. Emerging from the Veil, Thorne looked unimpressed with being in the rain, but the black coat spun from Death's power did not absorb a drop. Smiling at the woman, Astoria did not move from her spot. She wanted to remain where she was, pretending to be wrapped in the embrace of the two gods she loved.

Pressing a finger to her lips, Astoria said, "Don't tell Jola."

"So, I can tell my wife instead? How about Vesta?" Thorne blew a sodden strand of hair away from her nose. "Have you no concern at all about what this is doing to your sister?"

"Why do I have a feeling you're not talking about me standing in the rain?"

"No, but please, do tell me why you are."

Spider silk clung to her curves, making movement uncomfortable. "Because I like the rain, and I don't know how much longer I have to enjoy it. No one else was around, so I thought I could have a moment."

"Are you praying to them?"

"If you count longing for their arms as praying, then yes."

The dullaghan sighed, striding closer with a gleam of concern in the frozen depths of her gaze. "They summoned me. It's been a while since that happened, and I didn't appreciate it."

She knew what the older woman was talking about, and her brows rose in surprise. "They did?"

"Indeed. Because of you. First, to deliver a message from Life, and second, to negotiate."

Wrapping her arms around herself, Astoria shook her head. Dread bound her in chains, and tried to drag her down, but she stood firm. Even though she did not want to know what the message was, or what exactly the gods had wanted to negotiate with the Unseelie, it was clear Thorne intended to tell her.

"And?"

"Her Great Majesty has sworn she will not heal you. She understands your desire to end things your way and respects it. However, the gods would like us to allow access while you are in Diwan. Apparently, some of them are upset they might not get to say goodbye."

Lips twitching, Astoria wondered if the request had come from someone other than Dawn. She had spent enough time with the sky god's family to know her parents were as likely to tell her to stop being a child as they were to cave to her demands. But there was one god who could snap her fingers and have them all scrambling to please. Her time with Jen had been short, but she had loved being around the cheerful woman and her beloved Nexara. Even the bumbling god of crafting, Willowbrook, who followed them around with adoring eyes when he was not holed up in a workroom.

"You're talking about Ladies Jen and Nexara, aren't you? Lady Chaos would do anything for them, and we are... were friends. They're the only ones who I can think of who would want to visit."

"Actually, yes," Thorne said, brows furrowed in concern. "Though I imagine if we allow it to happen, your impetuous sky brat will be the first one to rush in. I remain amazed she hasn't already."

"You and I know the gods could visit without anyone's knowledge."

"A fact that weighs heavily on my mind now you're here."

Astoria wanted to ask the other woman to argue in favour of allowing the gods in. The only reason they would be there was to see her, and none of them were interested in trying to force the people of Diwan to worship them. It might even help ease tensions for the Unseelie to see it for themselves. She was pleased by Lady Eirian's promise not to heal her, but she could not shake the feeling there was another reason behind it. A sour taste at the back of her throat reminded Astoria of the god of time, and his control over the rest. He was the only reason the god of life would risk breaking her daughter's heart.

"Thorne, can I be honest?" she murmured, turning her face back to the sky.

"Always, Battle Hawk. You and I have fought side by side."

"I don't think Life is promising not to heal me because it's what I want."

Stiffening, the dullaghan stared at her, and the temperature dropped. "What are you saying?"

"Dawn might not love me, but she can't be taking the news of my impending death very well. Her mother adores her, and you can't tell me she would let a little thing like my wishes get in the way."

"It wouldn't get in my way if it were my daughter and her lover."

Chewing the inside of her cheek, Astoria knew what she would do in the same position. "If it was me, I'd be hunting me down and threatening all sorts of eternal pain for daring to run away from my child and breaking their heart. So why isn't she doing that? Why would she let me get away with it?"

"The god of time."

"Precisely. He must have seen something that is preventing Life from interfering. But what? Why is my death so important they would risk the balance?"

Thorne crossed her arms, staring into nothing. Neither spoke, the rain becoming the only sound. Whatever thoughts were going through the mind of the Unseelie Master of the Hunt belonged to her, and Astoria did not expect her to share them. Plucking the sodden fabric away from her stomach, the distant rumble of thunder surprised her. Storms were unusual in spring, but not entirely unheard of. Every few years they would roll across the land, providing unseasonable light shows for those happy to stay up and watch through the night. She hoped it would stick around long enough so she could enjoy it from a balcony with a nice bottle of wine and no one bothering her.

"We should get you inside." Offering an arm, Thorne waited for Astoria to accept the help. "Please, Battle Hawk, take it. If you slip and hurt yourself, I'll have to deal with your sister. And Jola."

"Don't forget Vesta," she said cheerily, slipping her arm through Thorne's.

"How could I forget her? You have been a reminder we were once on different sides of the battle line. And thanks to you, I've had to tell my wife about you and your mother taking part in a war against Annawyn's Unseelie. Not that I was aware Malena had never told the rest of your family."

"My father had secret dealings with Annawyn. There was no way Mother would risk him exposing the plans she was helping Oblivion with. I did my part and look where it got me."

Scowling, she did her best to pull the silk away from her legs so she could move easier. It clung tightly, and Astoria hoped they would not encounter Vesta on their way to her quarters. There were only two people she fancied hearing comments from about how they would peel the soaked clothing from her body. Biting her lip, the duine wished she could banish them from her thoughts. While Charnel and Dawn lingered in the shadows of her mind, she would not find peace in her decisions.

"Is it your fever? Your cheeks are very flushed." Thorne stopped next to her discarded shoes and pressed the back of her icy hand to Astoria's face in concern.

"No, it shouldn't be, but who knows? It's not like anyone is sure why it's happening."

She did not want to tell the woman her sister had married that she was flushed because her medicine addled brain kept offering images of her former lovers. It occurred to Astoria she should mention it to Jola just in case it was a sign her mind was being affected by either the medicine or the sickness. Either option seemed just as bad as the possibility it was her heart trying to convince her to change her mind about dying, because it would mean leaving Dawn and Charnel behind. Realising Thorne was staring at her with a raised eyebrow, Astoria huffed.

"I'm dying. Leave me alone."

"That's the strange thing, Astoria. I'm not convinced. As a dullaghan, my connection to these matters is complicated. My power is telling me you're dying, but it's also telling me you're not. I've felt this before... but I cannot explain it."

There was nothing she could say in response that made any sense, so the hawk shrugged. Part of her wanted to demand to know how much experience Thorne had around sick people, but the rest of her did not care. If anyone had told her that dying of cancer would be as big a hassle as it was, Astoria would have told them to take a long walk off a cliff. All she wanted was to spend time with her sisters and their families, and to know that when she was gone, they would not go back to hating each other for their choices after she abandoned them.

"I know you don't want to argue, or to question your fate, but Astoria, why must you be so selfish?"

Thorne's tone was icier than her power, and the duine clenched her jaw in frustration. It was not the first time someone in Eivor's circle had accused her of being selfish. None of them wanted to accept she did not want to be healed. She did not think it was some awful choice that she was making. Another part of her wanted to point out how hypocritical it was for leaders of the Unseelie to suggest she should use her connections to the gods to avoid the death chosen for her.

"I'm not being selfish."

"Yes, you are."

"Oh, fuck off, Thorne. This is my fucking life, and if I want to let the cancer take me, then I fucking will! How dare any of you try to force me to choose differently because you don't want to deal with the grief my sister will feel when I'm gone. Every time I went into a fight to liberate the victims of the slave trade, I could have died, and Eivor would have never known about it."

"If you can't see the pain you're causing, then you're stupid. Even more so if you don't think she wouldn't have grieved your death upon learning about it. We might be the Unseelie, but that doesn't mean we don't have friends among the Storm Queen's fleet. Eivor has known where you are for a long time, and she has worried about you every day. She knew the danger you faced but respected what you were doing."

"Maybe I should leave. I can say my piece once Silaine is here and then disappear into the forest to let this awful sickness do its thing. The fever will claim my life quick enough."

A hand wrapped around her throat, the impact of stone against her back stealing the air from her lungs. Eyes wide, Astoria did not struggle against Thorne's grasp. She knew better than to fight a dullaghan.

"Don't make me command one of my riders to take your name. They will do it without hesitation. Try to run away to die, and I'll make sure you live a long life in which you will spend your years making it up to my wife. Believe me, I have enough favours I can collect to make it happen."

Taking a heaving breath the moment Thorne released her, Astoria eyed the dullaghan warily. "Fine, I won't go die in the woods to spite you all for trying to convince me to be healed."

"Wonderful. I knew you could be as good a girl as your sister. It really is a pity my wife is so concerned about what your lover might do to Vesta if she digs her claws into you."

"Yes, a pity."

"Well, let's get you back to your quarters and out of that wet fabric. I'm not in the mood to be yelled at by Eivor, Jola, or Vesta. So, we won't be telling them about your little excursion into the rain."

TWELVE

"You should sit, Princess," Vesta murmured, hovering at her side with a hand on her elbow as though it would keep her from collapsing. "You're looking tired."

Dipping her gaze, Astoria bit back the snarky comment she wanted to reply with. They had gathered in the same garden they had been in when she arrived. After the rain, everything held a green freshness that made her want to roll around in the grass. It was her favourite thing about the spring rains. Everything felt renewed. Leaves glistened, and flowers bloomed, their faces turned to the sun in worship. Children ran around, chasing each other along pathways lined with stones to separate them from the sprawling lawn and garden beds. Someone had set up an awning over a table and chairs, and Astoria knew it was for her.

"I'm fine. Stop fussing. You're neither my mother nor my wife."

She jerked her arm away from the goblin, looking to the sky to search for the people they were waiting for. There were no gateway stones in Diwan, so the danann were flying in, carrying Silaine and her son. It left her uncomfortable to think of the danger her younger sister was in, but the nearest stones were in Talaroo, so the trip was not as long as it could have been. Another part of her was thankful the temptation would not be in her face. Without a portal in front of her, Astoria did not need to worry about feeling the urge to step through to the other side.

"You are not fine." Claws latched onto the silk of her dress, the general refusing to let her go. "And I could be, if you ask me nicely."

Astoria gave her a dark look, feeling the flush of heat ripple across her skin. It was getting worse, slowly draining away what little energy she could manage each day. All the medicines Jola and the other healers were feeding her helped, but short of placing magic suppressing restraints on her, they were clueless about how to prevent what was going on. It left them resigned to the fact it was not the cancer that would kill her, but her magic. Every time Astoria caught Jola and Eivor whispering to each other while giving her worried glances, she knew they were considering their options.

Rounding on the general without tearing her dress, she snarled, "Don't tell me what I am."

Unfazed by her response, Vesta arched a brow, lips twitching. "At least you still have some spark."

There was a ripple of energy behind them, and a hand landed on Astoria's shoulder. Feathers framed her vision, and the general's eyes widened in surprise. Gaze sliding sideways, she took in the sight of rainbow wings, her lips curling in delight. She did not need to turn around to know who had come to her rescue. Her relief was short-lived when it occurred to her King Tigernach would relay what he saw to Dawn. They were so close it was inevitable she would find out about Vesta's attention.

"So, you're still around, Vesta," he said, pressing in closer to Astoria's back.

Refusing to release her hold on the duine, she bared her teeth. "What are you doing here, Lord of Rainbows? The invitation was for the Raven Queen and her family."

"I am her family. She is my brother's wife, after all. And Tory is family to me, so it's only fair I come to visit her in her time of need. At least she'll have someone around to match her wit."

Twisting an arm around to snag a feather in her fingertips, Astoria tugged it slightly in warning. She did not need the flamboyant danann king starting a fight with the obsessive goblin. Not when it would likely result in her being hurt and anger her sisters in the process. Tigernach growled softly at her action, his head appearing in the corner of her vision as an arm slid around her waist to latch onto Vesta's wrist.

"You will release her, Vesta."

"Look, if the two of you want to go kick each other around in a training yard, do so. Just don't involve me. I will cut you both," Astoria said, keeping her tone cheerful. "But don't make me get Eivor."

Chuckling, Tigernach kissed her cheek and released his hold on the general. "Tell me why I'm not throwing you over my shoulder to take you back to the Vale, Tory? I've had a distressed pirate captain unleashing sudden weather disturbances on my city."

"Well, for a start, you can't fly with me over your shoulder. Dawn has tried. It doesn't help that I'm just that fucking good at shifting that none of you can keep your hands on me long enough to get far."

"And my niece?"

She sighed, giving Vesta a pleading look. The goblin still clung to her dress, the tips of her claws leaving holes in the silk. It was likely the garment was ruined for anyone else, but considering it did not make her itch, Astoria planned to wear it as much as possible until the end. Sorrow flickered across the general's face, and she retracted her claws, releasing her hold to step back with a curt nod. Making it clear she understood the duine wanted a moment of privacy, Vesta turned her attention to the guards surrounding them with hands on their weapons. No one would dare attack Tigernach, but his failure to greet Eivor first had left them unimpressed by his arrival. The Unseelie Queen remained with her consorts, watching warily, but willing to let her sister have a moment with the danann.

"Tigs, don't."

He turned her around in his arms, wings surrounding them like a wall made from colourful feathers. "She is hurting because of you, Astoria. That girl is the closest thing I have to a child. I expected better from you after all these years. You were supposed to help her grow, not break her heart."

"I'm mortal, and I was always destined to die. Besides, it's not like she loves me."

"Doesn't she?" Tigernach lifted her chin gently, examining the bruising on her face. "Oh, Tory. You're not doing well, are you? She should be here with you... and so should he."

It was impossible to hide the pain lancing through her at his words, and Astoria shrugged. "Let me fix things here, and then you can sweep me away to say goodbye to them."

"Your sister has been beside herself since Charnel delivered the news."

"She's always been the softer one of us. It'll be good to see her."

Holding her chin, Tigernach kissed her forehead and huffed. Lowering his wings, he released the sick woman and turned to greet her sister. With a wing curled around Astoria protectively, the danann smiled warmly at Eivor, Rhydwen, and Thorne. Meeting their gazes, she did not look at Vesta for fear of what she would see on the goblin's face. It was easy to remain tucked into Tigernach's side, and to let her mind drift into memories of cuddling Dawn while the god wrapped her wings around them.

"Queen Eivor, you are as beautiful as ever," he said, bowing slightly. "I apologise for my rudeness, but my concern for my friend was greater than my need to stick to decorum."

"I understand. If I hadn't, you would have known. Is Silaine close?" Eivor extended a hand for him to take, and there was a flicker of amusement in her blue eyes that surprised Astoria.

"Very. They had to make a few stops for Bard, but that's the joy of travelling with a child."

Rose ran over to join them; her face flushed from the game of chase as she grabbed Astoria's legs. "Who are you? I like your wings. They're pretty. Can I touch them?"

Peering down at her, Tigernach beamed in delight, and spread his wings as he dropped to a knee. "Aren't you a darling little one? You can touch them but be very gentle. I can feel every feather. My name is Tigernach, but you can call me Tigs. What is your name?"

Astoria was glad no one attempted to pull the girl away. She had seen how much the danann king adored children. Meeting Eivor's gaze, she smiled widely, hoping it would assure her sister that her daughter was safe. Tigernach would kill anyone who attempted to harm a child.

"I'm Rose. Are you Aunt Tory's friend?" Running her hands through the primary feathers of Tigernach's wings, the girl giggled manically. "I want wings. Can I have them?"

Murmurs spread across the waiting crowd, and attention shifted to the sight of a dozen danann drifting towards them on the breeze. Astoria sighed at the sight, reminded of her visits to the Rainbow Vale. The winged warriors were magnificent, and she questioned her decision to spend her last months in Diwan instead of where she could sit back and watch them train all day long. But she doubted Eivor would have been as willing to go to the city in the mountains as Silaine was to come to the castle where they had grown up. That was the part that mattered, not her enjoyment of the view.

As soon as the red-winged general of the danann army set his wife down, Silaine was running towards her sister. Tigernach's hand flattened against her back, a welcome bracing for the impact of having the younger woman fling herself into her arms. There was no sense to be made of the sobbed words spilling from her lips, and Astoria stared at Eivor in desperation, hoping their eldest sister would save her. Arms crossed and lips thin, the Unseelie Queen did not move, her eyes tracking the approach of the two danann who had claimed her sister as their Raven, and helped keep her from trying to free Diwan. Squealing in excitement, Rose let go of Tigernach and bolted over to the little boy clinging to Asthore.

"I'm Rose. Do you want to play chase?"

He tightened his hold on Asthore's leg, and Astoria poked Silaine's ribs to get her to turn and deal with her son. "Can your little one go play, Laine?"

Pulling back, Silaine blinked at her before turning to peer at the two children. "Oh, of course. Bard, go play with your cousin. You're safe here, don't worry."

Free to fold his wings back, Tigernach ruffled Astoria's hair and stepped away, moving over to join his brother. "Children always have the right idea. Nothing breaks tension like a good game of chase."

Not caring that they were being watched by all the adults in the area, Rose grabbed her cousin's hand and tugged him away from Asthore. "Maybe Keeran will give us rides. Is your name Bard?"

"Nadia, can you keep an eye on Bardhyl?" Redmond nodded to his older daughter, and she scowled, spreading her pale pink wings wide. "Don't give me that look. You can get to know your cousins."

Talaith darted over, offering her arm to the sullen danann. "I'm Talaith, and you can come with me. I know where we can find the best cakes and not have to share with the younger ones."

"But I'm supposed to watch my brother," Nadia muttered.

"That's what my brother is for. Keeran won't let them out of his sight."

Slapping a hand over her mouth, Astoria tried to muffle her laughter. Her sisters stared at her in confusion before exchanging wary looks. It had been years since they had seen each other, and neither knew how to approach their greeting. Their mates watched on, equally unsure, leaving the hawk as the only one capable of doing anything. Slinging an arm over Silaine's shoulder, she dragged her over to Eivor so she could sling the other one across her. Propped up between them, she nodded at the group of her nieces and nephews walking away while the two smallest ones chased Keeran.

"Look at what the two of you have done," she said, unable to hide her pride. "Mother and Father would be so proud of you. I am. You're doing incredible things and making a difference to the lives of so many. Certainly more than they ever did. Now, hug each other and don't piss me off."

"Are you bossing me around, Tory?" Eivor grumbled.

"I've been bossing you around since I was old enough to talk. Don't act like it's something new."

Silaine snorted, eyeing them sideways. "She's worse than she used to be. Tigs says it's because she has to keep Lady Dawn under control. It made her even bossier."

"Look, I'd like to see the two of you telling a god to get on her knees so she can fuck you with her mouth. When you can do that without blinking, come back and tell me I'm not allowed to be bossy."

Tigernach groaned, covering his face as he shook his head. "You're the reason my attempts to raise Dawn as a respectable god failed. Honestly, Tory, time and place."

"I'm dying, you pompous feather duster. It's always the time and place."

Behind them, Rhydwen snickered. "I love you, Tory."

"Don't encourage her," Thorne said, pinching the goblin in warning.

Rolling her eyes, Astoria caught the faint smile on Eivor's lips. "None of you have a leg to stand on. I've heard you, Tigs. As for you, Eivor, remember all the times we snuck over the border to those human towns? You'd get drunk, dance on tables, and behave worse than most of the pirates I've sailed with."

Gazes settled on the queen, with her ornate web of black and white braids adorning her head. She lifted her chin, regarding them all blankly before the corner of her mouth curled in smugness. Sliding an arm around Astoria's waist, Eivor decided she did not care what anyone thought. On the other side of their sister, Silaine did the same, though her smile was tense. No one needed to say anything to know it was because her older siblings had excluded her from their adventures.

"So, are we planning to stay out here?" Astoria winked at Tigernach, aware of the way he watched her closely. "In a hurry to run back to Dawn to report on me?"

He made a show of straightening his coat, eyeing Asthore thoughtfully. "Not right now. She is hoping we can make progress with the negotiations so she can come to you."

Feeling the brush of Eivor's magic in her mind, Astoria offered her a weak smile. "*I'm fine.*"

"*Do you want to see her? I'll agree if it's what you want. I know you love her.*"

Silaine's fingers dug into her hip. "*She's barely been back on the ship. Only long enough to tell her crew what is going on. We got here quicker because she opened the gateway and gave us the best winds.*"

Closing her eyes, Astoria finally admitted what she had been hoping for. "*I thought she might try to sneak in with you by pretending to be a danann warrior. But I'm glad she behaved herself.*"

"*She wanted to.*"

Eivor grunted, eyes narrowing as she glanced at the watching danann. "*I'm not sure I would have been able to excuse it, but I would've tried. Love makes fools of us all.*"

"If the three of you are done with your conversation, shall we show our visitors to their quarters?" Rhydwen joined their line, draping himself over Eivor as he grinned at the sisters. "Am I the only one with any manners today? It's nice to see you again, Queen Silaine. Motherhood suits you."

"No, it doesn't. I've already told Red and Moth, I'm not doing it again," Silaine replied, flashing a tense smile at her mates that received arched brows.

"Ah well, not everyone takes to it like my Songbird did."

Clearing his throat, Redmond lowered his wings and gestured in the direction the children had taken. "Do we need to find them before we go anywhere?"

Leading the way, Thorne gave the danann an amused look. "You'd have to be a Havard to find them. I swear this castle has places that only allow certain members of the family to enter. The number of times I've gone looking for them, only to give up because they're just not there."

"That's not reassuring."

Scoffing at them, Astoria wriggled free of her sisters and strode forward, thankful her legs did not betray her. "Thorne's right though. This is our family home, and it knows who belongs. Now, let's get you all sorted because it's been too long since we've been together, and I think everyone deserves a special performance. I've brought my best singing voice, so you better keep up, Laine."

"Considering your sister is the greatest performer on Tir, I think you're the one who needs to keep up," Ashore replied, striding over to offer her wife an arm, soft grey wings folded back to avoid people.

Following her lead, Rhydwen clung to Eivor. "I'm going to have to disagree. My Songbird has the finest voice. She could make the clouds weep in pleasure."

Eyes snapping to Astoria's grin, Tigernach darted over and slapped his hand over her mouth. "Don't."

Biting his finger, she cackled when he freed her. "I don't need to sing to make clouds weep."

When he covered her mouth again, no one batted an eyelid in surprise. "How is it she's so crude when the two of you are such lovely, polite creatures? Did your parents leave her in the barracks to be raised by the drill master? It's the only explanation I've got."

Pressing her lips together in mirth, Eivor nodded. "They did. Father thought he was raising a future arena champion like himself. General Vesta likes to call her a feral little thing, and it's true."

Happiness welled in her heart at the sight of them getting along. There would be arguments later, and she expected her sisters to scream at each other at some point. But for the moment, Astoria wanted to enjoy seeing her family together, even if it felt like she was missing something important. Better to focus on those who were present than to lament the absence of the two gods she loved. Eivor met her gaze, and the determination in her eyes filled her younger sister with suspicion. If there was anyone who could sense what was going on in her heart, it was the powerful mind mage staring at her.

Slumping in Tigernach's hold, Astoria wondered if it would be so bad if she let her sister decide for her. She had taken the steps she needed to bring her family back together after her decisions had so cruelly divided them. They had happiness, and the support of the people who loved them. Denying Dawn and Charnel the opportunity to be there did not punish her, but everyone else. It would only breed further resentment when what Astoria wanted was unity. Feathers brushed over her, a gentle reminder the man keeping her upright knew how the sky god felt better than anyone did. Offering him a smile, she did not resist his support.

Astoria met Eivor's gaze again and hoped the Unseelie Queen would take the choice away from her before her stubbornness ruined everything. Lifting her chin, the queen's mouth twisted in acknowledgement. The decision had to be hers because she was the only one who could command a change in the agreement the Unseelie had with the gods. To avoid a potential conflict, it had to be Eivor who extended the invitation. And they both knew Astoria would not ask her to.

THIRTEEN

"And I said to him that no, I didn't think it made a difference." Plucking the bottle of wine from the table, Astoria waved it at her sisters. "I was sure he was going to strangle me."

Eivor and Silaine stared at her in amazement before exchanging looks. Taking a swig of elderberry wine, the hawk leaned back on the lounge, shuffling around on the pile of pillows they had insisted she use. It was barely comfortable, but it was easier to keep her mouth shut than deal with the fuss they would make. Platters of food fought for space among bottles of wine; several glasses perched precariously among the plates with dark liquid half filling them. Reaching for a vine leaf roll stuffed with goat cheese, Astoria considered waiting for them to say something about her story and kept going instead.

"And while we stood glaring at each other on the deck of a sinking ship, I thought it was time to be bold. So, I grabbed his shirt, and I kissed the god of water while shit went up in flames."

Clearing her throat, Eivor looked flustered by the fragments of the memory lingering at the surface of her sister's mind. "And what did the other one do?"

"She wasn't there."

"Where was she?"

"I don't know. When I went flying, I wasn't expecting to find an abandoned ship run aground on a shoal. Nor did I think Charnel would be there. It was just one of those things."

"One of those things, she says," Silaine muttered, biting into a stuffed tomato. "Like we all go fluttering around the ocean, kissing gods while ships burn and sink at the same time. How are you still alive?"

"Pure tenacity."

Eivor laughed, stretching out a foot to kick her. "You've got more lives than a cat."

"You can talk! I'm not the one married to a fucking dullaghan," Astoria replied, shaking her head.

"Yes, the dullaghan are exceptionally good at fucking. Can't beat them in bed, that's for sure."

Not willing to be left out, Silaine smirked. "I'm mated to two of the most powerful danann alive. When they both bite me, I swear I'm never going to stop coming."

They stared at her in fascination, and Astoria leaned forward. "Dawn doesn't get the fangs when she grows her wings. What do you mean when they bite you? Do I need to go find myself a danann for a quick fuck before I die, because it sounds like I'm missing out on something fun. And here I thought Charnel's water cocks were the best thing I could ride."

"Excuse me?" Eivor gasped, eyes widening as she sat up to stare at her sister. "Water cocks? As in more than one? Because that's what I heard."

"We're getting ahead of ourselves. Let's start with the danann bite thing."

Laughing, Silaine tucked her legs up on her seat, lifting a glass of wine to her lips with all the smug confidence of a woman who knew how good she had it. Grabbing a cushion, Astoria threw it at her and gawked when her hand shot out to catch it. Throwing it back, the wolf winked. On the other lounge, Eivor cackled, her power curling around them to drink in the joy they were experiencing.

"You've changed so much, Laine. We should have been better sisters, and I'm sorry for it. It took me a long time to realise how messed up our lives were, but it wasn't until I found out about Father's deals and what the gods had done that I truly realised how little of it was our choice. They played us against each other for their own reasons, and now they're gone," Eivor said, her mirth fading into sorrow. "Lord Galameyvin has visited me a few times, but I don't tell Thorne and Rhydwen. He undid Annawyn's manipulations, so I remember some things. I know they had plans for all of us."

"I asked Charnel to speak to them about doing the same for me. There's a lot they made me forget. It's why I was careful to never let people know how much

I was aware of. If I'd said anything to you, then Annawyn would have found out. She might have killed me." Astoria sighed, tired of all the lies smothering their history like the smoke from a bushfire.

Dipping her gaze, Silaine swirled the wine in her glass before draining it to banish her feelings. "So, you're aware the danann use blood to work some of their magic. They can control the person whose blood is fresh on their tongue. Well, what you don't know is how fucking incredible it is when two of them have their fangs in you, and they both tell you to orgasm at the same time. I've forgotten my name too many times. Some days, it's a wonder I even bother to get out of bed."

"I'm sorry, they can what?" Covering her mouth, Eivor imagined what Rhydwen would do with an ability like the one her younger sister described. "How do you get out of bed?"

"How fresh on their tongue does it have to be? Like, do they have a few hours in which they can do it? Because I would absolutely take advantage of that if it was me. Can you imagine how hilarious it would be to make your lover come at random moments without warning?" Licking her lips, Astoria wished she could have done it to Dawn just to watch the god lose control.

"I'm thankful goblins don't have that ability. It's bad enough when Thorne uses her claim on my name to command my pleasure. So, the danann have a bite that allows them to control their lover's orgasm. What about the god of water and his cocks?"

Shuffling forward so she could refill her glass, Silaine nodded. "Yes, do tell."

"Give me a moment to marvel at my little sister wanting to hear about this." Holding up a hand, Astoria stared at her. "Because you were always such an odd one, Laine. Now you want dirty gossip."

"It's amazing what happens when you find yourself in the care of people who build you up instead of discouraging you from being anything more than the pretty musician in the corner."

Guilt had Astoria jolting back into the pile of cushions, and she stared at her sneering sister. "I did what I was told to do."

"Always the good little soldier, Battle Hawk. Tell me, do you plan to tell Tigs about the last time you saw his wife? Because the way I hear it, you were one of the last before she vanished."

Tapping her teeth together, Eivor said, "She can't. The best he'll get is what I can figure out from her memories. Yes, Tory was there during the battle, and afterwards. She saw what everyone thought was the last stand of the dragons and their riders, but it wasn't. They still exist, and our mother helped hide them."

A wry smile gave Silaine a calculating expression neither of her sisters was used to seeing. "Don't worry, as much as he wants to command the truth from you, Tigs won't. They ordered him to leave it be."

"Charnel was the only person I could talk to about it. Mother never let me speak. She always said the only way to keep secrets was to never remember them. Better to forget than to carry it close to the surface where anyone might read it in our thoughts. You have no idea how thrilling it was to fight alongside the dragons. I've never been the same since those days... nothing has felt right." Closing her eyes, Astoria let her thoughts drift to the quiet moments when she was safe in Dawn's or Charnel's embrace.

"Except them." Eivor gave Silaine a knowing look.

"You want to know about the tricks a god has? Well, Dawn's still figuring hers out, but I think you can imagine what the god of air might do to make things exciting. Charnel..."

"Is older than Tir and has more experience?"

Humming, Astoria nodded and opened one eye to peer at them. "And he's creative. His control over water in all its forms is flawless. Now, I know you think I meant cock cocks when I said his watery cocks, but I literally meant watery cocks. Charnel is like any other man, only has one of those things attached to his body, but he can make extras with water, and they can do things normal cocks can't."

The noise that came from Eivor's throat made Silaine laugh, and she waved at their eldest sister. "I think you broke the Unseelie Queen with talk about a god and his cocks."

"Look, I've been between a dullaghan and a goblin, and that's great. The contrast in heat adds a little something exquisite, but what exactly can those water cocks do?" Resting her elbows on her knees, Eivor stared intently at Astoria before gasping when her power latched onto the most recent memory of her time with Charnel. "That's... stars above, Tory. And you came here instead of being healed so you could spend a few more hundred years doing him?"

Giving her an annoyed look, Silaine huffed. "I hate that you can do that. It's an unfair advantage."

"He can make them change size and temperature."

"That's also unfair." She shook her head at Astoria, mouth open in stunned disgust. "And you left him? He's so pretty too. When he was in our quarters in the Vale, and Dawn was there as well, I wondered how you could ever leave either of them. Charnel seems like he would be the patiently dedicated to your pleasure sort of lover. The way he had Dawn melting with a few touches."

Stiffening, Astoria stared at the husk maker in surprise. "They were in a room together?"

"Yes. It was after he told me about your sickness. Why? Is that unusual?"

"Very. They can't stand each other."

"Well, they both love you, so maybe they have a reason to change." Silaine shrugged, examining the platters of food for something that struck her fancy. "Maybe we're not the only ones you're trying to fix."

Eivor rose from her seat, smoothing her hands over her skirts. "Please excuse me for a moment. No sharing titillating secrets I want to know about."

They watched her stride away, heading through the door to the bedroom. Astoria sighed, letting the exhaustion creep over her mind. She was enjoying the time with her sisters while everyone else kept away. After the early dinner they had shared with both families, it was exactly what they needed. No one had dared suggest they leave it for another day. Everyone was aware she was struggling. When they first gathered in her chambers, and servants had delivered a dozen bottles of different wines and platters of cold food for them to snack on, there had been an air of awkwardness between them. It had faded faster than Astoria thought it would once the first few bottles of wine were drunk.

"I can't help you," Silaine said quietly.

Lips twitching, she did not bother to look at her younger sister. "I wasn't asking you to. Husk makers might be some of the best healers, but even your power has limits. No one can fix cancer except the god of life. This is better, Laine. Let's enjoy what time we have, and when I'm gone, you and Eivor will have each other. We're sisters. We shouldn't be on opposite sides of a fake line."

"The Unseelie hate the gods."

"And you don't?"

"It's complicated." Silaine shrugged.

"Yes, it always is. I hate the old gods... well, most of them. But the new ones are deeply flawed people just like the rest of us. They have lived lives, and they have suffered. The last thing they want is to make things worse for anyone. Unfortunately, there will always be people who seek to use them to gain more power. That is the line we must agree upon."

The younger woman hummed thoughtfully. "You're talking about the religious sects continuing to spread across Tir, forcing people into worship, taxing them of their hard-earned belongings, and inciting wars against those who hold different beliefs from theirs?"

"All in the name of gods who want to live in peace with their friends and families."

"How can you say that when you sailed and fought under the banner of the sky god?"

Astoria knew it was borderline hypocrisy, but she also knew what Dawn believed in. "And what have we fought to do the whole time? She isn't out there attacking other ships just because she's a god. We share an enemy with the Unseelie. We kill slavers, we take the profits from those who benefit from exploiting the less fortunate. Communities in need receive all bounty from our endeavours. Rescued captives are taken to places where they can get help to heal and decide what to do with their freedom. Dawn stands for freedom and believes everyone should have equal opportunity."

"For how long, though? What will happen after you die? What if you're the one holding her to that path?" Shaking her head, Silaine picked up a bottle of wine, and examined the label. "Ah, raspberry. Haven't had this in a while."

"She doesn't love me. Certainly not in a way that would drive her to change everything she believes in."

"Grief changes people, Tory."

Returning to the sitting room, Eivor arched a brow at the frustrated looks they were giving each other. Walking over to Astoria, she pressed the back of an icy hand to her face, eyes narrowing in concern. The cold felt wonderful against her flushed skin, and the pirate groaned in appreciation. It faded swiftly when her thoughts caught up with what she was feeling. Her older sister should not have been so cold, which left one reason her fingertips were white.

"How was Thorne?" Scowling, Astoria pulled away from the soothing touch. "I'm not so addled with wine and medicine that I can't figure out the source of your icy hands."

"You've always been perceptive, Tory. Thorne is fine. She wanted to let me know she's been called away. River encountered a group of goblins where they shouldn't be."

Sitting up, Silaine inclined her head to the door. "Do they need help? I can ask Tigs."

"No, they'll handle it. Thorne will make them the usual offer. Queen Calista has been getting bold recently. I'm worried she might try something drastic to hurt us. We know there will be war between us eventually, but the longer we can avoid it, the better."

The thought of the goblin's Blood Queen harming her family filled Astoria with rage, and she felt her skin crawl with the heat of it. Frowning, Eivor stepped back, her gaze shifting from their youngest sister to the warrior sprawled out on the lounge. Even Silaine looked alarmed by the wisps of magic slithering outwards from the pirate. Taking a deep breath, Astoria attempted to bring her anger under control again.

"If you're ever worried about your children, Eivor, all you need to do is ask. They're more than welcome to stay in the Vale until any danger has passed. No goblin could enter the city uninvited."

Astoria watched the emotions flicker over Eivor's face before she nodded in appreciation. It was more than she had hoped for in such a short amount of time. She supposed it helped that Silaine had always been eager to reconnect with their eldest sister. They both suffered from the guilt of leaving her behind in Diwan to suffer the consequences of Oisin's invasion. Watching Eivor extend a hand to the husk maker had a weight lifting from her chest. If nothing went wrong, Astoria felt confident she would die peacefully with the knowledge her sisters would be there for each other.

Shooting a look over her shoulder, Eivor huffed. "I don't want you to die, Tory."

"Seems like you have little choice in the matter. Even the Raven Queen can't fix cancer." Smirking, Astoria settled back on her cushions and glanced at the windows to where the night sky was perfectly clear. "All I want is for the two of you to be family again. That's my dying wish."

"It's hard to be something again when we were never really it in the beginning."

"That's fair. It doesn't help that there's so many years between us. By the time Laine was born, you were over 1000 years old, and not exactly interested in raising your little sister."

Chuckling, Silaine surprised them by saying, "That's true. I wanted the two of you to have time for me, but you were both so much older, and you had lives of your own while I was just... me."

"Yes, but you're the most beautiful and talented of us." Eivor squeezed her hand. "There's no comparison to be had. I have a lovely voice, but neither of us comes close to what you can do."

"I wish I could paint like you."

Grimacing, Astoria wished she had an artistic skill like her sisters. "I'm good at killing people and shifting. I made it into an art form. And apparently seducing gods."

"I'm not sure that's a skill," Silaine muttered.

"Oh no, it is. Charnel was hard work."

Eivor snickered, returning to her seat to drop onto it without a care for elegance. "And Dawn?"

"Yeah, she was easy. It didn't take much, even though I was the naked stranger who'd flown in through the open door of her cabin on *The Storm*

Bird. All I had to do was bat my eyes and throw myself on the bed. She didn't question it until afterwards, and by then, I had her hooked like a fish on a line."

"Hearing you talk about gods like this is... strange. Though every time I look through your memories, it's hard to deny how much you believe in them. Not as gods, but as people."

"Possibly because they are people. Yes, they're gods, and their power is what it is, but they have minds and hearts just like ours. We are a reflection of them. When they hurt, so do we. Those who exist now are not the same as the ones who came before. They want to make Tir a better place for everyone."

A flicker of guilt had Eivor glancing away. "That doesn't mean we want them in our lives."

"Nor do they want to be. They have their own problems to worry about."

"We shall see. Tomorrow I will discuss the options with everyone, but not you. I'm sorry, Tory. You cannot be involved in this negotiation. While it might be because of you, you're dying and won't be around to face the consequences. This is our path to walk."

FOURTEEN

Leaving the smooth ocean behind, Dawn followed the tug of Charnel's presence at the back of her mind. Trees replaced the open blue; their crowns locked together in a delicate weaving of branches and leaves. Flowers gave colour to the green, bright pinks, yellows, and creams decorating the ground at her feet. A deep creek ran through a gully, the crystal-clear waters promising a cool embrace if she slipped off her boots and waded in. He was there, half submerged, with his arms and head resting on the rocky bank. Sunlight glistened off the surface, turning his lighter hair almost as dark as hers. It did nothing to hide the swirl of midnight lines covering his back and shoulders.

It was the first time she had seen him undressed, and Dawn could not resist admiring the smoothness of his skin, and the broad span of his shoulders. Her traitorous mind offered suggestions for how it would feel to cling to them while Charnel fucked her against the trunk of a nearby tree. The low chuckle from the water god suggested he had caught a hint of where her thoughts had gone. Making no attempt to turn around, he lifted his head and glanced over his shoulder at her. Lips pressed in a tight line, Dawn picked her way closer to the opposite side of the creek, careful not to slip on the rotting leaf matter blanketing the ground. She did not fancy the embarrassment.

"Have you had any news?"

"Not yet, but you only delivered them to the border yesterday. I suspect Queen Eivor will take her time deciding what she wants to do before we hear anything from Tigernach."

Doing her best to avoid staring at him, Dawn leaned against a tree. It stretched out over the creek, roots dangling into the water where time had eroded the bank out from under it. Given more, it would eventually collapse onto the far side, bridging the two until rot claimed its memory. Ants crawled across the bark, sensitive to the presence of a god. She found it amusing that while living things flocked to her mother, they avoided getting close to the rest of them. One of her favourite activities as a child was capturing animals and sneaking them into rooms where the god of life was, just so she could watch as they attached to Eirian. Snakes had been one of her preferred options. Something about seeing a snake curled around her mother had never stopped being hilarious.

"I hope she doesn't take too long."

Charnel rolled over, leaning back on his elbows as he regarded her. "She will take as long as she needs. This is not a simple decision."

"But—"

"Patience, Dawn. You must learn to wait."

She wanted to kick a rock at him or snap a branch from the tree to throw at his head. There was no point in it. The god of water would stop it before it reached him, and she would feel like a silly child. Charnel always made her feel that way, though she suspected it was not his intention. He was not the only one, leaving Dawn aware it was her understanding of how people perceived her behaviour that made her feel foolish. It was her. She was the problem. Not Charnel, not Astoria, not Cass, or anyone else.

"You're sulking, Tempest."

Opening her mouth to snap back, Dawn remembered her promise to behave better. "I'm sorry."

"Are you?"

"Mostly. I'm trying, Charnel. But I miss her so much it hurts, and I want to scream. I want to march into Diwan to take her back, and force Mother to heal the cancer taking her from me forever."

He sighed, and the golden-brown scruff covering his face drew her gaze. It was strange to see it grown out more when all her life, the other god had been the neatly trimmed man with disapproving eyes who went to great lengths to avoid her. Following the line of his chest to the water, Dawn realised he was naked, and she stiffened. The lines of their fractured connection disappeared beneath the surface, distorted by the current and the angle she was looking from. Charnel did not leave his spot, watching her as though she were a nervous animal, uncertain if she should bolt from a predator that could attack at any moment.

"I understand. You've done well so far, Dawn. Our Tory needs time to complete her task, and we cannot hurt her by interrupting. We will see her again; I am sure of it."

Rubbing her palms against her thighs, she nodded. "Uncle Emlyn said everything would work out the way it should if I didn't interfere. But how do I know I'm doing the right thing?"

"If he thought you were going to do the wrong thing, he wouldn't hesitate to stop you."

The more she stared at him, the more Dawn wanted to know what Astoria had experienced in his embrace. Desire pooled between her legs, the tattered threads of their bond urging her to repair them. Whispers caressed her mind, assuring her everything would be better if she went to him. Swallowing nervously, the Storm Queen shook her head, refusing the pull of their bond. No matter how much it wanted to be completed, she refused to join with a man who wanted nothing to do with her.

"That's true. He sees all. Do you ever wonder what exactly his plan is? Sometimes it feels like none of us has control over our lives that the god of time doesn't want us to have."

A broad grin gave Charnel an oddly boyish charm. "They're all the same, that lot. Chaos, Time, Choice. Pulling the threads of existence to guide us down a path to something they won't share. I learnt a long time ago to just let them. It's not like we can break free when we don't always know what the manipulation is."

"Yet everyone says the gods my parents replaced were the terrible ones."

"That's because they were. Mostly. Neriwyn and Gebael had their good moments. Perhaps if your grandmother had been better, Annawyn might not have become a monster. In the beginning, things were fine. Shianeni was never the nicest person, but it wasn't a horrible existence."

"And you believe a repeat is what Uncle Emlyn is working to avoid?" Rolling her shoulders, Dawn lifted her gaze to the patches of sky she could see through the canopy. "That's what they taught me."

Charnel hummed thoughtfully, shifting his position slightly. "It's what I choose to believe. I'm tired of living in fear of what more powerful gods might do to me. Alyah and Xhaiden once promised me happiness if I was patient, and I chose to hold tight to that because their heirs told me to have faith."

"They haven't given you a clue when you might pass over?"

"Why would they?"

She shrugged, refusing to bring her gaze back down to him. "Because it would give you time to prepare. Like Alyah did with her heir. She taught Viv what to expect once she was reborn as a god."

"Do you hate me that much, Tempest?"

Surprise had Dawn gawking at him. He had moved from the bank to the middle of the creek, and the water parted around him without the slightest splash. Drops clung to his skin like diamonds, his wet hair trailing over his shoulders as Charnel watched her. A faint smile tugged at the corner of his lips, and he stood, letting her see more of the incomplete lines swirling across his chest.

"I don't... you're the one who hates me, Charnel. All I've ever done is exist," she said, lifting her chin.

"You have so much to learn."

"Yes, people like reminding me about that. It's not like I'm not trying. I'm out there, fighting battles to make things better for mortals while the rest of my family hides away."

He cocked his head, and she felt a brush of approval across the bond. "Yes, you are out there. It's the best way you can learn, and I hope all the other young gods can do the same. By that choice alone, you've done better than some gods that came before."

"Then what else do I need to do?"

"Be patient, Dawn. Your temper gets the best of you too often, and when it does, everyone suffers."

Huffing, she pushed away from the tree, wary of slipping down the bank into the water where he waited to pounce. Eyeing the depth, Dawn wondered if he was using his power to raise the level so she could not see his lower half. It was hard to tell by looking, and she had no intention of using her power to discover the truth. When he laughed, she felt her cheeks burning, and stopped at the edge of the creek, arms crossed as she did her best to glare at him like her mother would glare at her fathers.

"And you don't have a temper?"

"Not one I let get the best of me. My restraint means that when I allow my control to slip, it makes more of an impact. Just ask your mother. The others underestimate me, and I'm good with that."

Water lapped at the toe of her boots, tendrils stretching across the leather like fingers. Fascinated, she let it distract her rather than risk her gaze lingering too long on where the water clung to his waist. It was better than eyeing the fine layer of hair shrouding some of the dark lines swirling across his chest. Chewing her lip, Dawn decided there was no point in remaining where she was. The longer she stayed, the stronger the pull became, and if they were not careful, they would do something they would regret. But when a cord of water wrapped around her ankle, she lifted her gaze to find Charnel closer than before.

"When you learn control, Tempest, you will be a force to be reckoned with. I can't teach it to you because water and air are not the same. We need each other, just like we need Earth and Fire, but none of us can walk the same path to become who we are. What is happening to Tory is heartbreaking, and I wish it wasn't happening, but if something good can come out of it for you, then Tir will be better off."

There was an understanding in his eyes that made her want to leap into his arms. Digging her fingers into her sides, Dawn wondered if it would be such a terrible thing if she did. Charnel had said it himself: they needed each other. The ache in her heart where Astoria lived was as painful as the ache where he belonged. It was a gnawing hole that could be repaired if she put her pride aside. Looking around at the place he had chosen to wait in, she wondered what the hawk would have said. A little voice that sounded too much like the absent woman scolded her for not taking advantage of an opportunity. Their relationship was a drawn-out battle, and Dawn suspected she was the one who needed to find the opening in Charnel's defences. If she could bring herself to stop being the child sulking in a corner.

"I don't know what I'm supposed to do," she sighed.

"There are many options. Just pick one."

She wanted him to close the distance, and to touch her like he had in the Vale. "But how do I know if it's the right option? Sometimes it's easier to throw myself into my piracy, battling the wrongdoings of unscrupulous mortals who would treat their own like cattle."

"The right one is the one you choose. Inaction..." Charnel shook his head, moving closer to the bank of the creek, the water clinging to him as he did. "Inaction is siding with those who do evil. You fight for the better of our people, and in their own way, so do your parents. Celiaen dances the delicate line between interfering too much and letting evil win. Your mother could destroy everything if she let her righteous temper get out of hand. Much like you. Galameyvin struggles to hold up the wall between himself and the world lest the reflection of his emotions drives him to madness like it did with Annawyn. As for Aiden? Death must do what it does best. Wait at the end of everything, guiding the energy back into the universe."

"No one tries to help me make sense of these things. They all tell me I'll understand one day. People look at me like I should have all the answers because I'm a god, but you're right, I'm just a child."

His hand was there, lifting her chin gently. "You are the storm that sweeps evil overboard where it is drawn into the depths to be forgotten. Why do you think I'm never far away?"

"You destroy what my crews leave behind."

It was difficult to avoid staring at his lips, or the bottomless blue of his eyes. Every hair on her body felt like it was standing, and Dawn struggled not to lean forward to kiss him. She pictured Astoria, but it did not help. All she could imagine was the duine woman urging her to do it before he moved away again.

"I admire what your fleet does. The task you set for them. That was all you, Dawn. Your desire to do good has saved countless people and continues to help more. They worship you for your deeds, not because you are a god. And as

I watch you with them, charming, and drawing a crowd, never trying to lord your power over them, I am filled with hope. Alyah and Xhaiden told me to be patient, and this is me being patient. One day, things will be as they are supposed to be."

"You've felt this hole for longer than I have. How can you wait?"

"I am the god of water, Dawn. There are few things more patient than me."

Licking her lips, she caught herself leaning forward and swayed back, breaking the contact between them. "I should go before I do something we'll regret."

Charnel half smiled, and for a moment she was sure she saw an ember of desire in his gaze. "True."

Mouth opening to reply, Dawn felt the disturbance in the air nearby. It rippled outwards from the Veil, icy in its touch. Snapping her teeth together, she shifted to where the dullaghan sat on the back of a black horse; the beast pawing at the ground. From her position higher on the bank, the rider could see how close together they were, and she felt guilt twisting in her gut like a knife. Staring at the woman, she thought she recognised her and wondered if she was one of those she had worked with years before to deal with a legion of Shadforthian soldiers attempting to take one of her favourite cities.

"Lord Water, Lady Air, I bring greetings from the Unseelie Queen," she said, swinging a leg over the rump of her horse to dismount. "She sent me because she thought you'd accept the message better from her wife."

Bowing his head respectfully, Charnel did not hide his eagerness for news. "It's good to see you again, Thorne. How are things in Diwan? Well, I hope. Is Astoria safe?"

"The Battle Hawk is safe. Extremely sick, but in the care of Jola and the other healers."

Impatience to know if they could see her had Dawn clenching her fists. She wanted to demand answers, but the calculating look Thorne gave her was enough encouragement to stay quiet. There was no good to be had out of acting rashly. It was better to let Charnel speak than to risk being denied access to Astoria.

"I'm glad she is. They'll make her comfortable. And your family?"

Thorne smiled warmly, pride robbing her features of their severity. "They're all doing very well. Eivor is thankful you brought her sister back to Diwan so they could spend these final months together."

"Did Silaine and her family arrive safely yesterday?"

"They did. Though I suspect the three sisters regret how much wine they drank last night. Eivor put on a good show, but Silaine looked rather... peaky. Astoria, however, looked fine, but she is being fed copious amounts of medicine. The fever is their biggest concern. They think her magic is trying to kill the cancer, which is causing her condition to decline quicker."

Gasping, Dawn reached for Charnel, the pain of touching him better than the pain in her heart. "Please, may we see her? I know she doesn't want to be healed, but Tory is... I... please."

Arching a brow, the dullaghan took a moment to study her before replying, "My wife seems to think your presence might convince Astoria to change her mind about being healed. Eivor and Silaine agree they don't wish to watch their sister die. The family has been through enough without Astoria using her death to bring them together in grief. So, despite what the Unseelie Council decrees, Eivor is granting the two of you permission to visit, starting the day after tomorrow."

Drawing her to him, Charnel huffed in relief. "Thank you. We promise to be on our best behaviour."

"I know you will be, but it is the Storm Queen we doubt."

"My word might not mean much, but I swear to you on Astoria's life, the only thing I want is to be there with her. She means so much more to me than she realises, and bringing her comfort is the least I can do after everything we have been through together. Tory is my heart." Clinging to Charnel, Dawn did not take her eyes off Thorne, frightened that if she did, it would all be a dream.

"We're not telling her you're coming. Please arrive at a respectable time, and not in the middle of the night. Besides, Jola is drugging her to ensure her body rests because the bloody stubborn woman won't stop wandering the castle grounds until she drops."

There was something in the dullaghan's gaze that told Dawn she had more concerns about Astoria than she was saying. Charnel's eyes narrowed, and he hummed in suspicion.

"What is it?"

Sighing, Thorne ran a hand through her hair. "They're worried they might need to cut Astoria off from her magic. The fever is bad. She said you used your power to soothe it, and I argued with Eivor that on that fact alone, we should allow you immediate access, but my wife wishes to have some time with her sisters before a pair of clingy gods take over. Her words, not mine. Though she's likely right."

"We respect Queen Eivor's desire for time with her sisters, but if it looks like it's getting worse, come for me. I won't leave this spot until you tell me I'm allowed over the border. And Dawn will be in Tallahmal with her mother. Tell Jola all she needs to do is send a list, and Dawn will bring all the supplies she could ask for from the spring valley. Including seeds. Plants from Life's gardens are the best on Tir."

"I'll do it anyway, list or not. Consider it a gift," Dawn said quickly, eager to offer anything she could to the Unseelie if it meant being able to see Astoria.

Smiling wryly, Thorne nodded and turned back to her horse. "Day after tomorrow. Arrive for breakfast. The family wants to meet you."

FIFTEEN

The last notes of the melody faded amidst sighs of admiration and the enthusiastic applause of the audience. Silaine held them captivated, and Astoria could not help but marvel at how much her younger sister had changed. She moved with confidence as she commanded the room filled with eager people who had heard stories of her gift. No one could mistake her for the timid woman who had constantly looked to her siblings and parents for direction. Asthore and Redmond mingled with the crowd, proudly boasting of their wife's talent. It was exactly what Silaine deserved, and the hawk was glad to cast off another layer of guilt.

When Eivor joined her at the front of the gathering, there had been nothing but mutual joy at performing together. Astoria had spent more time watching the reactions of the others than she had listening to the music. She had heard the two of them sing together more than anyone alive. Their families could not take their eyes off the two women. While there was some tension between the danann and the Unseelie, it was nowhere near as bad as she had feared it would be. A part of her was pleased Vesta had seemingly switched her attentions to bothering Tigernach instead of her, but another resented it.

"Are you going to join them?" Thorne perched on the end of the lounge they had insisted she use. "I've heard the stories of the three of you performing together. I think you should."

She wanted to, but her gaze drifted to the ever-watching healer. "Will Jola let me?"

"I don't see why not."

"Tell you what, I'll sing with my sisters if you loan me one of your riders to cuddle."

Her surprise was almost comical as she spluttered, "Pardon?"

Gesturing to where a cluster of dullaghan stood together to watch the show, Astoria smirked. "You lot are icy cold, and I'm struggling with my fever today. When Jola's brews wear off, it feels like my body is being cooked from the inside out. Maybe cuddling a headless rider will help."

"That's... I see your logic, and I will ask if anyone wishes to volunteer."

"I promise I won't get handsy. If that helps. I really do just want their cold."

"Have you tried swimming in the stream?"

Mouth twisting, Astoria dropped her gaze to where her hands rested in her lap. "No. I've had cold baths, but the stream? I can't. Surely you can understand why."

There was something odd in the way Thorne regarded her before pressing the back of her hand to her face. "Are Jola's medicines helping? You certainly have a rosy complexion."

"They are, but less so every day."

"I'll be right back. If no one else is willing, I'll sit with you. I'm sure Eivor will understand why I have her sister sprawled in my lap, even if no one else does."

Laughing as the Master of the Hunt moved away, Astoria could not help hoping none of the other riders wanted to put up with her company. It would provide her with a great deal of amusement to make Thorne suffer, and she suspected Rhydwen would find it hilarious. Sometimes she questioned how she could end up so different from her sisters. Eivor and Silaine were dignified queens, while she was the crude one best suited for life on a pirate ship. Watching the cluster of dullaghan gather around their leader, the hawk grinned and waved when faces turned in her direction. Several of them stepped back, shaking their heads, and gesturing at people nearby. Their argument was simple, and she respected them for it. But it surprised her when Thorne returned with a pair of riders trailing after her.

"Battle Hawk, I believe we have a deal. Meet Fern and Clove."

"Fern and Clove? Seriously, those are your names?" She arched her brows, fighting back laughter. "Ever thought about changing them? I've heard it's all the rage."

The one Thorne had called Clove rolled his shoulders. "I did."

"To Clove?"

"Yes. I like the smell of cloves, and I didn't like my old name."

Pressing her lips together, Astoria inclined her head. "Well, my apologies. I can't think of a better reason. And cloves smell good. You know, we use clove oil a lot on ships."

"If you insist on making mould or tooth ache jokes, I've been told I'm allowed to gag you."

Her eyes widened in delight, and Thorne sighed. Next to Clove, Fern looked amused by the situation, her blue eyes glittering with mischief that seemed out of place on a dullaghan. Leaning back on her cushions, Astoria tapped her chin thoughtfully, eyeing the two riders.

"Is that a promise, Clove?"

"Yes. Though you won't like it if I do."

"Oh, I'm sure I've gagged on bigger. It's the temperature I'm interested in."

Thorne squeezed her shoulder in warning. "Astoria, you said you would behave."

"He started it. I didn't bring gags into the conversation."

There was a faint smirk on Clove's lips, and he arched a brow slowly. "This is true. She didn't. You warned us about her filthy mouth, and I'm fully prepared to deal with it."

"We wouldn't expect anything less from a pirate," Fern said, and Astoria cooed in delight at the softness of her voice. "We also understand she's off-limits. So, this will be fun."

Her delight faded at the look Thorne gave her, and she huffed. "I will behave. I did say I was only interested in the cold. Besides, I'd hate to distract Vesta from Tigernach. She's finally leaving me alone, and it's blessedly peaceful. So, with that."

The three dullaghan watched her rise slowly, the slight stumble as she left the support of the lounge, bringing Thorne to her side. Smiling gratefully, Astoria refused to glance in Jola's direction, aware the attentive healer was waiting for an excuse to swoop in and feed her more medicine. She did not have the heart to tell her they were barely helping after an hour or two. It was better to pretend everything was working as intended. Astoria did not want to be confined to her bed yet, not when she wanted to watch her sisters work on repairing their relationship.

Leaning on Thorne's arm, she strolled around the edge of the audience to join her sisters. Spotting her, Talaith fetched a chair from a corner and brought it over to where Eivor and Silaine stood. Their gazes never left their sister, the concern twisting their features into mirrors of each other. Sharing a look with the dullaghan, Astoria kept the jokes she wanted to make about family resemblance to herself rather than risk upsetting them. Things appeared to be going well on the surface, but she knew it was like ice on a lake in winter. It looked solid, but all it would take was a crack in the wrong spot, and the whole thing would shatter.

"Well, what are we going to sing?" she demanded, grinning at them. "It's been a while, but I'm sure I can remember the words of something respectable. Unless we're ready for tavern songs? How about a shanty? I've gotten good at those."

Eivor rested a hand on her shoulder, nodding in appreciation to Thorne. "What about an old favourite?"

"The fox and the hound?"

"It was one of Father's favourites," Silaine said, fingers strumming her lute, eyes glittering with delight. "I've been meaning to ask you how many versions you've heard."

"Too many to remember. Stories travel the world in strange ways. I've even seen it performed by a cast of puppeteers who travel from town to town to put on their show."

She found it oddly comforting to be with her sisters while Silaine played the melody. It felt like no time had passed as her voice rose to blend with theirs, the faces of the audience blurring into nothing. The weight of Eivor's hand on her shoulder was an anchor to keep her from drifting deeper into the inferno consuming her body. One song melted into another, and Astoria kept her gaze on her elder sister, welcoming the soothing power wrapped around her mind. Those watching were oblivious to what was happening, and there was no need for them to know. Silaine's command over the instrument in her hands kept them distracted enough to only see three talented sisters performing together like they had before the war.

When Eivor decided she had done enough, she nodded to Silaine, and the husk maker leaned down to press a kiss to Astoria's head like a patient mother. Servants filtered through the crowd, offering food and drinks to those who were interested in it. Offering her hand while their younger sister set the lute aside, the Unseelie Queen wore a faint smile most people would not see as anything more than what it appeared to be. But Astoria knew it well and hoped she could avoid the lecture to come. It was harder to stand from the chair than it had been when she left the lounge, and she looked over to see if the two dullaghan were waiting for her. The burn of her skin looked forward to feeling the coolness of their presence.

"You're playing a dangerous game, Tory," Eivor murmured. "When Jola finds out you're lying to her…"

"Don't tell her. I'm not ready to be confined."

Silaine slipped in on her other side, head cocked. "Your fever is rising, Tory."

Huffing, she nodded at the lounge, where the riders sat like a pair of pillars draped in black. "I made a deal with Thorne for fever relief. They're going to cool me down."

"And you think that'll work?"

"It can't hurt… well, I suppose it could. But I'm already dying, so what have I got to lose?"

There was a twitch in Eivor's cheek, and she glanced at where Thorne stood with Rhydwen. "Time. That's what you have to lose. Why do you gamble with the days you have to spend with us?"

"Because I would rather have a few good days filled with laughter than more days filled with foggy thoughts and orders to stay in bed. This is not the battle I thought I would die in, but I'm determined to fight it my way. I'd like to visit the woods tomorrow with the children."

"No."

Reaching across their sister, Silaine touched Eivor's arm and said, "Why the children?"

Relief rippled through her when the two dullaghan rose to greet them, and Astoria smiled. "Because I'm the incorrigible one. There are secrets I must teach them, as is required as their aunt. Especially the middle ones. Call it secret middle child business if you must."

"Oh no, I am not letting you corrupt my children!" Groaning, Eivor happily relinquished her hold of Astoria to Fern. "But you'll find a way to do it, regardless of what I say. So fine. But Talaith is in charge."

Helping her to the lounge, Fern gave her a smug look that suggested she would find the woman's company delightful. "Dare I ask what secret middle child business means?"

Chuckling, Astoria's grin grew at the looks her sisters gave her. "It means torturing your siblings in a manner entirely unique to the middle child. You see, we're the ones people forget about. The eldest is the one on which parents pin all their all hopes and dreams. They're expected to become what the parents never could be. And the youngest child is the darling who can do no wrong."

For a moment, Silaine looked like she was going to argue, but her eyes widened, and she stared at Eivor in shock. "You know, I honestly don't remember ever getting into trouble. I mean, you all taught me to suppress my power, and encouraged me to devote myself to music, but I didn't get in trouble with anyone, really. I remember Mother and Father yelling at Tory a lot."

"It's true, they did," Astoria told Fern while Clove chuckled.

"Did you never realise why we encouraged you to play music?" Eivor arched a brow and gestured at the people crowding the room. "These people are here for you, Laine. You make them feel better. Sure, Mother didn't teach you to be a husk maker, but your talent for music had a way of healing people. I always thought you knew. That's why she had you spend so much time with the healers."

Turning to look for her husband and wife, Silaine shrugged. "I didn't, but Asthore figured it out. I guess it was obvious once I started learning to use the power in a more typical sense."

"You can heal with your music?" Clove stared at her in amazement.

"Yes. It's complicated, and you'd have to ask my wife for a better explanation than I can give. Something about me using it to channel my power outward into my audience. If you ask around, anyone with minor aches and pains will probably feel better than when they arrived."

"Our Silaine is truly the best of us," Astoria said, happy to boast about her sister.

Settling onto the lounge, she welcomed the dullaghan taking their spots on each side. Their power thrummed, the cold of the Veil coating them as though they were ready to step into it at a moment's notice. She wondered if they were doing it for her and hoped it would not cost them. Eivor studied them, eyes narrowing thoughtfully before she lifted her gaze to watch Thorne approaching. The Master of the Hunt moved with a predator's grace, people parting in front of her. It reminded Astoria of Dawn when the pirate captain commanded the deck during a fight. No matter the enemy, they always gave way to her presence.

"Remember what I said, Fern, Clove." Thorne slid an arm around Eivor's waist before kissing her wife. "Don't encourage Astoria, and if you think her fever is getting worse, throw her over your shoulder and take her back to her quarters. Jola will take care of the rest."

Clove leaned in closer, a challenging gleam in his eyes intriguing the warrior. "Are you going to make it easy for us to follow orders? Or are you going to be a pain in my arse?"

"You know what? I'm beginning to think you want me to be. Can't a dying woman just sit around taking advantage of how cold you riders are without having one of them trying to get her in trouble?" Mouth twisting, Astoria shook her head at Clove before turning to Fern. "Are you on the same page as him?"

She smiled, and the sick woman leaning against her felt the drop in temperature. "Perhaps. Clove and I have always been inseparable."

Caught between them, Astoria glared at Thorne and the smug look she wore. "I hate you. Can I have different dullaghan please? These two are trouble, and I don't need encouragement."

Laughing, Eivor looked at Silaine. "Well, at least she can admit it."

Tightening her hold on her wife, Thorne shook her head. "Sorry, they're the only ones who offered. If you're unhappy with the help provided, please take it up with someone who doesn't think you're an idiot."

"Ouch!" Astoria covered her heart in mock shock. "Fine, but if anything happens, I warned you."

"I have complete faith in Clove and Fern's ability to keep you contained. Do eat, or Jola will come over and yell at you. Something I believe you're trying to avoid."

Her heart felt full at the sight of the matching grins her sisters wore. It was not the same sort of banter Astoria was used to, but it made her happy. They had united to tease her, and that was better than fighting. So long as nothing went wrong, it was a foundation on which they could rebuild their relationship. Better to build it without her. Feeling Clove press closer, the hawk glanced at him and saw the look he was giving his leader. She knew the dullaghan were a family of sorts, and it did not matter which side of the line they stood. Something they had done the last time Astoria spent much time with them. The Unseelie and Seelie factions had united to help each other because one of them had been harmed. They were the perfect example of differences being set aside for family.

"Come on, there's someone I need to speak to," Eivor murmured to Thorne. "Will you be fine here, Tory?"

Silaine stretched up on her toes to examine the crowd. "I'll get her food, don't worry."

"There's no need to fret, my pretty magpie. Clove and Fern are more than capable of looking after her." Giving Astoria a pointed look, Thorne's lips twitched. "They know what they're allowed to do."

"No permanent damage, but we're allowed to leave a few handprints," Clove replied cheerfully.

"Exactly."

Crossing her arms, Astoria glared at her sister and the dullaghan. "You are the worst."

Smirking, Thorne kissed Eivor's neck. "I don't hear any complaints from this one."

"Stop tormenting my sister, Thorne." Pulling away, Eivor huffed. "Now, come along."

Watching them walk away, Astoria smiled happily. She did not mind the teasing, not in the slightest. It was better than being treated with the hostility she still occasionally felt she deserved. Tutting as she wandered off to locate food, Silaine left her ailing sister alone with the two dullaghan. Her head rested against the back of the lounge, the hard top of it digging into her skull uncomfortably. She found it somehow more pleasant than the ache of her bones. Everything hurt constantly. On each side of her, the chill of the riders seeped into her body, taking the edge off the burning.

"You're tired," Fern muttered. "Why stay here instead of going to bed?"

"Because I'm not ready to let this defeat me."

Clove cupped her cheek, his icy hand soothing the heat in her face. "Or you could view it as picking your battles. Push yourself too much today, and you will be weaker tomorrow."

"I don't need to be lectured."

"Are you hoping for someone to take charge of your wellbeing? I think you regret running away from the people who would have ignored your empty protests and done what is best for you."

Closing her eyes, Astoria thought of Dawn and Charnel, her mouth twisting with grief. "I don't know what Thorne told you, but I'm all talk these days. I've already given everything I have, and now I just want to make jokes, see my sisters happy and reunited, and to die quietly when I'm done."

Fern snorted, her hand resting on Astoria's stomach. "What Thorne told us is there are people who don't want you to die quietly. They want you to live. You are Astoria Havard, the Battle Hawk. You flew through dragon fire while we fought under the command of the Executioner. If you're to die, it shouldn't be at the whim of a disease that will leave you a fragment of your former self."

"Don't worry, I have no intention of letting that happen. A pirate always has a contingency plan."

SIXTEEN

She skipped dinner with her sisters and their families, deciding the day had been long enough. No one stopped her, and Jola had supervised Fern and Clove as they helped her back to her quarters. It was a challenge to keep her head high, to pretend she was not very aware her body was failing. In every glance sent her way, and with every gentle touch, they reminded Astoria they knew what was happening. What enjoyment she had found in the banter offered by her two dullaghan companions through the afternoon had faded when the cool of their power stopped soothing the fire of her magic. They had known before she admitted to it, but despite what they had joked about, there had been nothing but gentleness as they helped her leave the hall while Jola fussed over her.

There was food waiting for her in the other room, but Astoria could not bring herself to leave the lukewarm bath. Jola's medicines had taken the edge off her fever, allowing her to enjoy a cold bath without setting off the shivers. Her body had slowly warmed it until it was not quite cool enough to soothe the heat, but not so warm as to be uncomfortable. It was almost perfect, and the lavender oil helped her relax. She had nowhere she needed to be, no demands on her time, nothing except another restless night dealing with her aching body and the war her magic was waging on the cancer.

Resting her head back on the lip of the tub, Astoria kept her eyes closed and trailed her fingers through the water. She wished she was back on The Storm Bird in the bathing chamber the crew shared. There were strict rules about behaviour, but that never stopped Dawn from leaning against the wall to watch her while she washed. Then, when they got back to the cabin, the captain always left her satisfied. But it was not the sex she wanted. Astoria wanted to lie back against Dawn's chest while relaxing without a care for anything going on outside their bubble. It was something they enjoyed whenever they docked at the island the fleet called home, and they were free to live in the cabin on the hill overlooking the pristine bay with its glistening white sandy beaches.

It was easy to imagine the feel of Dawn's hands sliding over her chest, and her lips against her neck. "Fuck, I miss you, Dawn. I wish you were here."

"Tory?"

The caress of Dawn's voice against her ear made her smile. She knew the fever could make her delusional, and if it meant imagining the god was there, she was fine with it. Humming in appreciation, Astoria hoped the hands would resume their wandering.

"Astoria, open your eyes, love. I'm here." A hand left her chest to wriggle in between her neck and the bath while lips pressed to her forehead. "Shit, do you think you're hallucinating? What did the healer give you? Charnel, come here! I need your help."

She chuckled at the idea Dawn would call her watery counterpart for help. It was so completely preposterous Astoria had to open her eyes to confirm where she was. When she saw Charnel's face looming over her, his blue eyes dark with concern, she laughed harder. Splashing water at her vision, she wondered if she should get out before it got worse. If she could make it to her bed, then at least she could suffer in comfort until Jola found her. Though the stone floor sounded enticing for its coolness. The hallucination leaned in closer, his hand stroking her face as he hissed.

"She's burning up. I'm glad Thorne fetched us. Give me a moment, and I'll get her out."

Something cold slithered through her veins, forcing the heat back. Moaning in relief, Astoria closed her eyes again. She wanted to embrace the scene her imagination had provided. The thought of Dawn and Charnel working together to look after her was almost too much to hope for. Watery hands lifted her from the bath, allowing the captain to wrap her in a towel before the god of water slid his arms under her. Giggling tiredly, Astoria snuggled into his chest, deciding she rather enjoyed hallucinating.

"Don't go to sleep on me, my precious Fire Hawk. I need you to stay awake until I'm sure it's working."

Dawn hurried ahead of them to the bed so she could straighten the blankets before he set Astoria down. "Wouldn't it be better for her to sleep it off? She looks terrible."

He carefully set her down in the middle with a shake of his head. "No. If it's not working…"

"Then I'll get Mother."

"It's her magic doing this. That's why they're considering using magic suppressing cuffs, but I don't think it would help. All they do is cut off the connection, they don't remove the power. It would still be there, attacking the cancer like it can burn it out of her body."

Rubbing her face against the pillow, Astoria smiled at Dawn. "You are so beautiful, Dawn. I wish I could tell you how much I love your fucking face and how much I miss you."

"I know, Tory." Perching on the edge of the bed, Dawn started unlacing her boots. "You can tell me again when Charnel's power brings your fever down and you can think straight."

"Do you know how often I imagine being between you and Charnel? Stars above, it's my favourite dream to get off to. I really like the ones when he's using his watery cock powers on us while we take turns sucking his proper one. Real Dawn has no fucking idea what she's missing."

Groaning, Charnel covered his face, while the younger god stared at him in shock. Oblivious to the fact she was not hallucinating, Astoria flopped onto her back with a groan. Remaining beside the bed, Water showed no sign he intended to remove his shoes and climb in. Dawn resumed her task, kicking her boots off to the side. Out of respect to the Diwanians, she had left her weapons behind on *The Storm Bird*, not that she needed them. They were mostly for show. Her belt was the next thing to go, leaving her in her trousers and tunic. Settling next to Astoria, she pulled the ailing woman into her arms, lifting her gaze to meet Charnel's sad stare.

"Maybe you should join us."

Lips twitching, he arched a brow. "I'm not sure it's a good idea. She might get too excited, and in this state, it's impossible for her to realise what she's doing."

"True." Nuzzling the top of Astoria's head, Dawn chuckled. "So, watery cock powers?"

"Don't."

"Aren't I allowed to be curious about what I'm missing?"

"It's going to be hard enough spending time together without going there."

The sick woman snuggled into the pile of pillows, wriggling away from the arms of her lover. Shifting under the weight of Dawn's stare, the god of water sat on the edge of the bed, reaching over to brush damp hair off Astoria's face. He could feel his power working through her, lowering the fever. It had always fascinated him how much control he had over mortal bodies because of their water content, though he was careful not to reveal it to the other gods. While they were better than they had been before being reborn, the damage was done, leaving him with a healthy level of distrust. Drawing the drops of water from Astoria's hair, Charnel formed them into a ball above her head.

"What do you plan to do with that?" The suspicion in Dawn's voice made him smirk.

He knew what Astoria would have encouraged him to do, but then he would have had to dry her bed. The window was open slightly, allowing a cool breeze to circulate the air through the chamber. Sending the ball of water out, Charnel winked at his fellow god before returning his focus to why they were there. Dark shadows adorned her face, and letting his gaze trail down her body where the towel had come unwrapped, he saw the mottling of her skin. The magic bound to her was killing Astoria, and there was nothing he or Dawn could do that did not involve begging Life to intervene.

Understanding the expression he wore, the Storm Queen said, "She looks terrible."

"Her fever is coming down. Hopefully she'll be lucid, and we can talk."

"Do you think she'll remember any of this?"

Eyes snapping to Dawn's twitching lips, Charnel sighed. "You're going to ask her, aren't you?"

"Well, if you won't indulge me."

Slowly raising a brow, he pointedly dragged his gaze down the length of her body. "You don't want me to indulge you, Tempest. Because if I did, you would beg me to fulfil Tory's fantasy."

"Is that so?" A braid fell over her face, the burnt orange bow on the end reminding her of what Emlyn had said. "Would it be so terrible? Your bloodline is human. If you were going to pass over, you've had multiple opportunities, and none of them were bad people. Yet here you still are, lurking in my shadow, never far away, fucking my lover instead of me. Why?"

"You're right, I've had plenty of opportunities to pass over, all of them perfectly adequate."

"Only adequate?"

"None of them were strong enough for you. We're gods, Dawn. You were born this way, unlike your parents. They grew up mortal, they matured before they were reborn. Has it ever occurred to you I stay away so you can become you without my influence? I could have swept in once you were... old enough and shaped your growth to make you what I wanted. You're still so young, but the more I watch you, the more certain I am that I made the right choice."

Rolling over onto her back, Dawn huffed in surprise. She had never considered what he said, and mulling over it, she realised he was right. Everyone had expected him to swoop in to claim her once she was old enough. It had become a joke among the other gods that Charnel could not stand being near his mate. But learning it was because he wanted her to figure out her identity made her heart clench with guilt. All the years she had detested him for rejecting her, when he had been doing the right thing, left her wanting to beg Charnel's forgiveness. At her side, Astoria was muttering into a pillow, the flush of her cheeks fading, and Dawn looked at the other god, pressing her lips together.

"Why do you have to be so noble?"

Charnel snorted, a faint smile giving him a boyish look. "One of us has to be."

"I still want to know about your watery cock powers."

"Would you shut the fuck up?" Groaning in frustration, Astoria threw a pillow at Charnel. "Some of us want to sleep, and if you can't be quiet—hang on."

They watched her sit up in shock, eyes darting from one god to the other. Her hands patted her face before running over her neck and chest as though testing how hot she felt. Dawn did not move, unwilling to find out if the duine was coherent and risk ruining her chance. On the edge of the bed, Charnel waited, mouth twisted as he tracked every movement Astoria made.

"I'm not dead yet. I know that much. You can't be here, Eivor will—"

"Queen Eivor sent Thorne to fetch us when it was clear you were getting worse. Your sister wants what's best for you, my Fire Hawk. Right now, my power is keeping your fever down, just like it did the day you came to me, and I brought you to Diwan," Charnel said.

Her mouth opened and closed, but no words came out. Stretching her hand out, Dawn touched her side, making the duine whip around to stare at her. Their gazes met before Astoria looked around, taking stock of where she was, and her state of undress. Poking the towel wrapped uncomfortably around her waist, she felt her cheeks burn with embarrassment, which she decided was a pleasant change from the fever.

"I was delusional, wasn't I?"

"Well, you were fevered," Dawn replied, grimacing.

"I said things."

"To be fair, if you hadn't, Charnel and I wouldn't have talked."

Levelling an unimpressed look in her direction, Astoria snorted. "I heard the talking. Can't really recall what was being said because my thoughts were... I can't describe it. But I heard something about watery cock powers, which leads me to believe I said things."

She did not hide her bemused smile, and Dawn glanced at Charnel. "It's nice to know you fantasise about the two of us sucking his cock together while he uses said watery cock powers on us."

"Don't tease her, Dawn," he grumbled.

"Why not? I suspect you've got more than a few tricks up your sleeve."

"Indeed, I do."

Shifting to face him, Astoria drew her bottom lip between her teeth and did her best to look apologetic. "I didn't intend to cause any problems between you. Also, why am I so fucking hungry?"

"Because with the fever under control, your body is simply fighting the cancer as it should be without the effects of your magic. You're hungry because you need food."

"Right... And Eivor knows you're here?"

Cringing, Dawn remembered the greeting they had received from the Unseelie Queen before being brought to Astoria's chambers. "She does. I've promised to behave, and I refuse to do anything to ruin what time I have with you, Tory. You're all that matters."

Charnel stood, nodding at them as he stepped away from the bed. "There's food in the other room. I'll go fetch it while you sort yourself out, Tory."

The sound of his footsteps filled her with a sense of relief. Glancing at Dawn, the duine took in the way her eyes followed the other god from the room. It was a reminder of why she had chosen not to accept his offer to ask the god of life to heal her. Astoria did not want to be a distraction for them to waste their time on. They needed to sort out their problems, and work together to find two more people who would make them complete. As long as she was around, they would not do what they needed to.

"It's nice to see you tolerating each other," she said, keeping her voice low as she unravelled the towel around her waist. "Maybe my cancer will fix multiple problems."

"Tory."

Scoffing at the scolding look Dawn gave her, Astoria wriggled around to drag the damp length of fabric out from under her. "You might be a god, but I'm older than you, Captain."

A hand settled on her ribs, Dawn's thumb stroking one of the dark bruises left by her magic fighting her illness. "Even like this, you are my beautiful Battle Hawk. I'm sorry I've been such an idiot, Tory."

"Sometimes things must happen, even if we don't like it. You weigh up the consequences as you go and hope you don't break anything that can't be fixed."

"When I think about all those nights I left you alone in our bed. I should have been there, worshipping you instead of doing whatever nonsense had caught my attention. None of it was worth missing that time with you. Maybe if I'd listened to you, I would've realised I had everything I needed right in front of me."

"Hindsight is brutal."

Astoria moved from the damp patch on the bed and stretched out, resting back on the pillows. She was hungry, and tired, but with the two gods there, she was too anxious to get any rest. It felt like too much to hope she could help them come together at last. When Dawn shuffled closer, their legs touching, the hawk felt the thrum of power sending ripples of exquisite agony through her, and gasped. Charnel stood a short distance away, a tray of food in front of him, watching with a knowing gleam that told her it was the god of air's power reacting to his within her body. The sight of him in front of her while Dawn lay pressed to her side, had desire pooling between her legs, and Astoria did not know if she wanted them to realise what they were doing to her.

"If you want something hot to eat, I can ask the guards in the hallway to fetch something from the kitchens," he said, bringing the tray to the bed. "Otherwise, servants left this for your dinner."

She bit her lip, forcing herself not to make a joke. "This is perfect. You can feed it to me."

His gaze dropped to where she was patting the bed beside her. "Can I now?"

"I'm a dying woman, Charnel. You should dote on me."

Dawn chuckled, tugging the orange ribbon free from her braid to gather up Astoria's hair and tie it back. "She's got a point, Charnel. We should dote on her every need."

It took all her self-control not to squeeze her thighs together at the thought of them taking care of her every need. "That's right. Dote away, and I promise to do what I'm told."

"Ah, my precious Fire Hawk, since when have you ever done that?" Smirking, he placed the tray down on the bedside table. "Because I'd be surprised if you knew how."

"Old birds can learn new tricks."

The look in his eyes had Dawn clearing her throat. "I'm sure that between the two of us, Charnel, we can keep her from getting into any more mischief."

Grinning at them, Astoria wriggled her brows. "I'd like to see you try."

SEVENTEEN

For the first morning since the fever started, Astoria did not feel so terrible when she woke. There had been no restlessness caused by the burning of her magic, only the bliss of being curled between the two people she loved. Charnel's power kept the worst at bay, leaving her with the tired ache of her body battling the illness. She had never felt as happy as she was to wake up to the sight of Dawn sprawled across her while the god of water sat on her other side, back pressed to the headboard as he quietly read a book. It was as though someone had plucked a dream from her mind, spinning it into reality, and Astoria never wanted it to end. Not while she still breathed.

The hawk had hoped to have a quiet breakfast with them, but a summons to join everyone in the private family dining chamber had been waiting when she stuck her head out to speak to the guards. Without the fever ravaging her body and leaving her skin feeling irritated by everything it had contact with, Astoria had taken the time to dress herself in something different. Dresses were not her preferred garment, but Eivor had placed a couple of pretty ones in the wardrobe. The desire she had seen in Dawn and Charnel's eyes when she swept out of the small room adorned in layers of blue and green silk had been worth every moment spent fighting with the dress.

Swaggering into the dining chamber with a god on each arm felt like a bold move, but Astoria doubted it would surprise her sisters. The sight of them startled everyone except Eivor, Silaine, and their consorts. Dawn had struggled not to laugh when Tigernach all but fell off his chair when he realised they were there. While the sky god had done her best, his brother had not bothered to hide how hilarious he found watching the scene unfold. Out of everyone in the room, the only one who bothered Astoria was Vesta. She stared at them, jealousy twisting her features before she vanished into the shadows. But while she worried about the general, she silently endured Jola's examination.

"How long can you leave her before it comes back?" Jola huffed, eyeing Charnel like he was some sort of medicine she could use. "She's reading more like I'd expect."

"I don't know for certain, but I imagine not for long."

Eivor approached them, head held high, and a gratefulness in her expression that surprised her sister. "The fever has broken? Your power worked, Lord Water?"

Bowing, Charnel smiled, while Dawn squirmed on the other side of Astoria. "Thank you for letting us come. She was in a terrible state last night. Thorne fetched me just in time."

"I regret not doing it sooner," she replied, turning her focus to the duine held between the two gods. "Don't give me that look, Tory. I sent for them because you're my sister, and I love you. Even if you continue to refuse to ask to be healed, I don't want you to suffer more than you need to. Besides, when I considered what I would want if it was me, the answer was Thorne and Rhydwen holding me until the end."

She flicked her gaze at each god before huffing. "That's fair. I won't complain. Nor am I entirely surprised. But I am starving, so you better plan on letting me eat."

Talaith's hold on her little sister failed, and Rose ran over to throw herself at Astoria. "Aunty Tory! Aunty Tory! Can we play in the woods today like you promised?"

"Have you been a very good girl, my prickly blossom?"

Crossing her arms, Eivor glared suspiciously. "Is this what you were talking about yesterday?"

Unable to resist grinning, Astoria gave her sister a fake, innocent look. "Are you implying something, Majesty? I would never encourage my nieces and nephews to do anything bad."

Lips twitching as she remembered what Astoria was like with her younger siblings when they were children, Dawn said, "I wouldn't believe a word she says, Queen Eivor."

"Do you think you know my sister better than I do, little godling?" Squaring her shoulders, the Unseelie Queen did not sneer, but the gleam of her eyes suggested she wanted to.

"Not at all. However, if it gives you any measure of delight, the things she taught my younger siblings certainly caused my parents trouble... especially the toads in their bed."

Rose perked up, grinning at her aunt. "Am I allowed to have a toad in my bed?"

There was genuine amazement in Eivor's eyes as she regarded her sister. "You taught young gods how to prank their parents? The very gods our entire existence depends on?"

Smiling slowly, Astoria arched a brow and headed for the table on the balcony with Rose perched on her hip. "Would you expect anything less? I heard War screamed like a little boy. It turns out he's scared of frogs and toads. Anything slimy that hops. Apparently, I'm a bit of a bad influence. It's delightful."

Several of her children looked too excited by the prospect of spending time with their aunt without their parents around, and Eivor examined the two gods thoughtfully. Her gaze settled on Charnel, acknowledging that as far as divine beings went, he was tolerable. Cocking his head, the god of water stared back, waiting to hear what she had to say while Tigernach sidled over to Dawn, his wings folded back as much as he could, so they did not impede everyone else.

"Are you telling me Tory is responsible for the toad incident?" he whispered, but the other two heard him clearly. "I've not heard the whole story, but I've seen his face every time it's mentioned."

"My sister and I used to have competitions for catching small creatures. We'd pit the abilities of our animal forms that we retain in our natural state against each other. If you're telling me she helped a few children catch several buckets' worth of toads, I believe you." A smile softened the sternness of Eivor's expression. "And I'd tell you I'd have caught twice as many, so your parents got off lightly."

Holding up a finger, Dawn chuckled. "First, she did. Second, my younger siblings are triplets. So, take the mischief one child can get into, and triple it, then add Tory on top."

"I can't let her spend time alone with the children."

"Considering I'm not sure how long or how far apart we can be, I can assure you she won't be going anywhere alone unless we want to risk the fever coming back," Charnel said quietly, concern giving weight to his words. "And I fear it will be worse if it does. You must understand, Queen Eivor, I haven't stopped the illness. Her magic is an inferno wanting to consume the thing attacking its host, and mine is a wall keeping it contained. But the cancer is still there, and her magic wants to destroy it."

Dawn shook her head, frowning at his explanation. "I still don't understand. Mother refused to be helpful by explaining it, which isn't a surprise. She can heal anything except death, but she's not a healer."

"How can the god of life heal anything but not be a healer?" Pursing her lips, Eivor glanced at the table to watch everyone settling into their spots to eat.

"She was raised a warrior and a politician. In her mortal life, my mother was the queen of a human kingdom far from here. Healing magic wasn't her gift, but reborn as a god, it is. Though I'm not sure if it's healing exactly, or if she resets the body to how it's supposed to be. Like what she did for Lady Asthore after she fixed your sister."

Tigernach placed a hand on Eivor's arm when it looked like she had been struck. "Are you well?"

"What happened to Silaine that she needed the god of life to heal her?" Eivor hissed.

"Her former guard abducted her from Mowbray Valley. As punishment for escaping Diwan, Linnea, who we knew as Kerra, broke Silaine's hands and feet, as well as other bones, and caused internal injuries. A team of healers, including trained husk makers, saved her life, but the damage to her hands was permanent. At the time, Life was giving birth to the triplets and the gods couldn't come, but as soon as she could, Eirian visited the Vale and restored your sister."

They watched the pieces fitting together as Eivor stared at Tigernach in horror. "Oisin and Cathair delighted in telling me they'd had someone within the family since before the Fog, but I did not know it was Linnea. She was my sister's guard and lover, but I never had reason to delve into her mind. It must have been her who opened the gates and let them in. The whole time she was the snake in the grass."

"Your mother knew who she was."

"I know this probably means very little to you, Queen Eivor, but when I found out who Tory was and what had happened, I wanted to free you and Diwan," Dawn murmured, staring past her at the table of people. "But my Uncle Emlyn, the god of time, told me I had to leave you. He told everyone the same thing. We had to leave you here because if we did, you would become someone who does great things for Tir."

"If my rescue had come sooner, I wouldn't have my family, and I love Thorne, Rhydwen, and our children more than anything. It took me a while to realise a hundred years of suffering unimaginable things was worth the result. And you're right, I do great things for Tir… but so do you, Storm Queen." Swiftly turning on her heel, the Unseelie Queen started for the table. "Hence why we work together occasionally. Our values align, and by any standards, that makes us allies."

Astoria watched the four of them approaching, while Rose wriggled on her lap, giggling at something her father was doing. She had kept the seats on each side of her free, though it had been a challenge when so many wanted to sit with her. The two gods slipped onto the chairs, and the moment their hands brushed painfully against her arms, the hawk felt a weight lift from her. Part of her had not entirely believed it when they said Eivor had invited them to Diwan. There had been no threats of conflict, no claims that they had broken the agreement, and her sister had openly admitted to sending Thorne to fetch Charnel so he could keep her fever under control. But there was something in the way Eivor kept looking at Silaine that filled her with suspicion.

"What did you say to my sister?" she murmured, reaching around Rose to grab a slice of bread from her plate.

Giving her a tense smile, Dawn watched a dollop of cream slide across the thick layer of jam on the slice Astoria was attempting to eat. "She didn't know about what happened to Silaine, and I mentioned my mother had healed her. We had to explain. Have you got enough jam and cream?"

"Probably not, but it's hard with a child in my lap."

"Can I have some?" Rose lurched towards the bread, mouth open without regard for the fact her aunt had it positioned to take a bite.

Jam and cream splattered Dawn's face, and she heard a collective gasp from around the table. Astoria pressed her lips together, trying not to laugh while the child responsible happily chewed on her mouthful. Leaning forward, Charnel chuckled at the sight before returning to the slice of bread he was smothering in soft white cheese and honey, while a slice of bacon waited to be placed on top. Reaching over, Astoria swiped her finger through the jam and cream on Dawn's face, collecting it so she could stick it in her mouth. She knew they were being watched and decided not to care.

"Tasty," she said, making a point of swirling her tongue around her finger.

Dawn bit her lip, a gleam of desire making her dark eyes smoulder. "You knew that would happen."

"Children are unpredictable, so you can't blame me."

Repositioning where she held the bread, Astoria let Rose take another bite. She wanted to kiss the pirate captain, and to lick the traces of jam and cream from her skin. They had rarely spent much time together so far from the sea, so she wondered if the other woman would still bear the lingering taste of salt. Giving her a look that promised revenge, Dawn plucked a folded towel from the middle of the table and wiped the food off her face. Conversation had returned to normal, but an undercurrent of tension remained. Everyone was aware of the gods seated among them as though it was nothing unusual.

She carefully twisted, rubbing her foot against Charnel's leg, and watched him fold his slice of bread in half with its bacon, cheese, and honey coating. "I'm not going to ask."

"You don't know what you're missing," he replied, then took a bite, giving her a challenging look.

Chuckles drew Astoria's attention to Rhydwen, and she watched the goblin copying Charnel's combination. "Oh no, I'm sorry, Eivor. I didn't know he'd start a trend of mutilating food."

Baring his teeth at her, the red-haired Unseelie leader added an extra spoonful of honey out of spite. "He's one of the oldest people on Tir. If he says this is good, then I'm trying it."

"It's sweet, salty, and creamy, all your favourite things, my precious Fire Hawk." Charnel bumped his knee into hers, and she recognised the shade of blue his eyes took on when he was being mischievous. "I'm sure once you wrap your mouth around it, you'll appreciate my suggestion."

Choking on his version, Rhydwen stared at the god in admiration with watering eyes as he croaked, "And that's how you do it."

Eivor smacked his back, rolling her eyes at them, while Dawn covered her face with her hand. It was odd to see her flustered, and Astoria was unsure if she liked it. Had they been among the crew of *The Storm Bird*, Air would have happily piled on openly crude suggestions to what Charnel had said. She was clearly trying to be on her best behaviour in the hope it would endear her to her lover's family. Squealing, Rose wriggled off her lap, sliding under the table to crawl between people, and Astoria groaned in relief. As much as she liked children, they had bony elbows that always hit their mark.

Placing one of his cheese, honey, and bacon creations on her plate, Charnel arched a brow. "Well?"

"You're not going to let me avoid this, are you?"

"Have I ever?"

Lips curling wickedly, Astoria glanced at Dawn. "Fine, but only if she tries it as well."

"There are children present," Silaine said, shaking her head at them. "Actually, there are other people present. This is a family meal."

Remembering the stories they had swapped over wine, Eivor giggled. "I thought you liked conversations on the dining table, Laine. Or is it only when you're the centre of attention?"

"Speak for yourself! How did you seduce your husband the first time?"

Eyes darting between them while Charnel reached past her to place a plate in front of Dawn, Astoria wanted to laugh at the looks on the faces of her sisters' consorts. Seated among the younger ones, Tigernach looked a mixture of amused and appalled at the comments being traded back and forth by the two powerful daoine. Realising the three women had gotten drunk and exchanged stories, Dawn leaned closer to Astoria.

"You naughty hawk, Tory. What did you tell them?" The Storm Queen licked her lips, shifting her gaze from the food on their plates to the nonplussed god of water. "Did you tell them about his special skill?"

Chuckling, Astoria smiled innocently and picked up her slice of bread, folding it like Charnel had. "Eivor, Laine, and I are royalty. We would never talk about such matters. Isn't that right, sisters?"

Tutting, Jola waved a fork at each Havard sister. "They're daoine."

"That's a little offensive," Dawn replied. "I know a lot of daoine, and they're not all these amazingly seductive people who use their appeal to twist your mind."

"And how did Astoria convince you not to cast her off your ship when she stowed away?"

Biting into her food, the hawk snorted. Flustered, Dawn looked around for help from the others at the table who were not a daoine, but no one met her gaze. Not even Charnel.

"She was acting in self-preservation."

Sighing, Tigernach stabbed a fork into a small sausage. "The gods created the daoine to be incredibly beautiful. People are supposed to be attracted to them with little control over it. No other race walks around so comfortably naked and enjoying the way people stare at their glowing skin while coveting them."

"They're shape changers. Being naked makes it easier for them."

"He's right, Dawn," Charnel said. "Take it from a god who was involved. Not that I had much influence in the creation of the daoine. Kelpies, selkies, puca, merfolk, those are mine. The daoine are very much people of the land, not the water. All daoine feed their magic on the emotions of others, and rousing attraction makes it easier to feast. Desire is a weapon they learn to use well."

Rhydwen blew a kiss at Eivor. "When we first met, I called her the fucking entertainment."

"The children," she replied, giving him an unimpressed look.

Shoulders slumping, Dawn glanced at Astoria, as she silently ate her food. "Is that what you think of yourselves? The daoine are so much more. Look at everything you've achieved, Queen Eivor."

"Eat your food, Captain." The hawk pushed the plate closer to her lover. "Charnel's right, it's really quite delicious. I'd hate for you to miss out on something he can introduce you to."

Eivor smiled, and Astoria wondered if she was warming up to the younger woman. "Apart from our children, you are the youngest here, Lady Dawn. Some things take more than one generation to change, but I appreciate your enthusiasm. You're right, we are so much more than what we were made to be."

EIGHTEEN

Leaning back on her elbows, Astoria gazed at the patches of sky through the leaves. She longed to be up there, drifting on air currents, and pretending there was nothing more pressing to be worried about. Even with Charnel's power keeping her fever at bay, she had been told not to shift. It was the longest she had gone without flying since her power manifested. The only person she thought might understand how she felt was Eivor, but Astoria did not dare bring it up. Not when she knew what her sister had been through. A hundred years cut off from her power, unable to shape change, unable to slip through the thoughts of those around her, caged, and beaten. A little sympathy was not worth stirring those memories when she was trying to mend the rift between them.

Beside her, Charnel sat on the blanket, a book in his lap. The children had returned to their parents, leaving them alone in the small glade created within the walls of the city. Vines hid the surrounding stones, trees looming higher than the attempt to contain them. They were not the same kind as those found in the woods beyond the boundaries of the city, and Astoria knew her father had brought in specimens from many parts of Tir. It was not the only such section of the sprawling gardens of the only city in Diwan, and like nearly everything else, it was open to the general population. Their parents had always insisted on it, and Eivor had not hesitated to return that rule once back in power. There were a few sections reserved for the family only, safe areas where they could relax without the demands of duty.

"Where's Dawn?" Lying back, Astoria stared at Charnel, watching the flutter of his lashes against his cheeks as he read. "I didn't expect her to leave us alone for this long."

"We weren't alone. We had your sisters' children with us."

"Yeah, but they don't count."

He scoffed, brows furrowed as his gaze slid to her. "Since I know you're aware it's difficult for us to be together, I'm going to pretend you're not wanting to torment us."

"Torment you?" She gasped, covering her heart with a hand in mock dismay. "How could you say such a thing? I am hurt by your accusation! It is a knife in my back, and you're twisting it."

"Tory."

"I wasn't thinking of you... I was more amazed she was letting you be alone with me."

"You're worried she might be jealous?" Carefully draping the ribbon he had plucked from her hair between the pages, Charnel closed the book and set it to the side. "And what exactly does she have to be jealous about? Because I doubt she cares to learn about the secret passages in the castle that will let your nieces and nephews play tricks on their parents."

Rolling her eyes, Astoria watched a male splendid wren dancing on a branch above them. His vibrant blue feathers reminded her of the god seated beside her, and when two dainty brown hens joined him, their shrill voices expressing their opinions, she could not resist giggling. Following her gaze, Charnel watched the tiny birds scampering along the tree limb, their tails spread as they bopped around each other.

"What amuses you about them, my beloved Fire Hawk?"

"Do you really want to know? Or would you rather I come up with something less likely to make you sigh at me? Because I will. You're keeping me from being killed by my magic, so I don't want to push my luck."

"Are you worried I might withdraw my power if you upset me?" He looked troubled, and Astoria wanted to assure him she was not. "Because if that's what you think, then you don't know me at all."

"But do I know you, Charnel?"

Uncrossing his legs, the god twisted around onto his knees and put a hand on either side of her head so he could lean into her face. "I would never make you suffer without good reason, my beloved Fire Hawk. You invaded my thoughts from the moment I laid eyes on you. When Shianeni locked us away to sleep for a thousand years, you were what I dreamt of. The sight of you bathed in flames and blood, naked and fearless, after Xhaiden transformed you into something glorious? I've always wanted you."

Her breath caught, the scent of the ocean tickling her nose. It felt like she had been doused in a mountain lake, an icy chill settling into her bones. Forcing herself to swallow, Astoria resisted the desire to lurch upwards to kiss the god leaning over her. Turning his words over and over in her mind, she held his gaze and remembered the first time they had met before she took to the skies to scout the enemy. That meeting was one she had never forgotten, nor the way Charnel had drenched her in water as she shifted into her hawk form, leaving her waterlogged and unable to fly, while Alyah had lectured her on which path to take. She knew there was more, but the patchiness of those memories no longer mattered.

"For you, Astoria, I would drown the world," he murmured before capturing her lips.

Pushing up on her elbows, she met his hunger with her own. Too much time had passed since either of her gods had touched her, and Astoria refused to let an opportunity slip through her fingers. She wanted to be completely at his mercy. It had been one of her favourite places to be since the first time he gave in to her attempts at seduction. Part of her wondered why he had resisted for so long if what he said was true.

"Please Nel." She was breathless when he pulled away, but her gaze fell on the miserable face of the woman she loved. "Dawn. I was wondering when you would join us."

She shoved her hands into the pockets of her coat and regarded them. "Were you?"

Charnel did not move from where he held himself above Astoria, but the smug look he sent the other god told her it was on purpose. "You're right, my beloved Fire Hawk. She is jealous."

"No, I'm not."

"You can't lie to me, my Tempest. Not when I can feel your emotions so very clearly."

Gaze dancing from one god to the other, Astoria had a suspicion it was not just about her. They had spent more time together than they had ever done previously, and it was causing them pain. She knew enough about the gods to know those who belonged together, knew little peace when they were not with their mates. Even then, it hurt unless all of those who belonged in the knot were present. Without each thread of power binding them together, they were incomplete.

Biting her lip, she decided they needed a push, since she would not be around for much longer. "Oh, for fuck's sake, would you kiss already? Indulge a dying woman."

Dawn scowled at her, but Charnel chuckled. "Considering you're the dying woman, it should be about you, not us. If I kiss Dawn, she won't let it stop at that."

"Me? I can handle a little kiss!" Marching over, the Storm Queen dropped to her knees on the other side of Astoria, and grabbed Charnel's chin, leaning in to kiss him.

Licking her lips, Astoria did not bother to hide her delight. She watched Dawn attempt to withdraw, but each time she tried, she pushed back into the kiss. Her free hand settled on the duine's stomach, bunching the layers of silk between her fingers. It amused the hawk that Charnel did not control the situation. He did nothing while the god of air seemed unable to let go of his lips in complete contrast to her confident boast.

"This is even better than I imagined," she said, chuckling when the hand on her stomach flattened and nails dug into her. "Though I'm a little jealous that gods don't need to breathe."

Her words were enough to give Dawn the strength to break free of the kiss. "Fuck."

"Please do."

They looked at her, and Charnel arched a brow at the gleeful grin she wore. "You handled a little kiss wonderfully, Dawn. However, Astoria enjoyed it far too much."

"Why? Because I found the two of you kissing to be one of the most arousing things I've ever seen? After my delusional ramblings, it's no secret what I like to imagine about you."

Embarrassment and desire had Dawn's cheeks flushed bright red. "Astoria is trying to use her condition to push us together. I know you want to repair things with your sisters, but you can't just shove Charnel and me into a room and expect it to work out like one of your fantasies."

Lips thinning, Astoria refused to feel frustrated. "I'm not stupid, Dawn. But you know what I know? The two of you belong together, and neither of you will be truly happy until you're united and working to find your two missing pieces. I'm just the distraction you kept you from admitting the truth."

"You want the truth? I'm this close to dragging your stubborn arse to Tallahmal." Dawn held her fingers a hair's breadth apart. "Because I don't want you to fucking die. If you die, then part of me will die too."

"Ah, but Captain, your mother has promised not to heal me unless I ask. Dragging my stubborn arse to the spring valley will achieve nothing except to ruin my efforts here."

"Why don't you want to be healed? If you love me, then why do you want to abandon me?"

Removing himself from between them, Charnel sat back with his legs crossed and hands in his lap. "She has a point, Tory. Every time you refuse what we're offering, it feels like you're saying your love isn't strong enough to make you want to live. It says you'd rather die than be with us for longer."

Astoria groaned and shuffled to sit up, shaking her head. "That's not it... but maybe it is. Yes, I love both of you, but do you know how it feels to be the outsider in this? You belong together, even if you prefer to fight it. I suppose that's the nature of air and water. You scatter each other while depending on what binds you. But what you feel for me can never compare to what you will feel for each other once you stop avoiding it. And when you do, there will be no room for me. As it should be, because the gods are trying to avoid repeating the mistakes of the past. Loving you is killing me."

"No, that's the cancer," Dawn snapped.

"Fine, I'll be specific. Cancer is killing my physical body. Even before I knew I was sick, I realised being with you was killing me here." Astoria tapped her heart and her head. "I knew I had to leave you, and returning to Diwan to fix things with Eivor seemed like the best excuse to do so."

Charnel frowned, a flicker of hurt turning his eyes dark. "Even me?"

"Yes. I was planning to give both of you up. I wondered if I would find someone nice here if Eivor let me live." Thinking of Vesta, she snorted. "Well, maybe not nice."

There was defeat in the slump of Dawn's shoulders, and the way she stared at Charnel as he stared at Astoria. Squirming under the weight of their powers, she felt like the air was suffocating her. Drops of water clung to everything, making the silk of her dress stick to her skin. Her magic rolled around in it, revelling in the opportunity to soak in their combined effects when it had only ever had one at a time. A flicker of heat rippled across her body, fading again under the soothing influence of the god of water. But it was enough to make him stiffen, his eyes flicking to Dawn in concern to see if she had noticed it.

"Charnel, is her magic fighting yours?" the god of air whispered fearfully.

"I don't know..."

Chuckling, Astoria decided that if it was, and if she would die quicker, then there was no point beating around the bush. "There's only one thing I want for myself before I die."

Snarling, Dawn pointed at her. "You aren't allowed to die. I will make my mother heal you."

"Forget that. I want to enjoy both of you at the same time like I've dreamt about for nearly the whole time I've known you, Dawn. You don't have to touch each other, just put me in the middle."

Running his tongue across his teeth, Charnel cocked his head and studied her. "Are you suggesting we should turn you over so you can put that dirty mouth of yours to good use pleasuring your captain while I fuck you from behind? Because you haven't given us a good reason to reward you."

Desire had her clenching her thighs together, and Astoria remembered how much she loved and hated his ability to say the filthiest things while looking like he was talking about the most mundane subjects. Eyes wide, Dawn stared at him, her lips parted as though she had planned to say something before realising what he was suggesting. She wished she could tell the god of air about the times Charnel had restrained her with water and talked her into an orgasm without touching her.

"Is that a good idea?" The ability to speak returned to Dawn, and she looked nervous.

"Are you worried you'll like it too much, my Tempest?"

"No… I… it's just… she's not well."

Smirking, Astoria arched a brow to taunt the other woman. "Nothing wrong with my mouth. Last I checked, my tongue still functions just as well as it did the last time I fucked you with it."

Charnel waved at the duine, keeping his gaze on Dawn. "If you like the idea of all those layers of pretty silk pooled around her breasts while you hold her face to your cunt, and I fill hers with my cock until she can't take any more, then you'll take your clothes off."

She did not think she had ever seen Dawn stand so quickly to shed her clothes. Water moved to the furthest corner of the large blanket they had brought so they could have a picnic with the children. There was enough room for Air to kneel nervously in the middle. Her gaze kept darting around, never quite settling on her companions. Tugging the ribbon free of the book he had set aside, Charnel signalled for Astoria to crawl to him. Knowing what he wanted, she lowered herself when she reached him, allowing the god to gather her hair back, using the orange silk to tie it in place.

"Lie down, Dawn," Astoria said, turning around to study her lover. "And spread those legs for me."

Keeping her mouth shut, Air did as she was told. She felt the pull of the man watching her, even as Astoria's hands trailed over her legs. Part of her mind screamed it was wrong to be so aroused by the situation. Gods were not supposed to take mortal lovers any more after what had gone wrong with the ones before, but no one had stopped her because they understood the complexities of her relationship with Charnel. Sharing Astoria between them felt forbidden, especially when it brought them so close. Except the hands gently caressing her spread the embers of her desire, and Dawn whimpered when they trailed over her stomach, brushing the ticklish spots only Astoria knew.

"You are so beautiful, my captain."

Charnel kept back, watching the duine press kisses to the other woman's body. Her hands roamed, and he paid attention to the spots where they lingered, noting when they made Dawn squirm. They barely touched her breasts, which left him curious, but it was a question for later. When Astoria shuffled into position, carefully making sure her dress was not caught under her legs as she lowered herself to Dawn's cunt, his cock twitched eagerly. Her arse was in the air, legs spread to give him access, and he knew anticipation already had her soaking wet. The moment Astoria brought her fingers to open Dawn for her tongue, Air wrapped her hair around her hand, orange silk caught between her knuckles.

Moving forward on his knees, Charnel did not touch Astoria's legs, not wanting to distract her from her task until he had gotten a better look. Gazing down the slope of her back to where her face was pressed to Dawn's snatch, he undid the buttons of his trousers to free his cock. His counterpart had her eyes closed in pleasure, features twisting whenever the woman feasting on her sent sparks through her core. Gathering the skirts of Astoria's dress in his hands, he flipped them over her back to admire her bare arse. It did not surprise him she had skipped wearing undergarments. Trailing a finger down the crack of her backside, Charnel slid it between her wet folds, before shuffling forward to align the head of his cock with its destination.

He admired her unflinching devotion to bringing Dawn to her peak as he rubbed himself against her clit. Rocking back against his cock, Astoria lifted her arse a little higher to make it easier for Water to slide into her. When she felt him press at her entrance, she mimicked it with her fingers, pushing two into Dawn's cunt at the same slow pace Charnel set. Curling them to stroke the spot inside her captain that would heighten her pleasure, the duine could not help moaning when the cock suddenly shoved the rest of the way into her. His hands dug into her hips, holding her to him for a moment before he pulled out to slam back in. It forced her face into Dawn's vagina, her nose pressed against her clit.

"Hold her there, Dawn. Don't let her go until you come all over her face. If you don't, then I'll pull out and leave her unfinished," Charnel growled, holding the surprised stare of the woman beneath them.

Pulling her face back slightly to take a deep breath, Astoria nodded at Dawn before diving back in. The hand in her hair held her in place, encouraging her tongue to swirl around the sensitive bud in need of her attention. She knew how to make the other woman orgasm, but every rough stroke of Charnel's cock dragged her closer to hers, and she wanted to make it last. Pain spread through the left cheek of her backside, shortly followed by a smack on the right, and Astoria clenched around the penis inside her, pushing her arse higher in a silent request for more.

"Oh fuck!" Dawn sobbed, pressing her head in firmer as she ground against Astoria's face. "Yes!"

Her tongue joined her fingers, and the duine greedily lapped up the flood of arousal accompanying the clenching of Dawn's walls. The hand in her hair loosened, only to be replaced by Charnel's, and he pulled it tight but made no move to remove her face from the other god's cunt. His pace quickened, the force shoving Astoria into Dawn as though he were trying to fuck his mate through her. Adjusting the position of her head, she kept her tongue out and stiff, letting it spear into her captain with each stroke.

The hold he had on her hair changed as her walls fluttered around his cock. Shoving her head down, Charnel held her against Dawn's cunt, and his other hand closed over her throat. Hearing the whimpers of pleasure coming from the Storm Queen, Astoria attempted to coax a second orgasm from her as her own crested like a wave, breaking through her. Her lungs burned from the effort, demanding air as the edge of her vision danced with spots, but it felt like the pleasure would never end as Charnel filled her. She would die trapped between the two people she loved, and she would thank them for it.

"No more, please," Dawn whispered, her hand pushing the head between her thighs away. "She can't."

Free to breathe again, Astoria laid her cheek down, and did not move. She knew Charnel liked to stay buried in her for as long as he could after he finished. It gave her time to centre her thoughts and bring her emotions back under control. Without it, he knew she was likely to want to keep going until she collapsed.

His hands smoothed over her back, running down her spine to rub her arse. "You're such a good girl, my beloved Fire Hawk. This is where you belong, right between us. Completely ours."

"Charnel…"

Lifting his gaze to Dawn's, Charnel did not smile. "You need to go to your mother."

NINETEEN

The bliss of an excellent orgasm faded too quickly when she registered Charnel's words. His cock had not left her, and his hands pressed against her shoulders, keeping her still. As Astoria watched Dawn's legs shift from where they rested on each side of her and heard the scuff of the god moving, she wanted to struggle free. It was clear she had no intention of arguing with Water, leaving the duine to convince them they were making a mistake. By commanding Dawn to go to her mother, Charnel was drawing a line in the sand she did not want them to cross. Doing so would rob her of her free will, and as much as Astoria loved them, she wondered if she could forgive them for it.

"Don't listen to him, Dawn," she mumbled, the blanket scratching her cheek. "Please."

Staring down at her, the other woman looked troubled. "I know you don't want it yet, Tory, but it's the right thing to do. When you're healed, everything will be better. I will be better. I promise."

"Your mother said she wouldn't do it if I didn't want it."

He kept the weight pressing down on her shoulders, and Charnel said, "Don't worry about that, Dawn. Your mother owes me, so remind her of that if she tries to argue."

When Dawn hesitated to pull her clothes on so she could leave, Astoria felt a shard of hope her lover realised how wrong they were to defy her wishes. Sighing at her reluctance, Charnel slid his cock free and released his hold on her. Before she could move, ropes of water slithered across the ground to wrap around her, and Astoria whined. Despite her anger, she could not help the fresh desire fluttering through her and making her cunt clench with the need to feel him inside her. He knew how much she enjoyed it when he restrained her.

Astoria ground out, "Fuck you, Charnel."

"Ask me nicely once you're better, my beloved Fire Hawk." His hands brushed over the red marks he had left on her arse. "And believe me, you will be healed. I'm tired of denying what I want."

Pausing with her hands on the buckle of her belt, Dawn stared at him. "What do you mean?"

"Water possesses; it consumes. Given freedom, it takes what it wants. It erodes anything trying to stand in its way. I waited for over a thousand years to claim Astoria, and I can't just let her die when I want to spend as many years with her as I did without. She is mine, Dawn. Yours. Are you going to let her abandon us?"

Her mouth set in a firm line, and she shook her head. Watching Dawn resume dressing, Astoria could not ignore the tiny voice in her mind pointing out she had hoped someone would take the decision from her. Eivor had already done so by sending Thorne to fetch the two gods, and it made sense they would refuse to accept her choice to die. The watery ropes keeping her in place did not slacken, but Charnel rose to his feet, and Astoria saw the surprise on Dawn's face as she watched him tuck his cock back into his trousers. There was an ache in her shoulders from the position he kept her in, but the duine refused to complain. She had held it for longer without an issue, and the cancer would not make her admit defeat.

"Please don't hate me for this," Dawn said, dropping her gaze to meet Astoria's. "But he's right. I refuse to let you go, and maybe there's another way we can keep you. One I should have thought of years ago."

Even if the cancer could not make her admit defeat, the desperation in her captain's eyes did. "I know."

The moment she vanished, Charnel returned the ropes of water to the nearby pond. Her knees slid back, and Astoria collapsed onto her side, thankful the ache in her shoulders could find relief. Going over to the picnic basket the children had left behind, he retrieved a flask with one of Jola's concoctions for pain. Bringing it back, he knelt carefully and removed the stopper before pressing it to her lips.

"How do you feel, my beloved Fire Hawk?"

Between mouthfuls, she muttered, "Angry."

"Good, hold on to that emotion. You will need it." He glanced at the gateway in the wall surrounding the glade. "Because your older sister is coming."

Groaning, she accepted his help to sit up. The silk of her dress pooled over her legs, hiding the evidence of their relations from sight. Not that Eivor could not pluck the truth from her mind the moment she appeared. Astoria knew she had nothing to be ashamed of, and it was not a secret she was involved with the two gods, but it was the prospect of having her sister looking at her in disgust that sent a flicker of shame through her. Settling down on the blanket next to her, Charnel held out the flask, arching a brow when she squirmed. Her thighs were sticky, and she felt too aware of their combined fluids.

Eivor rushed into the glade, Vesta trailing after her. "Have you seen the children?"

Straightening, Astoria shared a look with Charnel, replying, "Not since they left earlier. They've been gone for a while. Talaith and Nadia were taking them back to the palace."

"Talaith, Nadia, Rose, and Bardhyl are missing. Luciana said they were going to find some toads, but no one has seen them since the other children left them."

"Nel, can you check all waters?" She turned to him, panic filling her.

He nodded, touching her cheek, and she was sure she saw relief in his eyes. "Of course. I shouldn't be gone long enough for your fever to return. Please be careful, my Fire Hawk. I love you."

No one blinked when he vanished, and Vesta's eyes narrowed when she made a show of sniffing the air, her shadows creeping closer. Struggling to her feet, Astoria refused to give the general the benefit of acknowledging what she was hinting at. She was glad her skirts had not been under her while she sat on the blanket, so there was no need to worry about the telltale wet patch. Approaching her sister, the hawk touched her arm.

"I'm sure it's fine. Talaith and Nadia are responsible girls, and they wouldn't let anything happen." Sharing a look with Vesta, Astoria wondered why they were so worried. "Unless you have reason to think there might be something else going on?"

"Queen Calista has made threats since we broke the treaty. Talaith knows she's not supposed to leave the immediate grounds without guards, but if she felt emboldened by Nadia, and your comments, she might have," Eivor replied.

"Take me to where they were last seen."

Nodding, the queen clutched her hand tightly and led her from the glade. "I know you'll find them."

Vesta scoffed, the sound of her boots heavy on the stone path. "We have guards scouring the gardens, headless riders searching beyond, but you know your dying sister will find them?"

"Yes, that's right!" Eivor cast a dark look over her shoulder. "Hawks are apex predators, and Tory possesses those abilities in her natural form. I've never encountered a better hunter."

"Is that so?"

Humming, Astoria swept her gaze across the gardens as they walked. "Your sense of smell is better than mine, but there's extraordinarily little I don't see. Between the two of us, we should be able to track down four children. Especially since I told them they're not to leave the castle grounds until they're at least 300 years old, and their powers have fully manifested."

"Right, because you were so well behaved."

"Actually, I was. Though much of that was because Father kept me busy training. By the end of the day, I was usually too exhausted to be interested in sneaking out into the city. Of all of us, they barely left me alone, which helped me learn things I wasn't supposed to know. People were so accustomed to seeing me there, they stopped noticing me and started saying and doing things they shouldn't."

"In a way, I can see how that makes sense. Hawks are good at camouflaging. I've seen them appear out of nowhere to snatch unsuspecting prey from the ground. Perhaps you have more of your hawk's abilities in this form than you realised," Vesta said, and Astoria glanced back at her.

"I've never thought of it that way. Perhaps you're right."

Silaine was standing with Asthore, clinging to her wife fearfully, while the other children huddled nearby. As soon as she saw her sisters, she ran over and grabbed Astoria's arm, yanking her close.

"Find my children," she growled, baring her teeth.

"I would've thought you'd be searching for them yourself. You know their scents better than anyone."

The wolf shot a look at the danann and the ring of guards surrounding them. "They won't let me just in case this is the goblin queen's doing. Some people are worried I might be a target of opportunity."

Cocking her head, Astoria wished she could take to the sky. Her ability to track was better in her bird form, and she could cover a greater distance. Feeling the soothing chill of Charnel's power still in her, she wondered if it mattered if she shifted. Dawn had left to speak to her mother, and when the god of life healed her cancer, there would be nothing to be concerned about. Clicking her tongue, she knew it was easier to act without permission when they were not present. Meeting Vesta's gaze, she nodded, and the general returned the action. With the safety of her queen's eldest and youngest children at stake, Astoria knew she could count on the goblin to let her shift once they were away from the others.

"Right then, General. Let's hunt. You smell the way. I'll keep my eyes open. Between us, we won't miss a thing." Gesturing for Vesta to go, she offered her sisters a faint smile.

No one moved to stop them, and when she glanced back, her heart clenched at the sight of her sisters clinging to each other for comfort. They were united by their desire to have their children returned safely. Sniffing carefully as they moved, Vesta muttered under her breath about the challenge of tracking four children in a place that saw so many visitors on top of the countless flowering plants filling the air with their perfume. Keeping her plan to herself until they were far enough away from her sisters, Astoria began unlacing the silk cords holding her bodice together.

"What are you doing?" the goblin grumbled, shooting an annoyed look at her.

"I'm doing what I do best. Hunting from the sky."

"You can't risk it."

Chuckling, she shed the dress, leaving it to pool on the ground. "Actually, I can. Those children are more important than me. Besides, Charnel and Dawn have taken the decision out of my hands. Despite my desire not to be healed, they refuse to let me die."

"About fucking time."

Thankful for the pain medicine banishing the ache of her body, Astoria reached for her magic. It leapt eagerly into her grasp; the shift sliding over her skin as easily as it always had done. She relished the feeling of her body twisting and contorting, feathers replacing her hair. The sharpening of her vision was as welcomed as the flapping of her wings. Vesta watched in admiration, a hand touching her scar while her lips curled into a smile. Launching into the sky, she settled into a height above the castle grounds that allowed her to see farther while not compromising her ability to spot minute details below. Giving a wave, the general continued to follow the familiar scent of the princesses she had known since birth.

It felt too good to be in the air again. She wanted to bask in the glory of flying, but there were things she needed to focus on. Dawn had blessed Diwan with perfect weather, and the air currents were gentle. There were no battling headwinds to drain her energy when Astoria could feel the demands of the cancer clawing at her. Circling higher, she trusted Vesta to alert her if she spotted anything, but she needed to look from above. Sweeping her keen eyes over the land, she spotted something on the outskirts of the palace grounds, heading toward the woods. Those woods filled her with regret as she remembered abandoning Silaine to fend for herself as Talaroonan soldiers closed in.

Swooping down, she drew Vesta's attention and set their direction. Moving quickly, she felt confident the goblin could keep up by shadow stepping as needed. Her eyes continued to search the ground for signs, narrowing in on a piece of fabric dangling from a branch near a small creek. Recognising it as the scarf Nadia had tied over her head to keep her hair under control, Astoria dove to wait for Vesta to reach it. The general plucked it from the branch for a sniff before nodding at the hovering hawk. Screeching in anger, she did not wait for the other woman to speak before winging her way higher. Wherever the children were, she would find them. There was nothing a team of goblins could do to hide them from her sight. She just hoped the two older girls would take no actions to put themselves and their siblings in further danger. Queen Calista would want them alive and unharmed.

But while she circled above the woods, searching through every opening she could find, Astoria felt the creep of the fever. It was moving faster than it had when she arrived in Diwan, and with it came the memory of Charnel claiming he believed it would be worse than before he used his power to lower it. Determined to find the children before it brought her down, Astoria threw caution to the wind. Keeping her wings steady, she wove in and out of the canopy, not caring when she got too close to a branch. Dawn was bringing her mother, and Life could fix anything she did to herself on her mission to find her nieces and nephew. She no longer knew where Vesta was, but she did not care. With the rage burning through her, Astoria was confident those responsible for taking the children would fall to her talons.

A scream tore from her when she felt something strike her wing. Pain coursed through her, and Astoria did her best to control her descent through the trees. Tearing at the arrow with her beak, there was little she could do to stop herself from hitting the ground, but she managed to force the shift into her natural form first. The last thing she needed was to be trapped as a hawk, and unable to communicate when Vesta caught up. She thought she heard Talaith shouting her name, while Rose sobbed, but she couldn't pick herself up from where she lay on the ground. Taking stock of her injuries, Astoria knew she had broken bones when she crashed, and the fever was crowding in on her with full force.

"Fuck! Astoria!" Vesta slid onto her knees beside the prone duine woman, shadows swarming them. "There's an arrow in your shoulder. What happened?"

"Someone shot me. I think the children are close."

Shivering, Astoria coughed and tasted blood. The general gasped, leaning over her to take in the trickle coming from the corner of her mouth. Pressing her ear to the duine's back, she attempted to listen to the rattle of her chest. Neither of them needed to say anything. They both knew one of the things she had broken when she struck the ground had been a rib or two, and they had punctured her lungs.

"Why were you in range?" There was anguish in Vesta's voice. "You stupid, stupid woman. Why?"

"Because the fever was returning, and I was angry," she rasped.

Stroking her head gently, the other woman contemplated what to do. She needed to keep going after the children, but she knew Astoria was dying. They both knew it. It was not the ending any of them had planned on for her, and it hurt that it was unlikely she could get the hawk back to her sisters to say goodbye. Leaving her to suffer slowly on the ground was not an appealing option. Leaning down, Vesta kissed the side of Astoria's head, and bit back a sob as her hand went for a knife on her belt.

"I will get them back, safe and sound, Battle Hawk."

Astoria understood. She could feel her lungs struggling as they filled with fluid, and the fever was consuming her in an inferno. If the general did not grant her the mercy of a quick death, then it would be a painful one. There was no reason to think that Dawn would arrive with her mother in time to save her, even though she knew Eirian could find anyone anywhere, if they were alive. Every moment Vesta delayed, the further away the children were taken. They could not risk losing them.

"Tell them I'm sorry," she whispered, trying not to cough up more blood. "And I love them."

The implications of what Astoria was saying hit Vesta like a boulder rolling down a mountain. "I will. Fly high in eternal peace, Battle Hawk. It has been my honour."

Her hand shook as she pressed the tip of the knife to the back of Astoria's neck. It would be quicker than a punctured lung and any other internal injuries, but she did not want to do it. Part of her hoped the gods would suddenly appear. Taking a deep breath when she coughed, splattering more blood onto the ground, Vesta forced herself to do it. As soon as she was sure Astoria was dead, she left the knife beside her, pressed a kiss to her burning cheek, and rose unsteadily. There was no time to grieve when there were helpless children to save. She just hoped the gods would not wreak havoc on Diwan and the Unseelie for what she had done.

TWENTY

Fire was everywhere, licks of flame reaching for her as though they wanted to offer comfort. Dying hurt, but Astoria had not expected to find herself in a place filled with fire. She had heard enough stories, and chatted with plenty of dullaghan, to know beyond the Veil was a frozen reflection of the living world. Not once had she been told anything about a wasteland of glittering darkness filled with fire. There was no point being angry about it when the lies they spread about beyond the Veil provided people with a sense of comfort. By the time anyone learnt the truth, they were dead, and there was no returning from death, no magical gift to yank them back to life.

Extending a hand to a bold tendril of blue, Astoria chuckled when it curled around her fingers. At least it could not hurt more than it did. She had thought dying would put an end to the pain, but it had not. Everything seemed wrong. Her body felt like it no longer belonged to her. Kneeling among the flames, the duine shook the tendril from her hand, watching it melt back into the rest. Staring at where it had been, she felt the pain increase as her eyes traced the faint black line left behind on her skin. It twisted around her fingers; swirls of familiar marks Astoria knew with every part of her could not possibly be what she thought they were.

"Except they are."

Lifting her gaze, she stared at herself. The other her mirrored the confused cock of her head. Bold swirls decorated her, melting into the tattoos Astoria had done when she was alive. Wings of flame trailed behind her, not quite the same as Dawn's, but the sort she envied. As though the other knew what she was thinking, she spread them, grinning at the wonder on the face of the kneeling woman.

"It's time for you to wake up, Astoria."

Shaking her head, she knew it was not possible. "I'm dead."

"Are you? I've been waiting for this for a long time. Really, for someone as reckless as us, it has taken too fucking long to get killed. Our poor Water, forced to wait with us." Sadness crossed her face before the other version of her straightened, her wings lifting. "But they never said Air would join us. I suppose after the separation of our threads, Air couldn't wait to follow. As for Earth..."

"I don't understand."

"You agreed to this. Well, maybe agreed is stretching it. They chose you, and Chaos bound us together. But they made you forget. You had to forget. Once you wake, you'll remember everything, but before you do anything else, we must save the children."

Astoria rubbed her face, confusion leaving her caught in a loop of thoughts. She remembered the sound of Talaith's screams when she plunged through the canopy of trees. Embarrassed rage burned through her. To be taken down by an arrow because she was being reckless was something she doubted she would live down. Barking out a bitter laugh, the duine reminded herself that she was dead. There was no need to worry about what people would say about how she died, and really, it did not matter since she had been trying to rescue her nieces and nephew. But lifting her gaze to the strange version of her standing among the flames with her hand extended in invitation, Astoria wondered if she was really dead.

"Yes, you died. Our goblin killed you rather than leave you to suffer. It had to be done. At least the scar won't be too bad, and it's easily hidden. We're wasting time, Astoria. Do you want the children and our goblin to be hurt because you can't accept what you are?"

The thought of precious little Rose or quiet Bardhyl being hurt while Vesta tried to help them filled Astoria with a desperate fury. "Fine. What do I need to do to save them?"

"It's simple. Take my hand and burn."

She slapped her hand into the waiting one offered by her mirror self. The surrounding inferno collapsed in on them, agony leaving her mind blank as the memories unravelled. All the careful manipulations throughout her life to ensure she never delved too deep into the rage burning within her. Just like her sisters, she resulted from deals her parents made, and Astoria did not know if she wanted to hate them for it. Not when each of them had found happiness. Hers was waiting for her to wake up and claim it.

Thoughts of what she would do when she got her hands on Dawn pushed aside the resentment she felt for Charnel. He had known what she really was because he had been there when Xhaiden bound them together. It had been his power that had soothed her when Chaos had first changed her. His touch that had kept the fires contained until it was time to set her loose on the enemy. And it had been Charnel who had calmed her when it was over, and the wall erected around the sanctuary where they had hidden the dragons with her blood binding it in place. In his arms, she had wept with exhaustion before Xhaiden had forced the power down, wrapping it in chains to keep it from being revealed.

Opening her eyes, she was greeted by dirt, leaves, and her blood. It filled her nose and mouth, but before she could do anything about it, there was an arrow in her shoulder that needed to be removed. Astoria twisted her arm, wrapping her fingers around the shaft awkwardly before she ripped it out. There was the barest hint of pain, like a memory, before her body healed. Tossing it aside so she could focus on sitting up and spitting out the remnants of her mortal death, she decided she really needed a bath. Her gaze fell on the knife lying on the ground where Vesta had left it after granting her the mercy of a quick death. As she stood, she picked it up, welcoming the comforting feel of a weapon when she had killing people on her mind.

Flames dripped from her fingertips, twisting around the polished silver of the knife. The desire to set the whole place on fire lingered at the back of her mind, but there were innocents in the woods who did not deserve to suffer because the goblin queen had sent people to kidnap her grandchildren. Standing over the arrow that had brought her down, Fire wondered if she could locate the archer. With her free hand, she plucked it from the ground, and let her power examine it. Rage belonged to her, so did the desire to consume, and both had filled the goblin who had shot it. Stretching her thoughts across the thin connection, Astoria let it sweep her away.

She appeared beside the goblin who had shot her, and it took him a moment to realise there was someone there. Shouting in surprise when her hand grabbed his shirt, he swung his claws at her face. Huffing when they sliced through the flesh of her cheek, Astoria swept her gaze over the area. A dozen of Queen Calista's people held the children with knives to their throats while Vesta had one dead goblin at her feet, and her claws embedded in the neck and shoulder of another, shadows billowing around her. The shout of the one in her grasp drew everyone's attention, and she watched the shock appear on the general's face.

"Astoria?"

"No hard feelings, General," she replied, returning her attention to the struggling man dangling from her grasp. "You shot me, you fucker. It hurt, but not as much as this will. Rose, Bardhyl, my sweetlings, close your eyes. I don't want you to watch this."

Counting five heartbeats to give the two children time to do as they were told, Astoria relished the feeling of the fire twisting across her skin. It was eager to consume the man who had hurt her. She kept her gaze on the group surrounding her nieces and nephew as the flames slithered down her arm. Talaith screamed when the goblin went up in flames, his agonised wails ringing through the woods. The delighted smile Astoria gave them when she let the smouldering corpse drop to the ground was enough to make several flee. In the time it took her to blink, the fire caught them in their tracks, gorging on flesh and bone.

"Now, release the children, and maybe I'll let some of you live."

Wings flared, and Nadia tossed her head back into the face of the soldier holding her. "Kill them all. Don't show them mercy, Aunty Astoria. Make them burn."

Her courage inspired Talaith to react, the slender princess grappling with her captor while the young danann leapt at the ones holding the younger two. Snarling, Vesta tore out the throat of the one she held before flinging herself at another, shadows leeching from the ground at her call. Careful to keep the fire away from the children, Astoria flung her power at all the goblins she could and shifted the knife in her hand. If she could not burn them, she could fight them, and the warrior side of her crowed in pleasure when the blade struck the goblin moving to help the one Talaith was fighting.

Flames leapt from the knife to the soldier, and she spun, pushing them away from the children. As much control as she had over her power, Astoria was unwilling to risk burning anyone who did not deserve it. Catching on, her niece shoved her opponent at her aunt, using her weight to carry them both into the god's arms. Slitting his throat rather than risking her flames hurting Talaith, she grinned. A quick look to check on the general provided Astoria with the sight of shadows tearing a man apart while Vesta fought the last soldier. The enemy woman hurled insults at her former commander, tempting the new god to set her on fire.

The temperature dropped, and the sound of horses surrounded them. Nadia huddled over the younger two, her pale pink wings shielding them from the sight of people being burnt alive. It did not prevent them from hearing it, and Astoria felt a pang of regret at the knowledge nightmares would plague them. At least Eivor could help them forget. Dullaghan moved among them, but there was no one left to deal with. Vesta stood farther away, blood and shadows covering her as she stared at the woman she had just killed, and the bodies of her victims scattered across the forest floor. Shuddering as she looked at the burnt husks, Talaith's gaze lingered on her sister and cousins before she flung herself into Astoria's grasp, a sob breaking free of her attempt to be strong.

"It's alright, my sweetling," Astoria murmured, holding her tight. "You're safe now."

Laughing nervously, the general took several steps forward, ignoring the dullaghan surrounding them. "I fucking killed you, Battle Hawk. You were dying from your fall, and I killed you."

"About that..."

"Talaith! Rose!" Thorne shouted, running to join them.

Breaking free of Nadia, Rose ran to her parent, crying as the dullaghan swept her up. "Mama!"

"Aunty Tory, what are you?" Talaith whispered, refusing to let go. "Are you a god?"

"Apparently. You should go to your mother and let her fuss over you. Then we'll get you back to the castle so the rest of your parents can stop worrying. I promise, no one will hurt any of you again." Kissing the top of her head, Astoria met Thorne's horrified stare.

Drawn by the smoke from her fires, Tigernach, Redmond, and the danann and pixies who had accompanied them, plunged down from the sky. Rushing to his children, the general did not spare a glance for the scene, but his brother drank everything in before turning to face the silent god standing among the smouldering corpses. His rainbow wings spread, apprehension filling his green eyes as he studied the sheen of fire dancing across her skin. Baring her teeth at him in glee, Astoria remembered the wings of her other self, and let the power flare outwards, feathers of flame surrounding her in a burning mockery of the danann.

"That's so fucking awesome!" Nadia pulled away from her father, laughing in excitement at her aunt. "I wish mine looked like that. You're the best, Aunty Astoria."

"How?" Tigernach asked, unwilling to come any closer.

Dismissing his question, Astoria nodded to Redmond and Thorne. "Take them back to the palace. My sisters need to know their children are safe. I'll clean this up."

"You're a god, Astoria. How?"

"Xhaiden and Alyah."

He recoiled in confusion. "You mean Tessa and Viv?"

"No. I mean Xhaiden and Alyah," she replied.

"But they've been gone for years."

"Indeed, and this has been waiting to happen since the beginning of the first war. So, like I said, Xhaiden and Alyah." She realised Vesta had come over to her and was doing her best to examine the back of her neck and head while shadows curled among her flames. "Yes, you left a scar. Consider it payment for the scars I gave you."

"They did this to you before the battle?" Vesta whispered, stretching out to touch her back, her shadows creeping across Astoria's body to follow the lines on her skin.

"Yes. Now, please, get those children back to the rest of their parents. Thorne, I'm sure you can trust King Tigernach and his people to take the girls, unless your mounts can cover the distance as quickly."

Turning to the Master of the Hunt, Tigernach bowed slightly in respect. "I would never harm them."

Her arms were wrapped around Talaith and Rose while Thorne shifted her focus from the god to the Lord of Rainbows. "I know. If you take them, we can get back faster through the Veil and prepare the others for... this. They need to be warned before the children can tell them about their adventure."

"Then we're agreed."

"We are."

While Thorne and Tigernach sorted out who would carry which child, several dullaghan circled Astoria. They stretched their hands out to brush her skin in amazement. She smiled in amusement, knowing they were curious about the heat radiating from her. Reluctantly leaving the new god, Vesta joined the others to argue over being sent back to the castle in the arms of a danann. Chuckling when Tigernach threatened to throw the general over his shoulder, Astoria enjoyed the sight of her crossing her arms and glaring at him.

"Don't get as handsy while carrying her as Dawn used to with me," she called out.

Tigernach gave her a disgruntled look. "I would never!"

In a hurry to get the children back, the danann leapt into the air, carrying their precious cargo. Watching them go, Thorne and her riders waited until they could not see them any more before turning their attention to the god. Stalking over to her, the Master of the Hunt held her gaze before pulling her into a tight hug. She shuddered as though she was fighting back sobs, and Astoria patted her awkwardly until she let go to step back. Looking around nervously, Fire was unsure how to proceed.

"Thank you," Thorne said, mouth twisting. "I suppose this explains why I couldn't make sense of your approaching death. The cancer was killing you, but you weren't going to die."

"The fever was the fire trying to hurry things along."

"You realise this makes things a little complicated?"

Laughing, Astoria waved at herself. "You don't say. If you want complicated, wait until I get my hands on Charnel. Because he fucking knew the whole time. He was there when they did it. As was my wonderful mother, War, Death, and Oblivion. They all watched while Xhaiden bound me to the flame."

"And when the war was over, they took your memories, and your mother's?"

"Yes. I've been walking around since then, carrying this power inside me, and waiting to die without knowing it. Imagine if someone had killed me during the Fog while the other gods remained imprisoned?"

She nodded in understanding before signalling to the rest of her riders. "We'll give you some time alone to deal with this. Try not to burn the woods down, there's people in it."

"So little faith."

"Well, you are a god."

A dullaghan sneakily stole a last touch before they left her. "And this doesn't make me your personal hearth. I know I'm hot, but after this, no more touching."

There was laughter as the riders summoned their mounts, and vanished into the Veil, leaving Thorne to shrug at the god. Snorting, Astoria flicked a hand at the dead goblins, each one bursting into flames. Eyeing them as she moved away, the Unseelie leader cringed and faded from sight. Alone among the evidence of what had unfolded, she struggled to keep her mind from reaching for the ropes binding her to Charnel and Dawn. While there had been people to kill, and children to rescue, Astoria had avoided thinking of them or feeling the aching need to be with her mates. Her captain was far away; no doubt being held back by the other gods under the instruction of the Lord of Time. It was Charnel's proximity that hurt the most. He had known what would happen. It was the only explanation.

Staring at the ash left behind by her rage, Astoria felt his arrival. "Don't fucking touch me."

"My beloved Fire Hawk."

"No, you don't get to call me that right now, Charnel. You knew the whole time, and maybe I could have accepted that, but you orchestrated what happened earlier. I should have realised something was strange when it happened, but I was just so happy to be with both of you. And you knew Dawn wouldn't be able to resist going to her mother at your command."

"Emlyn told me."

Laughing bitterly, she recalled the smouldering flames from the remnants of the dead. "Of course he did. I suggest you go to Tallahmal and explain everything to Dawn. You owe it to her. Perhaps start at the beginning when my mother gave me to Xhaiden."

Charnel's presence was agony. She wanted nothing more than to throw herself into his arms, to feel the soothing touch of his power against hers. But her anger was stronger than the pull of their bond, and Astoria refused to let him touch her until she was ready to forgive him. When Dawn found out, she suspected he would pay for deceiving them. What bothered her was how her lover would react when it was revealed the former gods of chaos, choice, and death had been part of it. As had her father's predecessor. There was no knowing how many of the others were aware until they revealed it. Astoria hoped for Dawn's sake, they had kept her mother out of it because she knew the other option would be unforgivable.

"I love you, Astoria," Charnel said, and she felt the ghost of his touch across her skin. "I always have. You're right, I need to speak to Dawn before something bad happens. When you're ready, I'll be waiting for you like I have since the day Xhaiden and Alyah told me what you would become."

"Just go, Lord Water. My family is waiting for me, and I have a lot to tell them."

TWENTY-ONE

The moment she appeared, Thorne held out her coat, the heavy black fabric strangely icy against the heat of her body. Avoiding the stares of her family and their closest, Astoria shoved her arms through the sleeves, slipping it beneath her wings before fumbling with the clasps. She felt the power of the Veil woven into the garment, reminding her the magic of the dullaghan spun it from the wall between life and death whenever they passed through. It was why they all wore much the same thing, and it always looked like the perfect fit. With it secured, the god of fire realised she had been worried at the back of her mind that anything she wore would catch alight.

"Thank you," she murmured, meeting Thorne's gaze for a moment before shifting her focus to Eivor and Silaine. "I'm not sure this is a conversation to be held out here. Or with the children present."

Lips twitching, Rhydwen cradled Rose tighter. "You're on fire today, Astoria."

Stares shifted to him, and Astoria bit back a laugh. It threatened to spill over, destroying any semblance of sanity she still possessed. She needed to either laugh or cry. The question was which option would win. The brush of Eivor's magic skirted the edge of her mind, unable to slip through the cracks like it used to. Stiffening, her sister held her gaze, lips pressed together as she did her best to read Astoria's expression. They were sisters, and the Unseelie Queen had watched her grow up. Her shoulders dropped, and she nodded in understanding.

"Go clean up, Tory. We'll meet in an hour on the balcony and have tea while we talk."

"Would it be too much to ask for snacks with the tea?"

"I didn't think you needed to eat anymore."

Her eyes darted to where Vesta lurked among the soldiers. "Well, I died today. Forgive me if I want something sweet when I recently believed I'd never eat again."

"Don't worry, there will be food," Eivor replied, a faint smile softening her features. "We could all use a treat after everything that has happened today. It might be a long evening."

Astoria studied the facade of the castle, her gaze sliding over the vines trained across the lower walls and the ornate balconies, light reflecting off thousands of windows, and the swirl of carvings artisan crafters had dedicated years to producing. It had been her home, and the memories unlocked by her rebirth betrayed the sanctuary she had believed it to be. Annawyn and Gebael had stalked the halls, turning Eivor into a weapon, while her mother had held secret meetings with Alyah, Xhaiden, and Oblivion to devise a plan to safeguard the future of the Ravens and the dragons. She had watched it all with Neriwyn's hand on her shoulder, unable to stop them from burying the knowledge in her mind. Layer upon layer of manipulation, and the protection of their plans was bound to her blood and the power Chaos had chained her to.

"I'll see you there."

She did not wait to hear any more of the conversation. It was easy to turn her focus to the chambers they had given her, where she knew a bath waited. The glimpse of herself in a mirror as she trudged to the tub, shedding the coat as she went, had her halting abruptly to stare. Wings of shimmering flame trailed behind her, almost dragging on the ground. They lacked the solid nature of Dawn's, but she wondered if she could make them that way. For now, she just needed them gone, absorbed back into her power. Dirt covered the front of her body, blood mixed in from where the arrow struck, and where Vesta had severed her spine at the base of her skull. There was no point trying to examine the black lines decorating her skin until she was clean.

Not wanting to wait for the tub to fill when she was so filthy it would be a waste of time and water, Astoria turned on the cold tap and climbed in. Sitting as close to it as she could, she let it run across her skin, washing away the traces of what had happened in the woods. Tears burned as they trickled down her cheeks, leaving tracks in the dirt on her face. Grabbing the washcloth sitting on the corner beside a bar of peppermint scented soap, she started scrubbing. It did not hurt, and she desperately wanted it to hurt. She wanted to tear the flesh from her bones until there were no traces of her blood, or the marks left.

Hands soothed over her head, encouraging her to slide forward so she could lean back to wash her hair. Trusting her older sister to hold her steady, Astoria closed her eyes and let the water flow over her head and face, taking the blood and dirt away with it. Her tears continued to fall, lost with the rest as she ignored the feeling of someone using the cloth and the soap to clean the rest of her body. They were gentle, and Silaine's voice filled her ears with the soft words of a lullaby their mother had sung for them. She wondered if her sisters used it to soothe their children when they needed it.

"I had a feeling you would be a mess once you got back here," Eivor murmured, encouraging her to sit up. "Your mind might be impenetrable, but your face is the same."

In an attempt to amuse her, Silaine said, "At least you don't have to worry about cold baths."

"Laine..."

"What, Eivor? It's true! I bet you wouldn't be complaining about never having frozen hands and feet. No more purple fingers, toes, nose or ears, and the pain it gives you."

Reminded of the affliction her sister endured, Astoria frowned and wondered if it was why Eivor had pressed her hands so firmly to her. "She makes a good point. There are frozen places in this world where I can finally go swimming. I wish I could show them to you. There are black and white birds called penguins that dive beneath the ice to hunt for fish. I bet they would love your magpie form."

Eivor huffed, unimpressed by the suggestion she might visit a frozen region. "That doesn't sound fun. Just cold. And I suspect if you tried visiting there now, you'd melt it."

"Am I really that hot?" she whispered.

"She's teasing you, Tory." Squeezing her knee, Silaine set the cloth and soap aside. "How are you feeling? This must be a lot to handle. Tigs said you didn't know this would happen."

"It was Mother."

"I don't understand."

Even if Silaine did not grasp the implication of what Astoria had said, Eivor did. She knew about the deals their parents had made, and her glimpses into her middle sister's mind had allowed her to see some of those interactions. Reminded of that fact, the Unseelie Queen stared at the shimmer of fire dancing across Astoria's skin and wondered if she could unravel the manipulations remaining in her mind. No matter what had passed between them over the years, if there was a god she could trust, it was her sister. Her stubborn nature would make it a challenge for the others to bend her to their will.

"Mother was a Raven through and through. Her loyalty belonged to her flock, and she plotted behind Father's back with Oblivion, and several gods to safeguard the Ravens when they forced Shianeni to do something about Annawyn. I was part of the price. In return for Chaos helping Oblivion, the Ravens, and the dragon riders, she gave me to Xhaiden to use."

Her sisters stared at her in horror while she took a moment to calm her raging thoughts.

"First, he changed my magic, making it easier for me to shift. Then he bound this power to me, turned me loose on the old Unseelie army when they fought the last of the riders, and when the battle was over, used my blood to seal the wall around the sanctuary Oblivion had built for the Ravens, and what remained of the dragons and their riders. That's why no one has found the Executioner."

Sighing, Eivor said, "Because a warrior makes for the perfect host for fire. You already live with the balance between an all-consuming rage and peace. Fire wants to burn and consume everything in its path, but it needs to be contained, to be reduced to a nurturing warmth that helps instead of harms."

Turning to rest her back against the side of the tub, Silaine muttered under her breath before thumping a fist against the floor. "I was always jealous of how they treated the two of you, but now I realise you suffered far more than I ever did. Father bargained with Annawyn and Gebael and let them do things to you,

Eivor. Mother sold Tory to other gods and tried to give me to War. Our parents were awful."

She had to laugh, or she would go insane, and the look Eivor gave her told Astoria she was not the only one. "They were, but they were also good to us. Everything they did had consequences for Tir, but I'm not sure we can say they're negative ones. I mean, sure, I'm not happy to be a god, but I agreed to it, and I love Dawn. Now I get to keep her forever."

Growling, Eivor punched her shoulder. "How dare you die to save my children!"

"I'm sorry!" Jerking away from the next blow, Astoria huffed at her older sister. "But I would do it again. I'd rather die saving them instead of wasting away in pain until someone took pity on me."

"Vesta is a mess over what she did."

"Did she tell you?"

"Yes. She said they shot you out of the sky and the damage from falling left you fatally wounded," Silaine replied, not turning to look at her sisters. "You saved our children, and we'll always be grateful. But that's who you are, Tory. What happened when Talaroo invaded was not you."

Closing her eyes, Astoria remembered the god who had visited her before the invasion, and the commands he had threaded through her mind. "It got each of us to where we had to go. You needed to find your danann, and bring about the return of the Ravens. Eivor needed to suffer while waiting for the Unseelie to come so she could become the balance to the fanatics who worship the gods. And I needed to fly through the open door of a ship's cabin so I would find Dawn."

"Did they know where we would end up?" Splashing water at Astoria, Eivor perched on the edge of the tub. "Or did they just take the word of the gods they bargained with, that good things would happen?"

"Mother knew she would die by Oisin's hand. Alyah warned her an old enemy would claim her life if she returned to Diwan instead of sending me alone and joining Oblivion."

Scrambling to her feet, Silaine gestured at her sisters. "We can't change what they've done, and every moment we spend feeling angry about their choices is a moment wasted. They're gone, as are the gods they bargained with, but we're not, and neither are the ones we love."

Turning off the water, Eivor slid from the tub and moved around to join her younger sister. "You're right. Our anger changes nothing and gets us nowhere. It's fine to acknowledge it, but let's not dwell."

Appreciation for her sisters filled Astoria's heart with relief. No matter what had happened and what was yet to come, they would be fine. She would destroy anyone who tried to harm her family. Heat chased across her skin, the flames of her power turning the lingering drops of water into steam that drifted into nothing. Climbing out of the tub, she shook her hair, feeling how dry it was. The sheen of her existence remained in place, refusing to retreat beneath her skin, and Astoria wondered if it was something she would need to learn to live with or if it was being stubborn after spending over a thousand years waiting to be reborn. If that was the case, she did not blame it for wanting freedom.

"I'd offer you a towel, but you don't need it," Eivor muttered, eyeing her with a hint of jealousy.

"Before we join the others, we need to decide what I'm doing about Oblivion." Locking her stare on Silaine, Astoria tried to ignore the prickle across her skin from the chains linking her to Dawn and Charnel. "Because I'm the only one who can break the wall keeping her and the others in their sanctuary. I swore an oath to release them, but..."

Running her tongue over her teeth, the Raven Queen did not look at her sisters. "I refuse to bend the knee to Oblivion. That's something I've made clear from the beginning. The new Ravens are mine, not hers. We were born, not made. Our path is our own, and I will not let her ruin what we have built."

"What about Tigernach?"

Crossing her arms, Eivor huffed. "Leave her. It's not like we need her or the dragons."

It was tempting. For the sake of her sisters, Astoria knew it was what she wanted to do. No one could force her to keep to the promises they had made her swear when they used her blood to seal the locks on the cage protecting the last of the dragons and the original Ravens. But casting her mind over the memories, she could not help the trickle of fear down her spine. Other than

Charnel, each of the gods who had been present back then possessed a new form. Most of whom she liked. Chaos and Choice were wonderful women she got on well with, though she now questioned their friendship. They had known what she was, and what lurked beneath her skin, waiting to be released.

"I want to, but I'm not sure if I'm strong enough to deny the combined determination of the other gods if they decide they want Oblivion released. If Tigernach finds out I hold the key to his wife's location, there's nowhere I can hide from him. Our best hope is that Time has seen a reason for the wall to remain in place. Should Emlyn declare I'm not to release them, no one will question it."

"Likewise, if he decides the other way?"

"The gods don't argue, even when they don't like what he asks them to do. I don't trust him. He pulls the strings of our existence, walking us down a path he claims is the best, but how do we know? The best for who? Besides, I've been told the story of what Life and Death did to Annawyn to force her to pass over, and I think I should be frightened of them."

Her admission surprised the other two women, and Silaine shifted nervously, gaze darting to the door. In saying it out loud, a sense of relief struck Astoria. She was a god, just like them. No less powerful or important to the balance of the world, but admitting she feared them was more than simply acknowledging a perceived power difference. It was a recognition that no matter what, she would be an outsider to their circle. What she had been through left her unwilling to claw out a place among them. Covering her mouth, Astoria laughed nervously, drawing the attention of her sisters back to her. Shaking her head, she could not stop the laughter spilling from her lips.

"I think she's broken," Silaine muttered.

Eivor rolled her eyes, huffing in annoyance. "Of course she is. She's a Havard."

"I think I'm the god of the Unseelie," Astoria said between bubbles of laughter.

"No, thank you."

"You don't understand. I'll never be one of them. I will always be an outsider."

Cocking her head, Silaine appeared troubled by the comment. "Surely they'll welcome you. You're a god, and the mate of Life and War's daughter."

"I don't want them to. Yes, I love and trust Dawn and Charnel, but the rest? I didn't mind Chaos and Choice, but now I remember everything, and I'm angry with them. They all knew. They all used me."

Agony bit at her heart, and Astoria doubled over in surprise. Rushing to her side, her sisters helped her through to the bedroom and over to the bed, where she collapsed on the mattress. The bitter mocking of the power fuelling her existence told her what was going on. Her heart shattered when she realised what it meant. She had been sure Dawn would rush to her side the moment she could, and it had never occurred to her that Charnel might decide it was time to repair the tattered threads of power binding Water and Air together. Worse, it had not occurred to her that Dawn would agree to it.

"What's wrong, Tory?" Eivor pulled her head into her lap, smoothing her brown hair out of her face.

"Dawn and Charnel," she whimpered.

Silaine gasped, and the Unseelie queen glared at her. "She can feel them together. Asthore has told me a lot about the gods, and apparently it hurts the excluded one when the others of a bonded group are together. It's the first time, so she's not used to it yet."

"Fuck that." Shaking her head, Eivor pitied her sister. "I'm sorry, Tory."

"I thought she would come to me as soon as she could." Sobbing, Astoria clung to her sisters and wondered why Dawn had done it. "I thought I would be the first bond she completed."

"You feel betrayed."

"Yes. How could she want to complete the bond with him after what he did to us? He knew the whole time. Dawn should be just as furious with Charnel as I am."

Curling around her back, Silaine cuddled her older sister tightly. "Fuck them. If they want you, they can crawl. Make them grovel for your forgiveness. Let them find out what happens when they cross a Havard."

"Who are you, and what did you do with my little sister?" Eivor chuckled, running her fingers through the hair of both of her sisters. "I like this version of you, Laine. It suits you."

Sinking into the comfort of her sisters, Astoria found a smile that felt right. Her power gathered the shards of her heart, melting the edges to stick them back together. Whatever Charnel hoped to achieve by seducing Dawn first did not matter. She was Fire, and her flames burned hotter with the right fuel. They were the ones who needed to be sorry, not her. Thousands of years of being the good little soldier had ended the moment she had been reborn, and Astoria refused to cower. If they wanted her, they could grovel on their knees just like Silaine suggested. They could beg at her feet for what she was willing to give them.

"Help me get dressed. You promised tea and something sweet to eat," Astoria said, wiping her tears away as she sat up. "Fuck! I just realised I can never get drunk again."

Arching a brow, Eivor tutted. "Well, that's just unfortunate."

TWENTY-TWO

Resentment simmered in Dawn as she stared out at the lake while her mother gently brushed her hair. She knew she was a coward, and everything she had done since she felt the agony of the bond to Fire snapping into place was a mistake. Astoria would never forgive her, and she would not ask her to. There had been nothing except anger and pain seeping across the frayed ropes connecting them, and it grew worse with every passing day. But it was the absolute despair screaming over the bond each time she surrendered to the need to be with Charnel that broke her. Dawn hated herself for letting her uncle convince her to do it with his claims it was for the best.

"Whatever you want to do, my little love, I will support you," Eirian said, setting the brush aside. "I know Emlyn has his plans, but sometimes we need to tell him to fuck off."

Watching a trio of swan folk drifting over the mirror-like surface of the lake, Dawn sighed. "I should have gone to her straight away. We've abandoned Tory, and she has every right to hate us."

"Believe me, Emlyn won't be coming anywhere near Tallahmal for a while. I'm beyond furious about what they've done. Him, Tessa, Viv, Aiden... your father. They all lied to us for years. They looked Astoria in the eye, and never said a word. Not to her, or you, or even me. As for Charnel? Well."

"I think Tory will probably forgive everyone. But not me or him. Especially not me."

"Because you did what Emlyn told you to do?"

Shoulders slumping, Dawn glanced at the messy bed on the other side of the room. Guilt rapped sharp knuckles against her heart when she remembered the peace she had allowed herself to embrace while wrapped in Charnel's arms.

It was wrong to enjoy it when they were missing Astoria. At least she could appease the pain by remembering the regret in his eyes. They had accepted and completed their bond, but it was not a joyous occasion. Not without her.

"Yes."

Eirian's fingers worked through her hair, separating parts of it to begin a new braid. "I'm frightened of Emlyn. His power over us is... he would have stopped you from going to her if you hadn't done what he wanted. I wish I understood how he's able to trap us, but I don't."

"Uncle Emlyn only wants what's best for us." Jerking in surprise at how quickly she had defended the god of time, Dawn realised she was repeating what she had been told all her life. "He's trained us well, and we're all so desperate to avoid repeating the past."

"And maybe it's the truth. How would we know?"

"Because Pa and the others can see variations of the future as well? If something really horrible was going to happen, Pa would see it. I mean, I know he can see something, and that's why he gives those little warnings to certain people in our lives. But we'd never turn on Tir! That's what I don't understand."

Frowning, the god of life plucked a thin blue silk ribbon from a pocket and worked it into the braid. "You were born like this, my little love, and you don't feel it yet. The danger isn't us turning on this world, it's others like us that are still out there, drifting among the stars. Every time we create a new god here, we split power from one of them, and maybe one day, all of our kind will be bound in physical form. We can't remember if this has happened before. There's a chance we've played this game before, and that's why we know we should fear the Nothingness waiting beyond the stars."

"The Nothingness?"

"You didn't think our kind had always existed?"

Dawn pursed her lips, twisting her hands in her lap as she considered what she had thought. "I mean, I guess I did. We are the fabric of existence, as Tessa likes to say."

Humming in amusement, Eirian gently wrapped the end of the ribbon around the braid, tying it off. "Our kind was born from the cold, and the dark, where nothing existed but the Nothing. And Nothing hungers. It hates being alone, and it desperately wants more. It made us for a reason."

"So it made us, and we made the universe?"

"No, the universe is what happened when we were born. Tessa likes to say the Nothing exploded, casting existence outwards at a rapid pace, and flinging our kind with it. That's why we remember dancing with the stars. Because we danced, and they formed between us. But I always wonder if this is an endless cycle. Maybe this isn't the first time the Nothing has exploded, and maybe one day it will consume everything until there is nothing again, only to repeat the cycle out of its desperate loneliness."

She wanted to shake off the feeling of dread that had settled on her skin, but Dawn doubted it would work the way she hoped. It seemed strange to consider why they existed. Cocking her head, she lifted her gaze to the distant sky, wondering if somewhere among the stars, the last fragment of the entity composed of the threads now living in her, Charnel, and Astoria, wept in loneliness. They had left it behind, one fourth of a being that wanted nothing more than to be reunited with the rest of itself.

"I need to fix things with Tory and Charnel. We need to work together to find our Earth."

"It might not be that simple, Dawn," Eirian said, plucking an orange ribbon from her pocket before she started work on a second braid. "You can't just pick a person from the crowd and decide to make them a god. Though I understand where you're coming from. Did you never think about the rest of you before?"

Shrugging, Dawn realised it had never really crossed her mind. She had been determined Jen would make a wonderful god of earth, but beyond that, she had ignored it. Not once had she bothered with searching for someone to be Fire and knowing the previous god of chaos had bound that power to Astoria before she had been born, Dawn wondered if the reason she had done nothing was because she had already known. Part of her had recognised the hawk belonged to her, even if she had been too blind to see it.

"Not really beyond wanting Jen to be Earth."

"And why did you want Jen?"

"I don't know." She chewed on her bottom lip, thinking back to when she set her sights on Jen. "I guess because Pa was constantly singing her praises. She was his heir, and sometimes it felt like he was more interested in her than me. He made her seem like perfection. Maybe I thought that if she became my mate, everyone would be happy. And you say things about her mother..."

Gently securing the ribbon around the end of the braid, Eirian chuckled sadly. "I suppose we did. Emlyn has admitted he manipulated my memories when I was young and absolutely in love with Tessa. There's no way to regain those, not even when we were reborn. That should terrify me, but maybe it's for the best that we don't remember our feelings for each other."

"Why don't you hate him?"

"Because I'm too tired to hate anymore. Is it wrong that I just want peace? I spent years alone, hating others for the parts they played in my life, and now I'd rather spend my time loving my family."

Turning on her seat to stare at her mother, Dawn frowned. "Why let me do what I do?"

Eirian stroked her cheek, smiling sadly. There was a flicker of fire in her eyes that made Dawn shiver. She knew how powerful her mother was and had heard all her life that it was better if she stayed out of things. While War dabbled in politics, and some lorded over their city of creatives, Life, Death, and Thought remained tucked away in their valleys, doing nothing more than existing.

"Better you fight for justice than I do. My anger could destroy our world, but yours is a little less troublesome. I feel content knowing you're fighting the darker sides of our nature."

Arching her brows in surprise, Dawn realised she had never considered it as a reason for her mother's willingness to let her leave in the beginning. Her mother had never tried to stop her, or talk her out of her plan, even while others did their best to convince her it was a bad idea. All Eirian had done was make her promise to be true to her heart. It was a reminder that Life had always told her to fight for what she believed in, and Dawn passionately believed in protecting those who needed it, especially women and children.

"Do you think Uncle Emlyn was right when he said Charnel and I needed to be united when we went for Tory? If I run to her now, do you think I might make things worse?" She hated how timid she sounded, but her mother was the only person she knew it was safe to let down her guard around.

Wrapping her arms around her daughter, Life sighed. "I think he had good reason to caution you. Astoria is the god of fire, and you are the god of air. Your power will make hers more destructive."

"Maybe that's why we had as many bad days as we had good, and why she would seek Charnel when she needed peace. He soothes her, and I'll never be able to offer her the same."

"I think she'll need you equally. Too much water, and a fire will go out."

Perking up at Eirian's comment, Dawn nodded in excitement. "That's right! Oh, that's why he said she belonged between us. Because I'll feed her flames and keep him from dousing them."

"I'd rather not think about my daughter's sex life, but I suspect you're right." Eirian kissed the top of her head, smiling sadly when Dawn clung to her like she was still a small child. "You are my precious lightning bug, and I will always be here for you. I suppose that's why they never told me. They knew I wouldn't keep it from you, no matter what arguments my brother presented. I refuse to lie to my children."

Dawn was angry on her mother's behalf. She had seen the cold shoulder Eirian was giving Aiden and Celiaen, and the way Galameyvin regarded them with bitterness. Turning her thoughts back, she realised Celiaen had always encouraged her to work harder to please Astoria, and he had constantly given her suggestions to fix things when they fought.

"Oh, Ma, Pa tried to help me see." Pressing her lips together, Dawn felt terrible for her father when she thought about what he had likely seen. "I should talk to him about the best way to grovel for Tory's forgiveness."

She cleared her throat to cover her uncomfortable chuckle. "Or you could go to her. I think you owe it to Astoria. Just be honest with her. She loves you, and she needs you."

"I'm terrified of losing her, Ma. My list of mistakes over the years..."

"We all make mistakes, my love. There is no such thing as a perfect person. Everybody has faults."

Smoothing her hands over the simple cotton dress she had put on after her bath, Dawn wondered if she would be welcomed back into Diwan. There was no reason for Eivor's court to put up with her again. No one had dared question how Astoria's rebirth as a god would change the situation with the Unseelie, but Dawn had seen the way Queen Eivor treated her sister. Despite everything that had happened in the aftermath of Talaroo's invasion, the three sisters had found it in their hearts to forgive each other. A little thing like one of them becoming a god would not change that. If anything, she could picture the Unseelie embracing Astoria as a weapon for their cause.

"How do I do this?" Pulling away from her mother, Dawn suspected she could not swagger into Astoria's presence like an overconfident pirate captain.

"In private. Go to the palace, find a spot out in the open where no one will disturb you, and where there's nothing to set on fire. A rooftop perhaps. And just be honest. Tell her everything that happened between you and Charnel and what Emlyn told you. She's older and wiser than you, Dawn, and she has seen how we treat what the god of time tells us. You're my daughter. You like to keep your truths close, but sometimes we must let in the ones who love us the most."

The stories of her mother's escapades were told frequently among the community surrounding her family. As a child, she had loved to listen to the elves who had been her father's companions when they talked of her parents' exploits. But her favourite had always been the quiet one whispered in her ear by War in which he told her about the time her mother had grovelled at his feet for forgiveness and finally admitted she needed him. Knowing how much she needed Astoria, Dawn wondered if Celiaen had liked to tell her that story because he had seen that one day she would need to do the same.

"Thank you, Ma. I love you," Dawn said, smiling faintly at the older woman. "I know you were never fond of Astoria, but I hope you can accept her."

Snorting, Eirian patted her shoulder. "I didn't dislike her. Something never quite seemed right about your hawk, but I could never work it out. Now I know what it was."

"The power waiting to be reborn?"

"Precisely."

"She told me the dullaghan could sense something strange about her. They could tell she was dying, but at the same time, she was not. Or something like that."

Cocking her head, Life clicked her tongue as she nodded. "That makes sense. She was dying, but a mortal death for an immortal life skews things. I wish you could have been with her. The two of you deserved that, but it hurts to watch someone you love die, even when you know it's temporary. They die, and there's always the doubt it'll really happen."

Dawn understood what her mother was saying, and she did not need to admit seeing Astoria die would have broken her. Rising from her spot on the window bench, she crossed to her wardrobe, pulling open the carved timber door. It seemed strange to see her clothes in such a small space after admiring the chambers dedicated to clothes Astoria and her sisters used, but they did not have brownies running everything. Every day, a different selection of garments appeared in the wardrobe; an offering handpicked by whichever brownie was dealing with her. They were always happy to fetch something specific when asked, but Dawn rarely bothered to. She preferred to accept her choices without complaint while staying in the spring valley.

"What are you thinking?" Eirian watched her trail fingers over the clothes.

Settling on a dress made from spider silk, Dawn smiled. "This. Today, I am not the Storm Queen, or the fearless pirate captain. No, I'm simply Air begging her beloved Fire for forgiveness."

Joining her daughter, Eirian helped her change out of the simple dress. The spider silk slipped through their fingers, soft and translucent, each layer adding another element to the illusion of colour. There were no laces or buttons to deal with, simply the twist of fabric in the right places. Examining her reflection in the mirror, the result pleased Dawn. When she turned around and craned her head to admire the back, she was thankful whoever had made the dress had left it fully exposed, so she did not need to worry about damaging it with her wings. But it was the sight of the partially complete swirl of black lines decorating her skin that held her fascination. She looked forward to discovering what Astoria's marks looked like, and what her own would become once they bonded.

A knowing smile lifted Eirian's mouth, and she trailed a finger over the lightning bolt running down the side of her face. "Tessa told me the marks incorporate any tattoos the god has before rebirth."

"Viv had tattoos?" Eyes wide, Dawn wondered what they were. "I hope Tory doesn't make me wait too long to see hers. Do you think she can still shift into her hawk form? Would that have changed?"

"I think those are questions you'll have to find out for yourself. Considering I can shift forms, you and Tessa can grow wings, and Aiden discovered he can shift like a dullaghan. I think it's safe to say she still can." Cupping her daughter's cheek, Life smiled. "Go to her."

There was nothing she needed to get, and tugging at a section of silk, Dawn nodded. She knew exactly where Astoria was in Diwan, but her mother's suggestion of a rooftop clung to the front of her thoughts. The one she ended up on was small, overlooking the city from high above it. Her toes dug into the cool stone while she turned her gaze to the night sky. Casting shadows over her spot was the larger central tower, its pointed roof dark against the star kissed night. Pale moonlight added to the shift of darkness, making Dawn regret not remembering the time difference between Diwan and Tallahmal.

"Bold of you to come here," Astoria said from behind her.

Closing her eyes, Dawn did not turn straight away. "I know I'm going to make a mess of this, but at least I know I'm doing it on my terms. Well, I think I am. Who knows, it's not like Emlyn tried to stop me."

When she was ready, she turned to stare at the other god, and it felt like her breath had been stolen. Astoria glowed with fire, a sheen of power dancing across her skin. A pair of wings flared out behind her with flames instead of feathers, and Dawn summoned her own before dropping to her knees.

"Oh, Tory, you are beautiful. I'm not worthy of you."

TWENTY-THREE

Astoria crossed her arms, and her eyes raked over the kneeling woman. In the moonlight, Air shone like a pale beacon, the light-coloured fabric of her dress pooling on the floor while her wings framed her. Flicking a hand, she cast balls of fire into the air surrounding them, their glow illuminating the rooftop. It became bright enough to study the desperation etched into Dawn's expression, and the soft shades of pink and blue draped across her to match the feathers of her wings. The god at her feet was not the commanding pirate she had first met, but she was no less alluring.

"Yes, I know," she drawled, refusing to listen to the whisper at the back of her mind pleading to touch Dawn. "I'd ask where you were after I was reborn, but I already know."

"There is nothing I can say or do that will ever excuse my absence. All I can ask for is your mercy."

"I assume your uncle had something to do with it. He pulls all the strings."

Bowing her head, Dawn nodded. It was difficult not to take pity on her when Astoria had seen how tightly entwined Time kept his fellow gods. They danced to his tune, accepting his direction with no arguments. If he had demanded they keep Air from rushing to the newly reborn Fire, they would have done what they were told. Pressing her lips together, she studied the other woman and debated if she wanted to know what else Emlyn had forced his influence on. She knew Dawn as well as she knew the back of her hand, and no matter how angry she was, her heart was certain there was no way she would have chosen Charnel first. Emlyn had to have insisted on them completing their bond.

"Did Charnel tell you everything?" Astoria whispered, arms dropping to dangle at her sides.

Lifting her dark eyes to gaze at the burning god, Dawn sighed. "I assume so. Everyone involved has admitted their part. Ma is furious. She banished Pa and Aiden from Tallahmal until she's less upset with them."

"I'm glad to hear she was unaware. To be honest, I was terrified she had been, and how it would impact you. You have such a close relationship with your mother."

"She's happy it's you."

Startled, Astoria pressed a hand to her chest. "She doesn't like me."

Dawn did not answer straight away, preferring to take the time to admire the way the red silk of Astoria's dress clung to her. Gone were the dark shadows beneath her eyes, and the pallor of sickness, replaced by the sheen of fiery power. But it was the hints of midnight lines swirling across her skin that drew Air's attention. She wanted nothing more than to slide the silk from Fire's shoulders so she could examine her body. It felt like every familiarity she had gained over the years was gone, and she would need to relearn the older woman's form. Something Dawn looked forward to more than anything.

"No, you unsettled her, and she couldn't work out why. She thinks it was because you were a god in waiting. Her power sensed yours, but it didn't click in her mind. Why would it? She didn't know."

"Curious, but when I think back over it, the only gods who were consistently nice to me were the ones who knew the truth."

The agony of being so close to Dawn without touching her was testing Astoria's resolve. She had not realised how bad it would be. Without thinking about it, she took a step closer to the other god, a hand outstretched, but she did not touch. Hope flared in Dawn's eyes, the eager swirl of her magic trying to coax the flames to embrace it. Slamming a wall into place around her power, Astoria lifted her chin and tutted. All her training had come into use once she got over the first day of learning the feel of her power, and now she was mostly confident in her control.

"I might be newly reborn, Captain, but I still have better discipline than you. You won't be swaying me so easily," Astoria said, arching a brow before turning her back on the kneeling woman. "While I understand you had pressure on you to do certain... things, it doesn't excuse the pain you caused me."

Slumping, Dawn curled her wings around her but found no comfort in the brush of her feathers. "No, it doesn't. Nothing does, and I know it. I didn't enjoy my time with Charnel. It felt wrong because I was doing what I was told. Uncle Emlyn insisted we complete the bond, so when we joined with you, we could control your power a little better. I think he was badly explaining how my power would make yours more destructive, but Charnel risks harming you, and we need to work together to find the right balance."

Frowning, Astoria considered the theory. It made sense. Without air, a fire would die, much the same as when it was exposed to too much water. She suspected the god of time had seen futures in which she had wreaked destruction upon Tir with Dawn at her side, and a distinct lack of Charnel's influence in their lives. Astoria let the flames leap from her palm, watching their hungry dance across her skin, and up her arm until she needed to stop them before they reached the sleeve of her dress. Several outfits had been lost to her power in her efforts to learn where the line between safe use and destruction sat.

"I'm not so foolish as to deny the truth in that."

"Part of me wishes it wasn't you, Tory. Not because I don't love you, but because I'm terrified our love could destroy the things we care about. What if we accidentally set *The Storm Bird* on fire?"

The risk she posed to the ship had crossed Astoria's mind, and her wings flared. "I know I cannot return to the crew. As much as I love my place there, I won't risk our family."

There was a hint of confusion in Dawn's voice as she said, "Our family?"

"You've never realised the crew is a family?"

"I mean... I guess..." Dawn huffed, and Astoria chuckled. "They are a family. Cass is definitely the mother, and now I feel like I've been neglecting them."

Snapping her hand shut to banish the flames, the god of fire turned back to her kneeling mate. "You told them I was dying, so I'm sure they understand your absence. Besides, they're used to you not being there."

"While you're not wrong, that doesn't make it any better. And now, if you can't be there, I'm going to be pulled away more and more because I want to be where you are."

"As wonderful as it is to witness you experiencing this revelation, I'm more interested in how you intend to earn my forgiveness." Taking a few short steps forward to tower over Dawn, Astoria gazed down, doing her best to hide the desire burning through her. "Because if you think you can just appear here to offer a few excuses, and everything will be fine, then you're sorely mistaken."

"I don't," she murmured, keeping her eyes downcast.

She wanted to touch Dawn, to feel the softness of her skin against her fingertips. It would hurt, but the whisper of her power promised it would be an exquisite pain she would never want to end. Drawing her bottom lip through her teeth, Astoria reached out and buried a hand in the other woman's hair. Agony tore through her, almost bringing her to her knees. The whimper spilling from Dawn's lips gave her strength, and she tightened her hold on Air's hair to tug her head back. Meeting the dark gaze of her mate, Fire let her power spill from her fingertips, flames dancing across the dark tresses to caress the sun-kissed skin beneath. Keeping it controlled was a challenge, but Astoria was determined not to let it get the better of her.

"You're beautiful like this." Admiring the swirl of orange across Dawn's cheek, she wondered if it mattered if she forgave her before they completed their bond. "The sight of you on your knees, desperate for my attention, might be one of the most delightful things I could imagine."

A flare of mischief had Dawn's lips twitching, and she stretched out a hand to grab Astoria's ankle. "You might be standing, my pretty Battle Hawk, but you're as desperate for my attention as I am for yours."

Fingers of wind twisted around her legs, making her skirt flutter. They wound upwards, a reminder of how well-versed Dawn was in using her power to bring her to her knees in need. It held an intensity that made Astoria's eyes flutter shut. The moment her grasp on Air's hair loosened, the younger god let her wings vanish, and rose slightly, placing her other hand on Fire's hip.

"I will gladly spend the rest of eternity apologising to you, Tory."

Astoria followed her lead, and the wings of flame faded. "Why the rooftop?"

"Because I didn't want to risk harming anyone," Air said, running her hand up the inside of her leg to her knee. "It seemed like a good idea at the time, but I regret the lack of a bed."

"Awfully bold of you to assume I'll let you take me to bed."

Her thumb drew circles over the sensitive spot at the back of Astoria's knee, and she smirked. "No matter how cranky you get with me, I always convince you to let me take you to bed."

Desire made her clench her thighs together, but a thread of resentment kept her from crumbling beneath the combination of physical and magical touch that usually worked in Dawn's favour. Tilting her head back, Astoria gazed at the sky, twisting the silky strands of Air's hair around her fingers. She found a new braid, the tip of the silk ribbon catching her nail. There was power in it that did not belong to either of them, and her eyes narrowed in annoyance. Snarling, she made the balls of fire flare, casting more light onto the rooftop as she stepped closer to examine Dawn's head.

"Who put this in your hair?"

Letting go of Astoria, Dawn ran a hand over her head to find the braid she was holding up. "My mother made a couple of new ones today. Why?"

"Because this is not an ordinary ribbon." Unravelling the braid, she pinched the offending silk between her fingertips. "I don't care why you wanted these in her hair, Lord Time, but they're not staying."

Eyes wide, Dawn watched it turn to ash. Running her hands through her hair, she searched for the other braid her mother had done. When she located it, she focused on the ribbon so she could discover what Astoria had noticed. Feeling the thread of her uncle's power, her shoulders dropped, and she undid the knot at the end to pull the braid apart. Thrusting her fist containing the silk out, Air could not resist the shiver that ran down her spine when Astoria's power encased her hand, consuming the ribbon.

"Why would she do it?" Dawn muttered, searching her mate's face.

Standing over her, Astoria ran her hands through her hair and gave silent thanks when she found no more ribbons carrying Emlyn's power. She did not blame Dawn for their presence. The god of time was the most manipulative of them all, and it was her duty to protect the woman at her feet. Especially since Charnel had proven he was happy to accept whatever commands were given to him by the other god.

"Your uncle told her to." Tilting Dawn's head back, Astoria brushed her thumb over her lips.

"I hate how he seems to know everything."

"Let's not talk about him, my beautiful captain. Every moment wasted on Emlyn is a moment we could have been kissing. What happened isn't your fault, and I don't intend to let him manipulate you again if I can manage it. So, stand up, kiss me like you missed me, and take me somewhere far, far away from anyone or anything we might accidentally destroy."

Dawn shot to her feet and grabbed Astoria's hips, pulling her in. "Are you sure?"

"Are you questioning me?"

"No, my love."

The initial brush of her lips was teasing, prompting Astoria to growl in warning. Wrapping an arm around her waist, Dawn chuckled and brought her other hand up to bury it in her hair before kissing her. She marvelled at how hot Astoria was, the flicker of flames leaping from the god of fire to dance across her skin. Warmth filled her, and her power screamed in delight. Thinking of the little stone cabin on the cliffs she liked to visit when she needed to be alone, Dawn kept a firm hold on her mate. Their lips never parted, even when she transported them to the location she pictured in her mind.

Wind whipped around them, tugging at dresses and hair, while the roar of the sea crashing into the cliff filled their ears. Astoria pulled away, licking her lips as she looked at where Dawn had brought them. On one side, the cliff dropped away, and her gaze settled on the small cabin perched away from the edge. Sloping back from the ledge, grassy hills stretched as far as they could see, with nary a tree to be spotted. There were white splotches scattered over the green, moving occasionally as they grazed. Her sharp long-distance vision had remained through her rebirth, and Astoria marvelled at the flocks of sheep before turning her attention to the building.

"Who lives there?"

"I do sometimes," Dawn replied, half-shrugging. "I found it one day, and it was empty. No one has ever tried to reclaim it. It's where I go in the middle of the night when I leave you alone in bed."

Lips thinning, Astoria arched a brow and marched towards the cabin. "Is that so?"

"There's no one else out here. Just the sheep and the birds. That's why I come."

"Because there's no one to worry about."

Nodding, Dawn kept close behind the other god, wondering what she would think of the small space inside. The heavy timber door was weatherworn but wrapped in wards. As was the rest of the building. Trailing her fingers over it, Astoria breathed in the layers of power before she pushed the door open. Her gaze danced over the few pieces of furniture decorating the room. Sunlight filtered in through salt-stained glass, illuminating a bed, two chairs, and a table. There was no air whistling through the chimney, but she sensed the ward on it to prevent the raging wind from entering. Everything was whitewashed, and the blue blanket thrown over the bed had Astoria turning to Dawn in amusement.

"Is that the colour of my eyes?"

Blushing, the Storm Queen glanced down. "It's my favourite colour."

"Shall I light a fire?" Moving into the cabin, Astoria flicked her hand at the hearth.

"I should have told you years ago that I love you." Rushing across to her, Dawn grabbed her arm and pulled her close. "So fucking much, Tory. You didn't deserve how I treated you, and I will never stop being sorry for what I've done. But if you let me, I will spend eternity worshipping at your feet."

Threading her hand into Dawn's hair, Fire smirked. "I know you will. Now shut up and kiss me."

Happily following the command, she slid her hands over Astoria's shoulders, seeking the neat bow at the back of her dress. Without breaking the kiss, Dawn worked to loosen the laces, eager to slide the red silk free. Careful not to impede her efforts, Fire hooked a finger through a twist of pale material, tugging it away from Air's body. Her dress was easy to unravel, leaving it on the floor long before the red dress joined it. Smoothing her hands over Astoria, the younger god sighed in joy at the sight of the dark lines twisting across the moon kissed skin she adored.

"Beautiful doesn't do you justice," she murmured, dropping her lips to Fire's shoulder to kiss a swirl of midnight ink. "I cannot think of a word that does. Not even resplendent. You are everything, Tory."

Walking backward towards the bed, Astoria drew Dawn with her. "I need you."

Regret twisted her heart. "The first time will be quick. When the bond repairs, it will rob us of control, but everything that comes afterwards is that much better."

"Forewarned is forearmed." Falling back onto the bed, Astoria propped herself up on her elbows. "Though in all honesty, I doubt it'll take much either way."

Crawling onto the bed, Dawn trailed kisses over her legs, memorising every fracture mark she found. Her tongue swirled over them, enjoying the smoky taste of Astoria's skin. Even though their climax would be over quickly because of the bond, she wanted to make whatever she could last. There was enough light to admire the pattern of flames caught up in a whirlwind of lines occupying most of her thigh. Glancing from the marks to Astoria's face, Dawn smiled at the sight of her bottom lip caught between her teeth.

"I'll never stop being thankful it's you."

Swallowing, Fire could not help the flash of guilt sweeping through her. "Why don't you show me your thanks by coming up here and kissing me?"

Grinning, Dawn carefully picked her way up Astoria's body and straddled her before cupping her face. "I was going to stay down there and kiss you, but if you insist."

She did not think she would ever get used to the agony of touching Dawn. The demanding caress of her lips and tongue sent sparks of exquisite pain down her spine. They fed her desire, and Astoria squirmed, desperate to feel something more. Nipping her lip, Air chuckled and adjusted her position so she could grind their cunts together. Pleasure swept through her, and Fire whimpered when she felt her power straining against the walls she had put around it. It wanted to sink into Dawn's with every touch, and she knew it would become impossible to hold it back.

"You're mine, Tory," Dawn murmured against her lips. "Always and forever."

All it took was another slight change of position, and Astoria rubbed against Dawn. Agony, unlike anything she had felt before, washed through her, sweeping away the wall that restrained her power. Pleasure joined it, robbing her of the ability to think about anything except the woman pressed against her body. It was an orgasm unlike anything she had experienced before, and it seemed like it would not end. At the back of her mind, Astoria was aware of Charnel's absence, the tattered threads of their bond pulling on her heart. But there was something else fluttering without an anchor, a shadowy reminder they were missing another.

When the rush of their bond completing faded, Astoria groaned softly. "I see what you mean."

Eyes widening, Dawn rolled off so she could examine the other god's body. "Just when I thought you couldn't get any more beautiful, Tory. Now my mark is all over you, and it'll never fade. You're mine, and I'm yours. Forever."

The brush of her fingers over the new lines decorating her skin had Astoria whimpering. Dawn's touch left a trail of pleasure behind it, promising the next round would be better. Their power curled together, content to bask in the established bond. Shuddering, Fire wriggled away so she could roll onto her side to stare at her mate's body bathed in the sunlight. She had barely glanced at Dawn's markings out of a desire to avoid becoming distracted. They had changed since the last time she had seen her naked. Running a finger over one of the new lines, Astoria wondered what her own would look like when completed.

"I love you so much, Dawn." Her finger lingered on a small flame marking Air's hip. "I might not have known you would exist when I agreed to this, but I'll never stop being thankful for it."

Wriggling closer, Dawn reached out to cup her cheek. "Before we go again, I want you to tell me everything. I've heard all the other versions, but they're not yours, and yours is the one that matters."

"Before I do, can you steal some wine from your parents?"

TWENTY-FOUR

Brushing a stray braid from Dawn's face, Astoria waited to be sure she remained asleep. Her snores were comforting, but as much as she wanted to remain curled up in bed with her, there was an itch she needed to scratch. Padding softly across to the door, Fire slipped through the gap she opened, taking care to shut it as quietly as possible. Evening bathed the cliff in an eerie light, giving the green of the hills a strange glow. A flock of sheep had moved closer, and Astoria suspected they had not belonged to anyone for a very long time. Wrapping her arms around herself as she walked over to the edge, she stared down at the distant water, enjoying the sound of it beating its foamy fist against the stone.

"212 years ago, a stubborn young human thought he could make his father proud by expanding their farm. He built the cabin before buying his first flock of sheep and bringing them out here. Of course, his father told him he was a fool. They were not sheep farmers, they were cattle farmers, and he was certain his son would fail."

Rolling her shoulders, Astoria sneered and refused to glance at where Emlyn stood a short distance away. "Must you be here? Surely you know you're unwelcome."

"The young man lasted a decade before he threw himself off the cliff."

"Wonderful. Why don't you show me how he did it?"

Chuckling, the brown-haired man waved at the air in front of them. "I understand your hostility, Astoria. You've always been an intelligent one, and I appreciated the challenge you gave me when Talaroo invaded Diwan. The number of times you almost went the wrong way and missed meeting Dawn. I was a fool to think my initial instructions would work on someone altered by Chaos and War."

She inhaled sharply, head swivelling around in a manner that reminded Emlyn of a hawk. "Excuse me?"

"You heard me. I know your hearing is as keen as your sight, even after rebirth."

"Are you telling me that if you hadn't intervened, I wouldn't have found my way to Dawn?"

He shrugged, shifting so he could stare at the cabin. "Indeed. You would have spent years running and fighting until you died. Charnel would have tracked you down, but the feelings you have for them would be different. The way things happened? It meant you fell in love with your mates first."

"While I'm thankful to have fallen in love with them, what I really want to know is why." Letting her arms fall, Astoria was aware of her power flickering at her hands, the dance of flames caressing her fingers. "What have you seen that drives you to manipulate all of us the way you do?"

Fear crossed his face, and Emlyn ran a hand through his hair with a shake of his head. "It's best not to talk of it, lest we draw it here by giving it attention. All we can do is delay the inevitable."

It felt like something cold had slithered down her spine, and the fire at her fingertips died. "That from which the source of our existence came? You're telling me it will come for us?"

"Eventually, yes. It's a matter of balance. Too few of us, and we'll destroy Tir long before it comes for us. Think of me what you will, but I assure you, everything I do is to prevent destruction from reaching this place sooner rather than later. Would you prefer I didn't?"

"I would prefer you were truthful."

Pointing at the cabin where Dawn slept, Emlyn bared his teeth. "If I had told her of your existence, she would have torn the world apart to get you. You know what she's like; how impulsive she is. Just like her mother. I've seen how you would have reacted if I'd allowed things to unfold that way."

The wind tugged her hair, whipping it across her face as she stared at the setting sun. It cast layers of colour along the horizon, but she could not bring herself to appreciate the beauty. Astoria did not want to admit he was right. Thinking about the damage Dawn would have done to be with her made her stomach clench with fear. Any of them were dangerous alone, and she understood why it was better for them to be together. As a whole, they balanced each other out.

"Has it occurred to you I gave Eirian those ribbons to go in Dawn's hair, knowing you would end up here? Or that I told Charnel to leave her alone yesterday so she would be free to seek you."

"You wanted to give me more reasons to dislike you?" She arched a brow, glancing at him. "Seems counter-intuitive for a god who likes to pull the strings to make everyone else do what he wants."

Emlyn snorted, giving her a knowing look. "I'm the god of time. I see the future, Astoria. How you feel now will change. In fact, you're already less angry with me than you were yesterday because you're intelligent and capable of reason. My methods might agitate you, but they get the job done."

Frustration made her want to scream at him, but it was impossible to string together a logical argument for why he had done the wrong thing. She had been raised to put the needs of the many before her own. Grinding her teeth, Astoria hoped he could see the conflict in her stare. Stretching out a hand, Emlyn swiped a finger through the flames coating her skin, capturing one in an orb of his power. It sat on his fingertip, trapped in a frozen state, while he examined it thoughtfully. Fascinated by the threads holding it, she could not resist letting her caution fade so she could take a closer look.

"All of us are beautiful in our own way. There's an overlap in some of our powers, and it's always interesting to see how each individual god embodies what they are. My mother and my sister are vastly different gods of life because Eirian had the right upbringing. I haven't seen a future in which you're driven to pass over, so I like to think Xhaiden and Alyah made an excellent choice in binding you to this."

"Tell me, Lord Time, did my mother know the path her daughters would walk before they were born?" It was a question she was desperate to know the answer to. "Because it feels like the way she raised us was preparation for the trials we would face."

Closing his fist around the captured flame, Emlyn nodded. "She knew some of it. Alyah couldn't see everything. That's not how the power of the god of paths works. But she saw enough to know Malena would have three daughters who would change the world. It was on her advice that your mother accepted your father's attempts to woo her after she lost her mates, despite her relationship with the danann, Erin."

Sorrow replaced the low simmer of her anger, and Astoria rubbed her face. "My mother married my father because a god told her their children would change the world. I suppose I've heard worse reasons."

"At least your mother didn't marry a man to have a daughter she intended to kill to keep one of her mates imprisoned. I had to instruct Gebael to threaten to kill Eirian as a newborn."

Recoiling in horror, Astoria stared at him. Dawn had never told her the story around her mother's birth, and hearing Emlyn speak so dismissively about it, she understood why. Like everyone born before the Fog, she had grown up aware of how selfish and terrible the former god of life was. It had never occurred to her just how terrible Shianeni might be. That she was willing to raise a child simply to kill her to ensure another god remained imprisoned seemed the antithesis of her existence. Emlyn regarded her in amusement before redirecting his focus to the cabin.

"She's going to wake up soon. I suggest you return to her before she gets curious."

Eyes narrowing, she considered arguing with him before deciding not to. "I have one question for you."

"No, you won't set fire to your sister's palace for any reason, including having sex with your mates." Cocking his head, Emlyn blinked at her, his expression oddly blank.

"And with that, I'm going back to bed."

"But you need to forgive Charnel."

Stopping, she inhaled sharply and pressed her lips together without turning to look at Time. "I will when I'm ready. You can't imagine how much his actions hurt me."

"Can't I?" he replied softly. "Our positions aren't exactly the same, but I had to leave Tessa in a terrible situation for years because it was in Tir's best interests. I know how much it hurt her and everyone else involved. And I know how much Charnel hated doing it, because so did I."

"Well, he can suffer alone until I'm satisfied."

"The longer you wait to forgive him, the harder it will be. You'll hold that anger in your heart until it becomes part of you, and you'll never really let it go. It'll fester like a bad wound, tearing you and the others apart. Where you lead, Dawn will follow, no matter what."

The thought of causing pain to her bonded left an uncomfortable churning in her gut. She cast a glance at him over her shoulder, taking in the way he stood with his hands shoved into the pockets of his coat. There was an air of regret surrounding him, the slump of his shoulders suggesting the conversation had stirred terrible memories. For a moment, Astoria considered offering him comfort, but a shift in the air reminded her of his warning that Dawn would wake soon.

"Thank you, Astoria."

Huffing, she rolled her eyes. "If you'll accept advice from someone older than you, Lord Time, stop doing that. Just because you had visions of me doing something doesn't mean you need to acknowledge it."

"Ah, but I enjoy unsettling people."

"This does not mean I intend to fall in line with the rest of the gods."

His chuckle was the only answer Astoria received. As soon as he vanished, she felt a weight lift from her lungs, allowing her to breathe easier. She did not know if it was simply the influence of his power, or if she had been more anxious over Emlyn's presence than she wanted to admit. Striding to the cabin, Fire's relief faded as quickly as it had arrived. The door was yanked open, but Charnel appeared between her and Dawn. Snarling at the sight of him, Astoria launched herself at the older god.

"Tory, no!" Flinging her hands out, Dawn used a gust of air to stop her from hitting him. "This is not the way! You don't have to forgive him but at least let him speak before you try to set him on fire."

Charnel turned to her, taking a step to close the gap between them. "Her mark is perfect on you, my Tempest. Thank you for being the voice of reason."

Stiffening when he cupped Dawn's face, Astoria fought back the urge to incinerate him. Flames flowed across her skin like silk, leaving a circle of ash at her feet. A wind caught them, and when Charnel pulled the younger god into his embrace, her control slipped. It became a whirl of fire dripping from her fists, circling her legs as though it were waiting to be set loose.

"Let her go," Astoria said, surprising herself at how steady her voice sounded. "You came here to talk to me, Charnel. Leave Dawn out of our fight before you ruin any patience I have for you."

Night was closing in on them, but enough light lingered for her to see the reluctance on Dawn's face. Knowing how content she felt in the arms of the other woman, Astoria understood why Air did not want to leave his embrace. They had denied each other for so long that fear of losing their fragile connection was as strong as their need to draw her into it. The emotions swarming down the chain binding her to Dawn told Fire everything she needed to know. Shoulders slumping in defeat, she shook her head, the flames fading as her control slammed back into place.

"Did Emlyn tell you to come as soon as he left?"

Clinging to Charnel, Dawn growled, "My uncle was here?"

"We talked."

Shifting the woman leaning against him, Water inclined his head at the open door to the cabin. "Shall we go inside? Or go somewhere else entirely? This is Dawn's sanctuary, and I wouldn't want to taint it for her. I know a place we can go where you can vent your anger safely if you need to."

She did not want to go anywhere of his choosing, but Astoria knew she was being irrational. Charnel had always done his best to guide and protect them, and no matter how angry she was with him, he would not put Tir at risk. The tattered threads of their bond stretched towards him in anguish, begging to be allowed to weave together with his. It was a pain Fire felt in every part of her existence.

"I know you have our best interests at heart, Lord Water, so lead away."

"Are you sure?" Dawn said, prying herself from his grasp to extend a hand to her. "I don't mind if we stay. We're already here after all…"

Meeting Charnel's eyes, Astoria knew she was going to regret her choice as she slid her hand into Dawn's. The fading light vanished, replaced with hazy sunlight. With it went the cool wind whipping in off the ocean. Pain coursed through her, more intense than what she experienced when it was only two of them. An angry voice at the back of Fire's mind told her to let go of the other woman, but her fingers refused to cooperate. They wanted to remain locked between Dawn's, using the younger god as a bridge between her and Charnel. She was supposed to be curled around them, and they around her.

Sand crumbled beneath her feet, drawing Astoria's gaze down. "A beach?"

"For now," he replied, jerking his head toward the smoking mountain. "Soon enough, it won't be much of anything. It's why I knew this place was safe for us to talk."

Closing her eyes, Fire let her power seep down through the earth, seeking the heart of the volcano. She felt the destruction bubbling away, steadily building towards its release. It felt different to ordinary flames, as though it only partially belonged to her. There were aspects of their absent fourth melded into the heat that left Astoria feeling like she had drunk too much wine. A sense of coolness slid over her body, soothing the burn of her skin, and urged her to release the magma from her grasp.

"Let it take your anger, my beloved Fire Hawk. You can give the volcano everything burning in your heart." Charnel's lips caressed her ear, and she could not help letting her head fall back against his shoulder.

She did not know when he had stepped in behind her, or when Dawn's hands had settled onto her hips. What she knew was it felt too easy to do what Charnel suggested. The fire at the heart of the volcano was as hot as her own, and Astoria let her power sink into it while she melted into his touch, the shadows of the earth gobbling it up. Emboldened by the way she relaxed instead of struggled free, Dawn ran her hands up, stroking sensitive spots along her ribs and the sides of her breasts. When her thumbs brushed over her nipples, Fire opened her eyes to stare at the smirking god in a daze.

"I like the sight of you like this, Tory," Dawn murmured, leaning in to kiss her.

Astoria's mind was sluggish, and she could not decide if she wanted to force it into focus. "What?"

"You draped across Charnel while he holds you in place for me."

His chuckle was an icy breath over the heat of her cheek. "We're supposed to be talking, Tempest."

"Or hear me out. We forget talking and fix this properly."

"As much as I'd like to, it'll only make things worse. I'd never take advantage of Tory."

A shard of hurt cut through the contentment encasing her heart, reminding Astoria of why they were there. "Except you already have. All those years when you kept the truth a secret while happily fucking me. You might not have initiated it, but you took advantage of my desire to satiate yours."

"Yes, I did. Because you told me to. Or are you conveniently forgetting our negotiations before they locked away your memories and buried the power you had access to before you were reborn?"

Startled, Dawn drew back, lips parted as she regarded them. "Excuse me?"

Keeping his power wrapped around the god of fire pressed against his body, Water scowled. "After Astoria sealed the shield into place surrounding Oblivion and the dragon riders, we talked. We knew if things went according to plan, Shianeni would lock most of us away, leaving her alone and unaware of what she was. Gebael promised to keep an eye on her, but I had my doubts. But we also knew it was likely our release would come while she was still mortal."

"Forgive me for thinking you would tell me the truth first," Astoria grumbled.

"You were there when they told me I couldn't!"

Tapping a finger on each of their noses, Dawn arched a brow. "Are you telling me that when Tory had knowledge of what was going on, she gave you permission to engage in a relationship with her, while she didn't know what was going on?"

"Yes, that's what happened. Except I thought he would tell me, despite what the others demanded. Clearly, I was wrong to assume loyalty to his future mate would be stronger than his desire to do what some other gods told him to do. Or he could have killed me."

The arm around her waist tightened, and Charnel growled into her hair. "I wanted to! Do you remember when I disappeared for a few days after the first time you kissed me?"

Reminded of the hurt she had felt at his absence back then, Astoria frowned, holding Dawn's gaze. Watching the confusion churn in the dark eyes of the other woman, she wondered if hers looked the same. It was short-lived, and Air bared her teeth, anger spreading through her power.

"Emlyn trapped you to teach you a lesson."

A weight formed in her gut as Fire realised she was missing information. "What do you mean?"

"Lord Time can trap a god in a moment of time. He can do it to the whole of Tir, but not for long, as the damage it can do to the world is significant. I was going to tell you everything, and he knew. When I refused to back down, he imprisoned me until I ceded." Pressing his face into her hair, Charnel breathed in the smoky scent of her. "That is why I did what I was told. You thought I was gone for a few days, but for me, it was much, much longer. It felt like an eternity cut off from you both."

She could not imagine what he had experienced. Casting her thoughts over her conversation with Emlyn, Astoria wondered if he had manipulated time while they spoke. If he had, she suspected she would never have known. No one would know when the god of time tugged on the threads of his power, holding Tir in an inescapable net. He was their puppet master, and they were the dolls dancing to his tune.

"Why didn't you tell me?" Dawn whispered, horror in her eyes.

"Because he's your uncle, and because he would have known. I told you he had given me instructions, and I obeyed them. Which is exactly what happened. You didn't need to know he had forced me."

Covering his hand on her stomach with her own, Astoria wondered why she was not as angry as she thought she should be. "I understand, Nel. Your fear of Emlyn is reasonable. We should all fear him."

Trapping her fingers between his, Charnel pulled her tighter against him. "As long as we keep our heads down and walk the path he has set, we can avoid more wars."

"We need to find our Earth."

"Shouldn't we focus on us first?" Stepping in closer, Dawn slid an arm around Astoria to rest her hand on Charnel's hip. "Because we need to find our balance before we make the last of us physical."

Pressed between them, Astoria felt the thrum of their power stroking hers, and the faint ache of desire became a throb of need. "We can do that, but until Earth has been reborn, we're incomplete. Once we're whole, we'll be stronger."

Happily kissing her neck, Water chuckled. "Besides, it might take a while to find the right person."

"That's right."

Dawn smirked and kissed the other side of her neck. "Does this mean you forgive Charnel?"

Aware of what they were doing, Astoria squirmed, but did not try to escape her spot between them, too caught up in the happy purr of her power. "Maybe. I haven't decided."

"Well then, I think it's about time you kissed our beautiful Fire, don't you, my Lord Water?"

His free hand found its way to Astoria's chin, and Charnel gently turned her face towards him so she could see the desire darkening his gaze. "Yes, I think it is time I kissed my fiery wife."

TWENTY-FIVE

His lips on hers felt like coming home. It did not matter that they were standing on a desolate beach beside a rumbling volcano, or that Dawn had turned the sky dark with rain-laden clouds in her excitement. All that mattered was the cool press of Charnel's mouth, and the soothing stroke of his power across hers. She burned for his touch even while it felt like he was drowning her beneath a wave. But for every drop dousing a flame, there was a touch of breeze to feed it. They held her between them, the threads of her existence tugged back and forth by theirs, keeping her from sinking into an inferno or becoming nothing more than a spluttering ember.

Pulling back, Charnel chuckled when she whined in disappointment. "Always so eager, my beloved Fire Hawk."

"It seems like being reborn didn't rob her of the lust of the daoine." Rubbing her nose over Astoria's cheek, Dawn loved the way her smoky scent blended with his salty one. "Fire is insatiable."

She wanted to deny the truth of Dawn's words, but the familiar fog of desire drifted over her thoughts. There was no point arguing when she wanted nothing more than to feel Charnel sinking his cock into her while the other woman sucked on her breasts and stroked her clit. Astoria held his gaze, pursing her lips in what she hoped was a challenge instead of the plea lodged in her throat. Stepping back, he arched a brow before turning to stare at the blue sea surrounding the volcano. The wind made his loose black linen trousers flutter and tugged at the sandy coloured tunic. He looked at home on the beach, and staggering out of Dawn's arms, Astoria dropped to her knees a short distance from him. Sand cracked beneath her, taking on a reflective sheen in the sunlight.

"Nel," she murmured, extending her hand in his direction.

Water crept across the beach towards her, foamy fingers eating away at the glassy layer her power had created. It made her sink into the damp sand, and Astoria enjoyed the moment of cool against her skin before her heat hardened it. Charnel did not turn back, remaining at the edge of the sea while Dawn approached to stand behind her. Running her fingers through Fire's hair, Air kept quiet, aware something was happening that she did not understand. She felt their emotions across the bonds, and knew they were mostly blind to each other until they repaired the tattered threads between them.

"I'm going back to the cabin."

Swivelling around, Astoria frowned and grabbed her wrist. "No, don't leave."

"You and Charnel need to be alone. There are things you need to say to each other that you won't if I'm here. Besides, he and I were alone, and then you and me. It seems only fair."

Astoria released her hold, letting her arm drop to her side. Her fingertips brushed glass, and tendrils of water latched onto them, curling around each until they had formed a web on her hand. Glancing at Charnel, she realised he had tilted his head to watch them from the corner of his eye. If Dawn left, there would be no one to keep her from surrendering completely to his power. Sensing her nervousness, Air kissed the top of her head, murmuring assurances into her hair before stepping back to vanish.

Staring at the water creeping around the edge of the melted sand, Astoria said, "You didn't stop her. Do you really think it's a good idea for us to be alone?"

"Dawn did the right thing."

"We belong together."

He tutted, and the tendrils of water encasing her hand spread further up her arm. "Yes, but we also need time to be in pairs. Do you think the other gods are constantly together?"

"Well... no. I know they're not." Mouth twisting, she huffed and attempted to brush the water from her arm, only to have it spread, creeping over her bare skin. "Charnel, please."

More water swept across the sand, surrounding Fire as he turned to face her. "You're frightened of me."

"Only a little. I'm as frightened of you as the campfire is frightened of the rain."

Charnel smirked, flexing his fingers. Water filled the sunken pit of glass and sand, covering her lower legs while more of it twisted around her thighs. The tendrils gripping her arms crept upwards, spreading thin strands over her shoulders. Where they clung to her skin, Astoria felt the cool, soothing touch of his power, and in between, the fiery sheen of hers remained. She reminded herself he would not intentionally cause her physical harm and reached into the recess of her mind for the calm place that had sheltered her during every battle she had fought. It was simple to sink into it, and to draw the simmering rage of her power in with her. Shoving it down, Astoria built a wall to control it easier.

"But unlike the campfire, your flame is unquenchable. No matter how much of mine I surround you with, you're the eternal fire of existence. The raging heat burning inside every living thing. All I can do is calm your power by taking the edge off and soothing the rage."

She marvelled at his ability to walk across the sand without sinking into it. Water chased at his heels like an eager hound, escaping the sea through the pull of his power. At the back of her mind, Astoria felt the molten heat of the volcano churning impatiently. It left her wondering if lava would flow after her like the water chased Charnel. Amusement tugged her lips as he reached her, his thumb brushing over the upturned corner of her mouth. There was a beautiful symmetry in his choice of location, and for a moment, Astoria imagined the sight they would make walking towards each other, with rivers of water and lava following in their shadows. No matter what the water tried to do, it would never quench the fire at the heart of the world, and she understood it was what he wanted her to realise.

"I have loved you since the first time I saw you. Alyah and Xhaiden told me Malena's middle daughter would become Fire, and I accepted that. But I didn't love you until I saw you. Xhaiden and Neriwyn wanted me there, but they didn't need to tell me who you were. I simply knew. When we met properly before the battle, you were beautiful, bold, brimming with confidence, and you burned even without Fire bound to you. But after it was…"

Casting her mind back to the day they had met before the battle with the mad god's Unseelie army, Astoria remembered how she had seen him through the crowd. There had been Ravens and dullaghan between them, but all she had noticed was the sandy-haired man standing alone at the edge of the gathering. It had been before Xhaiden revealed her fate, and before he bound the threads of Fire to her.

"I am still that woman," she murmured, lifting her face to gaze at him.

"Stars above, Tory. There's so much I wish I could change, but what if Emlyn is right and this was the best path? We can't know what would be different without the meddling of Time and Paths, and I don't know if I want to dwell on it. Not when I can accept this is how it is, and I'm thankful to have you."

Pressing her cheek into the hand cupping her face, Astoria did not argue. As much as she hated all the deception, she would not change who she was bound to. They were perfectly imperfect, but once they found the person to become Earth, they would be magnificent.

"It's fitting we do this here." Circling her, Charnel gathered her hair in his hand and tugged her head back. "The first time I had you was on a beach. I adore the sight of you spread out on the sand."

The cords of water keeping her from moving her arms tightened as more slid from the pool surrounding her. Before landing in Dawn's bed, if anyone had tried to restrain her during sex, Astoria would have cut off a hand. Or their head. But she had found more pleasure than she expected in it, especially when Charnel was in control. With her rebirth, she understood why they had always made her feel safe, why she was comfortable letting them have their way with her.

"Are you going to drag this out even though it won't last long the first time?" Shifting slightly to spread her knees further apart, Astoria craned her head back to pout at him.

He arched a brow, and the watery ropes slithered across her thighs, tightening when her pout turned mischievous. "It will only end quickly once we join. That doesn't mean I can't take my time teasing you."

Releasing her hair, Charnel returned to stand in front of the god trapped on her knees. He kept his hands clasped behind his back, watching her intently while his power wrapped around her. Dropping her gaze to the water, Astoria bit her lip when it tugged her arms back, forcing her to arch slightly. Thin tendrils circled her breasts, squeezing as they formed a web. Every line of water settling against her skin turned to ice, and she moaned when they encased her nipples, hardening despite the heat of her body. She did not need him to say it to know he had never dared make the water as cold before her rebirth. Charnel barely gave her a moment to adjust to the change of temperature before a finger of water stroked along her cunt.

She attempted to squirm away from the cold, whimpering when it moved with her. "Fuck! Please, Nel."

"What's the matter, my beloved Fire Hawk?" Cocking his head, Charnel smirked. "Doesn't it feel good?"

"Yes... no... stars!"

Hardening into ice, the finger pressed into her soaked entrance. It was only his power keeping it from melting when her heat surrounded it. Watching the flicker of flames shimmer across her skin, Charnel wondered how long it would take before she came. He wanted to lay Astoria out on the sand and bury himself in her and become lost in the overwhelming pleasure of their bond snapping into place. At the edge of his awareness, he felt fragments of her emotions. They were scattered, unlike the thrum of anticipation seeping across the bond from Dawn. Keeping his gaze on Astoria's parted lips, he stepped forward, bringing a hand to her cheek to trail his fingers over it. Water flowed over her body, twisting around her neck while a second watery finger wriggled into her arse.

"I'm looking forward to doing so much with you, Tory." Gripping her chin, Charnel held her gaze, watching the flutter of her lashes as she tried to resist the pleasure. "But first, I need you to come for me."

Astoria had always found it impossible to resist his gentle commands, and the desperate ache to please him had grown stronger in rebirth. The tendrils around her neck tightened, sending her over the edge she had been clinging to from the moment Charnel had slid the ice into her. Her moans caught in her throat with the pressure from the water restricting her ability to breathe as pleasure swept through her. With his power surrounding her, it felt like it would never stop, and Astoria let it take her. There was no need to breathe or think. All she had to do was surrender to Charnel.

Stroking her hair, he withdrew the ice from her holes, chuckling when she whimpered. "You're exquisite like this, my beloved."

It took several blinks to bring her vision into focus, and Astoria stared at him. "Please Nel."

The water fell away slowly, giving her time to shift her arms to hold herself upright. Stepping back, Charnel took a moment to enjoy the sight of her slumped forward, head hanging between her arms, and the tumble of her dark hair like a waterfall. It had lost some of the brown, turning deep red in streaks as though there were embers tangled in the silken strands. Sunlight brightened them, making her glow against the pale sand. Taking several more steps back, Charnel wished he had Chaos's power to make his clothes vanish, so he did not need to take the time to undress while his fiery mate waited for him.

"Tory."

"Yes?" Lifting her head, Astoria straightened with a broad grin, and he watched the flicker of flames across her skin before he undressed. "Don't be so impatient, Charnel. I was mulling over the fact that despite our inability to die, our bodies still seem to think they need to breathe and react the same way to a good choking as when we're mortal. A pity about the bruises, though."

Pausing with his tunic halfway over his head, he was thankful she could not see his face. "What?"

Laughing as she settled back to straighten her legs, Astoria used her heels to knock sand into the glassy depression her power had created. Charnel realised he would not get an answer and finished pulling the tunic off so he could stare at her. Her head had fallen back, hair hanging free, and gaze locked on the sun. There was no doubt in his mind that she was basking in its warmth, but a niggling voice reminded him of what Life and Death had done with the help of the nearby star. Astoria had no need of a specific affinity for its gifts. She was fire in all its glory. She was everything he had ever longed for.

Cursing under his breath when his eagerness to get his trousers off sent him tumbling to the ground, Charnel waited for her laughter. Her silence was louder than the rumble of waves stirred by his power. When he got back to his feet, he found her unmoved, but flames dripped from her hair. The sheen coating her skin had taken on a brilliant white glow, reminding him of Eirian during the war with the mad god. Frustrated by the memory of the god of life, he summoned the waves closer, letting them leap to meet the flames of his mate.

Her eyes opened, and Astoria gazed at him expectantly. "Don't tell me you're nervous."

"I'm admiring the view." Charnel turned his power in on himself. "It's quite spectacular."

"Just wait until later when it's improved."

The water kept the sand firm as he walked over to join her. Smirking, Astoria spread her legs, inviting him to drop to his knees between them. When he placed his hands on her thighs, the flames caressed his fingers before sinking into her. Despite the vanishing fire, the glow remained, and Charnel felt the heat. If he had been mortal, touching the god would have been impossible unless she controlled her power. Running his hands across her legs and over her stomach, he drew water along with them, relishing the steam their combined powers created. Touching Astoria was agony; exquisite pain that left Charnel hungering for more. He needed to feel the beat of her heart match his own, and to know there was nothing keeping them from being as close to whole as they could be without returning to the stars.

Sliding his hands over her breasts and along her neck, Charnel cupped her cheeks so he could lean in to kiss her. "You're mine, Astoria. My Fire Hawk. My burning heart of the universe. My wife."

Drawing her knees up so she could dig her heels in and lift her hips to rub against him, Astoria groaned in delight when his cock slid over her clit. "Prove it, my Lord of Tides."

Charnel reached down to position the head of his cock at her entrance. "I'm sorry."

"It's only once." Shifting her weight onto one elbow, Astoria buried her hand in his hair.

He knew the bond snapping into place would sweep them away the moment they joined. Capturing her lips, Charnel gave no other warning before driving his cock into her welcoming warmth. His kiss swallowed Astoria's scream of pleasure when their powers entwined, but he felt her nails dig into his scalp. It was a fleeting pain, lost in the agony of their connection. There were flickers of flame, and the press of water, each sensation drowned beneath the overwhelming inferno of her. She was everywhere, and everything, consuming him until he was nothing more than steam drifting from her skin. All Charnel could do was sink into the drumming of her heart, letting it set the beat of his own.

"Nel," she whispered against his lips. "Come back to me."

Pulling back slightly, he met her gaze, drinking in the sight of flames dancing in their depths. "There you are, Fire Hawk. I thought you had unravelled me for a moment."

"I did."

Groaning when her walls tightened around his cock, Charnel felt himself growing hard again. "If we weren't gods, I'd fear dying in your embrace."

Astoria chuckled, hand sliding free of his hair to rest on his shoulder as she gently rocked against him, enjoying how he twitched inside her. "But what a wonderful death it would be!"

Ropes of water wrapped around her arms, pulling her back against the sand. Charnel remained buried in her, the fingertips of one hand trailing across her gleaming skin, following the new lines that had joined the rest. Her legs tightened around his waist, and Astoria lifted her chin tauntingly, eyes chasing over the markings on his chest. There were flames dancing across his collarbones, trapped in a swirl of wind, leaving her wondering what they would look like once the marks from their fourth joined them. At the back of her mind, she felt Dawn's impatience, and the ripple of hope they would join her in the cabin on the cliff.

Sliding an arm beneath her leg, Charnel lifted it over his shoulder, withdrawing his cock slightly before pushing it back in. "This time we'll get to enjoy it."

Astoria struggled to meet his slow thrusts. "Who said I didn't enjoy the last time? There's no reason to torture me like this."

More water slid across her limbs, keeping her trapped in place. Ice hardened on her nipples while she felt the press of a watery finger into her arsehole. Charnel's mouth twisted in smug delight when she whimpered, a rope threading around Astoria's neck. He watched her eyes flutter shut, flames dancing between the threads of his power. Each slow thrust felt like coming home, even though he knew something was missing. That two others were missing. Without them, they were not truly complete.

Lowering himself to press his nose to hers, he murmured, "I love you."

The tightening of his power around her throat accompanied the shift in his angle. Her orgasm rolled in slowly, pushed along with each lazy thrust of his cock matched by the icy version buried in her arse, and Astoria sunk down into the pleasure. It made her toes curl, sand turning to glass beneath her hands as her power spread through the ground. Feeling Charnel spill into her before going still, she enjoyed the blissful haze, and the sparks shooting along her spine, keeping her on the edge of too much. Astoria knew he could coax her over again if he wanted to, and part of her hoped he would. But they needed to return to Dawn.

"I love you too," she said, straining against the restraints to kiss him.

Nipping her bottom lip, Charnel chuckled. "As much as I want to fuck you again, my beloved Fire Hawk, someone else is getting impatient. Shall we go to our Storm Queen?"

TWENTY-SIX

Slipping free of her place between Charnel and Dawn was a challenge to pull off without waking them. Lingering at the end of the bed, Astoria admired their naked bodies sprawled out on the pale sheets, sunlight filtering in through the window. Time was something she had long since lost track of while trapped in their arms. It bothered her she did not know how long it had lasted, and she could not help but wonder if it had been Charnel's plan. As long as they remained lost in each other, and the agony of their connection, then they kept the outside world at bay.

Her toe snagged the discarded red silk of the dress she had worn when Dawn came to her. Plucking it from the ground, Astoria slung it over her shoulder and eyed the bed regretfully. They would be angry with her for sneaking away, but deep down, she knew the longer they stayed in the isolated cabin, the harder it would be to leave. The power grumbled in reluctance, reaching for them. It did not want to be separated from its mates, and grinding her teeth, Astoria yanked it back. Flames twisted across her skin; their colours muted as though they were sulking. She wanted to be amused by their behaviour, recognising them as an extension of her emotions rather than entities of their own.

Turning her mind to the chambers in Diwan, Astoria cast a glance at her mates before vanishing from the cabin. Darkness greeted her when she arrived at her destination. No flickering lanterns or welcoming fire lit to bring warmth to the room. Servants had left wood in the fireplace, and she waved her hand, igniting the tinder. A second motion had the lanterns bursting into light, oil providing ample fuel for her flames. Casting her gaze around the room, the fact it was perfectly tidy came as no surprise to Astoria as she focused on a stack of papers sitting on the table, pinned down by a glass ball that gleamed in the light. When she took a closer look, Eivor's elegant writing brought a smile to her face.

It was a simple message, a reminder the family expected her to join them for meals when she returned, and that her sisters hoped she had found what she needed. Beneath it was a pile of drawings Astoria recognised as Bardhyl's and Rose's work. Resting her hand on them, she welcomed the flood of affection they stirred. Leaving them there with the weight keeping them safe, she wandered through to the bedroom, her power reaching out to light the lanterns and banish the dark. The empty bed made her hesitate, her unhelpful mind offering the memory of Dawn and Charnel curled up among the sheets back in the cabin. She knew from the lack of reactions across the bond that they remained asleep.

Aware of the state of her body, Astoria decided a bath was called for before she faced her sisters, and the scrutiny of those among the family with an overly sensitive sense of smell. Dragging the dress off her shoulder as she passed the chair in front of the mirror, the god dropped it over the back. The bathroom was dark, and she left it that way as she crossed to the tub. Not bothering to turn on the hot tap, Astoria summoned a ball of fire to provide enough illumination to locate a bar of soap and some oil to add to the water. Finding a bottle on the table of supplies, she uncapped it for a sniff. Humming in appreciation of the blend of lemongrass and peppermint, the god returned to the steadily filling bath and tipped some in.

"So, you're back."

Glancing over her shoulder at the woman emerging from the shadows, Astoria chuckled and replaced the cap on the bottle of oil. "Shouldn't you be asleep, General Vesta? Or is lurking in the chambers of your queen's sister part of your job description now?"

"My chambers are not so far away. I saw the light in your windows and knew you had returned. Considering you've done your best to avoid me, I thought I'd take this opportunity to corner you," she replied, coming to stand on the other side of the bath. "Of course, I don't need to ask to know where and what you've been doing. It's written all over your skin."

"Careful, General, you almost sound jealous."

Taking the oil back to the table, Astoria trailed her fingers over the selection of soaps. She did not want something that would clash with the scent she had added to the water, and finding a peppermint one at the end, she turned back to the staring goblin. The thin line of Vesta's lips betrayed her attempt to maintain a blank expression, and the god did not resist grinning while turning off the tap. Slipping into the bath, she appreciated the moment of cool before her power warmed the water to the point of steam.

"I want you to destroy Calista."

Choking, Astoria blinked at the goblin staring down at her. "I'm sorry, could you repeat that?"

Vesta grunted, mouth twisting in frustration. "She won't stop; she'll never stop. The babies won't be safe until she's dead. I can't return to do it, so I'm asking you. Kill the Blood Queen and protect your family. You're a god, you can pop in, set her on fire, and leave."

"Well, when you put it like that..."

Before the general could say anything else, Astoria dunked her head into the water, running the soap through her hair. Resurfacing, she arched a brow at the sight of the older woman perched on the side of the bath, elbow digging into her leg while she pressed the heel of her palm into her forehead.

"I know what I'm asking of you, Astoria."

"You're asking me to help you protect the people who matter most to you." Running the soap over her body, the god sighed. "I understand, but I don't know if I'm allowed to."

"Can you ask?" She gave her a hopeful look.

She did not know how to respond. The vengeful side of her wanted to forget the bath and go straight to where the goblin queen was, tucked away in the Spire, surrounded by her loyal people. Remembering the fear on her nephew and nieces' faces was enough to make her long to tear Calista apart. Feeling the soap melt in her grasp, Astoria grimaced and gave Vesta a pointed look while holding her hand up to watch the goop drip from her fingers. Eyes widening, the general stared at it like she was clueless about what was going on. Unwilling to let it all go to waste, she quickly finished washing herself.

"Pity it wasn't her face you melted."

"Tell me how you really feel, General." Screwing up her face at the mushy feeling of the remaining soap, Astoria flicked some off. "What made you turn your back on her?"

The guilt on Vesta's face surprised the god. "Your sister. I came here with Rhydwen, and my orders, but Eivor was not what I expected. She has a way about her that people struggle to deny, including me. Away from the Spire, I was free to be honest about how terrible Calista is."

"What happened to Tristan? When I last saw him, he was standing with Oblivion, and Briallen Altira, with their dragons behind them, while I sealed them shut in their sanctuary. Rhydwen was rather upset I didn't know more, which leads me to ask, who is he? Because clearly, he's not just a dragon rider."

"Why are you asking me?"

Draping her arms over the sides of the bath, Astoria rested her head against the back. "Well, I'm the one who can free the dragon riders, Oblivion, and the other remaining original Ravens. You're asking me to kill Queen Calista, and I have a feeling there might be someone with a bigger reason to do it."

Shoulders slumping, Vesta huffed. "Yes, Oblivion would. As would the dragon riders, and not just because of Tristan. I've never been able to work it out. When Shianeni sealed us all away, he somehow ended up with us after the dragons stole him as a small child and left his mother to heal from their fire. Calista never got over it, but I know he was the fortunate one to grow up away from his people. Especially away from his grandmother."

Frowning, Astoria remembered her initial confusion when she met Rhydwen. She had asked others how a goblin had come to be a dragon rider, but no one had given her answers. When the Fog descended upon them, she had forgotten it all. But those green eyes Rhydwen and Tristan shared were unmistakable. Just like they were in Rhydwen's children.

"Which of Rhydwen's sisters?"

"The eldest. Princess Penelope. She's the spitting image of her mother, and just as cruel. Perhaps worse. What they did to Tristan during the imprisonment was truly terrible. They punished him for being stolen when he was nothing more than a babe, as though he was to blame for what the dragons did."

"But what happened to him?" she whispered, anger and horror sending flames rippling across her exposed skin. "And how did he end up in the Spire when none of the other First People among the dragon riders joined their kin during the imprisonment?"

"When the Fog fell, he vanished. Maybe he returned to the dragons?"

Disappointment flooded across the bond, chased by a wave of anger. Groaning, Astoria flicked water at the goblin perched on the side of the bath. She knew Dawn and Charnel would join her soon, and they would have plenty to say. Her thoughts were too busy chasing each other around to be overly concerned by their reactions to her sneaking away from them. Mulling over what little information she had, Fire had to wonder if it would not be better for everyone if she killed the goblin queen. It might avoid escalating the conflict between Calista's forces, Eivor's Unseelie, and those who served the gods. Releasing an enraged husk maker like Briallen Altira and the dragons on Tir seemed like a dreadful idea, and as a god, she knew she had a responsibility to protect the people of the world.

"You need to go, General."

"Why?" Cocking her head, Vesta stared at her in the faint light cast by the ball of fire.

She felt the tugs of their attention, the unspoken demand for her return. "Because I snuck out of bed and left my mates asleep. Now they're awake, and aware of my absence."

"They know you're too good for them, and it makes them insecure."

"Or they're angry because I left without telling them."

There was a smug curl to her lips. "You're not denying their insecurity."

"There's no reason for them to be insecure!" Splashing more water at the goblin, Astoria knew they were coming. "But please, you really do need to leave. We can discuss murder plots tomorrow and question the overgrown feather duster king about what he knows. There are danann among the dragon riders."

"You're afraid of starting a war."

"Of course I am! Aren't you? Isn't there enough conflict already without me releasing the Executioner, her band of vengeful Ravens, and what remains of the dragon riders?"

Leaning down, Vesta poked her chest with a fully extended claw. "Then end it. You're the fucking god of fire, Battle Hawk. I've watched you burn her army before, so do it again."

Her heart plummeted when she felt their presence. "General, don't."

"They could have at least put on clothes."

Dawn's snarl made Astoria close her eyes. The tip of Vesta's claw pricked her skin, the pain fading as quickly as it came, but her low chuckle was confirmation she had done it on purpose. Dropping in temperature around her, the bathwater turned to ice, and it cracked when she moved. A hand slid into her hair, the familiar touch of Charnel's power curling around her as he tugged her head back.

"Why did you sneak away from us, my fiery wife?"

Meeting his gaze, she wanted to hate the desire pushing to the front of her feelings. "Because one of us had to, or we wouldn't have left that bed. Some of us have things to do."

"If you'd told us you wanted to come back here, we would have," Dawn said from where she lurked out of sight. "But why are you here, goblin? In the bathroom, while she bathes."

Dragging her claw down Astoria's chest to where the icy water clung to her, Vesta bared her teeth at Air. "I needed to talk to her about matters concerning the family."

Clenching her thighs together, Astoria was thankful she was in the bath, and the goblin could not smell her arousal. "It's fine, Dawn. General Vesta was just about to leave."

"No, it's not fine, Tory. You left without telling us, and then we come here and find you in the bath, naked, with the woman who killed you, and who has attempted to seduce you previously." The air crackled, and Dawn stomped over to the bath to stand over Vesta, lightning dancing across her skin.

Nose flaring, the Unseelie general dragged her gaze over the god of air. "Careful, little brat. You might be a pretty god, but I'm not afraid of you."

Charnel's hand tightened in her hair, but she could not take her eyes off the other two women, even when his mouth brushed against her ear. There was something mesmerising in the way Dawn glared at Vesta despite the lack of effect on her. Neither did the miniature storm gathering around the god.

"Well, isn't this unexpected?" Charnel murmured.

Slipping from the edge of the tub, Vesta ignored the lightning, and her hand shot out to grab Dawn's chin, claws digging in hard enough to draw blood. The storm worsened, making Astoria fear for the general. She knew what the other god's temper was like, and the last thing they needed was for Dawn to harm the commander of the Unseelie army, or to unleash a cyclone on Diwan. It would only drive a new wedge between her and Eivor. Releasing her hair, Charnel stepped around the end of the tub in case things took a turn for the worse. Taking advantage of her freedom, Astoria shifted onto her knees, leaning on the side to eye the distance to Dawn. Her arm was close enough to grab so they could vanish if needed.

"You should be afraid of me, goblin." Dawn wrapped a hand around Vesta's wrist, lightning darting along her fingers to dance across the general's skin. "Killing you would be like squashing a bug."

Astoria froze when more lightning spread from Dawn to Vesta. "Think about what you're doing, Dawn. Please stop before you hurt her. General, please let go."

Outside, thunder rumbled, and Charnel moved closer, prepared to pull the two women apart. "Let go, Dawn. Now. Before you make a mistake we can't recover from, I need you to remember where you are, and who she is."

Lifting her chin, Vesta smirked. "Listen to him, little brat. I'm too much for you."

Aware of the shadows swarming across the floor, Astoria flung more balls of fire into the air above their heads. She gasped when the darkness twisted around Dawn's legs, drawing the lightning down into their depths. Following her stare, Charnel stepped back in shock, while the god of air looked down in amazement before snapping her gaze back to the goblin. The smirk remained on Vesta's lips, smug and taunting.

"How?" Dawn whispered.

"I'm not in the mood to reveal my secrets to a bratty little godling." Digging her claws in tighter, Vesta pulled her closer. "But if you do anything to upset Astoria again? We'll talk."

Eyes narrowing, Charnel closed the gap between them and trailed a finger over the scar on the general's face. "How did you escape Astoria's attack all those years ago with only this?"

Frowning, she retracted her claws and released Dawn. Glancing at Astoria, Vesta cocked her head. None of them spoke, waiting for her to answer Charnel's question. The events of the battle still melded into one, and her fight with the goblin general was lost among countless others. It was unsurprising. So much had happened that night.

"I don't remember," she said finally, confusion making her hesitate. "She attacked first; I remember it clearly. Astoria was bathed in fire, striking me with her talons before shifting into her natural form to grab a sword from one of my burnt soldiers so she could fight me..."

"And?" He turned her face towards his.

Her mouth opened and closed, no words escaping her confusion. Turning back to Astoria, the general ignored the others. Covering her scar with one hand, Vesta shook her head.

"Why don't I remember what happened after our fight?"

Shrugging, Astoria replied, "I haven't been able to recall it at all. It was a messy battle."

"We fought, and then I was retreating with the others. The healers struggled to save my eye because you nearly took it out with your talons."

She watched Dawn and Charnel share a look. Peering down at the floor, Astoria studied the thick layer of shadows clinging to the goblin, and the legs of the two gods. Whatever they thought was going on, she wished they would give her a clue. They could mind speak across the bonds, something she suspected they were doing without her. Touching Vesta's arm, she sighed tiredly.

"You should go to bed, General. Perhaps you'll remember more in the morning after you've had some sleep. But you really do need to leave so I can yell at my mate for threatening the peace."

Biting her bottom lip, the confused general cast a look at Air and Water. "Breakfast?"

"Eivor left a note to remind me I'm expected at family meals."

"We won't mention what happened here."

Snorting, Astoria smiled knowingly. "You don't want Rhydwen to find out you asked me to kill his mother?"

"Not yet." Carefully moving away from the bath, Vesta gathered the reluctant shadows to her, snarling when it seemed they were ignoring her to cling to Charnel and Dawn. "Try not to make a mess of the place, and I'll try to be civil to the brat in public."

They watched her fade into the darkness, biding their time until their powers confirmed the goblin had left. Rubbing her face, Dawn gave Astoria an apologetic look that only lasted a moment before her earlier anger returned. Aware she needed to deal with their frustration over her departure, Fire hauled herself out of the bath, climbing over the side furthest from them. Her power evaporated the lingering water, leaving her dry. Flicking a hand at the bath, Charnel vanished the contents, eyeing her thoughtfully.

"What do you know about General Vesta?" he said, dismissing Dawn's anger.

"Honestly? Not a lot, except for the fact she's never gotten me out of her mind."

"I have a feeling she's the reason Emlyn wanted you to return here and repair things with your sisters. Well, one of many reasons. It makes sense. Just because Alyah and Xhaiden allowed me to know about you doesn't mean they told me everything. Think about it."

Dawn scoffed, crossing her arms to stare at him in disbelief. "Are you suggesting she's Earth?"

"She grounded your power, Dawn. You tell me."

Rubbing her head, Astoria banished her balls of fire and walked out of the bathroom. "I need to sit down for this conversation, and I really wish we could get drunk right now."

TWENTY-SEVEN

If there was one thing Astoria liked about being a god, it was no longer feeling physical exhaustion. Going without sleep was not an issue, even if her mind was tired of chasing around in circles. They had spent the night talking and arguing, but in the end, they had decided there was no point to the discussion until they had information. Aware they might not be welcome at breakfast, Charnel and Dawn had agreed to remain in the chambers until she had smoothed things over with her sister. She needed to make things right with Eivor because they wanted her to examine Vesta's memories of what happened during the battle, and afterwards. It was their first step towards discovering the truth.

Wrapping her arms around herself as she stood down the hall from the door separating her from her family, Astoria wished she had thought to arrive sooner. If she had been the first one there, she would have been free to hide in a corner to be stared at in batches. She knew she was being ridiculous. They were her family, and so far, they had done nothing but embrace her. Even after her rebirth. Flames slipped free of her control, dancing across her hands without damaging her dress. Dawn had teased her about it, promising to find her later to take advantage of the loosely flowing skirts, and her inability to say no.

The door opened, and she stiffened at the sight of Eivor slipping through the gap. Her sister gave her a bemused smile as she strode towards her, hands on her hips. Dropping her gaze to the floor, Astoria wondered why she was so nervous about joining her family for breakfast. They stood in silence, and she suspected the older woman was giving her time to settle her thoughts. She could always count on Eivor to know what she needed, even if she did not always give her a chance to appreciate it. Taking a deep breath, Astoria lifted her head to smile grimly at the queen, admiring the pale blue of her dress.

"I'm sorry for disappearing without notice."

Eivor arched a brow, reaching out to hook a finger on the neckline of her dress so she could examine the new swirls covering her skin. "I hope you made them beg first."

"There was begging involved."

"And?"

"We agreed the problem is Time. He manipulates things." Her gaze darted to the door, and she wondered if Vesta was at breakfast. "I'm not actually sure how long I was gone."

"A few days. Dare I ask?"

"Have you ever lost track of time because you were... busy?"

Lips thinning, Eivor fought back a smile. "Perhaps. Though it's harder for us mortals to do, considering we need to stop to eat and rest. Do gods have a recovery time?"

"Not really, no."

"But something is bothering you."

It did not surprise Astoria her sister had picked up on her turmoil. "Something strange happened when I got back here in the middle of the night. Vesta paid me a visit."

Her anger was as palpable as Dawn's had been, and Astoria was surprised Eivor was not surrounded by her own miniature storm. "She did what? Why would she do that? I thought I'd made it clear to her you were off limits. What did she do?"

"Nothing really, but her presence upset Dawn when they joined me. When she's angry, she summons a storm, lightning on her skin and everything. It didn't hurt Vesta."

"How did she end up in the position to find out it wouldn't hurt her?"

"Vesta taunted Dawn a little. Honestly, they were equally responsible. But there were threats, contact was involved, and your general grounded the lightning with her shadows. We were all flabbergasted. And then Charnel asked a complicated question."

"Which was?"

Chewing her lip, Astoria shrugged. "How did she escape my attack?"

"I see," Eivor murmured, shoulders slumping as she turned to stare at the door. "No wonder she's out of sorts this morning. She asked for a private audience with me after breakfast, and I suspect she wants me to examine her memories. You want to ask the same thing because you think someone has meddled with her mind like they did with yours. Why though? Why would they bother with Vesta?"

"Eivor—"

"Unless she knew something about what the gods did in that battle. But wouldn't you remember it now? When you were reborn, it unlocked all your memories."

Astoria touched her sister's shoulder, wondering if she should summon Charnel and Dawn. "You know why we're concerned. She grounded lightning from the sky god herself like it was nothing."

"No. No, I'm sorry, but you must be wrong. Perhaps the girl was restraining herself, and what you thought you saw was nothing more than an illusion. It just looked like Vesta did it."

The door opened, and Thorne appeared. She studied them in concern, glancing back into the room for a moment before stepping out into the hallway. Thankful no one else followed the dullaghan, Astoria leaned against the wall, watching her sister take a few steps to embrace her wife.

"What's going on?" Settling her icy gaze on Astoria, Thorne pulled Eivor against her chest. "Vesta won't stop pacing the room, and we're beginning to worry. Jola threatened to sedate her if she didn't calm down. She keeps muttering about fucking everything up."

"In our defence, she caused this. She came to my bathroom in the middle of the night, and then didn't leave when I asked her to before Dawn and Charnel arrived," Astoria said.

"I'm sure it was a misunderstanding, and there's no reason for the Storm Queen to unleash anything on Diwan. You can convince her of that, can't you, Astoria?"

Resting her head against her wife's chest, Eivor groaned. "No, that's not the issue. They think the old gods did something to Vesta and want me to examine her mind."

Frowning, Astoria studied Thorne and wondered if the Master of the Unseelie Hunt knew enough about the god who had helped create her people to judge if it was something Xhaiden would have done. "Tell me, dullaghan, would the former god of chaos have sneakily bound a power to someone?"

"Other than you?" she replied.

"Yes. Other than me."

Tightening her hold on Eivor, Thorne laughed in disbelief. "You think Xhaiden did something to Vesta? Are you insane? Did rebirth burn the sense out of you?"

"Rude."

"Other than killing her or involving others, the only way we're going to get answers is for me to examine Vesta's mind. I assume that's why you haven't gone to Chaos for answers. You don't want to involve the others because you don't trust them," Eivor said, wriggling free of Thorne's grasp. "You said the god of time is manipulative."

"Yes. All we know for sure is if we step onto the wrong path, he will interfere. Lord Time has powers the rest of us cannot defend against, and we fear him. Chaos is his wife."

Thorne shoved her hands into her pockets; mouth twisted in concern. "Astoria is right. Lord Time is a god to fear. What do you think they've done to Vesta?"

Opening her mouth to answer, Astoria snapped it shut when the general slipped from the shadows. She looked tired, and there were scratches on her scars suggesting she had been fussing over the marks. They looked at her, and Eivor held out a hand, the calming influence of her power spreading from it. Meeting Vesta's gaze, Fire hoped she saw her concern.

"They think I might be one of them." Vesta was matter of fact, her gaze shifting from Astoria to Thorne. "You can sense the end of people. What is mine?"

"It's the same as always... oh." Shaking her head, Thorne avoided looking at her wife. "Upon reflection, it feels a lot like Astoria did. Which explains why I thought it felt so familiar. Vesta is dying in the manner that we all are, but she's not."

"No!" Eivor snarled, fists clenched. "Absolutely not. They took my sister, and they're not taking my general. You will make Chaos undo it, Astoria. I don't care what reasons the old one had, fix it."

Every instinct she possessed as a god told her there was no undoing it. That once the threads of a power were bound to a person, nothing could change it. From the look on Thorne's face, Astoria believed the dullaghan had come to the same conclusion. Looking between them, an air of agonised rage surrounded the Unseelie Queen. She beat a fist against the wall before collapsing against it, forehead resting on the cool stone while her wife rubbed her back. Covering the scars on her face, Vesta sighed.

"Why me?"

"Don't ask me, I still don't know why me," Astoria replied. "But we think you might be Earth."

"Because I resisted the storm brat's lightning?"

Lifting a hand, she formed a ball of flames above her palm. Staring into the flickering depths, the god admired the vibrant colours. At the back of her mind, Charnel and Dawn waited eagerly for the invitation to join her. There was no point delaying their participation or risking the concerns of the rest of the family. It surprised her none of the others had pushed their way out into the hallway to find out what was going on. Particularly King Tigernach. He was on the other side of the door, the taste of War's power surrounding him like an enticing blanket Fire knew she could twist to her own purpose if she desired it.

"*Come,*" she whispered across the bonds to her mates.

Vesta snarled, stepping closer to Astoria as shadows gathered at her feet. A swipe of her claws through the ball of fire sent embers fluttering to the ground, where shadows were swift to swallow them. Hearing Eivor gasp, the general looked at her queen in horror, realising what she had done. The cool thrum of Charnel's power against hers assured Fire the other two had joined them. Hands pressed to her back in comfort as the newly arrived gods took their place on each side of her. Their presence had the dullaghan dipping her head in greeting, while her wife pointed at them in anger.

"Undo it!" Eivor sounded desperate, and Astoria saw the anguish in her eyes. "Please. I can't lose Vesta to you like I've lost my sister. It isn't fair!"

"But you haven't lost me, and you never will. We will always be family. I made mistakes in the past, but I will never abandon you again. My home is here, not the eternal valleys," Astoria replied, feeling Dawn stiffen beside her. "I will protect Diwan and my kin for as long as Tir exists."

A swirl of air tightened around her, and the god commanding it leaned closer to murmur, "You can't promise that. Your place is with us, as ours is with you."

"Then it's a good thing gods can travel anywhere instantly. Besides, I can hardly return to The *Storm Bird*. The god of fire on a timber ship? Not an ideal combination."

Eyeing them in annoyance, Vesta settled her attention on Charnel. "What do you think? You're older than anyone else here, and you fell alone from the stars, leaving the other parts of yourself to wait for their turn to take a form. If I was Earth, would you know it?"

He shook his head, stepping clear of his mates. "When I reach out for Earth, I feel the broken threads of our bond, and it feels the same way Fire's did. Before Dawn was born, Emlyn told me what she would be. He called her the missing piece. I never really gave his words much thought, but mulling over them now, I remember he specifically said, the, not a. If Earth had not been bound to someone, then Dawn would have been a missing piece, not the. This implies she was the last one to take physical form."

"Can you trust your memories?" Eivor crossed her arms, scowling.

"Yes, I am the god of water. Nothing remembers quite like water does. Why Vesta? When we created goblins, we bound them to the earth, to dark places where shadows grow, and she is a mountain among her people. Our paths have crossed in the past, and I've always admired her strength, the persistence with which she stood for what she believed in, the way she nurtures those who matter to her while giving them their freedom to grow. She would be a fine Earth, and being bound to her would be an honour."

Startled by his words, Vesta could not hide the faint flush of her cheeks. "I don't think anyone has ever flattered me quite like that, Lord Water. Doesn't mean I want to be a god."

"Do you think most of the new gods asked for their fate? I don't know how much of their story you've been told, but I assure you, if given the choice, they would have picked mortality. War, Death, Thought, they agreed to their path out of love for a woman who had no choice in what she became. They believed that together, they could make things better for everyone else because they had been mortal. Every single person who has taken on the power of a god has done so because of that belief."

"Including me," Astoria said, glancing at her feet sheepishly. "Well, what Alyah and Xhaiden told me made me believe if I didn't accept the power of fire, things would go badly for Tir."

Thorne stroked Eivor's hair, gazing at her wife adoringly. "Xhaiden wouldn't have forced anyone to take on the burden. If Vesta is what they suspect, then she agreed to it long ago."

Crossing her arms over her chest, the general drummed the fingers of one hand on her shoulder while the other dug into her elbow. "But I'm not likely to remember without first dying. I've got no faith in any of you being able to sense the power in me since the little godling never realised what Astoria was."

"In my defence, I wasn't exactly looking for it!" Dawn grumbled, clinging to the chuckling god of fire. "But point taken. You'd have thought I would have sensed something. My mother knew Tessa was the next god of chaos before she was reborn. So shouldn't we be able to recognise her?"

Charnel glanced at the dining room, where everyone else waited. "Tessa was Xhaiden's heir, and your mother is Life. Heirs are different. Remember how Jen's magic felt?"

"She felt like my father."

"Exactly. In Tory's case, there was no god to be connected to, so Xhaiden could bury the power." His lips curled in delight, and Astoria could tell he had thought of something. "But you're onto something about your mother knowing. She might sense the power in Vesta like she did with Tory."

Pulling away, Dawn grinned. "You're right. She didn't know Tory was Fire, but she sensed something wasn't right about her. If you want me to, I can ask her to come."

Aware the focus had shifted to her, Eivor clenched her jaw, and stared at Vesta. They stood in silence, the thrum of anticipation making Dawn fidget while Astoria poked her arm. She understood why the younger woman was eager to find out the truth. If Vesta was their fourth, their dynamic would change, and she was uncertain if she was ready when they were barely working out how the three of them fit together. At least they had already established an emotional connection before her rebirth. There was nothing between them and the general, and while she found the older woman undeniably attractive, Astoria was clueless to how the other two felt. Neither had mentioned it, nor had she asked.

"After breakfast I will examine Vesta's memories, and if I find anything suspicious, then you can ask the god of life to visit. Is that fine with you, or would you prefer something else, Vesta?" Eivor looked resigned, the downward turn of her mouth bothering Astoria.

Ever the sensible one, Thorne nodded and gestured at the door. "I think it's a good plan. Now, I'm surprised no one has tried to find out what's going on, so why don't we join them?"

"No one has come out because I'm discouraging them from doing so."

Laughing, Vesta covered her face with a hand. "When Astoria returned, I thought my dreams had come true. This was not the outcome I expected. I hoped I'd be lucky enough to steal a few kisses from the woman who had haunted my thoughts for a millennium... if she deigned to let me offer her companionship in her final months. But this? It's a lot."

Offering her his arm, Charnel smiled faintly. "A millennium is a long time to dream of kissing a person you fought during a very hectic battle."

"I know."

Watching the goblin slip her arm through Water's, Astoria swallowed to dislodge the lump that had settled into her throat. Eivor and Thorne led the way to the door; wary glances sent over their shoulders at the three gods. Slipping an arm around her waist, Dawn squeezed her gently, offering a faint smile. It was meant to be assuring, she knew that, but the gesture frustrated part of her. Even the thought of seeing Dawn and Charnel interacting with her family failed to shift her mood. All Astoria could think about was what they would learn after breakfast and staring at Vesta as they followed the others into the chamber, she realised what bothered her the most.

She was afraid they were wrong. If the same gods had not selected Vesta as they had selected her all those years ago, it meant the decision on who would become Earth fell on them. Having the choice taken from them by a god who could see the paths ahead felt like the safer option. The more she thought about the goblin becoming their fourth, the more Astoria suspected there was an excellent reason Alyah and Xhaiden picked her. Vesta was the sort of person who could keep them from doing anything stupid. She would balance out Dawn's impulsiveness, and her temper, while offering Charnel someone solid to cling to who understood the weight of millennia. As the god of earth, Vesta was perfect for them, and they would never have looked at her if left to find someone themselves.

"I can hear your thoughts churning," Dawn murmured, her gaze sweeping over the occupants of the balcony. "We'll figure this out together, Tory. Maybe this is for the best."

"That's what I'm pondering. Maybe they knew it was better to decide for us?"

Before Dawn could answer, Rose squealed in delight at the sight of them and flung herself from her seat to run over. Small arms wrapped around their legs, her beaming smile distracting Astoria from her thoughts. Grinning, Dawn picked the girl up, tossing her in the air to catch her with a carefully controlled gust of wind that made her scream in glee. Propping Rose onto her hip, the Storm Queen wandered over to the table to sit on the chair she had vacated, while Charnel and Vesta settled into seats opposite her. Lingering on the edge of the room, Astoria studied the people gathered for breakfast, marvelling at how the danann contingent had melded in. She wanted the same for her mates.

Meeting her gaze across the table, and over the heads of the people between them, Vesta nodded at an empty chair. "Well, come on, Battle Hawk. We've got a busy day, and food always helps."

TWENTY-EIGHT

Astoria threw herself on a lounge, yanking the cushion out from under her head so she could hug it to her chest. She ignored the disapproving huff her sister directed her way, opting to stare at the mural adorning the ceiling. It was Eivor's work, the swirls of paint complimenting each other perfectly to depict a field of wildflowers surrounded by a forest. Passing her, Dawn poked the pillow and snorted in amusement when she growled. Watching her linger by her legs, Astoria did not bother to lift them. Realising she wanted to sit alone, the god of air shrugged and wandered over to a different seat. Part of her wanted to feel bad for refusing Dawn's company, but she needed to deal with the mess of her thoughts.

"I know something is going on, and you're not excluding me, Eivor!" Silaine's voice carried across the room, prompting Astoria to look at the door. "She's my sister too, and I want to know."

Catching Thorne's amused gaze, Astoria bit back a chuckle. The dullaghan was standing to the side of the door while the Unseelie Queen leaned on the frame with her nails digging into the timber. Silaine had a foot shoved through the gap, a hand clinging to the door above Eivor's. It was amusing to see her sisters engaging in a battle of stubbornness, and she was not the only one enjoying the show. Seated on a lounge opposite her, Charnel and Vesta were craning around to watch the women.

"Just let her in. If she's anything like you, then this will take all day, and we'll resolve nothing. I'd really like to sort this out before we go insane," Vesta said, turning to flash a smile at Astoria before propping her feet up on the low table between them.

Eivor let go of the door and got out of Silaine's way, scowling as she stomped over to where her general sat. "Fine, if that's what you want. Now move so I can sit with you. If you want me to examine your memories, I need to touch you."

Arching a brow, Vesta gestured at Astoria. "Correct me if I'm wrong, but I recall you just diving right on into her memories without being within arm's reach."

"Yes, but she's my sister, and from the day she was born until the day she died, her mind was an open book to me. Silaine is the same. It's not something I can achieve over a few years. And yes, I could dive in from a distance, but trust me, you don't want me to."

Perching on the side of Astoria's lounge, Silaine contemplated them. "So, would someone like to explain what is going on? First Tory was gone for a few days, then she returns with her mates, who she has clearly forgiven for their transgressions, and now you're being all secretive about something to do with General Vesta. With said gods in attendance."

When the queen nudged her, Vesta dropped her feet to the floor and shuffled closer to Charnel to make room. The moment Eivor settled on the lounge, an odd look appeared on her face Astoria did not recognise. It was not the blank expression she normally wore when slipping into someone's mind. Rolling onto her side, Fire watched her sister, realising her focus had drawn the attention of the other two gods. Giving a little shake of her head, Eivor cupped Vesta's cheek, her expression shifting.

"Why don't you lot explain it while I get on with this? Vesta and I will be unavailable for conversation until I'm done. Interrupt us, and I will give you nightmares for a week."

Snickering at the comment, Dawn gestured vaguely. "If anyone could do it, it's you."

Eivor gave the younger woman an unamused look before placing her other hand on the goblin's leg. "I'll be as gentle as I can, but you need to let me in. If you fight, it will hurt."

"You're not the first mind mage to go digging through my head," Vesta muttered, settling against the back of the lounge. "I'm the second oldest person in this room. I've done this before."

Curious, Dawn pointed at Thorne, where she lurked near the door. "She's older than you?"

"Indeed," she replied, inclining her head in amusement. "We were the last species to be created before the original gods realised their mistake in making everyone immortal. You didn't know?"

"No, I didn't. Not that I've asked about the order in which the gods created people. I mean, I know for the mortals, it went daoine, elves, and then humans because they worked out they needed to shorten lifespans, or they wouldn't get as much entertainment out of people as they hoped. Mother likes to complain about how unpleasant my grandmother was, and how the others did little to stop her."

Rolling his shoulders uncomfortably, Charnel glanced away. "Eirian has always feared becoming her mother. At one point, we were concerned she'd drive herself down that path. Neriwyn and Gebael weren't helpful, but they were afraid of Emlyn. We created the First People as ideas came to us. Goblins were fourth after the danann, brownies, and pixies."

Brows raising, Silaine looked like she had been struck. "Wait, are you saying Tigs is the first? The oldest? There's no one older than him... and they created my mates right after him."

"No, the brownies were first. Shianeni wanted her servants."

"You didn't know?" Dawn grinned at her. "But we have so much fun teasing Tigs."

"Don't you give me a hard time when you didn't know either." Silaine scoffed.

"Fair. I just like teasing him about being old. No wonder he gets so uppity. He really is old. Not as old as Charnel, but I'm not complaining about the experience that comes with age."

Thorne chuckled, the curl of her lips taking on a smug edge as she settled her attention on Charnel. "If she's anything like Rhydwen, you have my sympathy. The young ones have so little discipline."

Glaring at her, Dawn crossed her arms and huffed. "Who's going to tell Silaine what's going on?"

Reminded of why they had gathered in the sitting room, Astoria returned her attention to the pair of frozen women. Eivor's closed eyes and blank expression was confirmation she remained deep inside Vesta's mind searching for answers. She wanted it to be over so they could know if their suspicions were on the right track. But as much as she needed answers, she did not want her sister to do any damage.

"We suspect General Vesta might be one of us," Charnel said, and touched the goblin's leg, studying the line of her face. "Eivor is looking for evidence of alterations to her mind."

The disbelieving laugh that spilled from Silaine's lips had Astoria smirking. Looking at each of them, the Raven Queen waited for someone to say something. Thorne peeled away from her spot, crossing to the lounge to stand behind Eivor as though she sensed something the rest of them did not. Swinging her legs off the lounge, she sat up and set the cushion aside. If the dullaghan's shift was a sign it was done, she did not want to be lying down when her sister delivered the news.

Sobering, Silaine rubbed her forehead. "Of all the things you could have told me, that was not one I expected. What will you do if Eivor finds evidence?"

"I'll ask my mother to examine Vesta. She sensed something strange about Tory, so we're hoping she might sense the same strangeness again," Dawn replied. "None of us want to approach the three gods who have the answers because we don't trust their motives."

"But you trust your mother? Not that I blame you. Your parents are wonderful, and I owe them a lot."

"You don't owe them. They never expect payment for helping people, other than in the form of said people living their lives to the fullest. That's all they want. People living in freedom and happiness."

Leaning over the back of the lounge to examine her wife, Thorne smiled. "We might not be the biggest supporters of the gods, but we appreciate their efforts to protect free will, while also doing their best to ensure the right people fight injustice."

The amused look Dawn gave her spoke volumes about what she thought of the comment. "Yes, they do their best to ensure the right people fight injustice."

Grinning, Silaine reached over to poke Astoria's shoulder. "She's talking about them, isn't she?"

"Of course." Resting her elbows on her knees, she kept her gaze on the two women, lost in memories. "As long as the god of time approves, things happen. Including keeping secrets from one's mates. It's wonderful. So much freedom for mortals, and little for the gods. We must dance to his tune."

"Can you refuse?"

"We can try, but how do you stop doing something when you don't know if you're doing it? Because he's so careful to nudge things without your realising. All you can do is hope his earnest words about only doing what is best for Tir are the truth, and not the greatest deception in existence."

Eivor withdrew from Vesta with a groan, and Thorne rushed to guide her to sit back. "I remember why I prefer not to delve too deeply into the memories of people several thousands of years older than myself. How we kept our sanity all those millennia is the greatest mystery."

Aware it had taken a toll on Vesta as well, Charnel placed a hand on her shoulder, and Astoria felt a brush of his soothing influence as it surrounded her. The general was slower to move than her queen, and she leaned into Water's touch as though embracing the effects of his power. She envied his ability to offer comfort when her power did the opposite. Glancing at Dawn, she observed the worried twist of her mouth and the constant bounce of her legs.

"Remind me not to agree to that again," Vesta mumbled, resting her cheek on Charnel's shoulder. "It feels like I drank far too much last night and then fell down an entire castle's worth of stairs."

"Let me fetch some tea," Dawn said, jumping to her feet. "I should have done it sooner, but we were talking, and it slipped my mind. Or do you want something stronger than tea?"

Giving a slight shake of her head, Eivor held up a hand. "Don't rush off right away."

"But surely you need something to drink after that?"

"Patience, Dawn." Giving her a look, Astoria did not blame the other god for feeling a need to be productive. "Besides, you might need to go further than the kitchens."

"Oh, yes, of course. I didn't think about that."

An awkward silence fell on them while Dawn sat back down on the chair she was occupying. Remaining propped up on Charnel, Vesta wore a look of resignation that sunk into Astoria like an anchor. She did not need her sister to say it out loud to know they had found evidence. One of the old gods had meddled in the general's mind. Between Eivor's discovery, and Thorne's confirmation that Vesta felt like she had before her death, Astoria wondered if there was a need to bring the god of life into it. They could keep it to themselves, dealing with the issue as a family fighting their battles together. If Vesta was Earth, it would ensure their group remained close to Diwan and the Unseelie because there was next to nothing that could convince either of them to leave Eivor.

"I feel like we all knew this would be my answer, but yes, Vesta's memories have undergone alterations. Not as much as Tory's were, but she also wasn't spying on things she shouldn't have been." Eivor gave her sister a pointed look, and Astoria grinned sheepishly. "The main area of modification is the battle, but someone has been in there more recently, which makes me think something happened that they didn't want people to know about. Perhaps she remembered something when the First People were released from the Veil. Or felt an urge to search for Tory or Charnel that would have unravelled the plan."

Heaving a sigh, Vesta sat up and rubbed her face. "Why me?"

"Why not you?" Thorne shrugged. "If I was going to pick someone to make a god, I'd pick you."

Crinkling her nose, Silaine giggled. "I don't know you as well as they do, but if I had to pick between you and Tigs? I'd go with you. The man is wonderful, and I love him like a brother, but no. Just no."

Her comment broke the tension looming over their heads, and Eivor and Vesta burst into laughter, followed by Dawn. Smiling indulgently at them, Thorne winked at Astoria, while she glanced between the dullaghan and the god of water. Charnel was pensive, his stare locked in the distance. Flickers of emotion crossed the bond, but nothing she could make sense of. He was a lot more complicated than Dawn, and her unabashed glee over what Silaine had said could not be mistaken for anything else.

"Fine, I accept that, compared to many other options out there, I am a better choice. I wish there was a way for me to remember why I agreed, if I did indeed do so, that didn't involve asking more gods for help. Or dying," Vesta said, looking at each of them solemnly. "The woman I am now is very different from the one I was then."

Clasping his hands in his lap, Charnel inclined his head. "Alyah and Xhaiden were my friends, and they tried to protect me from Shianeni and Annawyn as best they could. I want to believe they had a good reason for what they did. Maybe Alyah saw what would happen if you weren't the one sent to Diwan to free Eivor and her people, and knew it had to be you. My power doesn't let me see the future, but I'm not stupid enough to deny that sometimes we must trust we're on the right path. Here we are casting suspicion on Emlyn's motives, but can you imagine the weight of what he sees? Because I can't. As Eivor mentioned, how any of us keep our sanity with all the years we've lived is a wonder, but Emlyn's power encompasses time and all the variances our steps create. That is too much."

Dawn nodded slowly, mouth twisting as she looked at the ground. "That's why he keeps to himself, mostly. Too much time around more than a handful of people is overwhelming."

A sliver of pity dug into her heart, but Astoria was unwilling to let go of her resentment for the god of time and his manipulations. "Well, he wasn't born yet when Xhaiden and Alyah picked Vesta and I... and to be honest, I want this dealt with before I decide what I'm going to do about the Executioner and the dragon riders. Because releasing them back into Tir will change a lot of things."

Uncomfortable with the prospect of not releasing them, Silaine rubbed her face. "I'm not sure I should be a part of that decision, but then again, I am the leader of the Ravens now. Thorne and I are probably two of the most biased people who could be involved."

"True," Thorne muttered. "The Executioner can command the Hunt."

"Not to mention the thrill dragon riders will experience if they get to destroy the goblins in revenge for what we did. Perhaps if I'm the god of earth, I can convince them those who have sworn loyalty to the new Unseelie deserve mercy. And then offer to help them destroy Calista." Shrugging, Vesta almost looked excited by the idea.

Gesturing around the room, Dawn nodded slowly. "You'll be hard pressed to find anyone who disagrees with the plan to destroy the Blood Queen and her loyalists. I'd have done it myself already, but gods aren't allowed to do that sort of thing. She's one of the largest buyers in the slave trade."

Vesta flexed her hands, claws appearing. "I know what I'd like to do to my former mistress. The things she has done. And to come after the children? No more. You know, I'm not sure I want to be a god, but the image in my mind of how Calista will react is glorious."

"Ah yes, revenge is always a good reason to become a god," Thorne said, moving around the end of the lounge to perch next to her wife. "Would you like me to kill you now?"

"Trust a headless rider to be eager to kill someone."

"I'm offering you a minimal pain and blood free option. After all, the touch of the dullaghan ensures an almost instant death. Saves you the mess of being stabbed in the heart."

Rubbing the back of her neck, Astoria grinned. "Or the back of the skull."

"Having to die sounds unpleasant." Dawn pulled a face. "Not sorry to have missed out."

Eivor snorted, looking between them all with an expression Astoria knew well. It was one she had been on the receiving end of more times than she could count for as long as she could remember. She wished she had a bottle of wine to mockingly salute the older woman, just to see it become the narrow-eyed scorn that always made her laugh. The look was enough to have Dawn huddling back in her seat, and Silaine pursing her lips, glancing away to avoid having it linger on her for too long. When it landed on Vesta, the goblin flashed her pointed teeth at the queen, amused by the attempt to scold her.

"Put it away, Your Majesty. You know it doesn't work on me." Vesta rose from the lounge, gaze dancing over the three gods. "I have a pile of reports waiting for me."

It was a message they understood, and Astoria watched Dawn and Charnel nod at the general. She wished she had paperwork to help clear her thoughts. The moment they gave her space, she planned to shift forms and go for a fly. Clear skies were a freedom she could embrace, and Astoria wondered how her mates would react to the change in her hawk form.

Meeting her gaze, Eivor frowned, and lifted her chin as though she knew what her younger sister was contemplating doing. "I think it's a good idea for everyone to take some time to sort through their thoughts and feelings before we decide about bringing in the god of life or killing anyone."

Grunting, Vesta shrugged and started for the door. "Let's not forget our plans to destroy your husband's mother. She's gone too far with her recent attack, and I will not let her get away with it."

"I agree," Dawn said, drawing startled looks from the other gods. "She tried to take the children. I know you're not overly keen on us gods, Eivor, but you're Tory's family, which makes you mine. Anyone who tries to hurt this family will find out what happens when you piss off the Storm Queen."

A slow smirk curled the corners of Eivor's lips as her gaze settled on the god of air. "Is that your way of assuring me you have no plans to steal my sister away from me?"

"Or your general... if she turns out to be Earth. Gods have the benefit of being able to transport themselves anywhere with a thought. My parents always taught me home is where your family is."

"Truer words have never been spoken," Vesta said, glancing back at them. "We should have afternoon tea, just the four of us."

Charnel nodded, gesturing at Astoria and Dawn. "We'll be there."

TWENTY-NINE

She did not know what Dawn and Charnel were doing, but their presence in the palace was oddly comforting. For the three of them to be in the same place, and for that place to be somewhere that had previously refused to welcome gods, left her with an ember of hope. They could find their balance while aligning themselves with those who shared their views. It would have been easy to return to the little island in the middle of the ocean that the Storm Queen's fleet called home, and to spend her days assisting in the coordination of the missions the pirates ran while Charnel continued to keep the ships out of watery trouble. But her family was in Diwan, and her heart wanted to be there to protect them.

Wandering the halls, Astoria had no clue where she was hoping to end up, and the noise of her thoughts refused to let her pay attention to anything else. She danced from one dilemma to the next, barely able to linger for long enough to satisfy the twisting anxiety they caused. The only thing she knew for certain was she wanted to remain in Diwan. If knowledge of her presence helped keep enemies away from her mortal family, then she owed it to her sister to do what she could. Just picturing her nieces and nephews reminded her of all the things she had done wrong in her life.

But thinking about Eivor and Silaine's children pulled her thoughts down the uncomfortable road to Vesta. The general had barely left her mind since she walked out of the sitting room. If she was honest with herself, Astoria could admit that the older woman had been on her mind from the moment she accosted her in the hallway. No one other than Dawn and Charnel had ever ingrained themselves in her thoughts the way the goblin had. None of the lovers she had taken had clung to her like they did, and it was that aspect which convinced her Vesta was what they suspected. She did not need more to confirm the truth when her instincts screamed so loudly.

A hand shot out through an open doorway, grabbing her arm to yank her into the quiet room, where someone shoved her against a wall. Startled, Astoria let the flames dance across her skin, but the prick of claws, and Vesta's amused chuckle quickly had them fading. Waiting for the older woman to speak, she swept her gaze over the chamber, taking in the soft glow of sunlight around the edge of the heavy drapes. It cast just enough illumination to make out the bookshelves covering most of the walls, and the desk in the corner. She knew it was not the general's office, but the smell of ink clung to the air, and there was a lounge in the opposite corner with a blanket hanging off it, suggesting someone used it.

Stroking her cheek with a claw, Vesta buried her nose in her neck. "I can smell them all over you, and I can't decide if I hate how it makes me crave you more, Battle Hawk."

"What?"

"I should have realised there was something more going on. When Water and Air arrived in Diwan, all I could think about was what I wanted to do to them. The last thing I ever thought I'd imagine was pinning the bratty daughter of War and Life to a wall so I could listen to her beg while I fucked her with my fingers. Let alone what I imagined about him."

Astoria blinked slowly, turning over the admission in her mind while the goblin continued to nuzzle her neck. "She begs prettily. That's why you were in a mood after they arrived. I thought it was a jealous disappointment that you'd lost your chance to have your way with me."

"Oh, it was," she murmured, lips caressing the god's skin. "But my desire for them unsettled me. Craving a pair of gods like they're everything I need to survive was unexpected. Only now it makes perfect sense why I reacted the way I did, and I know I can do this without feeling guilty… or starting a war."

Claws dug into her chin, holding her still so Vesta could kiss her. The flames screamed to be released, fiery fingers wanting to pull the goblin closer. She clung to her power, fear of hurting the other woman keeping her from enjoying the taste of her lips and the graze of sharp teeth. Aware of a hand sliding down her leg to tug the silk of her skirts upwards, Astoria could not resist moaning when the other one left her chin to settle on her throat. Even though Vesta's sharp claws could not harm her, the prick of them sent shivers down her spine, and fed the desire pooling between her legs.

"You smell so fucking delicious, my feral Battle Hawk."

She wanted to bury her hands in the general's wild curls, but resisting the urge, Astoria flattened them against the smooth wall against her back. "How did you know I was there?"

Chuckling as she licked the god's cheek, Vesta continued to lift her skirt slowly. "The shadows told me. My command of them has always been exceptional, but I know better than to deny that it grew a great deal after that battle. Nor will I deny they seem particularly in tune with the three of you. They constantly tell me where you are. At first, I thought it was my paranoia making them pay more attention."

"So last night, it wasn't the lights that told you I was back."

"No, but I needed a logical explanation."

Fingers found her thigh, the barest tips of Vesta's claws tracing lines over the skin she had exposed. Shifting her stance slightly, the general pressed a knee to the wall beside her leg, pinning the silk in place. Nose flaring, Astoria wondered if Charnel and Dawn knew what she was doing, and if they could feel the desire stirred by every slight touch the goblin graced her with. The cool touch of shadows around her lower legs felt strangely like being pulled into the ground's embrace.

"Vesta," Astoria murmured when the hand slid over her thigh to cup her cunt. "You're playing with fire. Quite literally. This is not the time or place."

Drawing her claws in, Vesta slid a finger through the evidence of the god's arousal. "Empty words when you're this wet. But you're right, this isn't the time or place. I'm not even sure whose office this is. When I finally have you, it won't be against a wall with the fear of being caught hanging over us."

"Is that so? I thought you might avoid dying so you wouldn't end up as a god."

"And deny myself millennia of having you on your knees, bound and at my mercy? Not to mention the cocky brat who thinks she deserves you despite the pain she caused you."

Tilting her head back, Astoria gazed at Vesta. "Sounds like you've got a plan. What about Charnel?"

"I'm looking forward to him." Tightening her hold on the god's throat, she smirked. "Earth and water have a unique relationship, so I'm sure the gods will as well."

The prospect of Charnel and Vesta working together to pleasure her and Dawn made Astoria want to grind against the general's hand. Swallowing, she felt the claws dig into her neck and imagined what the goblin could do with them. Once she was reborn, they would have an eternity to find out. Rubbing her nose against Fire's cheek, Vesta purred when the smell of her arousal grew.

"Do they appreciate how fortunate they are to have a duine?" Her finger stroked along the entrance to Astoria's cunt, the claw slowly extending, and Vesta pressed the heel of her hand firmly against her clit. "You might be a god now, but deep down you're still a needy little whore who was made for this."

Vesta's low tone was a caress, pebbling her skin despite the flames wanting to break free of the control she was barely clinging to. She knew she had to keep herself from hurting the goblin, but every stroke of her finger had Astoria struggling. Shadows slithered further up her legs as though seeking the fire threatening to burst from her skin. Knowing what they had done to Dawn's lightning, she wondered if the general could tame her power in the same manner. It almost tempted the god to surrender to the slow build of her desire, and let Vesta coax an orgasm from her.

When the tip of a claw brushed against her clit, Astoria whimpered and grabbed the general's wrist. "No more, please. I don't want to hurt you."

Baring her teeth, Vesta growled, pulling back slightly. "You're denying me?"

"Yes."

Her eyes widened in surprise when the general laughed, a delighted grin curling her lips. The shadows slithered higher, keeping Fire in place while Vesta stepped back. Bringing her finger to her mouth, she licked the claw clean, gaze never leaving Astoria.

"Delicious. Just like I knew you would be."

"This can't happen. Not yet," she said, feeling the shadows curling around her fingers to consume the flames that had escaped her grasp to drip from her hands.

"Fine, but I'm not willing to be reborn until Calista is dead."

The words hit like a punch to the gut, and Astoria stared at her. She felt the concern of her mates across the bonds. Aware they would rush to her side if they thought it necessary, Fire sent assurances that all was fine back to them in the hope Dawn and Charnel would stay away. If they joined them, the conversation would become muddled, and that was the last thing she wanted. Easier to discuss their path without their interference. Particularly when the pirate queen was prone to making rash choices.

"If I release the Executioner, her Ravens, and the dragon riders, they will go after Calista for revenge. Lord General Valerian will want justice for his people."

Humming in appreciation, Vesta remembered the formidable general who had ruled the dragon city of Bellenden. "Yes, I imagine he will. We had a few encounters, and he was not a man to cross. But the Blood Queen has an army, and she won't stop coming for our family until she's dead."

"What do you propose we do?"

"I know you're not allowed to kill her for me, and setting the Spire on fire is out of the question. There are innocents in the city who don't deserve to die because of her. So, I want you to go to Calista and threaten her. Ensure she knows gods protect her grandchildren and they won't be merciful if harm comes to them. Then you can free the Executioner, and the rest. Set them on a path of justice."

She wanted to rub her face, but the shadows held her in place. "I want to kill her."

"What will the other gods do to you if you try?"

"Well, I assume Time would stop me. Unless it was the best option. It's impossible to know what might happen until we try. But if I killed her, it wouldn't be good for the Unseelie. You established the Council as anti-god and welcoming me treads a delicate line."

Nodding slowly, Vesta did not disagree. "We can't risk everything we've built here. You can't kill Calista, but I'm not a god. That means I can kill my former mistress."

"Hence why you refuse to be reborn until she's dead."

"Exactly. And if I die trying, at least I know it won't be the end."

It felt wrong to conspire with Vesta while Charnel and Dawn were elsewhere. Not just them, but her sisters. Eivor and her consorts deserved to have a say in what happened, especially Rhydwen. He was Calista's son, and Astoria did not know if he held any affection for his mother. Killing her without warning him was a betrayal of the family they hoped to build. A family that trusted each other and did not keep secrets without a good reason. Whatever move they made directly against the goblin queen needed to be done with the agreement of the whole family.

"Maybe I can threaten her, ensure she knows Diwan, the family, and the new Unseelie have gods protecting them and they won't let anyone hurt their people. But if I do, it's only with the blessing of Eivor and the others," Astoria said, lifting her chin to stare at the general unapologetically. "I have acted alone too many times in the past, and that must change. As much as I want to burn the bitch alive, I can't run off to do it like mine is the only opinion that matters. And you can't ask me to. That's not fair."

The shadows tightened on her for a moment before falling away, retreating to wherever Vesta drew them from as she sneered in frustration. "What if my request has nothing to do with what she's done to the family? I served the Blood Queen for thousands of years, and maybe I want her gone for all the terrible things she did before Rhydwen was born. Before all of this happened."

"And that's fine. Let me free the people who can see that through without risking us landing in trouble with the one god who can make our eternal lives exceedingly difficult. If we fuck up, Emlyn can imprison us. There's a reason Dawn and Charnel did what they were told, even though it hurt. Time controls all of us."

"He can what?"

"Ask Charnel about it. He has experienced what Emlyn can do."

Rubbing her face, Vesta turned away. "So, gods aren't free to do whatever they like?"

"Not if it has an adverse effect on the path he has chosen for Tir. As long as we don't step over the line, he seems to leave us alone. But we don't know where the line is. Maybe I could kill Calista without repercussion because it suits his vision. Or maybe trying to do so would earn me a time out like a naughty child. He could take me away from my family until I bend to his will."

"Do you think he knows we're having this conversation right now?"

Uncertainty raged through her, making Astoria glance at the corners of the rooms. She wanted to believe she would sense another god if they were lurking out of sight. They could shroud themselves, but Time was something else. If any of them could hide from the rest, she suspected it was him. Part of her wanted to scream at the world that they were being deceived, and the gods of life and death were not the most powerful of them all. Opening her mouth to reply, she snapped it shut again when the weight of what she wanted to say froze her tongue.

"Fuck," Vesta groaned, casting her eyes around the room as she drew the shadows to her.

"It's not like that. I don't know what everyone is capable of... I mean, I don't even know what I'm capable of! Dawn says her parents can do things the previous gods couldn't, but she didn't have the memories they did to know what her possibilities were. Neither do I."

"And I'll be in the same boat, so to speak. We'll find out what our capabilities are, but in the meantime, we need to focus. Calista must die."

Astoria did not disagree, but she did not want to go about it the wrong way. "I should bring down those wards keeping the Executioner and the rest locked away. They're bound to my blood, and only I can break them. What's the point of putting it off?"

Running a hand through her wild curls, the goblin huffed. "Does the Lord of Rainbows know the truth about his wife's location? He won't forgive you for keeping it from him."

"I don't care if he can or can't forgive me. If the Executioner wanted him to know what her plans were, she would have told him. She didn't."

"And your sister? Silaine is the new leader of the Ravens."

Mouth twisting, she contemplated how her sister would handle the return of the first Raven. "My sister is more than strong enough to stand up for the flock she has gathered. The Executioner is who she is, but the new god of death is loyal to Silaine. He wouldn't let Oblivion ruin everything. Besides, Aunty Liv always had a soft spot for her."

Vesta studied her, lips thinned. "Thorne and the Unseelie dullaghan would side with Silaine if a conflict emerged between the two Raven leaders. Family first. Always."

"Really? You know that for sure?"

"It's something we've discussed many times over drinks. We call it the 'what if' game. Pairs well with brandy and candied fruits. Thorne prefers Silaine to Oblivion because only one of them wields a sword with an unquenchable desire for blood and the power to control the dullaghan. And Silaine is family. If something happened to her sister, Eivor would salt the earth to help her. I suppose you're all the same. Allowed to fight with each other, but if anyone else comes for one of you, you're a united force to be reckoned with."

"Why did you betray Calista?" Astoria stepped away from the wall, flinching when the silk of her skirts settled into place. "Not the reasons you like to give, but the one you hold in your heart."

"You."

Stunned by Vesta's answer, she stared with her mouth open. Chuckling, the goblin closed the small distance between them, her blunt fingertips caressing the god's face before pushing her jaw up.

"I told you; you've never left my thoughts. Princess Astoria Havard, the secret obsession of a blood thirsty goblin general. Eivor is the queen I wish I had served all my life, but I also knew you would come home. Giving my loyalty to your sister ensured I walked a path of redemption, hoping to be worthy of the ferocious Battle Hawk who haunted my dreams for over a thousand years."

The intensity of the dark gaze pinning her in place had her desire returning. "Vesta."

She kept her fingertips on Astoria's chin. "Go free the Executioner and her flock. Let the dragons loose on Tir and remind them it was Calista who encouraged Annawyn. Tell Briallen Altira that it was her name that Tristan screamed while Calista tortured him. When he broke, it was their daughter's name he sobbed. Dragons are creatures of fire; they will answer the god of fire's call. Send them after the Blood Queen, and when she's gone, you can kill me like I killed you."

"You want me to return the favour?"

"Seems fair." Leaning in, Vesta brushed the tips of their noses together. "And then we can spend all the time we want locked away in a remote location, just the four of us. No doubt Charnel and I can think of new ways to make you beg. As for the Storm Queen? I'm looking forward to having her on her knees."

Unable to resist the smirk tugging at her lips, Astoria said, "She is good on her knees."

"And I imagine the pair of you will look gorgeous at my feet, trussed up and unable to stop Charnel and I from doing whatever we want to you. You will be mine, Battle Hawk. I knew it from the moment I saw you. Now, go do what you need to do while I have tea with the other two. We have things to discuss without you distracting us."

As much as she wanted to kiss the smug expression from Vesta's face, Astoria knew she was right. "Fine. But warn my sisters in case Tigernach senses his wife. Not to mention the dullaghan. They can't resist the Executioner if she calls."

Tapping her cheek, the general nodded. "I will. Go. Set the Blood Queen's downfall in motion."

THIRTY

The shadows whispered, telling Vesta everything she needed to know to locate the two gods. Shrouded in darkness that danced to her command so easily, the general slipped through the palace, ignoring the fragments of light and sound demanding her attention. Her nose was still filled with the scent of Astoria and the deliciously smoky flavour of her arousal. There were many things in her life she regretted, and a determined voice at the back of her mind assured her becoming the god of earth would not be one of them. Vesta did not know when she had accepted the possibility, but she knew she felt better for it.

Arriving in the elegant audience chamber several floors up, Vesta admired the wall of glass separating the room from a wide balcony overlooking the gardens. Her shadows crept across the floor, latching onto the two gods with no encouragement from her. Scowling at them, she wondered why she had ignored their behaviour. From the moment Dawn and Charnel arrived, the unruly shadows had sought them, leaving her overly aware of their presence. Not a moment had passed when she had not felt them, and Astoria, wherever they were within the palace grounds. If she had been listening to her power, Vesta knew she would have realised sooner that things were not as they appeared to be.

Darkness slipped from her like silk, and Charnel's knowing chuckle had the goblin squeezing her thighs together. Remaining in her spot in the corner furthest from the pair on a lounge, sunlight bathing them in a soft golden glow, Vesta remembered the first time she had seen the god of water. It had been during the creation of the goblins, and he had been there, watching from the shadows, with Alyah and Xhaiden beside him. While Annawyn had helped Calista rise, it had been his hand that had grasped hers, pulling her to her feet with the same secretive twist of his lips he wore while they regarded each other from opposite ends of the room.

"What did you say to her?"

His voice was a silken caress, and Vesta squared her shoulders, refusing to let them see how easily they affected her. "I asked her to kill Calista for me."

Startled, Dawn struggled up from her spot sprawled across his lap. "What?"

"She said no. We discussed our options, our mutual desire to see the Blood Queen pay for her crimes, and then I sent our hawk on her way." Clenching her fist, Vesta met Charnel's gaze and flattened it against her thigh. "By that, I mean I've sent her to free Oblivion and the dragon riders."

"It needed to be done," he replied, gesturing at the low table in front of the lounge. "Will you join us for afternoon tea?"

There was no hesitation in her steps, or in the shadows swirling around Water's feet, tendrils seeking to creep up his legs. Sweeping her gaze over the pot of tea and the cups arranged around it, Vesta wondered if he had known she would find her way to them or if the servants had provided extra cups just in case. Perching on the edge of the lounge opposite theirs, she reached for a cup, scoffing when a twitch of Charnel's lips accompanied the steam rising from the spout of the teapot.

"Handy trick. One never needs to fear their drink is the wrong temperature with you around. I hate tepid tea."

"You'll find I'm full of handy tricks. The thing about being overlooked as lesser is people never realise how powerful you really are. Isn't that right, General?" Slinging an arm over the back of the lounge, Charnel stroked Dawn's hair with the other, tucking a braid behind her pointed ear.

Lifting her chin, Vesta did her best to keep her focus on pouring tea into the cups and not following the steady motion of his fingers through the dark tresses of the woman curled against him. If someone had told her a year earlier that she would be driven to distraction by the thought of what the god of water could do with his hands, the goblin would have laughed in their face before eviscerating them. But there she was, pouring him a cup of tea while trying desperately to ignore the slither of ice through her veins, and the weight of the air in her lungs that threatened to vanish when she flicked a glance at Dawn.

"I should have seen it." Cocking his head, Water sighed. "For all my boasts of having an impeccable memory, I forgot. It seemed so inconsequential back then."

Frowning, Dawn glanced up to study the twitch of his cheek. "What do you mean?"

"The day they began creating the goblins, Alyah told me to go to her. I had already learnt to be frightened of what Shianeni, and the others might do, so I was trying my best to be invisible. But I did what I was told, and I helped Vesta stand. Annawyn was beside me, her hand grasping Calista's while mine was entwined in hers."

Lips twitching, Vesta arched a brow. "I'd forgotten as well. Until now. You think she knew, even then?"

"Of course I do. It wasn't your path, or Tir's she was looking at, but mine. You came into existence, and she saw a path for me that led to being whole. At least, that's what I believe happened."

"I am not a good person."

Settling back on the lounge, she cradled her cup and gazed at the swirl of steam rising from the deep brown liquid. The smell of it was soothing, hints of chamomile promising a blend to calm the storm in her mind. Vesta wished there was a way she could give them the contents of her thoughts, the dark caverns of her memories. It would have been easier than trying to work out how to put everything into words. For all her thousands of years of existence, she had never felt so off kilter as she did while facing them. They had history, they knew each other, and she was an outsider.

It surprised her when Dawn said, "I think the definition of a good person is more complicated than you are giving it the freedom to be. What is a good person? There are many who would argue I'm not one, and just as many who would disagree. My mother doesn't believe she's good most of the time, yet she would sooner die than put the people of Tir at risk. Even before she was reborn, she considered herself a monster for the choices she made and the power she possessed, but was she?"

Mulling over her words, Vesta felt the cool slither of her shadows curling around her in comfort. "You're right. Of all people, I should know better. I was the one who fought to keep Calista's twisted desires under control, who stood between her and committing genocide on many occasions. But for every good thing I tried to do, every life I fought to save, I probably destroyed twice as many."

"You are one goblin, Vesta. I am the god of water, Lord of Tides, master of merfolk and kelpies. Do you think I bat an eyelid when they consume the flesh of those who stumble into their grasp? Yet most people would not consider me to be an evil god." One of her shadows crept across the back of the lounge where Charnel sat, and he stroked it with a faint smile. "Do you know how many people I have sent to the depths of my oceans, their screams swallowed by my lack of mercy?"

Desire flooded her again when his bright blue eyes pinned her in place. Vesta felt every brush of his fingers over the shadow that was ignoring her command to leave him. Men had always been playthings to her, creatures to take pleasure from in between courting beautiful women. They had been trophies to boast about. A flash of Astoria's amused smile crossed her mind, reminding her of how the Battle Hawk had watched her flirt with Tigernach. He had been a trophy she had wanted to collect for a long time, but compared to the smirking god opposite her, the danann king was nothing.

She suspected Charnel knew the effect he had on her as she said, "There are many who would argue water is evil."

Removing herself from his grasp, Dawn snorted and leaned forward to pluck a cup of tea from the table. "I'm beginning to believe he planted the idea to become a pirate in my mind."

There was something decidedly smug about his smile, and Charnel flicked his gaze towards the windows. "Water hungers more than people realise. The difference between water and fire is patience. It's easier to fear the one that is going to consume you immediately, but patience is far more terrifying. They don't realise they're drowning until it's too late."

Meeting Dawn's gaze, Vesta knew the other woman had not considered the possibility of what he was saying. Reflecting on all the things she thought the god of earth might experience, the goblin wondered if her often insatiable needs were because of a forgotten power lurking far beneath the surface. She could imagine Earth being as deeply hungry as Water, their existence a constant craving to consume everything, to cover their world with themselves. People would fear Astoria, fear the power of Fire, while turning a blind eye to the dangers of the rest of them.

"If I am your fourth, I hope you will be patient with me," she murmured, sipping her tea, and relishing in the perfect warmth of it. "I have no desire to be reborn until we've dealt with Calista."

"Because you fear you won't get your revenge on her if you're a god?" Dawn grimaced.

"Indeed."

"Plenty of people wouldn't understand, but I do. If we cannot do anything to her because we're already gods, then hopefully you will be able to. Obviously, there is also the concern of how people will react to you becoming a god when it's time. You are an important member of the Unseelie Council."

Eyes widening, Vesta scolded herself for being so surprised at Dawn. Shame twisted through her, a reminder that, like so many others, she had viewed the young god of air as a brash child instead of an insightful woman who battled to free mortals and help countless people in need. There was no doubt in the goblin's mind that the Storm Queen was a complete brat when she wanted to be, but she was also a keenly intelligent woman who shared a lot of the same beliefs.

"Knowing Eivor as I do, I imagine she is currently working on a plan to deal with any upset my potential future might cause. I should probably step down from my position until we know for certain if I am Earth or even a different god. Perhaps I'm not your fourth, but some other. Either way, if it came out that I knowingly continued to serve on the council while suspecting I was a god, it would undermine everything. At least by stepping down, I should avoid doubt being cast on my previous actions. Sometimes, the only way to proceed is by being openly honest."

"You're right. The last thing we need to do is destabilise the Unseelie Council." Air nodded slowly, her furrowed brows suggesting she was contemplating their options. "If we need to remove ourselves from Diwan, we will. Whatever is necessary. I know we didn't get off to the best start, General Vesta, and I apologise for my part in it. Recent events have taught me things about myself."

Stiffening when the temperature dropped, Vesta shared a look with the two gods before turning to greet the new arrival. She wondered if Eivor had sent Thorne to find her so they could discuss council matters. When a dullaghan stepped free of the Veil in their headless form, Dawn shouted in alarm, a gust of wind swirling around them. It did nothing to stop the frozen fingers from brushing against Vesta's shoulder, only tearing them away after it was too late. A second dullaghan shot out of the Veil, tackling the first to the ground while Charnel and Dawn rushed to her side.

"Vesta?" Cupping her face, Dawn held her gaze as the ice spread through her, slowing her heart to a stop. "How do we stop this, Charnel?"

"You can't. No one can. She was gone the moment she was touched," Thorne said, standing behind them, her blue gaze locked on the dead woman who had done so much to help Diwan and who she had considered a friend.

A groan came from the floor, and Dawn snarled, rising to her feet while the other god cradled Vesta's corpse. Flinging her hand out, she drew the air from the lungs of the woman who had killed the general. Listening to her choke, it surprised her when Thorne snapped out a hand, smacking her arm down.

"You will not kill my sister, Storm Queen."

Focusing on the struggling dullaghan, Dawn realised who it was. "Fuck. Rain! Why?"

Ice-blue eyes that mirrored Thorne's locked on her, and the Seelie Master of the Hunt rasped for breath as the god of air released her power. "Time."

"I believe she's trying to say the god of time gave her Vesta's name and sent her to kill her." Extending a hand to her sister, Thorne shook her head. "Which answers the question of Vesta's future. Were you given a message to deliver to them?"

It was strange to stare at the two powerful dullaghan, her focus dancing from one to the other, desperately trying to pick out the slight differences between them. In the past, when she had encountered them together, they had always been different genders, never the same. They were almost identical. Shaking her head, Dawn sunk back down into the lounge to study the woman in Charnel's grasp.

"How long do we wait?" she whispered, meeting his patient gaze.

Stretching her fingers out, she brushed a stray coil of hair away from Vesta's face. The goblin wore form fitting leather armour, leaving little exposed, but at the base of her throat, Dawn was sure she could see the faintest glimmer of midnight ink against dark skin swirling down beneath the layers adorning her.

"Lord Time said you need to go to Fire as soon as Earth awakens." Rain leaned on her sister, gaze wary as she regarded the gods. "She's bringing down the barrier and needs all three of you to stop her from losing control. Which I'd really rather appreciate since my mate is with her."

"Cami is with Tory?" Swinging her focus back to the pair of dullaghan, Dawn frowned. "Why?"

"They tasked Camellia and Merle with delivering the means by which Fire could complete her task. Her blood sealed it, so to bring it down, she needs to shed blood again. Making a god bleed is no small ask."

A sudden gasp accompanied the flicker of the tattered bond that had fluttered in the void for her whole life. Power slammed into them, the suffocating whisper of the depths of the world. Shadows swarmed the room, blotting out the sunlight while Charnel murmured softly to Vesta. Eyes darting to the watching dullaghan, Dawn saw the darkness encroaching on them, her heart hammering in fear for their safety. The only thing she could think of to calm the fog was kissing the newly reborn god, her lips crashing into Vesta's hungrily. Hands grabbed her, claws digging into the back of her neck as Earth refused to let her go.

"You couldn't wait to kiss me, could you, little brat?" Vesta murmured against her lips. "But we need to go to Astoria right now. I'd rather she didn't destroy Tir before I got to see you on your knees at my feet."

Charnel rested a hand on their heads with his narrow gaze locked on Vesta. "How do you know?"

"Because the power warned me before it took over. Someone could have mentioned it's fucking painful to be reborn. Worst experience ever. As for you, dullaghan, I'll deal with you later."

THIRTY-ONE

There was something unsettling about leaving Charnel and Dawn behind again. At the back of her mind, Astoria felt their surprise, but her pleas for them to remain in Diwan kept them from following. She suspected they knew where she had gone. Or where she intended to be when she gathered her courage. Her power heard the call of the extensive wards surrounding the region where Oblivion and the dragons had taken refuge. Powerful people had built it before turning to her to provide the blood sealing it closed. Something she had gladly done, knowing one day she would release them back into Tir.

Perched on a rock, the god of fire watched the waves eating away at the stony beach. There was no glistening sand inviting her to laze in the sun, only the dull grey of rocks, and the distant whistle of the osprey who had made the stretch of coastline their home. Astoria wondered if the countless birds living in the area were aware of what lurked on the other side of the wall of magic. She knew they were too small to be preyed on by the bigger dragons, but hatchlings often used birds to practice their skills. Before they had sealed the occupants in, Oblivion had shown her all the preparations they had made. Farms had been established, and herds of beasts let loose in the mountains and forests to help feed the dragons.

She turned her gaze to the shimmering wall of power further down the beach. No ships dared sail near it, and Astoria studied the way it cut out into the ocean. It was easy to imagine the ruins of broken vessels washing up on the shore, dashed to pieces by unforgiving storms. The wall was invisible to most people, and she had heard the stories warning crews from sailing near the region. When she returned to the others, Astoria hoped she remembered to ask Charnel if he had purposefully made the waters surrounding the region treacherous as protection.

Aware the longer she delayed, the more impatient the other two would grow, Astoria slid from her spot on the weather worn rock. Part of the reason she was dragging her heels was the anticipation of Emlyn appearing to put an end to the plan. Every sound and movement had her twitching in dread, gaze searching for the god of time. Or any of the others. Death, War, Chaos, and Choice all knew about the sanctuary. They knew it was bound to her blood, and she had sworn an oath to release the people living in it. But as she picked her way across the shore towards the rolling green hills, Astoria faced a problem she did not know how to get around.

As a god, she was invulnerable. Lifting a hand to let the flames dance along her fingers, she wondered how she was going to shed the blood needed to unravel the layers upon layers of magic woven together to create the wall. With her memories fully restored, Astoria remembered how much blood she had given to the wards to bind them. There was no way the few drops she could manage before she healed would be enough. Which led her to her second problem. In her hurry to do as Vesta asked, the need for a sharp blade to cut herself with had not entered her thoughts. Smoothing her hands over the silk of her dress, Astoria reminded herself she was no longer a mortal bound to a power she could barely touch. She was a fully reborn god with the abilities that came with it.

"Ah, there you are!"

There was a familiarity to the voice calling her attention to a cluster of rocks surrounding a pair of taller stones. Settling her gaze on the smiling elf with long red hair, Astoria chuckled in relief. Beside her, the scowling man was far more familiar. He was leaning against one of the taller stones, a lute in his grasp, and hanging from his hip was the ominous sword that had always left her unsettled. Now she heard the faint whisper of its voice against her mind, though the words were unclear. The first time Astoria had seen the weapon, it had been bound to a different person, but she was thankful it was on this side of the shield instead of with its mate on the other. Poking her companion, the elf huffed when his scowl deepened.

"Don't be an arse, Merle. They sent us for a reason," she grumbled.

"Forgive me if I'm in no hurry to do this, Camellia." Merle continued to play the unfamiliar song without looking at the confused god. "I'm not ready to meet her yet."

The god of chaos's champion shook her head, sending Astoria a pleading look. "I'm sorry about him, Astoria. You're looking good. Congratulations, by the way. When I heard you'd been reborn as the god of fire, I was so thrilled for Dawn. Though I am curious about how you plan to continue sailing with her."

"I don't. Things are complicated." Cocking her head, Astoria realised she could hear more than one voice whispering against her mind, and her eyes narrowed in suspicion. "Captain, what are you hiding?"

He arched a brow, glancing at her. "Nothing that concerns you."

"Oh, I wouldn't be so sure about that. Considering I left Tigernach in Diwan, and he doesn't know what really happened to the Executioner, do you want to annoy me?"

"Tigs doesn't know?" He looked startled as he lowered his instrument. "I thought you would tell him once you were reborn and remembered everything."

"No. She didn't tell him back then, and it's not my responsibility to do what she should have done. I'm just here to start a war so I can kill a goblin general and claim my fourth mate."

Merle adjusted the strap securing the lute to him and slung the instrument across his back before picking up a wrapped object at his feet. "I've got a gift for Briallen Altira."

Clearing her throat, Camellia said, "Tessa and Aiden worked on them together. They didn't tell us why, just that they're an apology to her. Something about fixing the lingering link to Eclipse."

Clasping her hands in front of her, Astoria sighed. "Yes, that makes sense. It nearly killed Briallen when Gebael separated her from Eclipse. The only thing that saved her was Oblivion. I guess remaining with the Executioner was enough to keep her alive."

Unwrapping the objects, Merle revealed a pair of sai that reminded Astoria of the two swords. There was something about them that drew her power in, and her fingers twitched with the need to snatch them from the cloth. Lifting her gaze to the shimmering wall of magic, it reminded the god of what Vesta had said. Dragons were creatures of fire. A gleeful voice at the back of her mind cooed that by all rights, dragon riders were hers. Dawn often joked all those with wings served her despite previous loyalties, and the water bound belonged to Charnel. Her focus returned to the sai, settling on the clear stones set into the hilts. She knew black gems adorned the two swords.

"Tessa said we need to stab those through your hands and into the shield." Merle looked troubled as he glanced away. "I know you're a god, but it makes me uncomfortable."

Astoria cringed in agreement, no longer eager to pick up the weapons. "When they bound the wall to my blood, I had to give up a lot. My mother kept me from dying. I was wondering how I would shed enough to unravel the wards. Those pokey sticks are my answer."

"Pokey sticks?" Camellia snickered.

"Jabby jabs? Oversized toothpicks?"

Groaning, Merle shook his head. "Can we just get on with it?"

She understood his desire to move matters along. There was only so much procrastination could do for her before it became a simple choice. Free them or not. For a moment, she felt tempted to leave them be, but Astoria was unsure she could make peace with herself if she did. Breaking oaths was not something that came naturally to her. Looking back at the ocean, she remembered the gleam of desperation in Vesta's eyes. If they wanted to know the truth about what the general might become, she needed to set the Executioner free. Queen Calista had to die, and the goblins needed to be freed from her cruel chains.

"There's no point putting this off," she murmured, and drew her power around her.

Not waiting to see what they would do, Astoria kept her shoulders squared as she marched towards the wall of magic. It called to her, and she knew then that fragments of the power Xhaiden had bound to her had become part of the shield. Closing her eyes as she moved, the god summoned her wings, letting the flames slither over her skin to form the translucent feathers she curled forward to block out distractions. The anxious side of her wanted to stop and look at every little thing. Hearing Camellia's shocked gasp, Astoria remembered few people had seen her wings, let alone the flaming hawk her other form had become.

"Impressive."

His voice came from the side, and she reluctantly stretched her wings back so she could see the human captain Death had refused to be parted from. "I thought it best to put on a good show. We don't know how the Executioner will react when she meets you. Arranged marriages don't always end well."

"She's not my wife," Merle growled.

"How much time have you spent arguing with Eclipse about that? Because remember, I was there when Gebael bound that sword to Briallen Altira. Do you know what Oblivion called her? Wife. Some ties are inescapable."

There was a resigned determination in his eyes when he met her concerned stare. "Aiden is going to offer her the chance to put the sword down. Freedom from being the Executioner."

"You mean he's going to offer her the chance to die? Because I was also there when Gebael took Eclipse away from Briallen. It nearly killed her. Oblivion has never lived without her sword. They're one and the same. If she accepts the offer, it will kill Tigernach. The pompous feather duster loves her more than life."

"We know. Celi is prepared to let Tigs go if that is what he wants."

Laughing, Astoria shook her head and waved a hand dripping with flames at him. "But you're not."

"Don't be silly. Of course I am. There is nothing between Tigs and I."

"Now, I'm still learning what I can do, but I can see when you think about the Lord of Rainbows. It's rather peculiar. I wasn't paying attention earlier, but passion burns brightly. You're in love with him, and no matter how much you deny it, I know the truth."

Camellia skipped to the other side of her, and the knowing smirk she sent Merle's way told Astoria the elf had her suspicions. "Some emotions are a fire. Love. Passion. Hatred. They burn in us, threatening to consume all others. And some of us have known for years that Tigernach is obsessed with you. Rain complains about it all the time, and Slade just laughs."

"I don't appreciate you gossiping about me with your mates." Merle shot an annoyed look at her. "Surely you have better things to do. Like keeping your charges out of trouble."

"Right. Because it's so easy to keep three headstrong gods out of trouble. And have you met the dullaghan? Honestly, no one is as gossipy as them."

The wall was close enough to send shivers down her spine, and Astoria flared her wings outwards, cutting them in front of the two champions. Reaching out, she trailed her fingertips over the magic before making a fist to pound against it. Her companions gasped when flames rippled outwards, slowly spreading over the shield until it became a shimmering beacon. Anyone close enough to the region to see it would spread the story of the day the sky turned into a blanket of fire. More than that, it was a signal to the people contained within that their freedom was coming. Swiping her hand through the flames, Astoria cleared a doorway to allow them to see the land beyond so they could watch for the dragons.

Glancing at Merle as he unwrapped the two sai, Astoria pressed her lips together. She did not know how she felt about the weapons or knowing Death and Chaos had worked their gifts to create more blades like Eclipse and Oblivion. There was no need for weapons capable of killing immortals anymore. Not when the new gods had made the First People mortal. A timid whisper in a dark corner of her thoughts reminded her there were things to fear beyond the stars. The pull she felt for the sai was a test and an offering. Death was giving her the chance to claim a champion to kill Calista for her without telling the others.

"Are dragons as terrifying as they sound?" Merle asked, passing a sai to Camellia.

Her gaze found the dark shapes in the distance that her companions could not spot. "They are magnificent. Don't worry, I won't let them eat you when they get here."

No one needed to tell her what came next. Aware Charnel and Dawn could sense her anxiousness, Fire assured them across the bonds that she was fine. Sucking in a deep breath, Astoria pressed her hands to the wall of churning magic, sinking her power into it until she connected with the threads she had left behind. Merle's touch to her arm had her glancing at him, the concern in his dark gaze surprising her. On the other side, Camellia was a cold pillar of determination as she shrouded herself in the safety of the battle-hardened commander she had once been. As a soldier, Astoria appreciated the elf feeling a need to wear that guise.

"I really don't want to do this."

The women stared at Merle with matching unimpressed expressions, and his shoulders slumped. One hand rested on the hilt of his sword as though he could draw comfort from the weapon, while the other grasped the sai. Astoria wanted to say something to assure him it would be fine; except she did not know what would happen when the two blades were driven through her hands into the shield that kept them from the land beyond. Nor did she know if it would hurt when it happened.

"Don't think, just do it, Captain," Camellia said, her dispassionate tone reminding Astoria of her father.

"Easy for you to say. Not all of us made committing war crimes into a hobby."

Shaking her head, Astoria did not banish the images of what she had done over the years. "If it makes it easier, think about all the times you've wanted to stab the other gods. This is your chance to vent the frustration I know you feel about their antics."

He grunted, mouth twisting as he aligned the tip of the sai with her hand on the wall. "You're right. I have wanted to stab them so many times. Sometimes they're so thick, it drives me mad."

Pain tore through her the moment the blade pierced her body. It doubled when Camellia drove the second one through her other hand, and Astoria bit her lip in the hope she could stop herself from screaming. The two champions stumbled back, but the god did not hear what they said. Pushing through the pain, she relaxed her grasp on her power, letting it wash through the wall. Flames clawed at the sai pinning her in place, but echoes of Death and Chaos seemed to draw them into the weapons. Her blood seeped into the power, calling to what had been woven into it more than a thousand years earlier.

Astoria knew she needed to focus on tearing it down and sunk her flames into the fabric of the shield.

It filled her mind, each delicate weave tasting of the person who had poured their gifts into securing a place where they could find safety until the mad god was gone. She recognised the touch of her mother's power, and the threads of other Ravens who had drifted through her early life as doting aunts and uncles. The blades piercing her hands became anchors, providing Astoria with a focus to draw the power into. As she worked, she heard the whispers of the sai grow louder while the flames took hold inside the stones, burning with an almost blinding brightness. What did not find a home in the weapons flowed into the god until lines of fire spread across the ground, swirling around her like a storm.

She felt the dragons approaching. The burn of their fire waiting to be released called to her, and her power screamed in answer. But in the distant recess of her mind, Astoria knew something else had changed. There was a tug she had not felt before that had nothing to do with the collapsing wall of wards that left her overfilled with power. Soothing hands held her up, siphoning what they could to keep her from burning the world. When the shield fell, Astoria went with it, her knees barely noticing the welcome of the ground while someone gently pulled the sai from her hands. Lips caressed her cheeks; soft murmurs promised she was not alone. Leaning into their embrace, she slowly opened her eyes, flinching at the light.

"Dawn?" she rasped, staring at the woman cradling her bloodied hands. "Wait..."

Claws pricked her side, Vesta's amused chuckle startling her. "Time sent a dullaghan to kill me. Apparently, my presence was required to stop you from destroying Tir."

Recalling the soothing power that had drawn the flames from her, Astoria understood it had been Earth and Water working together. Dawn's power would have made things worse, feeding the inferno until it consumed everything. The arms keeping her upright tightened, Charnel's forehead resting against the side of her head. She appreciated the ice flowing through her veins as it helped her thoughts and power settle into clarity. In the distance, the dragons grew closer, their forms a dark cloud against the blue sky.

"Merle and Camellia?"

"We're fine," Merle replied, his voice heavy with nervous anticipation. "It comes in handy travelling with a skilled shield mage blessed by Chaos. Camellia protected us."

Inhaling deeply, Astoria stretched her wings out and extracted herself from Charnel and Vesta's hold. Ignoring their protests, she plucked her hands from Dawn and grabbed the pair of sai from the ground where the god of air had tossed them. They thrummed in her grasp, voices singing sweet songs only she could hear. Rising to her feet, Fire turned her gaze to the sky, seeking the pale grey dragon she had flown on so long ago. No two dragons were the same, and among the swarm flew birds of darkness, dragging memories of her mother from where she kept them buried. The Ravens were in her blood, their power carrying a promise of withered landscapes ripe to feed an inferno.

A roar ripped through the air like thunder, and the grey form she was waiting for slammed into the ground a short distance away. Two women climbed down from the mighty creature, and they heard Merle's groan. Astoria suspected he was struggling with the demands of the sword he was bound to, as well as the inevitable pull he felt for the ancient duine striding towards them. She was as striking as the god remembered, her bone white hair fluttering in the breeze while ice-blue eyes remained locked on the nervous man.

At her side, Briallen Altira swept her gaze over the four gods, and the two champions, before settling on Astoria with a flicker of recognition and the lifting of her chin. Merle stepped forward to greet Oblivion, his hand on Eclipse's hilt, but whatever he planned to say was silenced when she grabbed his shirt, pulling him in so she could kiss him. Exchanging looks, the four gods did not know what to do, and Camellia wrapped herself in a shield in anticipation of something going wrong, a hand on her axe.

Rolling her eyes, Briallen came to a halt in front of Astoria, eyes dropping to the sai in her hands. The whispers cooed in delight, knowing she was the one for them. Holding them out, Fire nodded, not letting go when the dragon rider placed her hands on them. Her power wrapped around the other woman, finding the fragile remnants of the bond forged between Briallen and Eclipse by the previous god of death. It was easy to weave them into something new, claiming the husk maker as her champion.

"Are they bound to the others?" Briallen whispered, holding Astoria's gaze.

"No. They're... we're something new. I'm sorry I took so long to fulfil my oath."

There was relief in the dragon rider's eyes as she glanced at Oblivion. "Thank fuck, I'm free of her. Now, where's my husband? Tristan vanished along with the other First People among us, but unlike them, he did not come back. My daughter is missing her father."

Clearing her throat, Vesta drew Briallen's attention to her. "About that. We don't know where he is. While we were imprisoned, he somehow ended up in his grandmother's hands but vanished when we were freed. No one has seen him since. If Calista still has him, she's keeping it secret."

Withdrawing her hands and the sai from Astoria's grasp, Briallen squared her shoulders. "Well then, it's about time the Unseelie felt the wrath of the dragon riders. I will get Tristan back, and if I must burn down the Spire, I will. Are you going to help me, Princess Astoria?"

"Yes," she replied without hesitation, and Charnel's sigh made her glance at him. "But first, we need to talk. Tir has changed a great deal. Annawyn is gone. As is Gebael, Neriwyn, Shianeni, Xhaiden, Alyah, and Raghnall. There are more gods, and the Unseelie is no longer what it was."

"Tonight is a night of celebration. We will feast, and you can share everything."

Stretching her head high, the grey dragon roared before releasing a plume of fire. The other dragons responded in the same manner, and Astoria shuddered at the thrill it sent through her power. She wanted to roar with them, and the flames danced across her skin, her wings burning brighter at the prospect.

"I'm looking forward to it."

THIRTY-TWO

Slipping away from the festivities, Astoria found her way to where the pair of dragons pretended to slumber. In the background, she heard the music and laughter, the joy of freedom carrying through everything they did. She did not blame them for celebrating, but she hoped it was not premature. Tir had changed so much since the Fog ended. War had forced the gods to change, and with them, the nature of Tir had shifted. It was something she felt in the fabric of her being, the thrum of existence burning at her core.

The grey and red dragons lifted their heads at her approach, calculating gazes tracking her progress towards them. Surrounded by the creatures, Astoria had soon learnt she could hear them speaking to each other. She knew dragons and their bound riders could communicate with each other, but with her rebirth, she had gained them as hers. Not just her either, if Dawn's wide-eyed wonder was anything to go by. If the god of air was bound to them as well, it made sense, but Fire could not help hoping it was not the case. When the grey dragon lowered her head towards her, the god realised she wanted them for herself.

"We feared you would never return."

Closing her eyes as she ran her hand over the scaly snout bigger than her, Astoria smiled. *"I'm sorry it took me so long to come for you, Igraine. They took my memories."*

Chuckling, the dragon nudged her as gently as she could. *"No doubt with good reason, Battle Hawk. How fares your mother? I see she did not come with you to greet her kin."*

"My mother is dead. She and my father fell when Annawyn's servant, Oisin, invaded Diwan. I fled, as did my youngest sister, leaving our eldest behind to deal with him. It is a shame I will always live with."

Snorting, the red dragon blew warm air over her. *"Sometimes running is the right thing to do, Lady Fire."*

She leaned against Igraine, enjoying the thrum of power passing between them as she stared at the stars. The pair of dragons sensed her need, and the red brought her head in, caging the god where she stood. With a hand pressed to the second beast, Astoria felt a sense of peace she barely recognised. It made her question if her constant need to move had been her instincts telling her something was incomplete. There was no longer a desperate urge to fly wherever the currents took her, only a deep-seated sense of belonging. In the corner of her mind connected to the dragon's, she drew pleasure from the murmur of their voices. Somewhere, a pair of dragons cooed to their hatchling, while elsewhere, several argued over the best approach to scout the unfamiliar region now open to them.

"I never realised how noisy you are," she said, rubbing a scar on the red dragon's face.

"Don't start nagging, Ysgarlad. She's new to hearing us. Even our riders don't realise how much we speak." Igraine snapped her jaw, and Astoria felt a thrill at the sight of the dangerous teeth. *"Can you still shift forms? We've never encountered new gods."*

Exhaling, Astoria wondered if anyone would complain if she shifted and went for a flight with the dragons. The longer she considered it, the more she wanted to follow through with the idea. To avoid anyone accidentally burning themselves, she had vanished her wings when she realised how fascinated people were by the feathers made from fire. It had not helped that every chance she got, Vesta had run her fingers through them, keeping her on edge with a desperate need to touch the newest god. Dawn had taught her how sensitive wings could be, but she had not tested her own to see if they were the same.

"You need to work on your mental shields. I suppose you're not used to keeping dragons out. We're very nosy, and it's strange for us to feel this connection to a god," Igraine said, her chuckle scratching at Astoria's mind in a way that reminded her of Eivor.

"Oh. I'm sorry."

Ysgarlad snorted, a puff of steam escaping between her lips. *"I'm disappoint-ed I cannot eat the goblin general. We know her crimes. That she is now a god is baffling."*

It was not her place to defend Vesta's past when the woman would be the first to admit to what she had done. Nor had they been given the time alone they needed to discuss everything, so Astoria was clueless as to what had occurred between the older woman and the previous god of chaos. All she needed to know for the moment was the threat she posed to Tir was something her mates could mitigate. They had stopped her from doing something terrible when the wall unravelled. At least they understood why it had been bound to her blood. No mortal could have survived. There was simply too much magic.

"I don't know why Xhaiden and Alyah chose her, but she is not the same woman you know of. She's changed. We all have. And now everything will change again. Those of us born before the Fog have long thought the dragons gone forever, and mortals don't even know you exist. I fear there will be war because of it. The only immortals are the gods and their champions. Even the Unseelie Council stands for something different. They fight for free will and equal rights, defend against slavery, and they refuse to let the gods meddle in mortal affairs. Which is also about to go through upheaval because my sister, Eivor, is the Unseelie Queen, and I am the god of fire."

Shifting her head, Igraine forced the god to stop leaning on her. *"Family is only family when it wants to be. God or not, if you and your sister love each other, then you will find what works."*

Nose flaring, Astoria sensed the approach of the god she both longed for and feared. Shadows clung to Vesta, trailing from her to seep into the ground like tree roots. Raising their heads, the two dragons huffed at her in distrust, the rumble of their emotions making Fire flinch. They were so loud, reminding her of what Igraine had said. She needed to practice shutting them out, for her sake and theirs. In the pale moonlight, Vesta knelt, head bowed respectfully to the towering creatures guarding her mate.

"I know it's too little, too late, but I am sorry for what we did to your kind," she said, and across the bond, Astoria felt how deep her sorrow ran. "We were so entrenched in Annawyn's control we forgot to listen to ourselves when we knew what we were doing was wrong. Nothing can make up for that, but we'll do our best to try. Whatever you need to rebuild a home for your kind, we will help."

Snaking her head forward, Ysgarlad growled, baring her teeth. "*I should eat you.*"

Vesta's eyebrows rose in surprise. "I can hear you!"

"*Yes, you are a god. We can speak to you, but only our Fire can hear all of us,*" Igraine replied, lowering her pale grey head to nudge Astoria forward. "*There are some nice caves in the cliff. Too small for dragons, but perfect for a pair of gods who need privacy.*"

"Is she telling us to get a room?"

Rolling her eyes, Astoria crossed her arms, and did not move closer to the kneeling woman. "Yes."

"*You're the one who kept thinking about how it felt when she touched your wings.*" Chortling, the grey dragon nudged her again, steam billowing around the god in encouragement.

"Really?" Earth drawled, rising to her feet as the shadows crept towards Fire. "How much of her thoughts are you privy to, Mighty Ones? Did she have any specific desires?"

Snapping her teeth, Ysgarlad shuffled back. "*She will work on keeping us out.*"

"*Yes, she will. For all our sanity.*" Eyeing them knowingly, Igraine stretched her wings. "*And better to discover now if her desires have any influence over us. Here it is safe. We have our dens.*"

Eyes widening, Astoria realised what the dragon was suggesting. "Well, fuck. I didn't think of that."

Shadows curled around her legs, clinging tighter with each step Vesta took. The dragons retreated slightly to give them the illusion of privacy, but she felt their encouragement in her mind. Her flames swirled down to meet the creeping cold, the colours melting into the darkness that did not seem as black as it had earlier in the day when the woman in control of them had been mortal. There was an earthy tone to them, like the darkest soil waiting to swallow her whole. Vesta cupped her face tenderly, keeping her claws retracted as she brushed her thumb over Fire's lips.

"They can't hear us now," she whispered across the bond, the tentativeness of the attempt making Astoria smile. *"Can you bring yourself to trust me, Battle Hawk?"*

The matter of trust seemed so strange when the familiar agony of being in contact with one of her mates was twisting through her body. She wondered what it would feel like when the four of them finally curled up together, the connection as close as it could be without them shedding their physical forms to return to the stars. Vesta slid a hand into her hair, and the prick of claws told Astoria the gentleness was fading. When her head was tugged back, she groaned in delight as the action had her squirming.

"You're mine, and no one is going to stop me from doing exactly what I want to you."

Cool lips claimed hers, and for a moment, Astoria thought the other woman was trying to draw the heat from her through their mouths. A hand settled on her arse, sharp claws digging in as Vesta pulled her tightly against her body. She surrendered willingly, letting her dictate how long the kiss lasted. The shadows slithered up her legs, twisting around them like cold silken cords. The similarity to Charnel's ropes of water had her imagining how it would feel when they worked together. Breathing heavily when Vesta pulled back, Fire realised they were no longer in the grassy courtyard where they had been talking to the dragons. Instead, the dark walls of a cave surrounded them.

"Tell me what to expect," Earth murmured, running her hands over the neckline of the silk dress that hid the body of her mate from her. "I've been around long enough to know it will be different. Does it ever go away? This agony we feel when we touch. Or will we simply learn to enjoy it?"

As Vesta slid the dress from her shoulders, Astoria felt the shadows creep around her waist. "I haven't been a god long enough to know if it gets less. But I don't think it goes away. Not completely, and only when we're all together. It's part of being torn apart, just like the fracture marks on our skin."

Her sharp inhale was loud in the darkness. "I forgot about the marks."

Eager to see what Earth looked like, Fire summoned orbs of fire to cling to the roof of the cave. She gasped in surprise when the light caused parts of it to glisten. There was no entrance framing a starlit sky, but the dragons and the other two gods felt close enough to assure her they were still in the same area. Fascinated by the cave, Astoria cast more orbs around it, quickly realising there was a reason Earth had chosen it. Distracted by the beauty of the crystal veins running through the stone, she did not notice the other god stepping back to strip away her clothes.

"This might not be a comfortable bed in which we can take our time, but all things considered…"

Returning her focus to Vesta, Astoria admired her standing naked in the flickering light. "It's perfect. I can't think of a better or safer place. I can't hurt anyone if I lose control."

"Except the worms," she replied, chuckling nervously.

"It won't last long the first time. Well, no, that's misleading. Dragging it out is possible. The bond takes over, robs us of that moment, and we can't stop it."

"But it's just the once?"

"Yes."

Cocking her head, Vesta flicked her fingers at Astoria. The shadows swarmed upwards, tugging at the silk dress clinging to her until it slid to the ground to pool around her feet. She felt the weight of her mate's gaze. It seemed strange to feel self-conscious, but the possessive gleam that appeared in Vesta's eyes, and the smug twist of her lips, suggested there was nothing to fear. Watching her prowl closer, Astoria examined the dark swirls adorning the taller woman, trying to memorise how they looked before they changed.

There was a strange sound. A grinding of rock against rock close behind her that sent Fire jolting forward in alarm. Catching her before she tripped on the dress tangled around her feet, Vesta chuckled and dipped her head to graze her teeth along the exposed side of Astoria's neck. When the sound stopped, she carefully walked Fire backwards until she had her pressed against the smooth quartz pillar in the middle of the cave. The pale crystal glittered in the firelight, its depths becoming oddly murky, shadows creeping over the surface in anticipation of what Vesta had planned. Her hands settled on Astoria's wrists, slowly lifting her arms above her head.

"I want you to trust me, my feral Battle Hawk."

Shadows smothered her hands, twisting down her arms until they reached her elbows, and she let them pin her in place. "Do I wear an invisible sign begging the three of you to tie me up?"

Trailing a claw down each of Fire's arms, Vesta smirked. "One only we can read. But tell me to stop, and I will. Unlike them, I don't have years of experience learning what works for you. I don't know what you like, and you don't know what I like. If you say no, I'll listen."

"And here I thought you were the general, and I the good little soldier."

"Not today. When I was in the space between dying and becoming this, the power told me Fire is the burning heart of our existence. I'm glad the first time is fast, because I want to feel your heart beating in time with Tir. There is molten stone churning in the centre of our world, the dance of our being waiting to erupt if given the chance. But as wonderful as the dance is, Earth must always keep Fire contained." Leaning their foreheads together, Vesta sighed. "In a way, I will always be your general, and you, my obedient little soldier, who knows that she follows orders for the good of everyone else."

She did not know how she felt about what the other god had said, but a flicker of something in the darkness of her mind recognised it as truth. Fire consumed; it destroyed despite the good it could provide. At the core of her existence was destruction. Yet with each touch, Vesta calmed the inferno simmering within her, and Astoria did not want her to stop. Every brush of her lips, and the scratch of her claws, drew the flames deeper, shifting it into the ache of desire.

Fingers slid between her folds; claws fully retracted as they sought her clit at the same time Vesta kissed her hungrily. The merciless nip of sharp teeth against her bottom lip made her whimper as pleasure jolted through her, and Astoria rocked her hips, seeking more. A soft growl was all the warning she had before the other woman speared two fingers into her vagina, curling them against the sensitive spot inside her. The prick of claws grazing over her walls as Vesta stroked made her clench. If she had been mortal, Astoria doubted she would have enjoyed the danger of exposed claws being used inside her, but as a god, it was nothing but thrilling pleasure.

"Not yet," Vesta murmured, withdrawing her hand despite her mate's whine of frustration.

Sliding her hands down Astoria's legs, she used the shadows to help lift them around her waist, settling between them comfortably. Flicking her gaze up to where her power kept the other woman secured, Vesta shifted a hand around to support her arse, and hoped her control did not falter. She wanted to be confident it remained as good as it had been before she became a god, but there was no knowing until she tested it. Her other hand grasped Fire's hip, claws piercing her skin. The smell of Astoria's blood and arousal filled Earth's nose, and she leaned in to nuzzle the crook of her neck.

"I'm going to bite you, Tory, and I'm not going to apologise for it."

The press of teeth into her skin drew a pleading moan from Astoria's lips. Vesta adjusted their position so she could grind their cunts together. Feeling the tattered threads of their bond stretching between them, Fire twisted her hips, attempting to find the angle that would satisfy the power. A sharp pain cut through the pleasure and agony, feeding it as Earth bit her. It faded into something exquisite when she felt the swirl of a tongue, and the strange tug of the bite being sucked on while the teeth remained buried in her seemed to have a direct connection to the coil of pleasure waiting to overflow.

Drawing tight, the bond snapped into place, and Astoria was sure she was falling through the ground. Earth seemed to surround her completely, smothering her flames as though to make them a part of it. But unlike the water that had tried to drown her, she found herself cradled in a bed of molten embers, burning hotter than anything she had felt before. Vesta's kisses were there, a soothing reminder the thrum of the world beneath their feet belonged to another god. She was not falling; she remained pinned between a pillar of crystal and the firm muscles of a warrior who knew how to fight back the moment of panic. It was easy to listen to the steady thud of Earth's heart to bring her own in line.

"There now, beautiful." Rubbing her nose against Astoria's cheek, Vesta groaned. "I'm glad that was a once off. Well, once between each of us. I've still got the other two to go."

Chuckling hoarsely, she rolled her gaze up, realising the cave was glowing brighter. "Is it you or me doing that? Because I swear those crystals are shining with their own light."

"A bit of both. I think I channelled your flames into them."

"Useful skill. I wonder how long they'll stay like that."

Vesta carefully released the shadows, cradling Astoria to her as she sank to the ground. "You tasted even better than I imagined, Battle Hawk, and you definitely enjoyed it."

Resting her ear against the older woman's chest, Fire snorted. "I think it had a lot to do with who was biting me. Though I don't recommend trying to do it to Dawn."

"She'll come around once she sees how much you like it."

THIRTY-THREE

Vesta's claws running through her hair while she curled up in her lap filled Astoria with peace. She was perfectly content to remain where she was, the glow of the crystals surrounding them. Trailing her fingers over the swirl of lines decorating the other god's leg, she hoped their absent mates would be understanding. It made sense for each of them to slip away and complete the bonds alone rather than as a group. That way, each pair could have a moment of intimacy. But logic did not stop the uncomfortable churn of guilt over the fact they had not taken the time to discuss it.

"Do you think all the gods feel this insatiable need?" Vesta murmured, the tip of a claw brushing over a sensitive spot on Fire's ear. "I should feel satisfied, but all I want is to fuck you again."

Chuckling softly, she recalled her observations of Dawn's parents and the other bonded gods she knew. "I've had limited exposure to them, but yes, I do. From what I've seen, they can't keep their hands off each other. It's the entity the power was before it split. No matter what physical form it possesses, it will always want to return to being whole. Contact between us helps soothe it."

They felt his presence before he said, "It's why it hurts. Think of the contact like the edges of a wound healing. Except, this wound is in the very fabric of existence. We're all spun out of it."

Glancing up at Vesta, Astoria studied her pensive expression. Their watery counterpart had come alone, leaving the god of air back on the surface. Dawn was close and staring at the cave ceiling with its veins of glowing crystal, Fire sensed the younger woman's impatience to join them. Not bothering to sit up, she was thankful when Earth continued to run her claws through the tangle of her hair. It kept her calm, allowing her to think clearly, and she knew the flicker of flames across her skin had faded into nothing more than a sheen of warm orange, like embers in a banked fire.

"You picked a beautiful place, Vesta."

She hummed in agreement. "It was the dragon's suggestion. Well, they told us about the caves, and I found this spot. I won't apologise."

"Nor would I expect you to. I claimed our fiery wife on the shore of an ocean volcano, and our ever-impatient Tempest on the side of a mountain while a waterfall shielded us from sight. This is perfect."

Arching a brow, Astoria wondered why Dawn had not told her about Charnel's choice of location. "Are you going to make it a competition to find the most extreme locations to fuck Dawn and I?"

Claws dug into her scalp, tugging her head back so Vesta could smirk down at her. "Awfully tempting. Though, I do like the sound of a volcano. I saw one erupt once, and I'm in the unique position to say one in the middle of the ocean is the perfect place for us."

Watching Charnel wander around the cave, his hands stroking the glowing veins of crystal, Fire wondered if the woman holding her was feeling every touch. The gleam of Vesta's bared teeth suggested she knew what the other god was doing. Shadows crept across the walls to latch onto his hands, and Astoria did not miss the sharp hiss of Earth's breath when he twisted them in his grasp, drawing the writhing mass of darkness to his face. Whatever he whispered to them had the newest god stiffening in surprise. Her eyelashes fluttered, but nothing could hide the flood of desire across the bond.

"You need to teach me that trick, Nel," Astoria said, a hint of laughter in her tone to match her smirk.

"No, I don't think so. Earth and water share the dark places. Even in here, there is more water than there is fire, entwined within the rock and dirt. Air lingers where it can, simply doing nothing more than being present. She'll learn that skill as she gets older. Fire is the one that cannot truly sit still. You'll never possess the same patience as the rest of us, and the need to keep moving will never change."

"Why does that feel like an insult?"

He cocked his head, gazing at her while Vesta's hand roamed across her body. "It's only an insult if you let it be. We cannot change the nature of what we are. You told me you've always felt the need to move. You fly, you fight, you run. Remaining always in motion."

Something colder than the shadows curled around her ankles, but she could not focus on it. Vesta pinched her right nipple between two claws, the sharp tips almost breaking the skin. Hands clasped behind his back, Charnel ambled closer to gaze down at them, one side of his mouth curled in a knowing smirk. His eyes trailed over the length of her, taking in the completed mosaic of lines etched into her skin, before shifting his focus to Vesta. The slither of thin cords of water continued up her legs, and Astoria whimpered when they pooled at the back of her knees.

"She's very sensitive there," Charnel said, meeting Vesta's gaze. "Also, the insides of her elbows to wrists. Now, in the brief time I've spent with Dawn in this manner, I've learnt she's sensitive everywhere. Tory likes to be treated roughly, but our Tempest responds better to soft touches. You can drive her to the edge by simply stroking her skin."

Grinning, the general twisted the nipple pinched between her claws. "Oh, I've noticed this feral creature likes it rough. The smell of her arousal the first time I had her pinned against a wall to introduce myself was all the confirmation I needed."

Aware of the cords of water slipping from her, Astoria realised the point of Charnel's words was not to discuss her and Dawn, but to assess the woman beneath her. She wanted to scramble out of the way, but the claws digging into her scalp and nipple kept her in place. From her spot plastered against Vesta, she could see the water snake onto her legs, and the eager surge of shadows rushing to stop it. Fascinated by how they merged, she wished she had taken the time to figure out how to do it with her flames. The slight shift of Vesta's legs drew her attention back to the other two, suddenly aware Charnel stood beside them, his fingers lifting Earth's chin.

"I think I understand why they chose you, Vesta. We must be as strong as each other while recognising the need for give and take to maintain the balance. Tell me what you need."

She frowned, eyes darting to either side. "No one has ever asked me."

"They created you to be in a position of power, standing strong at the side of your queen in servitude to the gods. So, you did, and it became how you approached relationships. Strong and in command. If you want Tory to leave us alone, she'll go. Or if you want Dawn to join us in worshipping you, she'll be here in a heartbeat. Just say the word, and we will obey."

"Isn't it better for the first time to be a private moment?" Astoria muttered, her confusion churning as though a cyclone held her caught in its grasp. "The bond completing is—"

"Whatever we want it to be. Vesta wanted you alone because you're the one who has haunted her all these years. Understandably. I endured the same until Dawn was born. But Earth, Air, and Water are different. Ours is something more constant. We flow together."

Drawing her bottom lip through her teeth, Vesta looked befuddled. It seemed odd for her to be confused when Astoria was convinced the woman was smarter than all of them. She was a tactician with countless victories under her belt, and she had endured War's arenas, earning the respect of her fellow warriors. But the longer she sat in silence, the more concerned Fire grew about what was going on in Earth's thoughts.

"The first time sweeps control away from us. It's intense with two, but I can't help wondering what it's like with three." Her lips parted in wicked delight, tongue darting out to lick them. "So many possibilities to explore. For now, let's deal with the bonds so we can enjoy ourselves."

Shaking her head, Astoria could not help feeling like she was not seeing the first time as something special. "You shouldn't rush it. I know it happens fast, but it's still important."

Wrapping the thick brown hair around her fingers, Vesta yanked her head back. "Yes, it is. And I intend to share it with Dawn and Charnel. You can join us, or not."

The thought of being left out while the other three completed their bond stung. It had hurt when Dawn and Charnel had joined before she had gotten to see the pirate captain, and she wondered if it was fair to be upset. An unfamiliar voice suggested all she needed to do was sit quietly and be there. Her curiosity over what it looked like from the outside when the bonds between gods settled into place had her gaze darting between her mates.

"I'll stay," she whispered, remembering the physical pain that had swept through her when Air and Water had joined. "Whatever you want me to do, I'll do it."

A breeze swept through the cave, carrying a hint of salt with it. She felt the cool touch of it across her skin, but her attention remained on Vesta and Charnel's faces above her. Their eyes were locked in a silent conversation, and Dawn's arrival did not break their concentration. Nor did the impatient scuff of the young god's boot, and the clearing of her throat intended to draw their focus to her. Giving her what she wanted, Astoria shifted her stare to the woman standing a short distance away, nervously twisting her hands together. It was strange to see the jovial captain so unsettled, but part of her understood.

"Stars, Tory," Dawn murmured, taking a step closer to them. "Everything I've imagined about those marks over the years doesn't compare to the beauty of you."

It felt like her cheeks were on fire. Which was a sensation Astoria thought she had escaped, and one she found strangely hilarious. Her unintended giggle broke the intense silent exchange between Charnel and Vesta, the hand on her breast releasing it to slide down her body. Unable to tear her eyes off Dawn as claws stroked over her mound, Fire marvelled at the darkening of the power clinging to the younger god. Lightning danced across her skin, but there was no jealousy in her gaze.

Lips caressed Fire's ear as Vesta dipped her head in to whisper, "I think she appreciates the sight of you like this. Do you agree, my feral Battle Hawk?"

She recognised all of Dawn's tells and hummed in agreement. "When she blinks like that, she's trying to hide how much she's really affected by something."

"Well then, little brat, this is what I want." Pressing the tip of a claw to Astoria's clit, Earth chuckled. "I want you beneath me while Charnel fucks me from behind."

Dawn arched a brow in surprise. "Beneath you how?"

"Considering I want to feel both bonds completing as close together as possible..."

"Oh. That's an option?"

Chuckling, Charnel stepped back to give the women on the ground room. "We don't see why not. Who can tell us otherwise? I'm eager to experience it. This is all that remains between us and feeling complete."

When a second claw tip joined the first on her clit to pinch it, Astoria squirmed, whimpering at the sharp pleasure jolting through her. Shadows pounced, wrapping around her ankles to tug them apart. From the eager way Dawn stepped forward, it was easy to work out what Vesta had in mind. Letting the cool ropes of power spread her open, Fire arched her back, enjoying the firm grasp of the hand in her hair. The claws on her clit retracted, leaving bare fingers toying with the sensitive bundle of nerves. Growling when Air went to drop to her knees, Vesta used two fingers to spread open Astoria's cunt.

"You can watch while you strip, little brat."

Realising she was being used as a distraction, Astoria rolled her eyes in Charnel's direction, spotting him in the corner of her vision. He had already shed his clothes and stood watching them, hands clasped behind his back. The studious expression on his face was the one he usually wore when considering what he intended to do to her next. Arousal flooded her at the prospect of the two older gods working together to wring orgasm after orgasm from their other mates. She wanted to warn Dawn they were in trouble, but the press of a watery finger against her arsehole banished the thought.

"What do you want to do with her?" Charnel nodded at Astoria, and the finger slid in further.

Not glancing down at what he was doing, Vesta kept her eyes on Dawn. "She can sit back and watch. If she behaves, and doesn't come while we're busy, she can feast on her captain."

Dawn groaned, pausing in the middle of unlacing her boots. "That's an unfair challenge."

Gawking at her, Astoria was unimpressed by her lack of faith. "Just you wait and see."

"Good girl," Vesta murmured, releasing her hair while withdrawing both of her hands. "Now I want you to kneel with your back to the pillar, and legs spread nice and wide."

The water retreated, and Charnel smirked at how quickly she scrambled to do as asked. No longer feeling normal pain seemed like a mercy as she settled into the position Vesta had requested. It was one the silent man had bound her in many times, always careful not to leave her in it for too long. Knowing she did not need to worry, Astoria twisted her arms behind her back, fingers grazing over the warm crystal. A rope of water encircled her wrists, and the god controlling it gave her a wink.

"Look at them watching you, Tempest." Charnel moved to stand behind Dawn, running his hands across her shoulders and down her arms.

Rising from the ground with more grace than Astoria suspected she would have managed, the general prowled forward to bury her hands in Dawn's hair. Watching them kiss while Charnel pressed up against Air's back, Fire was glad she had stayed. In all her years of fantasising about Dawn and Charnel together, she had never imagined what they had become, let alone the presence of a fourth person. Vesta was entirely new to them; someone they needed to learn about despite their new affection for her. As four parts of a godly entity, they could not help but love each other deeply. Except, three of them had seen the terrible turn things could take when that deep love became entangled with hatred.

Nuzzling the side of Dawn's face, Earth purred. "I didn't get to tell you earlier that you're softer than I expected, and you taste like the cleanest mountain air. But it's that tempest lingering on your skin that torments me."

Meeting Charnel's kiss over Dawn's shoulder, she trapped the other woman between them. His arm encircled the pirate's waist, holding her tight with his cock pressed between her cheeks. The sight of them fed her arousal, and Astoria whined in disappointment when the kiss ended. Watching people have sex in front of her was nothing new, but they were hers. Their desire was a white-hot flame threatening to consume her, and she feared she could not control it. She needed to or she would never trust herself with her power.

Vesta guided Dawn to a spot she had made perfectly smooth. Glittering light surrounded them, the crystal veins still glowing with the flames of Astoria's power trapped within. It left the cave almost as bright as early morning. When Earth dropped to her knees in front of the younger woman, she slid her hands down her legs, encouraging her to open them. Complying, Dawn gasped when teeth grazed her thighs before a tongue found its way into her cunt. Leaning forward slightly, Astoria wished she could see what was happening from a better angle, but the tightening of the water around her wrists was a warning. Meeting Charnel's amused stare, she straightened, giving him her best pout.

"You taste sublime." Licking her lips as she settled back on her heels, Vesta waited for Dawn to lower herself to the ground. "I look forward to spending more time doing that."

Casting a glance at Astoria, Dawn chuckled at the impatient twist of her lips. Hands cradled her cheeks, drawing her focus back to Vesta as the ancient woman settled above her. Knowing Air was tasting herself on Earth's tongue as they kissed, Fire imagined it was her arousal they were sharing. Standing above them, Charnel admired the swirl of lines on Vesta's back before slowly lowering himself between their tangled legs. His hands smoothed over the toned arse in front of him, following the marks that would soon change again. Guiding his cock between them, Water was surprised when a shadow tugged it down, aligning it with Dawn's entrance.

"I want you to give her a taste first," Vesta said, grinning at him over her shoulder.

Obliging her request, Charnel pressed into the moaning woman's cunt. He did not get far before he understood why she had wanted him to. Rocking her hips back, Vesta slid over the part of his cock not buried in Dawn. Hissing, he grabbed a handful of her wild curls, yanking her head back while he pulled out. Her soft laugh promised she would do it again. Squirming, Astoria wished she was a part of it. The sight of Dawn pinned beneath Vesta and Charnel, while the god of water had the domineering woman arching in his grasp, was one she would cling to. It was a reminder he knew how to make them surrender.

"Are you ready?" He rubbed the head of his cock along Vesta's cunt, not releasing his hold on her hair. "Because I suspect this will be impossible to control in any manner."

Carefully rocking against Dawn, Earth groaned in pleasure. "Blood and bones, yes."

He went as slowly as he could, giving the two women a chance to find the right angle to satisfy the power thrumming through them. Agony struck Charnel and Astoria when Dawn and Vesta's bond snapped into place. It was all he needed to thrust his cock all the way in, letting the threads of their existence wrap tighter around them. In the distance, somewhere through the fog descending on them, they heard Fire whimpering in desperation. She sounded farther away than she was, but they only knew the cold press of a bitter fog, the damp earth reaching up to swallow them whole. Charnel felt like a million dew drops scattered across the soil, tumbling along under the push of a glacial wind. There were too many heartbeats pounding in their ears.

Heat enveloped them, the gentle caress of flames chasing the frozen depths away. It cut through the fog, turning drops into a mist that could break free of the greedy clutch of earth. Fire drew the wind into her embrace, churning it back into the sky. Free to slump back, Charnel stared in wonder at the woman running her hands over each of them. The concerned twist of her lips made Vesta question if she had made a mistake in her request. But it was Dawn's apologetic whisper for making her worry that brought a faint smile back to Astoria's face. She tutted at them, pulling the fire back until she was simply her again.

"Well, at least you can't do that again," she said, stroking Vesta's head as the god of earth slumped against her. "But it was fucking glorious. Honestly, I can't describe it."

Dawn mumbled, "You sounded like you were in pain."

"Oh, I was. It was the worst agony imaginable. But it's done, and you're all beautiful." Licking her lips, Fire dragged her gaze across each of them. "Might I suggest we go for a swim before we do anything else?"

Chuckling, Charnel reached out to brush the hair away from her face. "I know a place."

THIRTY-FOUR

Surrounded by dragons, Astoria giggled when a hatchling bounded up to her, the rough tongue leaving a trail of drool on her face. Running her hands over the rich brown scales, she listened to the jumble of the young creature's thoughts while its parents attempted to coax it away. Amusement rippled across the bonds to her mates, leaving her overly conscious about what they thought of her playing with the smallest of the dragons. Other hatchlings played nearby, wrestling with each other for a turn with the woman they felt an unfamiliar pull towards. They were too young to understand that with her rebirth, Astoria had become the god connected to them at the core of their existence.

"She's going to need another bath," Vesta said, the mischievous tone of her voice causing Astoria to whip around to stare at the other gods where they stood with Briallen, and her father, Lord General Valerian. "They're like over excited puppies. Who's going to tell her she's not allowed to keep them?"

Dawn snorted, gesturing at the dragons. "Probably their parents."

"I can hear—no, not again!" Spluttering when the hatchling licked her face, Astoria shot a pleading look at a larger dragon. *Do you mind calling them off?*

Chortling, Ysgarlad blew a puff of steam over them. *Gentle with the god, little ones.*

The brown hatchling whined, curling around her to blink at the adult dragon. Astoria felt pity for it and scratched the spot behind its tiny horns. Small wings fluttered in delight, the spikes of its tail smacking into her leg. If she had been mortal, she knew it would have done damage, and looking at the wincing faces of the riders watching from a safe distance, Fire suspected they avoided playing with hatchlings for their own safety. There were tears in her dress from the tiny deadly talons attached to each of their four feet, but at least her power seemed to protect her clothes from their fire. Escaping their affection was easy if she wanted it to be, but the idea of transporting away from the adorable babies and upsetting them bothered Astoria more than missing out on the discussion.

Inspired by a puff of wispy smoke from a hatchling, the god flicked her hand at an open spot. A ball of fire gathered there, bobbing above the ground like it was in a current. Catching sight of it, several of the hatchlings gave chase, drawing the attention of the others until they became a tumbling pile of baby dragons, fighting for the chance to catch it first. Laughter rumbled across her mind from the adult dragons enjoying the sight of their young battling over a ball of fire. Freed from their attention, Astoria drifted across to join her mates. Valerian eyed her in amusement, but she saw the wariness in his gaze as it slid from her to Vesta. It was a reminder the stain of what the old gods had done clung to the new, and those who had suffered would never forget.

"I hope I didn't miss anything important," she said cheerily, leaning against Dawn when the younger woman held her arm open in invitation. "Where's the Executioner? If we're going to discuss the Blood Queen, she should be here."

Briallen stiffened, a hand settling onto the hilt of a sai. "Liv found out Captain Merle was leaving with Lady Camellia. She's gone to stop her new husband."

Pressing her lips together, Dawn flinched. "Uncle Merle doesn't want to get involved with her."

"I wish him the best of luck escaping her. If she's chasing him, I'm free. Finally."

"She wouldn't hurt him, would she?"

Astoria understood the concern in Dawn's voice and hoped for the sake of her mate's family that Oblivion would not harm the charming soldier. He was Death's closest friend, and had been there for Dawn and her siblings, no matter what. She suspected it was not just Merle, but Tigernach, that Air was concerned for. When she had been weighing up her choice in bringing down the wall, she had considered the implications for the danann king, but not the human baring Eclipse. Knowing he was with the strong-willed champion of Chaos, she felt a little better about his chances of escaping Oblivion unscathed for the time being. Camellia would not let any harm come to Merle.

"Considering his companion, I doubt she'd get close," Charnel said, reaching out to squeeze Dawn's shoulder. "Honestly, the Executioner has met her match in Commander Camellia. Remember how well she handled Tigernach, Tempest?"

Sharing a look with her father, Briallen released her hold on the sai. "You're talking about the cheerful elf who arrived with you? No one can stand up to Liv, and I say that as someone who saw her pushing Gebael around without fear of repercussions. She'll walk all over her without hesitation."

Assured by Water's reminder of what Camellia was capable of, Dawn grinned. "Yes, and I've seen Camellia push my parents around to get what she wants. But it doesn't matter right now. Our families are in danger from the same woman, and unfortunately, we're forbidden from doing anything ourselves."

Valerian shook his head, his bafflement over her admission clear to all of them. "You are gods. Since when have the gods been forbidden from doing anything?"

"Since the god of time was born. He sees things the rest of us cannot and does what is needed to ensure we don't fuck up his vision of a perfect future for Tir. One where the gods are at peace," Charnel replied. "We don't know where the lines are before Lord Emlyn imposes his will upon us. But if he didn't want us to help you go after Queen Calista, then he would have stepped in already. So, here we are to help."

Tucking her hands into the pockets of the floor length thick leather jacket she had gotten from the riders, Vesta bared her teeth at the two mortals. "No one knows the Spire or Calista like I do."

"And yet you don't know where Tristan is!" Briallen snarled, jabbing a finger into the god's chest. "If you want to make yourself useful, find my husband before we rain fire down on the Spire."

"Mother, that's enough!" The soft voice of Briallen's daughter had them turning to watch the tall woman striding towards them. "They will help us find Father. There's no need for you to be like this."

Slipping her arm around Dawn's waist, Astoria scrutinised the newcomer, and the shadows curling around her. Glancing at Vesta, Fire noticed the curiosity overtaking her features when she saw the young woman. She suspected the former general was desperate to find out what powers had passed to the great-granddaughter of the Blood Queen. It was an unavoidable fascination when the magic clinging to her whispered alluringly.

"Morwenna."

Huffing, she shook her head at her mother. "No, Ma, don't tell me to keep out of this. Tristan is my father, and they took him from me before I really had a chance to know him. I'm more than old enough to fight this battle, and Viggo's hungry for a taste of the goblin queen."

Behind her, the massive form of her pale blue dragon lowered his head. "*You will not let your champion keep us from the fight, Fire Queen. We will find Mor's father.*"

Covering her face, Astoria sighed. "*I will do my best.*"

Viggo drew back as Morwenna joined the group with her gaze locked on Vesta. "You will provide us with detailed maps of the Spire and tell us everything you know about what Calista might have done with my father. While my grandfather and the dragons rain fire down on the city, distracting the goblin army, my mother and I can locate him, and extract him from wherever he is imprisoned."

The curiosity faded from Earth's face, replaced by concern. "Whatever you think you can do is irrelevant. Your grandmother and her sisters are as powerful as their mother. Calista picked each of the men who fathered them for the potential of their magic, and they are formidable. Lady Briallen might be a husk maker, but she is hardly as powerful as she could be, considering she isn't bonded to a pair of danann."

"Nor am I interested in being bonded to a pair of danann," Briallen replied, and her dragon grumbled in agreement. "After a thousand years trapped with Liv, the only relationship I'm interested in is the one I chose. If any danann dare come after me, they'll quickly learn why you don't fuck with a dragon rider."

Something about the wicked twist of Morwenna's lips had Astoria straightening. "The Blood Queen and her daughters aren't the only powerful ones in the family. My mama trained me well."

Meeting the bitter gaze of the grey dragon, Astoria frowned. She had a suspicion Morwenna was not referring to Briallen, but to the absent Executioner. It seemed logical that Oblivion would have played a part in raising the daughter of the woman who had been briefly bound to Eclipse. Gasping, she shared a look with Charnel, realising he had his own suspicions over the matter.

"How old were you when your father vanished with the Fog?" she asked softly, locking her gaze on Briallen so she did not miss the flicker of fear that crossed the other woman's face. "You conceived before I sealed you all in here, didn't you, Briallen? While you were bound to the sword."

Eyes widening in horror, Vesta recoiled, putting distance between her and Morwenna. "Blood and bone! The daughter of a royal goblin and an Altira husk maker bound to Death's sword. No wonder your power feels so different. I've been trying to put my finger on it."

Holding out her hand, Morwenna chuckled at the shadows flocking to her fingertips. "It's a bit of this, and a bit of that. Unlike my mothers, I cannot shape shift, but I'm a husk maker who can shadow step."

"You're a husk maker who can use the shadows to suck the life out of things."

"That too."

Stunned by the revelation, Astoria knew her sisters needed to meet Morwenna. "We should take you back to Diwan to meet with the Unseelie Council before we make any moves on the Spire. Even with the might of the dragons, your numbers are too few to defeat Calista and her army. You need the Unseelie."

"Do you really expect us to believe the great General Vesta has truly changed colours? That countless goblins have done the same?" Valerian snarled, a whisper of his blood lust rising with his anger. "Because I find it highly unlikely. And to suggest half the dullaghan have turned their backs on Death?"

"My father is right. The headless riders would never betray their god." Lifting her chin, Briallen avoided looking at her daughter while Igraine blew a puff of smoke over their heads.

"Actually, they didn't. He told them to go," Dawn replied, crossing her arms with a petulant scowl. "My parents gave everyone the freedom to choose their own path. They encouraged those with doubt in their hearts to walk away from the gods, and to do whatever they needed to do to hold us accountable."

"Accountable to mortals?" There was scorn in Valerian's gaze as he regarded Air.

"Yes. After what happened with the previous ones, we're determined to avoid a repeat. Tir doesn't need another war between the gods." Charnel rolled his shoulders, clearly unsettled by the prospect. "The last one nearly destroyed this world. I would take it as a personal insult if anyone started that nonsense again. Especially now that I have all my mates. This is one thing I agree with Lord Time about."

The dragons stared at the god of water, and Astoria smirked. She knew he could switch from the bumbling man who cowered before Shianeni and Annawyn to the commanding Lord of Tides without blinking. It was a transformation she enjoyed watching purely for the impact it had on his audience. He was showing them his stern but cordial aspect, the calm ocean before the storm rolled in. A wary voice whispered at the edge of her mind that they needed to watch their tempers until they understood how much had changed with the completion of the bonds. They had each come into the full strength of their powers.

Ever concerned with the possibility of war, Vesta studied Briallen before glancing at her mates. "We need to warn the Raven Queen. She needs to prepare her flock for the return of the Executioner and those who remain of the original Ravens. Not to mention her mates. General Redmond deserves the chance to prepare for a conflict with the Lord of Rainbows. You've barely repaired your relationship with your sisters, Astoria. Obviously, the Unseelie Council will side with the Raven Queen."

"The Raven Queen?" Briallen recoiled in astonishment. "No one mentioned anything about someone replacing Oblivion as the leader of the Ravens last night. She and the others may not take it well."

Aware it was her sister who might face the wrath of the Executioner, Astoria replied, "My sister, Silaine, was the one who made the danann aware daoine born as husk makers could become Ravens. Something Oblivion knew. General Redmond and Lady Asthore are her mates. Under her leadership, the new Ravens have flourished, their numbers growing with each year as they search Tir for their fellows."

"Their numbers are now greater than those of the originals." Dawn gave the dragon riders a smug look that made Astoria snort. "And it seems more are born each year."

Lips parted, Briallen looked like she wanted to say something, but it was Morwenna who said, "How many Ravens are there now? Are they all bound to danann?"

"Not all of them. You can't force a bond. Many danann and Ravens have not met their mates. I've asked my parents why, because to me, it seems logical that when a duine is born with the husk maker power, they would also awaken a connection to their mates. However, there are danann who don't even have their initial pairing. One of Camellia's mates is a danann warrior who never had a blood mage."

Valerian nodded, giving his daughter and granddaughter a knowing look. "Just like Callea."

"I always thought she didn't have a warrior because she bonded with a dragon," Briallen muttered. "Now I feel stupid for never asking more about how their bonds work."

"No, darling girl, she bonded with a dragon because she was alone. She found her home among us instead of War's army, surrounded by pairs of her fellow danann."

She did not know if Oblivion had intercepted Camellia and Merle, but Astoria felt tendrils of concern wrapping around her heart. At the back of her mind, the knowledge that what she had done in releasing the people sealed behind walls of magic for over a thousand years would have a far-reaching impact urged her to move. Back in Diwan, her sisters and their families were waiting for them to return. They needed to know what was going on, but a vindictive desire lit a fire in her, demanding to pay a visit to Calista. Not to bring down the Blood Queen, but to warn her. For so long, people had lived in fear of the goblins and their ruthless leader. Now it was her turn to live in fear.

Reaching for Vesta, Astoria licked her lips. "We're wasting time. You and I have a task."

"Are you suggesting we leave the dragon riders to do what they want and pay my old mistress a visit?" There was a delighted gleam in the god of earth's gaze when she bared her teeth.

"Yes, I am. No matter how much we tell Lord General Valerian and Lady Briallen, we cannot cover everything that has gone on or changed. Much of it is up to them to learn. All we can do is offer advice. Seek Queen Eivor in Diwan. The Raven Queen is also there. They are your best choice of allies for the war against Calista... and the husk makers here deserve the chance to decide their own path. Let them meet Silaine before they risk starting a fight."

Running his gaze up and down her, Valerian smiled sadly. "You're not the same blood-thirsty warrior I met before our downfall. Your mother would be proud, Astoria Havard."

As much as she wanted to relish the idea that he was right, and her mother would be proud of her, Fire could not forget how much Malena had done behind the backs of her family. Her parents had made deals with gods to decide the fates of their daughters without ever stopping to ask them if it was what they wanted. Not to mention what they had encouraged the three of them to do to each other. She did not know if she could ever properly forgive herself for the role she played in undermining Silaine's confidence for most of her life. Or for keeping the truth of what their father was doing with the mad god from Eivor.

"I'm sure she would be. After all, I've fulfilled her plans for me."

The way he frowned at her words reminded Astoria that few people knew the truth about Malena. She wondered how much Oblivion knew, and if she had shared her knowledge with Briallen or Morwenna. Glancing at Vesta, she looked forward to getting the other god alone to discuss the ramifications of the half-goblin woman. There was an agitation simmering along the bond to Charnel, and it added to her pile of concerns.

"If you wish to pack a bag, we can use the gateway stones to bring you close to Diwan," Dawn said, crossing her arms as she frowned at something that had entered her thoughts. "It would cause less panic than people seeing dragons for the first time. I can ensure the currents are in your favour if you decide to fly a small contingent there instead, but please remember, the humans and elves have forgotten you exist."

Placing a hand on her shoulder, Charnel offered Dawn a reassuring smile. "Why don't you oversee things here while I return to Diwan to meet with Queen Eivor and the others? Vesta and Astoria can complete their task, then head there to relieve me. You can fly."

"I'm sure a dragon would be happy to carry you."

"That doesn't mean I want to. I'm the god of water, not air. Up there is your realm."

They stared at the god of water, and Astoria grinned. She had never realised Charnel was uncomfortable with heights, but she stored the information away to be examined later. None of them dared tease him about it in front of the mortals or the dragons, but her connection to the mighty beasts told her his admission bothered them. She supposed it hurt their pride that a god did not wish to make use of their services. Rolling her shoulders, Astoria decided she needed to assert her power as the god of fire, and the one to whom the dragons were bound.

"Lord General Valerian, you are not to lead your people away from here until I'm able to guarantee the dragons won't be attacked on sight. There's too few to risk their future."

She saw the moment he quashed his desire to argue with her. At his back, the dragons rumbled their agreement, the hatchlings still chasing the ball of fire she had created for them. There were enough high-ranking dragons present for Astoria to be confident they would share her command with the rest. For the first time, she wanted to meet with the other gods so they could discuss the best way to ensure the fire-breathing creatures remained safe.

"As you wish, Lady Fire," he replied, bowing stiffly. "You're right. We can't risk the dragons."

"Charnel, let my sisters know where we've gone."

Winking at her, he vanished, leaving them to finalise their plans. Briallen looked ready to argue with the command, but Morwenna grabbed her arm, giving a shake of her head to caution her mother. There was a small part of Astoria that felt guilty over cutting their discussions short. A larger part of her knew they could talk until they were blue in the face, and nothing would come of it. They would circle the same topics from different angles without making progress. Sometimes they just needed to act, and hope the consequences were what they wanted them to be.

"Right, Vesta and I need to go put the fear of the gods into Queen Calista. It's about time she learns we will not let her actions go unpunished. No one fucks with my family and gets away with it." Setting her gaze on Morwenna, Astoria wondered what her sisters would make of the woman. "And as far as I'm concerned, that now includes the two of you, and all the dragons, with their riders."

THIRTY-FIVE

Arms wrapped around Astoria tightly, keeping her pinned to the other god's chest while shadows crawled through the room where they had appeared. Lips covered hers, stealing anything she might have said before Vesta was certain they were alone. There was a wall at her back, the consistent grooves pressing into her confirming it was made from bricks rather than carved from stone. She had never been to the Spire. As a duine, the home city of the goblins was a place out of her worst nightmares. All those created or born before the Fog knew that setting foot inside the Spire would be the last thing they did.

"I like you like this," Vesta whispered in her mind rather than stop kissing her. *"Trapped, and completely mine. For so many years I dreamt of you in this room, and now I'm glad for how it is. You're my feral wife, and I never have to let go of you."*

The shadows withdrew, seeping into the cracks of the room to leave it bathed in low afternoon light. Peeling away, Vesta swept her gaze across the chamber. Less interested in the room than she was in her mate, Astoria frowned when Earth's shoulders dropped. A wave of grief swept across the bond before a solid wall of stone slammed into place to prevent her emotions from leaking through to all of them. Curious about what had caused the shift, Fire turned her attention to the room in front of her. When they left the dragon riders, Vesta had suggested they arrive in the Spire in the quarters that had belonged to her.

"It's empty..."

A muscle twitched in her cheek as she glanced at Astoria. "Everything is gone. I didn't expect that. Maybe rifled through and destroyed but not expunged.

Part of me assumed she would want to keep it in place, so if she ever got her claws back into me, she could use it to teach me a lesson."

Reaching out, Fire cupped her cheek gently. She understood the impact of what the Blood Queen had done. It had stung more than she cared to admit, discovering they had disposed of all the evidence of her life as though she never existed. Though it was not Eivor who had been responsible for it, rather some nameless servant of the man who had invaded their home and killed their parents. Astoria imagined the pain was that much more because the order had come from someone who had commanded Vesta's loyalty for as many years as Calista had.

"At least someone else hasn't moved in," Astoria said quietly, hoping her mate understood where she was coming from. "She emptied them, but perhaps she still has some fragment of affection for you."

"Or no one wants to risk being tainted by my reputation."

"But they're just living quarters."

Giving her a bitter smile, Vesta walked into the middle of what had been her bedroom. No furniture remained to occupy the space, and it somehow made it seem both bigger and smaller at the same time. She trailed her gaze over the blank walls, wondering what had happened to the art that had once hung there. It was not the removal of her belongings that hurt, but the mystery of what had happened to items she had carefully collected for their beauty over her lifetime. Many of them served as reminders of the destruction the goblins had been responsible for. Trivial things that would not betray her wavering loyalty to the Blood Queen. At least she had taken those with the most sentimental value to Diwan with her, including a single brown feather preserved in glass.

"Social perceptions are funny things. People see connections in the oddest of places. To many, my betrayal tainted these rooms because they had been mine since the day the gods settled us into the Spire. Perhaps she has ordered them to remain empty for much the same reason."

"It's odd to think some lingering sentimentality might sway the Blood Queen."

Vesta lifted her chin, shadows writhing at her feet. "I've never dared ask if I might be her sister in the same way General Redmond is King Tigernach's brother, and Thorne and Rain are twins. Though their relationships are glaringly obvious. Still, I've often wondered. Not that it matters anymore."

"You feared you would turn out vicious like her?" Astoria took a step towards her.

"Sometimes. Annawyn played an overwhelming part in that. She always left me alone because you can't risk the one in charge of the army. Not like you can the figurehead."

Frowning, Astoria cast her memories back to the battle on the plains near the twin cities. "Do you think the mad god knew what they had done to you? She might have detected their meddling in your mind."

Grasping her hands behind her back, Earth snorted, casting a look at the woman who shone among the shadows clinging to her. "Would she have cared? Her rage was over what Shianeni, Neriwyn, and Gebael had done. If she was aware of what Alyah and Xhaiden were doing behind Shianeni's back, then it likely suited her to believe they were her unspoken allies. She may have even believed I would side with her, especially with how Shianeni treated Charnel."

"Was it really that bad?"

"Yes. We call Annawyn the mad god, and she was. Her own power drove her to it. But Shianeni was wretched. Well and truly wretched. The most horrid creature to ever exist. They threw me into the arena a lot in the early years, so I saw how she treated the others. Our precious Charnel was a favourite target, and he had no one."

Inhaling sharply, Astoria did not want to dwell on the thought of what he had gone through when she needed to keep her temper under control. That anger could wait for later, when she could safely let it burn as much as she wanted. Somewhere Charnel could come and assure her he had survived everything they had done to him. Because she needed to know nothing would sway him to leave them after all the years he had waited. He was finally whole, and Astoria wanted to give him everything he wanted.

"My feral Battle Hawk, save your fury for Calista." Shadows swarmed across Astoria, and Vesta narrowed her eyes as they latched onto the flames flickering over her skin. "There's nothing to be gained here. I only came to see if I could collect a few things."

Astoria closed her eyes, taking slow, deep breaths until she was confident her power was under control. The shadows curled around her legs were a cold weight, comforting in their presence. She appreciated knowing Vesta could soothe her fire before she did any harm. She hoped it would get easier to keep the power contained, but for the moment, despite wielding the precision over her magic she had possessed before her rebirth, Astoria knew she was struggling. Until such a time as she felt confident she was safe to be left alone, she would cling to Earth and Water.

When she opened her eyes again, Astoria found Vesta in front of her and smiled in relief. "Don't leave my side, General. Not if you don't have to. There are innocent people here."

Trailing her fingertips down the side of the younger woman's face, she nodded in understanding. "You'll be fine, my feral wife. But I promise I will never leave your side."

"I should be reassuring you before we confront your former queen."

"Perhaps, but we're not concerned I'll burn down the Spire if someone makes me angry. Besides, worrying about your temper gives me something to focus on, so I'm not tempted to rip this place apart from the foundations. And I could if I wanted to. I could move the very ground upon which it sits, every stone in the walls, and every speck that came from the earth. But I won't because you need me to be the rock holding your fire back, and I need to be that for you, so I don't do something unforgivable."

Unable to hold back her snort of amusement, Astoria turned her face to kiss the palm of Vesta's hand. "What a pair we are. We're both afraid of becoming reprehensible and relying on the other to stand between them and the line. But she threatened our family."

"That she did."

"Sometimes I still hear them screaming. Especially little Rose."

Reaching for her hand, Vesta clasped it tightly. "Shall we then? Because I'm looking forward to her face when she sees us. We should make as big an impression as we can."

Astoria cocked her head, lips twitching in delight. "What do you have planned?"

"This time of the afternoon, she'll be preparing for the night's festivities. Dinnertime at the Spire is hours of what Calista considers entertainment. Courses of food brought out between performances and the sort. Depending upon her mood, it might be fairly tame. Or it might be dreadfully bloody."

"I will follow where you lead. Tell me what you want me to do, and I will do it."

Lifting the hand she held to her lips, Vesta kissed their joined fingers. "Ever the obedient soldier."

She suspected the comment would have been an insult from anyone else's lips, but from her mate, the words were affectionate. Yet the truth of them remained. An obedient soldier was what she had been for most of her life, and Astoria knew it was time to break free of the chains her father had bound her in. He was dead, and she was a god. The only people she had an obligation to take orders from were her mates, and the other gods when it was within reason for the sake of their peace.

"You know our audience, Vesta," she said firmly, rolling her shoulders as she considered summoning her wings. "What will make the biggest impact? I doubt she'll show fear, but she'll feel it."

Pulled close by Earth's power, the shadows swallowed the low light filtering in through the windows. Wanting to see the view of the world outside, Astoria tugged on her mate's hand, leading her over to the frosted panes of glass. The fog of darkness shielded them from sight, but when she pressed her face against the window, Fire realised there was little need for it. Wherever the ground was below them, she had no hope of spotting it.

"By the stars!"

Nuzzling her neck, Vesta chuckled. "Did no one ever tell you what the Spire was?"

Shaking her head in amazement, she doubted anything could adequately describe the home of the goblins. "Being told about the massive tower built by the gods does not prepare one for the reality."

"I always wondered why they made this place, and why they chose us to inhabit it. While it's not the Rainbow Vale, it has a beauty to it that nowhere else possesses. The forests carpeting the ground are so dense sunlight barely touches the earth. They make the woods in Diwan seem bright in comparison. Every bridge connecting the smaller towers to this central one is perilous in the wrong weather for those who cannot reach out and pull themselves through the shadows. You've been in caves other than that last one?"

"More than a few. Why?"

"Because from a distance, the Spire reminds me of stalagmites." There was a wistfulness in Vesta's sigh as she attempted to draw Astoria away from the window. "Come on, we don't want to push our luck. For all we know, Lord Time is waiting for us to make a misstep so he can punish us."

Reminded of the looming shadow of the god of time, Fire huffed. She had no clue where he was, but it would not have surprised her if Vesta was right. For all they knew, Emlyn might be mere steps away, watching the variations, and preparing to act should they deviate from what he wanted.

"You still haven't told me what you want me to do."

Engulfed by shadows, Astoria let the earthy scent of Vesta's power fill her nose as the other god transported them to a new location. Almost instantly, she felt the prickle of magic that suggested they were close to a large crowd. It was a sensation she was still adjusting to, and from her sharp inhale, it was clear it equally unsettled the other woman. Holding tight to each other, they remained where they were while the shadows bled into the stone. There was no need for them when their power kept them unseen. No mortal could spot them, and the chance of another god being present was highly unlikely.

"What I want you to do, my feral wife, is burn. We're Earth and Fire, the two things all goblins fear. I shall plunge them into darkness, and you can light our way. Let them realise what walks these halls."

Sweeping her gaze back and forth along the wide hallway they had appeared in, Astoria smiled gleefully when she settled her sights on the heavy doors separating them from what she assumed was the great hall. Flames danced across her, gathering at her back to form into the glowing wings she delighted in possessing. Meeting Vesta's thoughtful stare, it occurred to her that the other god might contemplate spinning a pair of her own. It was easy to imagine the three of them taking to the sky together with wings of fire, feathers, and shadows. Letting the flames settle over her, Astoria inclined her head.

"As beautiful as always."

If she had been in her hawk form, she would have preened at the compliment. "I'm ready if you are."

Vesta swallowed, and for a moment, it looked like she might hesitate. "Before we go in there, I want to tell you how sorry I am for anything Calista might say about my history. There are things I'm—"

"Not proud of? We all have dark parts in our past."

She gave a single nod and moved forward to the doors. Pressing a hand to the carved timber, Vesta closed her eyes to picture the cavernous chamber beyond. With the memory of the boundaries held in her mind, it was easy to draw the darkness from the earth, and from the forgotten corners where dirt gathered. Screams sounded from within, alarmed shouts accompanying them. As soon as she was sure the shadows had plunged the great hall into complete darkness, Vesta tossed a smirk over her shoulder at Astoria and inclined her head at the door. Extending a hand to her mate, Earth waited for flame-touched fingers to entwine hers. Their power sent the doors flinging open, allowing them to see what sort of chaos they faced within, and to enjoy the results of it.

Glancing at Vesta, Astoria spread her wings. "Shall we, wife?"

Lifting her chin, Earth let the shadows settle like a fine mist. A fresh round of shouts directed attention towards the two gods striding down the middle of the room. There was no distinctive ring of swords being drawn, reminding Astoria the goblins had little use for weapons when they had their claws. She had seen what they could do with them. But whatever they thought they might do to defend themselves, it was increasingly obvious they were reluctant to follow through on those ideas. A part of her was disappointed. It would have been enjoyable to make an example out of a few goblins.

"Who dares enter my hall in this way?"

Flicking a hand toward the source of the voice, Vesta smirked when the shadows faded, revealing the room. "Don't you recognise your old friend, Calista? I'm insulted."

The woman seated on the massive stone throne at the head of the hall resembled her son more than Astoria had expected. Blood red hair tumbled across her shoulders, and she suspected that if the goblin queen stood, it would almost reach the ground. A pristine white gown encased her in a stark contrast to the colour of her hair. From what Vesta had implied about what the queen enjoyed, she suspected the white dress was a deliberate choice. All to display the results of her bloody fun.

"I recognise a traitor. No loyal friend of mine would have done what you did." Draping a leg over the arm of the throne, Calista stared at her former general. "But you're not the woman who left me. No, you're something else."

"Perhaps she's more intelligent than I thought," Astoria said, stretching her wings.

It was obvious when the queen's focus settled on her. "My, my, what have we here? You look tasty. I'll enjoy eating you."

Shadows lashed out, wrapping around Calista's throat. Alarmed by the attack on their queen, guards leapt towards the two women, completely unprepared for what they were. Rolling her eyes, Astoria spun a wall of fire down each side of the middle path. Fearful screams came from those clever enough to recognise the danger, and the scramble of bodies rushing for the door had Fire's lips twitching. They were the wise ones to flee any potential conflict before it began. Any who remained risked being killed if things went too far, and either of them lost their temper with the goblin queen.

"You are not worthy of addressing my wife!" Snarling, Vesta strode towards the throne, leaving her fellow god behind. "We're here to deliver a warning, Calista."

Summoning a ball of fire to float above her hand, Astoria chuckled. "Maybe less of a warning, and more of a threat."

Planting a hand on each arm of the throne, Earth leaned in closer to admire the flicker of fear she could see dancing in the depths of the queen's eyes. It was not an emotion she had ever thought she would witness in Calista. Vindictive rage coursed through her, and Vesta did not resist her desire to tighten the shadows around the neck of her former mistress. Her claws tore at them, unable to break through the ropes of darkness that were steadily robbing her of her breath.

"I never thought I'd see the day when you were at my mercy, my queen."

"What do you want?" Calista wheezed, struggling to speak with the shadowy noose at her throat.

"For you to stay away from my family. I'm not a general anymore. I'm barely even a goblin. The power that wears my skin and owns my memories is far older and hungrier than you could imagine." Keeping her face close to the goblin queen's, Vesta smiled. "You will cease your attempts to steal Queen Eivor's and Prince Rhydwen's children from Diwan. If you do not leave them alone, my wife will feel a need to burn the Spire to the ground, and I will ensure no trace of it remains."

Tossing her ball of fire into the air, Astoria ambled closer. "You sure I can't do it now?"

"Your dragons would be rather unhappy if you did. They want their vengeance."

"That, and my champion wants her husband back. I don't suppose you'd like to make it easy for everyone and tell us where Tristan is? His wife, daughter, and the dragons would like him returned."

Glee replaced fear, and Calista smiled. "My grandson is gone."

A chill ran down Astoria's spine, and she knew if it was true, then the wrath of Briallen and the dragons would shake Tir's foundations. "Are you telling us he is dead?"

"Yes."

"Astoria, be calm," Vesta said, glancing at her mate, and the flames spreading across the ground. "If you burn the Spire down now, you'll deny Briallen and Morwenna their justice."

She reined in the fire, drawing it back into herself. "You will stay far away from Diwan and from my family. If you do not, Queen Calista, then nothing will stop me from killing you, slowly and painfully."

Withdrawing her shadows, Vesta stepped back to join Astoria. Slipping an arm around her waist, she kissed her wife, taking her time to drink in the raging fire of her power. That the goblin queen was watching intently did not matter. If anything, it was an incentive to pull her closer until the soothing darkness of her magic was thoroughly entwined with the burning heat of the other god.

"She knew something had been done to you all those years ago," Calista said, straightening on her throne as though they had not threatened her life. "But she was never sure. Now I know what it was. Chaos bound you to the essence of a god. Not just you, but Malena's middle child."

Casting a look over her shoulder at her former queen, Vesta smirked. "That's right. I'm the god of earth, and she is the god of fire. But it's not us you should really fear right now. The dragons are coming for you, Calista. And they're angry. More than that, they're connected to their god, and it makes their fire burn all the hotter. Beware the wrath of a wronged dragon rider, my queen, because you're going to die."

"We destroyed the dragons."

"No, you didn't," Astoria replied, gathering her power in preparation to return them to Diwan. "Because I was used to secret them away. While I tore through your army, the Executioner led them away. Now they're free, and they're hungry for justice. You should run, little goblin queen. Run fast and far and never stop because they're coming for you."

THIRTY-SIX

She had intended for them to appear in her chambers, but somehow between there and the Spire, Vesta changed their destination. Chilly air surrounded them, a heavy darkness tricking her senses. Shoved against rough stone, Astoria did not fight off the hungry shadows swarming across her body to consume the flickering flames, or the demanding kiss that stole any words she might have said. Claws pierced her clothes, pressing into her skin hard enough to draw blood. The wall that Vesta had carefully placed between their bond to contain her emotions crumbled, giving Astoria a taste of the desperation coursing through her. A lingering hint of fear accompanied it.

"*I'm sorry,*" she whispered in Astoria's mind. "*None of that went the way I thought it would.*"

Drawing Vesta tightly against her, she let her take what she needed. "*What matters is we accomplished the task. We delivered our warning, and didn't destroy the Spire.*"

Breaking their kiss, she dropped her head to Fire's shoulder, breathing in the smoky scent of her skin. "You're right. We did what we needed to do. But I'm still sorry, my beautiful Battle Hawk. I didn't want to lose my temper like I did, but when Calista looked at you, and said what she did, something snapped."

"My darling, everyone knows how possessive you are. Does it really surprise you she knew how to set you off? In a few words, the Blood Queen pushed you to the edge. No one knows you better than she does, including us. One day it will change, but that won't negate the thousands of years you spent at Calista's side as her general. Don't feel guilty for reacting the way you did."

"But I know better."

Running her hand along Vesta's spine, Astoria chuckled. "It's only been a little while since you were reborn. Neither of us is in complete control of our powers, or anything else that comes with what we are. Honestly, if someone approached and dared flirt with you, I'm fairly certain I'd set them on fire."

The ripple of jealousy accompanying her words made Earth smirk against the warm skin of her neck. Nipping her gently, she tightened her hold on Fire. Her power thrummed through the stone wall that kept Astoria in place, tempting her to manipulate it. As much as she wanted to bind her mate where she stood and take her time to remind her there would be no one else outside of the four of them, they had a task to complete. Charnel's presence in the palace tugged at the bond, his patient calm seeping down it to take the edge off their lust.

"He's eager to know how it went," she murmured, trailing kisses along Astoria's jaw until she reached her lips. "I don't know why I brought us to the lowest level of the dungeon."

"My guess is you wanted a place where you could contain my power and in which you felt a stronger draw for yours. In here, we're alone, and safe. All you need to do is tell me you want to come here, and we will come." Summoning balls of fire to illuminate the room, Astoria sighed. "At least it's a storeroom, and not a prison cell. Perhaps we can clean it up and bring in a few bits of furniture for comfort. We can make it a safe place for you to retreat when you feel a need. With all, any, or none of us."

Kissing the tip of her nose, Vesta smiled adoringly. "Your consideration for my needs is more than I deserve after such a short amount of time. A part of me wants to resent the way our feelings for each other came about, but I can't think of anyone I'd rather be chained to than the three of you."

"It's funny, you know. I never fell in love with anyone. Silaine thought she was in love with that treacherous bitch, and Eivor had her first love. He was a good man, but not as good for her as Rhydwen and Thorne. Not me though. Lovers, and many of them, but never love."

"Until you met Dawn and reunited with Charnel?"

Astoria nodded slowly, frowning at the memory of the first time she met Dawn. "I knew the moment I saw her that I would love her until the day I died. Do you find that rather odd?"

"No, never. Because in the chaos of everything that happened when we met on the battlefield, I saw you, and you never left me, even though they took your memories of it. I'm glad they left me mine. As torturous as it was. I suppose if they had taken them from me, I wouldn't have insisted on being the one to bring Rhydwen here. Initially, Calista didn't want me to, but I needed to. For you."

Impatience rippled across the bond from Charnel to remind them he was waiting to find out how things had gone with the goblin queen. Sighing heavily, Vesta relaxed her hold, but did not step back. Cupping her face, Astoria pressed a gentle kiss to her lips, hoping it would convey her promise for later. They needed to prepare the others for what was coming and to discuss how to deal with the return of the dragon riders. She did not look forward to facing King Tigernach.

"Do you think we should change before we face the others?"

Humming thoughtfully, Vesta cocked her head and eyed the ceiling. "No, we should put him out of his misery. I imagine your sisters have been giving him a tough time. At least Dawn seems to be fine."

"She would be. You haven't seen her when she's around people who don't scare her. There's a reason Dawn commands the loyalty of a fleet, and they happily serve under her banner. But she's intimidated by Eivor and the others. Which I can understand because I feel the same about her family."

"To be honest, I'm not looking forward to meeting them."

Laughing, Astoria gave her another kiss. "They're not bad people. And remember, we're their equals. I'm sure War would appreciate how utterly feral you would go to protect his daughter."

"Feral?" Earth scoffed. "No one has ever accused me of being that. They created me to exercise restraint. You're our feral wife, not me."

"Oh no, I quite disagree. Especially after today. For the right person, you become the most fucking feral woman on Tir. And I love it. I bet when Charnel finds out, he'll do whatever you ask."

An extended hand accompanied her slow smirk. "Let's join him and find out."

The shift in the air was the first sign of their relocation, but it was Rose's excited squeal that confirmed where they had appeared. Vesta released her to spin and catch the energetic child before she collided with them. Surrounded by the lush gardens, Astoria was thankful they were under the shade of several towering gums, because it made the adjustment to daylight easier. Her gaze settled on her sisters, surprised to find them stretched out on a picnic blanket beside each other while Bardhyl cuddled his mother. Their partners were scattered around, and she found Charnel sitting next to a pond with several of the children, entertaining them with displays of his control over the water.

"It's about time. He told us you were in the palace," Eivor said, gesturing at the seated god. "Is it done? Please tell me you killed the bitch and saved us all some effort."

Clapping hands over her son's ears, Silaine gave their older sister an annoyed look. "Please watch what you say around the children! Honestly, I expect better from you."

Amused by the exchange, Astoria clasped her hands behind her back and gazed down at them. "I hope you don't expect better from me, Laine. Because I won't be minding my words. Someone needs to be a terrible influence on them, and I'm happy to fill the role."

"You would be. But you haven't answered my question. Is she dead?" Flicking a braid of white hair over her shoulder, the Unseelie Queen kept her gaze on the god.

"No, we didn't kill her. Nor did we destroy the Spire. We warned her to stay away from the family, and that the dragon riders want revenge." Shifting slightly, Astoria met Rhydwen's sorrowful green eyes. "I'm sorry, brother, but she claims your nephew is dead. We need to tell his wife and daughter, though I'm not sure how that will turn out. Did Charnel tell you about Morwenna?"

Grief twisted his delicate features, and at his side, Asthore placed a comforting hand on his shoulder. "We will welcome Lady Briallen and her daughter as family, Rhydwen. Because they are. No matter what has happened throughout the years, that hasn't changed. And at least here, you will get to know them properly. The real problem is Tigs."

Thorne levelled a blank look in her direction. "He knows about Oblivion."

"Ah." Grimacing, Astoria's eyes darted to where Redmond stood. "Where is he?"

"My brother is dealing with his anger in a training yard. Alone. Best to leave him to it. We knew she was alive, somewhere, but when he felt the connection return... I feel for him," Redmond replied, curling his crimson wings around himself as he stared at the sky as though he expected dragons to appear. "Charnel told us Liv and the old gods used you to seal the sanctuary. He'll be angry with you for a while, but he'll get over it. I'm more concerned about the apparent relationship between Liv and this Lady Briallen. Not to mention the daughter. Did she really call Liv mother?"

Cuddling Rose, Vesta nodded. "Aye, she did. And there's more."

"There is?"

"Morwenna is a husk maker with goblin shadow powers. They suggested she can use the shadows to draw the life from things." She hesitated, sharing a look with Astoria while contemplating if they should tell them everything. "Gebael bound Briallen to Eclipse for a time. She fought in the battle against us when old Endara and Ensaycal fell. Her daughter was conceived while she was bound to the sword."

There were several gasps from those who understood the implications, and Rhydwen looked at each of them in confusion. It surprised Astoria he did not grasp the seriousness of what it meant. She supposed none of them really knew the truth of it. For all they knew, Briallen and Morwenna had twisted the details to make them fear what she was capable of. Except deep down, her instincts screamed they had not exaggerated, but in fact, done the opposite, and hidden the full extent of what Morwenna could do.

"It will cause an uproar among my flock," Silaine grumbled, stroking Bardhyl's hair. "But we'll deal with it. Best to keep the old Ravens away from the new until we've met."

Eivor frowned, her black and white hair gleaming in the beam of sunlight she was sitting in. "Yes, things are going to be quite chaotic for some time. Imagine that. The dragons have returned to Tir."

"As has the Executioner," Thorne said, her lips twisted in conflict. "I don't know how I feel about it. At least Captain Merle respects our freedom, and the gods do what we ask."

"Even our resident ones?"

Scoffing, Vesta kissed Rose's head. "I'd like to remain in my post if the rest of the Council will accept my change. Neither Tory nor I want to leave Diwan if we don't have to."

"Well, if Eivor can't convince the Unseelie Council to let you remain, you can come to the Vale. Though, as gods, shouldn't you reside in one of the eternal valleys with the others?" Silaine helped her son stand so he could run over to join the others at the pond. "Or are you allowed to do what you want when it comes to where you live?"

The sense of Charnel's power intensified for a moment, and Astoria watched him spin a display of dolphins leaping joyfully across the pond. She saw the shimmer of a ward settling onto the body of water and wondered if he was doing it to prevent any of the children from getting into it. As he rose from the ground, the god smiled at the laughing youths before turning his attention to his mates. From the corner of her eye, she observed how Vesta watched his every movement with a hunger she could not describe. Aware of her attention, Charnel reached for Earth, caressing her cheek before kissing her gently while Rose giggled. Astoria watched her sister, biting back a chuckle at the confusion Eivor wore at the display. She supposed it was strange for them to see their fierce general accepting a kiss from a god.

When his hand touched her face, Astoria smiled, pressing her cheek into his palm. "I behaved myself. Didn't set anyone on fire, as much as I wanted to do so."

"And I never doubted you, my beloved Fire Hawk." His kiss was soft, a gentle reminder of his faith in her. "You need to stop fretting about your ability to control your power and remember how talented you are."

"He's right, Tory. You've always been the most in control of your gifts out of the three of us. No one has ever matched you in the ability to shift forms, and your prowess as a warrior is legendary. If anyone can master this power, it's you," Eivor said, rising from the picnic blanket while Silaine shook her head.

"It's perfectly understandable if you feel overwhelmed by your new power. I doubt any of the others who have been reborn felt completely in control from the get-go. In fact, I know Death didn't. We've talked about it. And apparently, Life really struggled after her rebirth. She still can't control the dandelions growing everywhere she goes."

Blinking at Silaine, Astoria remembered her younger sister enjoyed regular visits with the other gods. "You're right, Laine. But Eivor is also right. I just need time to relearn my limits. Vesta will need the same. Thankfully, it's something we can do together."

Sauntering over, Eivor elbowed her way between Astoria and Vesta, slinging an arm across their shoulders. "And we will support you. Don't worry about the Unseelie Council. In this matter, they can't deny me. You're family. Gods or not. Something we've all learnt the importance of since that awful day."

"We certainly need to stick together with the changes to come." Thorne drifted over, a faint smile tugging at the corners of her mouth. "Because the return of the dragons and their riders will shake the foundations of our world. People either believe they're long dead or never knew they existed."

"I've never seen a dragon," Rhydwen said from his spot on the ground with Silaine.

She inclined her head at him. "I saw a few once. They're huge."

Casting her gaze across the gathering of people who had become her family, Astoria regretted Dawn's absence. It was a stark reminder that she would come and go as she needed, filling her role as feared pirate captain and Storm Queen. She knew Charnel would do the same, following her to ensure her fleet was always safe, and the evidence of their battles was sent to the depths. They would make it work between them, but having a place to call home would help. Diwan was perfectly situated. And it was close enough to the Rainbow Vale for Silaine to visit. What mattered most was that they wanted to be a family.

"Thank you, Eivor," she murmured, bumping her hip against her sister's. "We have a long way to go, but I need you to know how grateful I am that you've welcomed me home."

If there was one thing Astoria could always count on Eivor to do, it was pick up on the emotions masked behind her words. "My darling Tory, no matter what, you will always be my sister. And sisters may fight with each other, so long as they remember they can always count on each other to stand against everyone else together. In our case, we had to learn it the hard way, but we're stronger for it."

"Are we?" Her gaze darted to Vesta and Charnel, who smiled reassuringly.

"Considering you're a god now, I'd say we're definitely stronger than we were before."

Laughing at them, Silaine poked Rhydwen. "Take note, Rhyd. We're not stronger because we're all happy, but because Tory is a god. Don't worry though, you're still pretty."

Rhydwen flicked a clump of his blood red hair over his shoulder, preening at her compliment. "Yes, I am the prettiest here. There's no denying it. I asked your husband to gift me some of his smaller feathers. They would look perfect in my hair. And I plan to ask Dawn to do the same."

"You want to wear their feathers in your hair?" Astoria gawked at him, and she heard Vesta's amused chuckle. "Why would you want to do that? I don't understand."

"Because we're family. I've got some of my beloved Songbird's feathers, and I plan to collect a few of yours. Thorne's horse graciously let me collect some of its tail, and Asthore has given me some of her feathers since they moulted while she was here. In goblin culture, we're expected to display tokens of our family as a mark of respect. This is our family gathered here, though Dawn isn't present."

"Oh, I don't know, I think I'm fairly present." Stepping into view, Dawn spread her wings and bowed to Rhydwen. "Please, take whichever feathers you wish. It would be an honour for you to wear them however you fancy. You have no idea how much it means that you would count me as family so quickly."

His emerald-green eyes settled on Eivor, and the prince smiled knowingly. "Someone once told me you can't fight everyone. Better to have people you can trust. A family with whom you can let your guard down. Family isn't always blood, and the best kind is the one you build for yourself."

It seemed strange to look around the private garden at the collection of people gathered there, and Astoria wondered what her parents would have thought. She doubted they could have imagined the family their daughters had built. Or the gaggle of children who brought laughter to the halls of the palace. Stretching her hand out to Silaine, she beckoned her younger sibling to join them. Bounding over, she slung an arm around Astoria, settling into position on the opposite side of Eivor. Vesta slipped free, moving to stand with Charnel and Thorne while the three sisters hugged.

"Do you think they'd be proud of us?" Astoria whispered to them.

Eivor smiled sadly. "I'd like to think so. After all, their secret plans led to this."

"You know, the first time I met him, Death told me they're at peace," Silaine replied, resting her head against Astoria's. "We can imagine they're proud of us, but it's more important that we are proud of ourselves and each other. Not to mention our partners. Through thick and thin, it's time we stick together."

"And that we shall. Though you lead a life with your flock of Ravens and the danann in the Rainbow Vale. But it's not so far, and there are gateway stones outside the border to make things easier now we have pet gods." Completing the circle by putting her arm across Silaine's back, Eivor gazed at them affectionately.

"It won't be easy, and we won't always get along, but what matters is we love each other." Kissing their cheeks, Astoria felt peace settling over her, calming the inferno of her power. "And despite everything, I've always loved both of you dearly. I always will. No matter what."

Their paths had diverged for a time, but they were back where they belonged and surrounded by the people who made life worth living. They were better together. Whatever the future threw at them, they would face it as a family, united in their desire to make Tir a better place for everyone, not just themselves. Together, there was no battle they could not win. They would fight for the peace everyone deserved, and they would do it hand in hand.

Acknowledgements

Well, wasn't that a sweet ending?

This book was supposed to be about healing, and it definitely mended something in me while I wrote it. My time spent with the Havard sisters has been amazing, and I hope you've all enjoyed their antics. Don't worry, they will all be back! Eivor, Astoria, and Silaine might not return as the main characters, but I promise they'll be popping in and out of other books. And the dragons? Oh, there is more of them coming. You'll get to see Briallen Altira again soon when we travel back over a thousand years to the fall of the dragon riders. This is the benefit of writing within one world. Side characters have the chance to tell their own stories. So, while the sisters have had their chance, and found their way back to each other, there are others waiting for an opportunity to do the same.

As always, Beau, my love, thank you for being my rock. You are my everything, and I thank the stars for each and every day I get to spend with you by my side.

Freya, I miss you more with every passing day. My love for you never fades, and I know you're proud of everything I've achieved. I just wish you were walking this road with me.

To my family and friends: thank you for putting up with me. I know I can forget a lot when I'm hyperfixated on writing, but I do love you all. To my parents and my parents-in-law, thank you for all your support. I am so grateful for the four of you, and I hope I keep making you proud. Kyle, if you're reading this after having finished the book, I don't want to hear a word of it the next time we cross the country to visit. No. Please. Don't.

Callai, I remain in awe of your strength. You inspire me. 2025 has been a wild year, and a life changing one. Hopefully, it keeps getting better. Thank you for being my friend.

Chloe, you should be writing. I'm waiting. Damn it, woman. Stop giving me reasons to nag you.

As for my wonderful beta team! You're all so amazing, thank you for helping me turn these books into something decent. Especially you, Anita. My gratitude for everything you've done knows no bounds.

Vii, beautiful Vii. Thank you for being with me through all of this. Your enthusiasm for my characters, and the love you pour into all the art you do for me gives me light. I can never fully express how much your friendship means, and I hope we have many more years of working together ahead of us. Because one of the first things I think of when I create another badarse FMC is: *will this character bring Vii joy to paint?* Well, I hope they do. Your excitement over them always brightens my day.

Finally, to my readers, thank you. Without you, there would be little point to this. I promise more baby dragons are in the future. As well as more disaster women with swords and magic who want to make their world a better place for everyone.

About the Author

Joyce Gee is based in Mandurah, Western Australia. Growing up among the rainforests of Far North Queensland, she loved to vanish into the other worlds hidden within the trees. When she isn't writing, she enjoys drinking tea with a book to read, pottering in the garden, camping with her husband and their two children, or escaping with her camera to capture the beautiful landscape of Western Australia.